Charles D. Hazen

Contemporary American Opinion of the French Revolution

Charles D. Hazen

Contemporary American Opinion of the French Revolution

ISBN/EAN: 9783337227463

Printed in Europe, USA, Canada, Australia, Japan

Cover: Foto ©Andreas Hilbeck / pixelio.de

More available books at **www.hansebooks.com**

CONTEMPORARY AMERICAN OPINION

OF THE

FRENCH REVOLUTION

BY

CHARLES DOWNER HAZEN, Ph. D.

Professor of History, Smith College.

BALTIMORE
THE JOHNS HOPKINS PRESS
1897

JOHNS HOPKINS UNIVERSITY STUDIES

IN

HISTORICAL AND POLITICAL SCIENCE

HERBERT B. ADAMS, Editor

History is past Politics and Politics present History—*Freeman*

EXTRA VOLUME

XVI

CONTENTS.

TO

MY FATHER

WHOSE LIFE HAS BEEN MY GREAT ENCOURAGEMENT.

PART I.

OPINIONS OF AMERICANS ABROAD ON THE FRENCH REVOLUTION

JEFFERSON   MORRIS   MONROE

INTRODUCTION.

In the closing quarter of the eighteenth century life moved swiftly in America as elsewhere. After a period of self-examination at once intense and profound, emerging in determined and confident effort, the people of this country succeeded in achieving their independence, only to be thrown at once into the maelstrom to which an imperfect and inconclusive development of the principle of nationality inevitably leads. Wrestling for another decade with the elements of disunion and anarchy inherent in the situation, they sought an issue from their troubles in the creation of a new constitution. No sooner was this accomplished than the regime thus erected was wrenched to its innermost core by a conflict, exceedingly bitter, of forces to some extent old but largely new. The young republic contended not only with ideas and sentiments of native historic growth and worth, but with certain new and very captivating ones that came, at least in their more striking and militant form, from that very Old World from which the New thought itself finally and completely free. A fierce ferment of discussion, occasioned not only by questions of American political and economic life proper, but also by the aspirations and efforts of another country, now broke out and filled the first decade of our national life with clamor and excitement. Party strife, which was, of course, inevitable under the new constitution, took on a color strangely foreign in character.

"The reason was," as Colonel Higginson points out, " that the French Revolution really drew a red-hot ploughshare through the history of America as well as through that of France. It not merely divided parties, but moulded them; gave them their demarcations, their watchwords and their bitterness. The home issues were for a time subordinate, collateral; the real party lines were established on the other side of the Atlantic."

I have attempted in this monograph to state the attitude of Americans toward these efforts of a foreign country that seemed so completely to eclipse their own problems in interest and significance. I have not attempted to write a history of party politics, to show how opinion worked itself out in acts, altering the life of the country. I have simply endeavored to show from the writings of the men of that time what that opinion was.

The history of American Opinion of the French Revolution falls naturally into two parts—the opinion of those who were in France at the time and who were consequently better informed than most of their fellow-countrymen, and the opinion of those who, remaining at home, were hardly a whit less absorbed by events passing in France, and who based their judgments upon whatever information they could get, good, bad or indifferent. This natural division has dictated the form of the present essay. These two kinds of opinion may be best studied separately, even though at the expense of some repetition, which, however, it is believed, is slight.

I desire to express my sense of great personal obligation to Prof. John M. Vincent, of Johns Hopkins University, for kindness in proof-reading and for many valuable suggestions in construction.

Northampton, September, 1897.

THOMAS JEFFERSON IN FRANCE.

FIRST IMPRESSIONS.

Whoever would know the condition of France toward the close of the Old Regime, and the trend of events at the ushering in of the New, would always do well to consult the writings of American diplomatists resident in that country after 1776, notably those of Thomas Jefferson and Gouverneur Morris. Our earlier representatives abroad, Franklin and Adams and Jay, have naturally far less to contribute to the illumination of that period of French history. Coming events in this case did not seem to cast their shadows before. This supremely momentous movement, followed with such absorbing interest by Jefferson and Morris, was certainly not foreseen in even the dimmest outline by many of the most sagacious observers of the decade preceding. The most weatherwise divined no coming storm. Franklin arrived in France in December, 1776, was received with perfect furor by the society of Paris and Versailles, and enjoyed, during the nine years of his residence there, a most remarkable popularity. He seemed, as John Adams afterward said, to have a reputation "more universal than that of Leibnitz or Newton, Frederick or Voltaire," a testimony made all the stronger when Jefferson said, in 1791, "I can only, therefore, testify in general that there appeared to me more respect and veneration attached to the character of Dr. Franklin in France, than to that of any other person in the same country, foreign or native."

"Benjamin Franklin," says Mr. Parton, "was the American who discovered France." But though he discovered France, he discovered no signs of a revolution germinating there. "There is not a single expression known to us in any of Franklin's letters or papers up to the time when he left France which shows that he expected any considerable change in the government of that country," says a recent writer.[1] Franklin has left behind no description of the economic, moral and political conditions of France in the years immediately preceding the great convulsion. That there lay hid in those conditions the germs of a sweeping and violent change seems never to have occurred to him. To be sure, he never had occasion or inclination to probe very deeply beneath the surface of French life. An old man at the time he entered upon his mission, far from enjoying good health, he made no journeys of importance through the country. Yet seeing a great deal of the political, literary, and scientific society of the capital, he would have caught whatever revolutionary premonitions were in the air and would almost certainly have recorded them. He was in France from 1776 to 1785. He enjoyed French society. Life as men lived it in France seemed to him full of fine pleasure and incitement, of which his pages are evidence, abounding, as they do, with praises of that people. He did not find them abnormally and disastrously organized, and when he sailed for home he carried with him, apparently, no presentiment of that eventful future that lay so near across their pathway.

Nor do we find any symptoms of an impending change in the writings of Jay or Adams. Adams, indeed, travelled across the country twice, in 1778 and 1780, but the observations he made upon his journeys, being very fragmentary and superficial, are of no value to the student of the Old Regime. In after years, in the light thrown upon French conditions by the Revolution, he recorded the impressions made upon him by the retreat of Madame du Barry and the palace of Madame de Pompadour. These remarks on morals, the position and manners of women, the importance of virtue as a foundation for society, are edifying, no doubt, but seem rather like afterthoughts.

---

[1] Hale. Franklin in France, II, 391.

But in the writings of Jefferson and Morris we see ourselves swept along in the broad, deep current of an actual
revolution. These were men of judgment, insight, and
wide acquaintance with affairs. Trained in the suggestive
school of American politics, absorbed in the practical operation of government, with a keen sense for the fitness or
weakness of institutions, and very observant, they were well
qualified to be critics of Frenchmen, French institutions and
conditions, French aspirations and struggles, as that country was about to enter upon an experience that, at the outset at least, seemed very familiar to Americans.

Jefferson and Morris are conspicuous among that small
band of men who have left us the impressions of spectators
of the great Revolution rather than of players in it. From
this fact that they were eye-witnesses who succeeded in
large measure in holding themselves aloof from the conflict
about them, arises the distinctive value of their testimony.
Not that they succeeded in leaving a perfectly objective
and impersonal portrayal of the rise and progress of this
great movement. The times were against them in this,
and so were their temperaments. But though now and
then entering the lists themselves, they remained on the
whole judicial and clearsighted observers, intent upon the
spectacle before them.

These men differed widely in most important essentials.
The one was what was termed in the parlance of the day a
"philosopher," an advanced thinker along new lines, an
undoubted doctrinaire, an optimist, enamored of democracy
with a love that did not pass. The other was first and last
a conservative by nature, a man to whom doctrinaires were
abhorrent, especially when they left the quiet and obscurity
of their closets to mingle in the fray of public life; a man
who held that academicians were made for academies and
not for parliaments; a man of vivacity and pungency and
wit, rather Gallic than English, somewhat of a cynic, too.
These men differed temperamentally. Their political ideas
were also sharply at variance, and when their tempera-

ments and their intellectual likings and dislikes interject themselves into their descriptions, we perceive in each a distinctly personal note. But this is not always the case, for while these men had strongly individual traits, they had traits in common as well. Both were intelligent, facile, acute, and penetrating. Both were strongly prejudiced men, though in inverse senses, but both were thoughtful and possessed discernment. Both were flexible, pliant, easily appreciative of different conditions than those to which they were accustomed at home.

The description which they have left us of France in the most interesting period of her history is continuous from 1784 to 1794, changing in 1789 by the passing of one of them from the scene and the entrance of the other upon it, with the consequent alteration of the note where the strictly impersonal one is dropped.[1]

In May, 1784, Congress appointed Thomas Jefferson to a foreign mission, to join Franklin and John Adams in Europe in negotiating treaties of commerce. Sailing from Boston in July he had a quick voyage and reached Paris, his destination, August 6. Soon after Dr. Franklin's repeated request to be relieved of his position was granted, and on the 10th of March, 1785, Jefferson was appointed to succeed him as Minister to France. Franklin had enjoyed a popularity in France probably unparalleled in the history of diplomacy. He had made America fashion-

---

[1] In the preparation of this chapter I have used both Washington's and Ford's editions of Jefferson's works. References are, however, to the former unless otherwise specified. Most unfortunately, and for no apparent reason, Mr. Ford's edition, at least so far as it deals with the period treated here, 1785-1789, is far less complete than the one brought out forty years ago. Of the sixty letters I have had occasion to use, forty-five are to be found in Washington and are not in Ford, twelve are in both, and three only are in the latter that are not in the former. Of the forty-five, many are of the utmost importance, as for instance more than a dozen official dispatches to John Jay, besides letters to Washington, Adams, Monroe, Lafayette, and Paine. That the later collection should be much less satisfactory than the earlier occasions surprise and regret.

able at this center of fashion, and his country reaped the benefit of his personal prestige. Jefferson was launched upon this new sea as the friend of the great Franklin and as the author of the Declaration of Independence, passports that quickly secured the favor of the French. He still further ingratiated himself with them by improving the occasion of Franklin's departure to make a neat epigram quite in the national taste. By the publication of his *Notes on Virginia* he caused the philosophers of the French capital to speedily recognize him as one of their own guild. The trans-Atlantic scholar and statesman appeared quite worthy of their esteem, his temper of mind commending itself to them as being essentially French. Appearing in France at the time its writers and thinkers were so zealously devising schemes of political and social regeneration, he was soon recognized as a master of the art, a "*connoisseur en révolutions.*" "He had acted one of the most prominent, as well as one of the most showy civic parts in the great trans-Atlantic drama," says his biographer. "He had preceded the French patriots in their present class of ideas. He had acted a high part where they were only commencing to speculate. He had reported the Declaration of Inpendence itself, and was generally supposed to be its author. He had overthrown and reconstructed the legal systems of a chief member of the confederacy. He had seen the practical workings of his labors. He was profoundly versed in the theories of government. With the same knowledge of the ancient ones possessed by the best educated Frenchman, he was far more deeply read in the legal and constitutional system and precedents of England than any man who could be found in France. . . . In respect to American systems there was, of course, no one who could pretend to vie in knowledge with this actual builder of those systems. And it was to England and America alone that the French patriotic party looked for precedents and for examples."[1]

---

[1] Randall. Life of Jefferson, I, 420-421.

Jefferson soon found himself on very good terms with the Government. His home became the rendezvous of that class of French reformers of whom Lafayette was a type, and who were soon to have their day. Touching the life of the country at many points, the criticisms that he soon began to make upon the social and political phenomena before him are always interesting, and possess no slight importance.[1]

From the beginning his criticisms assumed a tone of sharpness and distinctness that they never lost. His observations on the politics and society and morals of France are generally thoughtful and appreciative, but are, as a rule, unfavorable. He finds the social life graceful, attractive, polished, interesting, but after all essentially corrupt. He rejoices in the intellectual illumination, yet he finds the notion of the relative inferiority of other nations grossly exaggerated, even America being not more than half a dozen years behind this center of light in the things of the intellect. Though he apparently found life extremely pleasant in Paris, never for a moment was he dazzled. From the beginning to the end of his stay abroad he contrasts France with America, unfavorably to the former, be it in the domain of politics, or religion, or economics, or education, or social integrity. All this may be abundantly shown by extracts from his correspondence.

For the governments of Europe, Jefferson expresses, from first to last, the most extreme aversion. Those at home who in 1787 mentioned the desirable features of a royal government as a refuge for the distracted thirteen

---

[1] " The residence of Jefferson in Europe is one of the most curious portions of his life, less on account of what he did than of what he saw and thought. . . . It was in Paris he learned to abhor the whole social organization of Europe and everything then appertaining to it still existing in America; it was in Paris that he learned to hate the power both of the aristocracy and clergy, which till then he had opposed without any irritation."—De Witt. Jefferson and the American Democracy. Translated by R. S. H. Church. 123-124.

states were advised "to read the fable of the frogs who elected Jupiter for a king. If that does not put them to right, send them to Europe to see something of the trappings of monarchy, and I will undertake that every man shall go back thoroughly cured. If all the evils which can arise among us, from the republican form of our government, from this day to the day of judgment, could be put into a scale against what this country suffers from its monarchical form in a week, or England in a month, the latter would preponderate. Consider the contents of the Red Book in England, or the Almanac Royale of France, and say what a people gain by monarchy. No race of kings has ever presented above one man of common sense in twenty generations. The best they can do is to leave things to their ministers; but what are their ministers but a committee badly chosen? If the king ever meddles it is to do harm."[1] And again; "With all the defects of our constitution, whether general or particular, the comparison of our government with those of Europe is like a comparison of heaven and hell. England, like the earth, may be allowed to take an intermediate station."[2] Elsewhere, speaking of European governments in general, he says that "under pretence of governing, they have divided their nations into two classes, wolves and sheep. I do not exaggerate. This is a true picture of Europe."[3] And again he compares these governments to the relation of kites to pigeons, and says that we ought "to besiege the throne of heaven with eternal prayers to extirpate from creation this class of human lions, tigers and mammoths called kings; from whom let him perish who does not say, ' Good Lord, deliver us.' "[4]

This is no uncertain sound. It is not the sober thought of a judge, but is rather the war-cry of the republican militant. And we shall see that, despite the general baneful character of kingly government, Jefferson could say good

---

[1] Works, II, 220-221. [2] Ibid. 249. [3] Ibid. 100. [4] Ibid. 253.

things of it, and could earnestly advise a people who were ." ground to powder by the vices of the form of government,"[1] whereby out of a population "of twenty millions of people supposed to be in France . . . there are nineteen millions more wretched, more accursed in every circumstance of human existence, than the most conspicuously wretched individual of the whole United States,"[2] to put up with that form longer, to change it only slowly by breathing a new spirit into it. Jefferson never ceased to hurl anathema against this odious form of government, but he never showed clearly by any exposition of the abuses of French life a necessary and causal connection between the former and the latter, and he found it perfectly possible and apparently easy to praise this corrupt rule in many instances, and to extenuate it and plead for extreme moderation in altering it, acts little in harmony with the vehemence of his denunciations.

Writing to Mr. Bellini, soon after his arrival in Paris, Jefferson said: "But you are, perhaps, curious to know how this new scene has struck a savage of the mountains of America. Not advantageously, I assure you. I find the general fate of humanity here most deplorable. The truth of Voltaire's observation offers itself perpetually, that every man here must be either the hammer or the anvil. It is a true picture of that country to which they say we shall pass hereafter, and where we are to see God and His angels in splendor, and crowds of the damned trampled under their feet. While the great mass of the people are thus suffering under physical and moral oppression, I have endeavored to examine more nearly the condition of the great; to appreciate the true value of the circumstances in their situation which dazzle the bulk of spectators, and especially to compare it with that degree of happiness which is enjoyed in America by every class of people. Intrigues of love occupy the younger, and those of ambition the elder part

---

[1] Works, I, 394.   [2] Ibid. 394-395.

of the great. Conjugal love having no existence among them, domestic happiness, of which that is the basis, is utterly unknown. In lieu of this are substituted pursuits which nourish and invigorate all our bad passions, and which offer only moments of ecstasy amid days and months of restlessness and torment. Much, very much inferior, this, to the tranquil, permanent felicity with which domestic society in America blesses most of its inhabitants; leaving them to follow steadily those pursuits which health and reason approve, and rendering truly delicious the intervals of those pursuits.[1] In science the mass of the people are two centuries behind ours; their literati, half a dozen years before us. Books, really good, acquire just reputation in that time, and so become known to us, and communicate to us all their advances in knowledge. Is not this delay compensated by our being placed out of the reach of that swarm of nonsensical publications which issues daily from a thousand presses and perishes almost in the issuing?[2] With respect to what are termed polite manners, without sacrificing too much the sincerity of language, I would wish my countrymen to adopt just so much of European politeness as to be ready to make all those little sacrifices of self which really render European manners amiable, and relieve society from the disagreeable scenes to which rudeness often subjects it. Here it seems that a man might pass a life without encountering a single rudeness. In the pleasures of the table they are far before us, because with good taste they unite temperance. They do not terminate

---

[1] I, 444. See also the letter to Mrs. Trist, quoted above. " The domestic bonds here are absolutely done away, and where can their compensation be found? Perhaps they may catch some moments above the level of the ordinary tranquil joy we experience, but they are separated by long intervals during which all the passions are at sea without rudder or compass." (Works I, 394.)

[2] See also his remarks in regard to sending boys to Europe to be educated. In everything but the languages they could do as well at William and Mary College as at any school in Europe. I, 467.

the most sociable meals by transforming themselves into brutes. I have never yet seen a man drunk in France, even among the lowest of the people. Were I to proceed to tell you how much I enjoy their architecture, sculpture, painting, music, I should want words. It is in these arts they shine. The last of them particularly is an enjoyment, the deprivation of which, with us, cannot be appreciated."[1]

Thus the French were superior to us only in the grace and polish of their social life and in their achievements in the fine arts. These no doubt are important, and yet with such a man as Jefferson they could never pass for essentials, they could never blind him to the fact that "notwithstanding the finest soil upon earth, the finest climate under heaven, and a people of the most benevolent, the most gay and amiable character of which the human form is susceptible," France was "loaded with misery by kings, nobles and priests, and by them alone."[2]

That the Americans who were abroad at this time saw no portents of an impending catastrophe has been convincingly shown by Dr. Hale in his Franklin in France.[3] A striking illustration of this is to be found in the description Jefferson has left us of a trip he made through Southern France in the early summer of 1787, where even the faint tremors of coming change are not perceptible.

A JOURNEY THROUGH FRANCE.

On the 22nd of February, 1787, the first Assembly of Notables was convened in Versailles and the Revolution had begun. Jefferson was present at its opening and followed its proceedings with keen interest. But a week later he set out upon a journey to the baths of Aix, in Provence, whither he had been advised by his physicians to go.

Jefferson was away from Paris more than three months. This was the very year that Arthur Young was making the

---

[1] I, 444-445.   [2] II, 7-8.
[3] Hale. Franklin in France, II, ch. xix.

first of those memorable journeys for which he is held in such grateful remembrance by the students of history. Jefferson kept a journal of his trip, which has been published in the editions of his works. His account-book and several of his letters are also important as showing the impressions made upon him by the country through which he passed. The observations upon the conditions of France as recorded in the intervals of a leisurely journey, and apart from the influence of political considerations, are far more valuable as evidence than the general and sweeping utterances of the political doctrinaire which have been quoted above. Jefferson for a moment forgets the lurid character of the French government—of mammoths and kites and wolves, upon which he had spent much of his most energetic rhetoric, and his descriptions of France become less emphatic, less declamatory, less saturated with his all-pervasive political theories, also become more trustworthy as evidence, a better revelation of the conditions he portrays. Jefferson's journey extended from the last of February to the middle of June, 1787, and led him through Dijon, Lyons, Nismes, Arles, Aix, Marseilles, Toulon, Fréjus, Turin, Milan, Pavia, Tortona, Novi, Genoa, Monaco, Nice, Aix and Marseilles; thence to Aix, Avignon, Pont du Gard, Nismes, Montpellier, Narbonne, along the canal of Languedoc, Toulouse, Bordeaux, Rochefort, Rochelle, Nantes, L'Orient, Tours, Orleans and Paris, "upwards of a thousand leagues." [1]

Jefferson's notes are mostly on the agricultural conditions of the country through which he is travelling, and a few extracts from them will furnish the best information we have from any contemporaneous American source on the rural life and aspect of old France. [2]

Champagne, March 3. " The plains are in corn, the hills

[1] Ford. Jefferson, IV, 386-7. Letter of Jefferson to Martha Jefferson, Marseilles, May 5, 1787, quoted from S. N. Randolph's Domestic Life of T. Jefferson, 120.

[2] Memoranda taken on a journey from Paris into the southern parts of France, and of northern Italy, in the year 1787. IX, 313-367.

in vineyards, but the wine is not good. There are a few
apple trees, but none of any other kind, and no enclosures.
No cattle, sheep, or swine; fine mules.

"Few chateaux; no farm houses, all the people being
gathered in villages. Are they thus collected by that
dogma of their religion which makes them believe that
to keep the Creator in good humor with his own works
they must mumble a mass every day? Certain it is that they
are less happy and less virtuous in villages than they would
be insulated with their families on the grounds they cultivate. The people are illy clothed. Perhaps they have put
on their worst clothes at this moment, as it is raining. But
I observe women and children carrying heavy burthens
and laboring with the hoe. This is an unequivocal indication of extreme poverty. Men, in a civilized country, never
expose their wives and children to labor above their force
and sex, as long as their own labor can protect them from
it. I see few beggars. Probably this is the effect of a
police."

Burgundy, March 4. "All in corn. Some forest wood
here and there; broom, whins and holly, and a few inclosures of quick hedge. Now and then a flock of sheep.

"The people are well clothed, but it is Sunday. They
have the appearance of being well fed. . . Between Mai-
son-neuve and Vitteaux the road leads through an avenue
of trees, eight American miles long, in a right line. It is
impossible to paint the ennui of this avenue."

Dijon.—"The road in this part of the country is divided
into portions of forty or fifty feet by stones, numbered, which
mark the task of the laborers."

March 7 and 8.—From La Baraque to Chagny. "The
plains are in corn; the Cote in vines. . . . There is a good
deal of forest. Some small herds of small cattle and sheep.
Fine mules. . . . A farmer of ten arpents has about three
laborers engaged by the year. He pays four louis to a man
and half as much to a woman, and feeds them. He kills
one hog and salts it, which is all the meat used in the

family during the year. Their ordinary food is bread and vegetables. At Pommard and Voulenay I observed them eating good wheat bread; at Meursault, rye. I asked the reason of this difference. They told me that the white wines fail in quality much oftener than the red and remain on hand. The farmer therefore cannot afford to feed his laborers as well. At Meursault only white wines are made, because there is too much stone for the red. On such slight circumstances depends the condition of man!"

March 9. From Chalons to Macon. "Met a malefactor in the hands of one of the Marechausée; perhaps a dove in the talons of the hawk. The people begin now to be in separate establishments and not in villages. Houses are mostly covered with tile."

Beaujolois. "This is the richest country I ever beheld. It is about ten or twelve leagues in length, and three or four or five in breadth; at least that part of it which is under the eye of the traveller . . . The whole is thick-set with farm houses, châteaux, and the Bastides of the inhabitants of Lyons. The people live separately and not in villages. The hill-sides are in vine and corn; the plains in corn and pasture. The lands are farmed either for money or on half-stocks. The rents of the corn lands, farmed for money, are about ten or twelve livres the arpent. . . . When lands are rented on half-stocks, the cattle, sheep, etc., are furnished by the landlord. They are valued and must be left of equal value. The increase of these as well as the produce of the farm is divided equally. These leases are only from year to year. They have a method of mixing beautifully the culture of vines, trees and corn. . . . The wages of a laboring man here are five louis; of a woman, one-half. The women do not work with the hoe; they only weed the vines, the corn, etc., and spin. . . . I passed some time at the Château de Laye-Epinaye. Monsieur de Laye has a seignory of about five thousand arpents in pasture, corn, vines and wood. He has over this, as is usual, a certain jurisdiction, both criminal and civil. But this extends only

to the first crude examination, which is before his judges.
The subject is referred for final examination and decision
to the regular judicatures of the country. The Seigneur is
keeper of the peace on his domains. He is therefore subject to the expenses of maintaining it. A criminal prosecuted to sentence and execution costs M. de Laye about
five thousand livres. This is so burdensome to the Seig-
neurs that they are slack in criminal prosecutions—a
good effect from a bad cause. Through all Champagne,
Burgundy and Beaujolois the husbandry seems good,
except that they manure too little. This proceeds from
the shortness of their leases. The people of Burgundy
and Beaujolois are well clothed and have the appearance
of being well fed. But they experience all the oppressions
which result from the nature of the general government
and from that of their particular tenures, and of the seignorial government to which they are subject. What a
cruel reflection that a rich country cannot long be a free
one."

Dauphiné, March 15-18. "There are few châteaux in
this province. The people, too, are mostly gathered into
villages. There are, however, some scattering farm houses.
These are made either of mud or of round stone and mud.
They make inclosures also in both these ways. Day laborers receive sixteen or eighteen sous the day and feed
themselves. Those by the year receive, men, three louis,
women half that, and are fed. They rarely eat meat; a
single hog salted being the year's stock for the family.
But they have plenty of cheese, eggs, potatoes and other
vegetables, and walnut oil with their salad."

Languedoc, March 19-23. (Near Nismes.) "Many
separate farm houses, numbers of people in rags, and
abundance of beggars."

St. Remis. "A laboring man's wages here are one hundred and fifty livres, a woman's half, and fed. . . . There
are some châteaux, many separate farm houses, good, and
ornamental in the small way, so as to show that the tenant's

whole time is not occupied in procuring physical neces-
saries."

Aix, March 25-28. "The wages of a laboring man are
one hundred and fifty livres the year, a woman's sixty to
sixty-six livres, and fed. Their bread is half wheat, half
rye, made once in three or four weeks to prevent too great
a consumption. In the morning they eat bread with an
anchovy or an onion. Their dinner, in the middle of the
day, is bread, soup and vegetables. Their supper the same.
With their vegetables they have always oil and vinegar.
The oil costs about eight sous the pound. They drink
what is called piquette. This is made after the grapes are
pressed, by pouring hot water on the pumice. On Sunday
they have meat and wine."

On the way to Marseilles. "The people are in separate
establishments."

Toulon. "The people are in separate establishments."

In Italy. Jefferson had reached Vercelli. "The people
of this country are ill-dressed in comparison with those of
France, and there are more spots of uncultivated ground."

Frontignan, May 12. "A laboring man hires at 150
livres the year and is fed and lodged; a woman at half as
much. . . . More of the waste lands between Frontignan
and Mirval are capable of culture; but it is a marshy country, very subject to fever and ague and generally unhealthy.
Thence arises, as is said, a want of hands."

Le Saumal. Travelling via the Languedoc Canal. "The
barks which navigate it are seventy and eighty feet long,
and seventeen or eighteen feet wide. They are drawn by
one horse and worked by two hands, one of which is generally a woman. The locks are mostly kept by women,
but the necessary operations are much too laborious for
them. The encroachment by the men on the offices proper
for the women is a great derangement in the order of
things. Men are shoemakers, tailors, upholsterers, stay-
makers, mantua-makers, cooks, housekeepers, house-
cleaners, bed-makers, they *coeffe* the ladies and bring them

to bed; the women, therefore, to live, are obliged to undertake the offices which they abandon. They become porters, carters, reapers, sailors, lock-keepers, smiters on the anvil, cultivators of the earth, etc. Can we wonder if such of them as have a little beauty prefer easier courses to get their livelihood, as long as that beauty lasts?"

Bordeaux, May 24. "The farmers live on their farms. . . . They never hire laborers by the year [in the vineyards]. The day wages for a man are thirty sous, a woman's, fifteen sous, feeding themselves. The women make the bundles of sarment, weed, pull off the snails, tie the vines, and gather the grapes. During the vintage are paid high and fed well."

May 28 and 29. "The country from Nantes to L'Orient is very hilly and poor, the soil grey; nearly half is waste, in furze and broom, among which is some poor grass. . . . The people are mostly in villages; they eat rye bread and are ragged. The villages announce a general poverty, as does every other appearance. Women smite on the anvil and work with the hoe, and even are yoked to labor."

Near Rennes. "Some small separate houses, which seem to be the residence of laborers or very small farmers; the walls frequently of mud, and the roofs generally covered with slate."

Thus we see that Jefferson, after a long and leisurely trip through France, has left no very severe arraignment of the condition of the masses. He believed it would be better for them to live upon the farms rather than to be huddled together in villages, which is quite in harmony with the belief he always entertained that population should be scattered rather than greatly concentrated at a few points. But he finds numerous regions where this is the case. He believes the system of land tenure bad, owing to the shortness of the leases, three, six, or nine years, whereas longer leases encourage the cultivator to greater exertions.[1] But,

---

[1] Arthur Young expressed the same thought much more vigorously and picturesquely when he said, "Give a man the secure

though the condition of the agricultural class is better in this respect in England,[1] it is worse in Italy.[2] France holds a sort of middle ground.

He finds that the people seem to be, on the whole, well clothed and well fed. . To be sure, they eat but little meat, but their diet, which is vegetable, he thinks quite as good. Jefferson's testimony is quite as important for what he does not say as for what he does. Long before he left Paris he was indulging in his emphatic denunciations of monarchical and aristocratic government. He was declaring that five hundred persons could scarcely be found in America so wretched as twenty-four million and a half in France. Yet with this strong conviction of the inherent and unqualified badness of the government, and with this ready disposition to see its evil effects everywhere, we find the memoranda of this journey almost entirely free from condemnation. The picture that he paints is by no means black, though it may be rather sombre. Nowhere does he seem to find the condition of the masses intolerable. On one occasion, indeed, he does say that though the people of Burgundy and

---

possession of a bleak rock and he will turn it into a garden; give him a nine years' lease of a garden and he will convert it into a desert."—Travels in France, Bohn, 1890, p. 54.

[1] Jefferson to John Page. Paris, May 4, 1786 (I, 549); "I returned but three or four days ago from a two months' trip to England. I traversed that country much and own that town and country fell short of my expectations. Comparing it with this, I found a much greater proportion of barrens, a soil, in other parts, not naturally so good as this, not better cultivated, but better manured, and, therefore, more productive. This proceeds from the practice of long leases there and short ones here. The laboring people here are poorer than in England. They pay about one-half their produce in rent; the English, in general, about a third."

[2] In the memoranda quoted above Jefferson says, speaking of Northern Italy: "The women here smite on the anvil and work with maul and spade. The people of this country are ill-dressed in comparison with those of France, and there are more spots of uncultivated ground (IX, 337). Leases here are mostly for nine years. . . . A laboring man receives sixty livres and is fed and lodged." (Ibid. 340.)

Beaujolois are well clothed and have the appearance of being well fed, yet "they experience all the oppressions which result from the nature of the general government and from that of their particular tenures, and of the seignorial government to which they are subject." And he adds, " What a cruel reflection, that a rich country cannot long be a free one!" And, again, on seeing a prisoner in the hands of a policeman, his humanitarianism rises to the occasion and he thinks that possibly he is a "dove in the talons of a hawk."

But on the whole, Jefferson does not seem to have been moved by any great distress in the conditions of those whose lives he observed. There are none of those passionate outbreaks that one finds in Arthur Young's record of his travels. "The same wretched country continues to La Loge; the fields are scenes of pitiable management as the houses are of misery. Yet all this country highly improvable, if they knew what to do with it; the property, perhaps, of some of those glittering beings who figured in the procession the other day at Versailles. Heaven grant me patience while I see a country thus neglected, and forgive me the oaths I swear at the absence and ignorance of the possessors," [1] and " Oh! if I was the legislator of France for a day, I would make great lords skip again." [2]

This cannot have arisen out of the fact that Jefferson was not passionate, for that he most certainly was; nor out of any self-imposed limits upon the matter to be inserted in his journal, for though that is devoted, to be sure, mainly to a description of the topography of France and the agricultural methods, particularly the culture of vines, yet he constantly deviates from so strict a path and speaks of landscapes, birds, views, and works of art. [3] It is hardly

[1] Young. Travels, 19.   [2] Ibid. 71.
[3] Memoranda *passim.* See also letter to Comtesse de Tessé, II, 131-132, and letter to his daughter written on this trip, Ford's Jefferson, IV, 388.

conceivable that some references to the wretched conditions of the French masses would not have crept into Jefferson's writings had he been vividly impressed with their wretchedness. He was a man of quick sensibility, of lively humanitarian feelings, and yet he was not moved to indignation by what he saw. The upshot of the whole matter seems to be that Jefferson, though finding the lot of the average Frenchman a hard one, did not find it unusually hard. And such an opinion seems to be confirmed by a letter that he wrote to his friend Lafayette from Nice.

"In the great cities I go to see what travellers think alone worthy of being seen; but I make a job of it and generally gulp it all down in a day. On the other hand, I am never satiated with rambling through the fields and farms, examining the culture and cultivators, with a degree of curiosity which makes some take me for a fool, and others to be much wiser than I am. I have been pleased to find among the people a less degree of physical misery than I had expected. They are generally well clothed and have a plenty of food, not animal, indeed, but vegetable, which is just as wholesome. Perhaps they are overworked, the excess of the rent required by the landlord obliging them to too many hours of labor in order to produce that and wherewith to feed and clothe themselves. The soil of Champagne and Burgundy I have found more universally good than I had expected, and as I could not help making a comparison with England, I found that comparison more unfavorable to the latter than is generally admitted. The soil, the climate and the productions are superior to those of England, and the husbandry as good, except in one point, that of manure." . . . [France should adopt the system of long leases.] . . . "From the first olive fields of Pierrelatte to the orangeries of Hieres has been continued rapture to me. I have often wished for you. I think you have not made this journey. It is a pleasure you have to come, and an improvement you have to add to the many you have already made. It will be a great comfort to you to know, from your own inspection, the condition of all the provinces of your own country, and it will be interesting to them at some future day, to be known to you. This is perhaps the only moment of your life in which you can acquire that knowledge. And to do it most effectually you must be absolutely incognito; you must ferret the people out of their hovels as I have done, look into their kettles, eat their bread, loll on their beds under pretence of resting yourself, but in fact to find if they are soft. You will feel a sublime pleasure in the course of this investigation, and a sublimer one hereafter, when you shall be able to apply your knowledge to the softening of their beds or the throwing a morsel of meat into their kettle of vegetables." [1]

The tender sentiment of the closing sentences would, no doubt, be justified in any land and time.

This position is still further reinforced by the testimony of another American who happened to be in France at this time, Joel Barlow, of Connecticut, a liberal, who went to Europe in 1788 as the agent of a business enterprise, remaining there a number of years and playing a unique part in the great Revolution. Barlow landed at Havre, June 26, 1788, and reached Paris, July 3d. In his note-book, full for the first four months, he says, "I do not find that extreme wretchedness and poverty among the lower class of people in France that I had been taught to expect." [2]

---

[1] II, 135-136. Nice, April 11, 1787.
[2] Life and Letters of Joel Barlow, by Charles Burr Todd, 75.
The view given here of Jefferson's opinion of French conditions does not seem to me to be especially modified by a very interesting letter written by Jefferson to his friend, the Reverend James Madison, and recently brought to light by Mr. Ford. The letter was written at Fontainebleau, October 28, 1785, and runs, in part, as follows:
Dear Sir:—Seven o'clock and retired to my fireside; I have determined to enter into conversation with you. This is a village of about 5000 inhabitants when the court is not here, and 20,000 when they are, occupying a valley through which runs a brook, and on each side of it a ridge of small mountains, most of which are naked rock. The King comes here in the fall always to hunt.

THE PASSING OF THE NOTABLES.

Jefferson had delayed his departure for Southern France several days in order to be present at the opening of the Assembly of Notables, February 22, 1787. Early in January he had notified the government at home that such an assembly was shortly to be called. "This has not been done for one hundred and sixty years past. Of course it

His court attend him, as do also the foreign diplomatic corps, but as this is not indispensably required, and my finances do not admit the expense of a continued residence here, I propose to come occasionally to attend the King's levees, returning again to Paris, distant forty miles. This being the first trip, I set out yesterday morning to take a view of the place. For this purpose I shaped my course towards the highest of the mountains in sight, to the top of which was about a league. As soon as I had got clear of the town I fell in with a poor woman walking at the same rate with myself and going the same course. Wishing to know the condition of the laboring poor, I entered into conversation with her, which began by enquiries for the path which would lead me into the mountain; and thence proceeded to enquiries into her vocation, condition and circumstances. She told me she was a day laborer at 8 sous, or 4d sterling, the day; that she had two children to maintain, and to pay a rent of 30 livres for her house (which would consume the hire of 75 days); that often she could get no employment, and of course was without bread. As we had walked together near a mile, and she had so far served me as a guide, I gave her, on parting, 24 sous. She burst into tears of gratitude, which I could perceive was unfeigned, because she was unable to utter a word. She had probably never before received so great an aid. This little attendrissement, with the solitude of my walk, led me into a train of reflection on that unequal division of property which occasions the numberless instances of wretchedness which I had observed in this country and is to be observed all over Europe. The property of this country is absolutely concentred in a very few hands, having revenues of from half a million guineas a year downwards. These employ the flower of the country as servants, some of them having as many as 200 domestics not laboring. They employ also a great number of manufacturers and tradesmen, and lastly, the class of laboring husbandmen. But after all there comes the most numerous of all classes—the poor who cannot find work. I asked myself what could be the reason so many should be permitted to beg who are willing to work, in a country where there is a very considerable portion of uncultivated lands? These lands are undisturbed only for the sake of the game. It should seem then that it must be because of the enormous wealth of the proprietors which places

calls up all the attention of the people."[1] The objects of
the Assembly were unknown, though several are conjec-
tured. "But in truth nothing is known about it. This
government practises secrecy so systematically that it never
publishes its purposes or its proceedings sooner or more
extensively than necessary."[1] This was the chief topic of
conversation in Paris for some time.[2]

"This event, which will hardly excite any attention in
America, is deemed here the most important one which has
taken place in their civil line during the present century.
Some promise their country great things from it; some
nothing. Our friend de La Fayette was placed on the list
originally. Afterwards his name disappeared, but finally
was re-instated. This shows that his character here is not
considered as an indifferent one, and that it excites agitation. His education in our school has thrown on him a
very jealous eye from a court whose principles are the most
absolute despotism. But I hope he has nearly passed this
crisis. The King, who is a good man, is favorably disposed towards him, and he is supported by powerful family
connections and by the public good will. He is the young-
est man of the Notables, except one whose office placed
him on the list."[3]

---

them above attention to the increase of their revenues by per-
mitting these lands to be labored. I am conscious that an equal
division of property is impracticable, but the consequences of this
enormous inequality, producing so much misery to the bulk of
mankind, legislators cannot invent too many devices for subdividing property, only taking care to let their subdivisions go hand
in hand with the natural affections of the human mind." Jefferson
goes on to discuss the methods for subdividing. He insists that
provisions should be made so that "as few as possible shall be
without a little portion of land. The small landowners are the
most precious part of a state." The *Nation*, July 25, 1895. This
letter, written earlier than most of those mentioned in the text, does
not conflict with them in any essential matter, and is, after all,
chiefly significant as showing the importance Jefferson attached to
the wide diffusion of property in land.

[1] II, 91. Jan. 9, 1787.   [2] Ibid, 95. Jan. 14, 1787.
[3] Ibid, 99. Jan. 16, 1787.

Before leaving Paris, Jefferson wrote to Lafayette as follows: " I am just now in the moment of my departure. . . . I wish you success in your meeting. I should form better hopes of it if it were divided into two houses, instead of seven. Keeping the good model of your neighboring country before your eyes, you may get on, step by step, towards a good constitution. Though that model is not perfect, yet, as it would unite more suffrages than any new one which could be proposed, it is better to make that the object. If every advance is to be purchased by filling the royal coffers with gold, it will be gold well employed. The King, who means so well, should be encouraged to repeat these assemblies. You see how we republicans are apt to preach when we get on politics. Adieu, my dear friend." [1]

There, in the face of circumstances, the doctrinaire withdraws and the cautious statesman, willing to progress slowly, less eager for a complete and immediate overhauling of the entire state system, comes forward. A month later he writes in the same vein to Madame de Tessé: " My journey has given me leisure to reflect on the Assemblée des Notables. Under a good and young king, as the present, I think good may be made of it. I would have the deputies then, by all means, so conduct themselves as to encourage him to repeat the calls of the Assembly. Their first step should be to get themselves divided into two chambers instead of seven; the Noblesse and the Commons separately. The second to persuade the King, instead of choosing the deputies of the Commons himself, to summon those chosen by the people for the provincial administrations. The third, as the noblesse is too numerous to be all of the Assemblée, to obtain permission for that body to choose its own deputies. Two houses, so elected, would contain a mass of wisdom which would make the people happy, and the King great; would place him in history where no other act can possibly place him. They would thus put themselves in the

---

[1] II, 131. Feb. 28, 1787.

track of the best guide they can follow; they would soon overtake it, become its guide in time, and lead to the wholesome modifications wanting in that model, and necessary to constitute a rational government. Should they attempt more than the established habits of the people are ripe for, they may lose all, and retard indefinitely the ultimate object of their aim. These, Madam, are my opinions; but I wish to know yours, which, I am sure, will be better." [1]

Thus Jefferson thought that its possibilities for good were great if the Assembly should adopt a moderate instead of a radical policy, and should choose the best concrete model as a guide, rather than insist upon following out any purely experimental, though ideally more perfect scheme of its own devising. By the time Jefferson returned to Paris the Assembly had been dissolved and a change in the ministry had taken place. He was very favorably impressed with the achievements of this Assembly, both as being very worthy and desirable in themselves, and as preparing the way for a general and more complete reform.

Writing to Washington, August 14, 1787, he says: "The Assemblée des Notables has been productive of much good in this country. The reformation of some of the most oppressive laws has taken place and is taking place. The allotment of the state into subordinate governments, the administration of which is committed to persons chosen by the people, will work in time a very beneficial change in their constitution. The expense of the trappings of monarchy, too, is lightening. Many of the useless officers, high and low, of the King, Queen and Princes, are struck off." [2]

But the cries for reform were not stilled by what had been accomplished by the Assembly of Notables. The struggle had indeed but just begun. Jefferson, on his return, seems for a moment to have been surprised that the

---

[1] II, 133-134.
[2] Ibid. 251. "That of partitioning the country into a number of subordinate governments under the administration of Provincial Assemblies chosen by the people is a capital one.", II, 222.

improvements that had already been effected had not quieted the rising commotion and been frankly accepted by all as a sufficient achievement for the present, a good basis for further reorganization to be brought about slowly as ripening conditions might favor and permit. But he soon saw the reason for this uncertainty, this restlessness, and describes the succeeding quarrels between the Crown and Parliaments minutely. Jefferson, the political thinker, was a doctrinaire of the most radical type. Jefferson, the practical statesman, confronting actual conditions, seeking a feasible issue, knew how to adapt and trim, if not suppress his theories quite easily. He viewed all the efforts of the progressive party with optimistic sympathy. Yet he rarely lost his judgment, could criticise unfavorably as well as favorably. He plainly had a sober estimate of the capacities of Frenchmen for larger political life, and believed that they should enjoy the extensive political rights that were their due only after some training in practical politics. And even the attempts of the government to be liberal he regarded with something like open scorn. Speaking of the edict emancipating the Protestants, which was hailed as a triumph of enlightened legislation, he says, " The long expected edict of the Protestants at length appears here. It is an acknowledgment (hitherto withheld by the laws) that Protestants can beget children, and that they can die and be offensive unless buried. It does not give them permission to think, to speak, or to worship. It enumerates the limitations to which they shall remain subject, and the burthens to which they shall continue to be unjustly exposed. What are we to think of the condition of the human mind in a country where such a wretched thing as this has thrown the state into convulsions, and how must we bless our own situation in a country, the most illiterate peasant of which is a Solon compared with the authors of this law." [1]

---

[1] II, 350. Feb. 2, 1788.

The establishment of the Provincial Assemblies, which embodied the principle of electors, was to be the instrument of national salvation, and would in time circumscribe the influence of the Crown and increase that of the people. But events soon took another turn. The Notables had accepted some of the propositions of the Crown, but had ignored others, including those which had formed the real reason for their summoning—the financial schemes, the plans for new taxes. Jefferson speaks rather admiringly of their skill in passing over these. "Though the minister who proposed these improvements seems to have meant them as the price of new supplies, the game has been so played as to secure the improvements to the nation without securing the price. The Notables spoke softly on the subject of the additional supplies."

THE INTERLUDE.

But just because the Assembly spoke thus softly the agitation continued, and became more intense because concentrated upon these objects alone. The contest henceforth was between different powers, but it was the same contest, drawn all the more sharply because side issues, confusing or palliating, had dropped away. The contest between the Crown and Parliament was on for several months to come. The immediate occasion of the outburst was the registration of new taxes demanded by the Crown. These were opposed, and in the end successfully, by the Parliament, though the old familiar and heroic methods of the Crown were resorted to to enforce its will. "But to the delirium of joy which these improvements gave the nation, a strange reverse of temper has suddenly succeeded."[1] This was occasioned by the deficiencies in the revenue, which, as officially exposed, were frightful. The monarchy had evidently shown a disposition to economize, a disposition that seemed soon to vanish. "But expenses are still very inconsiderately incurred, and

---

[1] II, 222.

all reformation in that point despaired of. The public credit
is affected; and such a spirit of discontent has arisen as has
never been seen."[1] "The constitutional reformations," says
Jefferson again, "have gone on well, but those of expenses
have made little progress. Some of the most obviously
useless have, indeed, been lopped off, but the remainder is
a heavy mass, difficult to be reduced. Despair has seized
every mind, and they have passed from an extreme of joy
to one of discontent."[2] The Parliament refused to register
the new taxes and was compelled by a *lit de justice* to do
so, but only after having uttered the ominous word States-
General. "It is evident, I think," says Jefferson, when he
hears of this *lit de justice*, "that a spirit of this country is
advancing towards a revolution in their constitution.
There are not wanting persons at the helm, friends to the
progress of the spirit."[3] "Your nation is advancing to a
change of constitution," he writes again. "The young
desire it, the middle-aged are not averse, the old alone opposed to it. They will die, the provincial assemblies will
chalk out the plan, and the nation, ripening fast, will execute
it."[4] "The day before yesterday," he writes, August 15,
"the Parliament House was surrounded by ten thousand
people, who received them on their adjournment with acclamations of joy, took out the horses of the principal speakers
and drew their chariots themselves to their hotels."[5] Agitation at once attained a degree of intensity greater than any
hitherto known in the recent history of France, a faint
foreshadowing of what was to come. "From the separation of the Notables [May 25, 1787] to the present
moment," writes Jefferson, August 30, "has been perhaps
the most interesting interval ever known in this country.
. . . In the meantime all tongues in Paris, (and in France,
as it is said) have been let loose, and never was a license of
speaking against the Government exercised in London more
freely or more universally. Caricatures, placards, bons mots,

---

[1] II, 222.   [2] Ibid. 230-231.   [3] Ibid. 231.   Aug. 6, 1787.
[4] Ibid. 234-5.   [5] Ibid. 255.   Aug. 15, 1787.

have been indulged in by all ranks of people, and I know
of no well attested instance of a single punishment. For
some time mobs of ten, twenty and thirty thousand people
collected daily, surrounded the Parliament House, huzzaed
the members; men entered the doors and examined into
their conduct, took the horses out of the carriages of those
who did well and drew them home. The Government
thought it prudent to prevent these, drew some regulars
into the neighborhood, multiplied the guards, had the streets
constantly patrolled by strong parties, suspended privileged
places, forbade clubs, etc. The mobs have ceased; perhaps
that may be partly owing to the absence of Parliament.
The Count d'Artois, sent to hold a bed of justice in the
Cour des Aides, was hissed and hooted without reserve
by the populace; the carriage of Madame de (I forget the
name) in the Queen's livery, was stopped by the populace,
under a belief that it was Madame de Polignac, whom they
would have insulted; the Queen going to the theatre at
Versailles with Madame de Polignac was received with a
general hiss. The King, long in the habit of drowning his
cares in wine, plunges deeper and deeper. The Queen
cries, but sins on. The Count d'Artois is detested, and
Monsieur, the general favorite. The Archbishop of Thoulouse is made minister principal, a virtuous, patriotic and
able character. . . . I think that in the course of three
months the royal authority has lost, and the rights of the
nation gained as much ground by a revolution of public
opinion only, as England gained in all her civil wars under
the Stuarts. I rather believe, too, they will retain the
ground gained because it is defended by the young and
the middle-aged, in opposition to the old only. The first
party increases, and the latter diminishes daily, from the
course of nature." [1]

And in writing to Jay, September 22, 1787, Jefferson re-
affirms this opinion. He clearly saw that the contest which

---

[1] II, 257-259; see also 372. May 2, 1788.

resulted so disastrously to the Crown was not one between the Crown and the Parliament, but was in reality between the Crown and the people. That Parliament was only powerful in so far as it was the mouthpiece of the popular will was evident to him from the first. As soon as it ceased to hold that position it became as weak and selfish a factor in the struggle as the Crown. Speaking of the repeal of the stamp tax and the " impost territorial," and the substitution for- them of the *deux vingtièmes*, he says: " There can be no better proof of the revolution in the public opinion as to the powers of the monarch, and of the force, too, of that opinion. Six weeks ago we saw the King displaying the plenitude of his omnipotence, as hitherto conceived, to enforce these two acts. At this day he is forced to retract them by the public voice; for as to the opposition of the Parliament, that body is too little esteemed to produce this effect in any case where the public do not throw themselves into the same scale." [1]

Jefferson evidently had a high opinion of the Archbishop of Toulouse when the latter became Chief Minister, an opinion only strengthened by the policy he adopted at the outset—a policy of peace, in itself a commendation in the eyes of Jefferson. "There has long been a division in the Council here, on the question of war and peace. Monsieur de Montmorin and Monsieur de Breteuil have been constantly for war. They are supported in this by the Queen. The King goes for nothing. He hunts one half the day, is drunk the other, and signs whatever he is bid. The Archbishop of Thoulouse desires peace. Though brought in by the Queen, he is opposed to her in this capital object, which would produce an alliance with her brother. Whether the Archbishop will yield or not I know not. But an intrigue is already begun for ousting him from his place, and it is rather probable it will succeed. He is a good and patriotic minister for peace, and very cap-

---

[1] II, 278. Sept. 22, 1787.

able in the Department of Finance. At least he is so in theory. I have heard his talents for execution censured." [1] Again: " That he has imposing talents and patriotic dispositions I think is certain. Good judges think him a theorist only, little acquainted with the details of business, and spoiling all his plans by a bungled execution. He may, perhaps, undergo a severe trial. His best actions are exciting against him a host of enemies, particularly the reduction of pensions, and reforms in other branches of economy. Some think the other ministers are willing he should stay in till he has effected this odious, yet necessary work, and that they will then make him the scape-goat of the transaction." [2] That he favored peace, that he attempted to reduce the odious pension list and to introduce other reforms were elements decidedly in his favor in Jefferson's opinion. " In the meantime," he says, " The Principal goes on with a firm and patriotic spirit, in reforming the cruel abuses of the government, and preparing a new constitution which will give to the people as much liberty as they are capable of managing. This, I think, will be the glory of his administration. . . . Twelve or fifteen Provincial Assemblies are already in action, and are going on well; and, I think, that though the nation suffers in reputation, it will gain infinitely in happiness, under the present administration." [3]

Jefferson caught the premonition of a coming crisis [4] in the spring of the following year when the edicts for the suppression of the Parliaments and the establishment of a *Cour Plenière* were issued, and then registration extorted in a *lit de justice*, May, 1788. On the whole he seems to have approved these edicts, though he certainly did not approve everything they apparently involved. As issuing from the King alone they implied that with him alone rested all rights. Still Jefferson thought that they would, on the whole, prove beneficial and might be used to obtain

---

[1] II, 293-4.   Oct. 8, 1787.   [2] Ibid. 310-311.   Nov. 3, 1787.
[3] Ibid. 316.   Nov. 13, 1787.   [4] Ibid. 382.   May 4, 1788.

the larger freedom France desired. Speaking of our own new ·Constitution, he says, in writing to the Comte de Moustier: "There are, indeed, some faults which revolted me a good deal in the first moment; but we must be contented to travel on towards perfection, step by step. We must be contented with the ground which this constitution will gain for us, and hope that a favorable moment will come for correcting what is amiss in it. I view in the same light the innovations making here. The new organization of the judiciary department is undoubtedly for the better. The reformation of the criminal code is an immense step taken towards good.' The composition of the Plenary Court is indeed vicious in the extreme; but the basis of that court may be retained and its composition changed. Make of it a representative of the people, by composing it of members sent from the Provincial Assemblies, and it becomes a valuable member of the Constitution. But it is said the court will not consent to do this; the court however has consented to call the States-General, who will consider the Plenary Court but as a canvas for them to work on. The public mind is manifestly advancing on the abusive prerogatives of their governors and bearing them down. No force in the government can withstand this in the long run. Courtiers had rather give up power than pleasures; they will barter, therefore, the usurped prerogatives of the King, for the money of the people. This is the agent by which modern nations will recover their

---

[1] Speaking of this reform in the criminal law, Jefferson says: "This reformation is unquestionably good and within the ordinary legislative powers of the Crown. That it should remain to be made at this day proves that the monarch is the last person in his kingdom who yields to the progress of philanthropy and civilization." (May 23, 1788. II, 390.)

Of the reorganization of the Judiciary Department by the institution of subordinate jurisdictions, the taking from the Parliaments of all causes of less than 20,000 livres, the reduction of their number to about a fourth, he says, "Even this would be a great improvement if it did not imply that the King is the only person in this nation who has any rights or any power." II, 391.

rights. I sincerely wish that in this country they may be contented with a peaceable and passive opposition. At this moment we are not sure of this, though as yet it is difficult to say what form the opposition will take." [1]

Most of the innovations of this period Jefferson thought were decidedly for the better. " Two only must be fundamentally condemned: the abolishing, in so great a degree, of the Parliaments, and the substitution of so ill-composed a body as the *cour pleniere.* If the King has the power to do this the government of this country is a pure despotism. I think it is a pure despotism in theory, but moderated in practice by the respect which public opinion commands. But the nation repeats, after Montesquieu, that the different bodies of magistracy, of priests and nobles, are barriers between the King and the people. It would be easy to prove that these barriers can only appeal to public opinion, and that neither these bodies nor the people can offer any legal check to the will of the monarch. But they are manifestly advancing fast to a constitution. Great progress is already made. The Provincial Assemblies, which will be a very perfect representative of the people, will secure them a great deal against the power of the Crown. The confession lately made by the government that it cannot impose a new tax is a great thing; the convocation of the States-General, which cannot be avoided, will produce a National Assembly, meeting at certain epochs, possessing at first probably only a negative on the laws, but which will grow into the right of original legislation, and prescribing limits to the expenses of the King. These are improvements which will assuredly take place, and which will give an energy to the country they have never yet had. Much may be hoped from the States-General, because the King's dispositions are solidly good; he is capable of great sacrifices; all he wants to induce him to do a thing is to be assured it will be for the good of the nation.

---

[1] II, 388-389. May 17, 1788.

He will probably believe what the States-General shall tell him, and will do it. It is supposed they will reduce the Parliament to a mere judiciary. I am in hopes all this will be effected without convulsions." . . . " The English papers have told the world, with their usual truth, that all here is civil war and confusion. There have been some riots, but as yet not a single life has been lost, according to the best evidence I have been able to collect." [1]

THE STATES-GENERAL ONCE MORE.

Jefferson was convinced that a great deal had been accomplished for the good of France before the summoning of the States-General. The ministerial activity of Brienne received his warm approval.[2] The contest between the Crown and Parliament Jefferson characterized as " a contest between the monarchical and aristocratical parts of the government, for a monopoly of despotism."[3] Good men take part with neither and should take part with neither. But they are simply using the necessities of these two powers to pursue their own object, the attainment of a fixed constitution. He was convinced that the King and his ministers would " make great concessions to the people, rather than small ones to the Parliament." It is interesting to see Jefferson's moderation asserting its superiority in the midst of extreme political theories, to see how eagerly he grasped first at the Assembly of Notables, then at the Plenary Court, then at the States-General as furnishing the possible germ of a real national legislature. What improvements had been made would serve well as

---

[1] II, 438-439.

[2] II, 466. Aug. 12, 1788. To Carmichael: " I applaud extremely the patriotic proceedings of the present ministry. Provincial Assemblies established, the States-General called, the right of taxing the nation without their consent abandoned, corvées abolished, torture abolished, the criminal code reformed, are facts which will do eternal honor to their administration in history."

[3] II, 457.

the groundwork for future ones. What was necessary above all was peace. Nothing could be more unfortunate than a " hasty and premature appeal to arms." " There is neither head nor body in the nation to promise a successful opposition to two hundred thousand regular troops. Some think the army could not be depended on by the government; but the breaking men to military discipline is breaking their spirits to principles of passive obedience. A firm but quiet opposition will be most likely to succeed." This Jefferson thought would be the course of events. "This nation is rising from the dust," and it was rising so quietly and with such self-control and decorum that Jefferson thought it probable that it would, " within two or three years, be in the enjoyment of a tolerably free constitution, and that without its having cost them a drop of blood; for none has yet been spilt, though the English papers have set the whole nation to cutting throats."

As the year 1788 wore on the States-General loomed larger in the horizon, bringing with it a perilous preliminary question: Should there be one chamber, or two, or three? Should the Commons lead the way, or should they be skilfully checkmated? That the King would not stand in the way of the popular will Jefferson was convinced. "He is the honestest man in the kingdom, and the most regular and economical. He has no foible which will enlist him against the good of his people; and whatever constitution will promote this he will befriend; but he will not befriend it obstinately; he has given repeated proof of a readiness to sacrifice his opinion to the wish of the nation."[1] A greater possible danger may be found in the characters at court who may not all be of this conciliating nature, and from whom misrepresentations and evil influences may arise, and also in the constituted authorities. The Parliament, for instance, when threatened by the royal authority, called loudly for the States-General, but when

---

[1] II, 469-70.

they saw a sort of peril to themselves in these very States, they demanded them " in the form of 1614," that is, wished them in a form that would not command the confidence of the people and that would consequently not be as dangerous. "Here the cloven hoof begins to appear," says Jefferson.[1] Later events seemed to show that the nobles and clergy would combine to oppose great reforms, and that consequently the people would be thrown into the scale of the King. "This may end in liberty or despotism at his will," says Jefferson. "I think that both he and his ministry are in favor of liberty, and that having twenty-three millions and a half of the people on their side, they will call the other half million to order and show them that instead of having two-thirds of the nation they are but the forty-eighth."[2]

In the succeeding months before the assembling of the States-General, in the discussion of all those questions then agitating Frenchmen, both with reference to its composition and its work, Jefferson showed at every point the same wise moderation.

"If the *États-Généraux*, when they assemble, do not aim at too much," he says, "they may begin a good constitution. There are three articles which they may easily obtain. 1. Their own meeting, periodically; 2, the exclusive right of taxation; 3, the right of registering laws and proposing amendments to them, as exercised now by the Parliaments. This last could be readily approved by the court, on account of their hostility against the Parliaments, and would lead immediately to the origination of laws; the second has been already solemnly avowed by the King; and it is well understood there will be no opposition to the first. If they push at much more all may fail."[3]

"If the States stop here for the present moment," he says in another letter, "all will probably end well. and they may, in future sessions, obtain a suppression of *lettres*

---

[1] II, 485. Sept. 29, 1788.   [2] Ibid. 490. Nov. 2, 1788.
[3] Ibid. 506-7. Nov. 18, 1788. See also other letters of this period.

de cachet, a free press, a civil list, and other modifications of their government. But it is to be feared that an impatience to rectify everything at once, which prevails in some minds, may terrify the court and lead them to appeal to force and to depend on that alone."[1] "If the States are prudent," he says again, "they will not aim at more than this at first, lest they should shock the dispositions of the court, and even alarm the public mind, which must be left to open itself by degrees to successive improvements. These will follow from the nature of things; how far they can proceed in the end, towards a thorough reformation of abuse, cannot be foreseen."[2]

That France herself was not ready for greater reforms, even for certain rights considered as elementary and indispensable in English-speaking countries, Jefferson clearly saw. Some, he said, would try to obtain a habeas corpus law and a free press. "I doubt if the latter can be obtained yet, and as for the former I hardly think the nation itself ripe to accept it. Though they see the evils of *lettres de cachet*, they believe they do more good on the whole. They will think better in time."[3]

Jefferson once before had spoken with some bitterness of the backwardness of French political development. Writing to Mrs. Adams on the occasion of the meeting of the Notables of 1787, he had said: "The most remarkable effect of this convention, as yet, is the number of puns and bon-mots it has generated. I think were they all collected it would form a more voluminous work than the Encyclopedie. This occasion, more than anything I have seen, convinces me that this nation is incapable of any serious effort but under the word of command. The people at large view every object only as it may furnish puns and bon-mots; and I pronounce that a good punster would disarm the whole nation were they ever so seriously determined to revolt. Indeed, Madam, they are gone when a measure so capable of doing good as the calling of the

[1] II, 511.   [2] Ibid. 535-6. Dec. 4, 1788.   [3] Ibid. 543-4; 548.

Notables is treated with so much ridicule; we may conclude the nation desperate and in charity pray that heaven may send them good kings."[1] Another American travelling at this time in France seemed to hold an equally modest estimate of the political capacities of the French, and to hope they would treat the existing emergency in a spirit of moderation. "If the States-General are composed of wise men," writes Joel Barlow, in his diary, "they will consider that the small remnant of ancient provincial rights and the present opinions of the people are the materials with which they have to work in forming a constitution. As the former are variant and the latter variable, it will be necessary to conciliate and soften in order to impart to the people that portion of liberty which they can bear, and to impart to all alike. Such wisdom and the necessary integrity to direct it is hardly to be expected in a court like this. I presume there are not to be found five men in Europe who understand the nature of liberty and the theory of government so well as they are understood by five hundred men in America. The friends to America in London and Paris are astonished at our conduct in adopting the New Constitution. They say we have given up all we contended for. They are as intemperate in their idea of liberty as we were in the year seventy-five."[2]

Though Jefferson seemed to think that, on the whole, France was pressing forward to a good constitution, yet, when he heard Frenchmen flattering themselves that it would be better than the English, he had his doubts. "I think it will be better in some points, worse in others. It will be better in the article of representation, which will be more equal. It will be worse, as their situation obliges them to keep up the dangerous machine of a standing army. I doubt whether they will obtain the trial by jury, because they are not sensible of its value."[3]

---

[1] Ford's Jefferson, IV, 370-1. Feb. 22, 1787.
[2] Todd. Life and Letters of Joel Barlow, 83-84. Diary for Oct. 3, 1788. [3] II, 557. Jan. 8, 1789.

Though the outlook was, on the whole, encouraging, there were some possible difficulties in the situation. There was an economic danger. The winter 1788-1789 was unprecedentedly cold. For two months the thermometer varied between 18½ below freezing (Réaumur) and zero.[1] "We have had such a winter," says Jefferson in a letter to Madame de Bréhan, "as makes me shiver yet whenever I think of it. All communications, almost, were cut off. Dinners and suppers were suppressed, and the money laid out in feeding and warming the poor, whose labors were suspended by the rigor of the season. Loaded carriages passed the Seine on the ice, and it was covered with thousands of people from morning to night, skating and sliding. Such sights were never seen before, and they continued two months."[2] In his autobiography Jefferson speaks thus on this topic: "There came on a winter of such severe cold as was without example in the memory of man or in the written records of history. The mercury was at times 50° below the freezing point of Fahrenheit and 22° below that of Réaumur. All outdoor labor was suspended, and the poor, without the wages of labor, were, of course, without either bread or fuel. The government found its necessities aggravated by that of procuring immense quantities of firewood and of keeping great fires at all the cross streets, around which the people gathered in crowds to avoid perishing with cold. Bread, too, was to be bought, and distributed daily, gratis, until a relaxation of the season should enable the people to work; and the slender stock of breadstuff had, for some time, threatened famine, and had raised that article to an enormous price.[3] So great indeed was the scarcity of bread, that, from the highest to the lowest citizen, the bakers were permitted to deal but a scanty allowance per head, even to

---

[1] II, 590. March 13, 1789.   [2] II, 591. March 14, 1789.
[3] Jefferson says in one of his letters that supplies arriving from America reduced the price of flour at Bordeaux from 36 *l.* to 33 *l.* per barrel! II, 590.

those who paid for it; and in the cards of invitation to dine in the richest houses, the guest was notified to bring his own bread. To eke out the existence of the people, every person who had the means was called on for a weekly subscription, which the Curés collected, and employed in providing messes for the nourishment of the poor, and vied with each other in devising such economical compositions of food as would subsist the greatest number with the smallest means." [1] This distress, though somewhat relieved by shipments from the United States and the West Indian islands, continued till July.

Another possible danger that Jefferson detected lay in the size of the coming Assembly. "Twelve hundred persons of any rank and of any nation, when assembled together, would with difficulty be prevented from tumult and confusion. But when they are to compose an assembly for which no rules of debate and proceeding have been yet formed, in whom no habits of order have been yet established, and to consist, moreover, of Frenchmen, among whom there are always more speakers than listeners, I confess to you I apprehend some danger. However, I still hope for the goodness of the body, and the coolness and collectedness of some of their leaders will keep them in the right way, and that this great Assembly will end happily." [2]

The outlook, however, was on the whole encouraging. "The change in this country since you left it is such as you can form no idea of," he wrote Col. Humphreys, March 18, 1789. "The frivolities of conversation have given way entirely to politics. Men, women and children talk nothing else; and all, you know, talk a great deal. The press groans with daily productions which, in point of boldness, make an Englishman stare, who hitherto has thought himself the boldest of men. A complete revolution in this government has, within the space of two years

---

[1] Autobiography, I, 88-89.   [2] II, 580, 588; III, 8.

(for it began with the Notables of 1787), been effected
merely by the force of public opinion, aided, indeed, by the
want of money, which the dissipations of the court had
brought on. And this revolution has not cost a single
life, unless we charge to it a little riot lately in Bretagne,
which began about the price of bread, became afterward
political, and ended in the loss of four or five lives. . . .
The writings published on this occasion are, some of them,
very valuable; because, unfettered by the prejudices under
which the English labor, they give a full scope to reason,
and strike out truths as yet unperceived and unacknowl-
edged on the other side the Channel. An Englishman doz-
ing under a kind of half reformation is not excited to think
by such gross absurdities as stare a Frenchman in the face
wherever he looks, whether it be towards the throne or the
altar. In fine, I believe this nation will, in the course of
the present year, have as full a portion of liberty dealt out
to them as the nation can bear at present, considering how
uninformed the mass of their people is. This circumstance
will prevent the immediate establishment of the trial by
jury." [1] Thus, as the time for the meeting of the States-
General drew on, Jefferson was hopeful that a partial reformation of French conditions would be easily effected. He
did not think that anything more than a limited ameliora-
tion was possible or, considering the state of the public
mind, desirable.

Jefferson was present at the session of the 5th of May,
and his description, though not so vivid as Gouverneur
Morris's, is interesting. "The States-General were opened
the day before yesterday. Viewing it as an opera it was
imposing; as a scene of business the King's speech was
exactly what it should have been, and very well delivered.
Not a word of the Chancellor's was heard by anybody, so
that, as yet, I have never heard a single guess at what it
was about. Mr. Necker's was as good as such a number

---

[1] III, 10-12. March 18, 1789.

of details would permit it to be. The picture of their resources was consoling, and generally plausible. I could
have wished him to have dwelt more on those great constitutional reformations, which his ' rapport au roy ' had
prepared us to expect. But they observe that these points
were proper for the speech of the Chancellor. We are in
hopes, therefore, they were in that speech, which, like the
Revelations of St. John, were no revelations at all." [1]

But there were difficulties arising. Necker had not satisfied the " patriotic " party because in his speech he had
" tripped too lightly over the great articles of constitutional
reformation." " It is now, for the first time, that their revolution is likely to receive a serious check, and begins to
wear a fearful appearance," writes Jefferson to Jay.[2] He
had hoped the majority of the Nobles would side with the
Third Estate in their desire to form a single chamber, but
this apparently was not to be. They would consent to
equal taxation, but five-sixths of them were thought to be
decidedly for voting by orders. "Were this single question accommodated, I am of opinion there would not occur
the least difficulty in the great and essential points of constitutional reformation." " But on this preliminary question," he continues, " the parties are so irreconcilable that it
is impossible to foresee what issue it may have. The Tiers
Etat, as constituting the nation, may propose to do the business of the nation either with or without the minorities in
the Houses of Clergy and Nobles which side with them. . .
In fine, it is but too possible, that between parties so animated, the King may incline the balance as he pleases.
Happy that he is an honest, unambitious man, who desires
neither money nor power for himself, and that his most
operative minister, though he has appeared to trim a little,
is still, in the main, a friend to public liberty."

Jefferson's letters for May and June are full of the exciting events of those weeks. He describes the insistence of

---

[1] III, 22-23. May 8, 1789.   [2] Ibid. 26. May 9. 1789.

the Third Estate upon its position, its final assumption of the title and rights of a National Assembly, the 20th of June, the Tennis Court oath, the announcement of the Séance Royale, which he said was the work of a reactionary and desperate court which had succeeded in "browbeating" and intimidating "M. Necker and shaking the King." The noblesse were in triumph; the people in consternation. Jefferson's own views at this crisis are given in his memoir. "I was quite alarmed at this state of things. The soldiery had not yet indicated which side they should take, and that which they should support would be sure to prevail. I considered a successful reformation of government in France as insuring a general reformation through Europe, and the resurrection, to a new life, of their people, now ground to dust by the abuses of the governing powers. I was much acquainted with the leading patriots of the Assembly. Being from a country which had successfully passed through a similar reformation, they were disposed to my acquaintance and had some confidence in me. I urged most strenuously an immediate compromise; to secure what the government was now ready to yield and to trust to future occasions for what might still be wanting."[1]

He proposed a compromise to Lafayette and another member of the Third Estate, M. de Etienne. He writes to the latter, June 3, 1789: "After you quitted us yesterday evening we continued our conversation (Monsieur de Lafayette, Mr. Short and myself) on the subject of the difficulties which environ you. The desirable object being to secure the good which the King has offered, and to avoid the ill which seems to threaten, an idea was suggested, which, appearing to make an impression on Monsieur de La Fayette, I was encouraged to pursue it on my return to Paris, to put it into form and now to send it to you and him. It is this, that the King in a *séance royale* should come forward with a Charter of Rights in his hand, to be signed by himself and by every member of the Three Orders. This

---

[1] Autobiography, I, 93.

charter to contain the five great points which the Resultat of December offered, on the part of the King, the abolition of pecuniary privileges offered by the privileged orders, and the adoption of the national debt, and a grant of the sum of money asked from the nation. This last will be a cheap price for the preceding articles; and let the same act declare your immediate separation till the next anniversary meeting. You will carry back to your constituents more good than ever was effected before without violence and you will stop exactly at the point where violence would otherwise begin. Time will be gained, the public mind will continue to ripen and to be informed, a basis of support may be prepared with the people themselves and expedients occur for gaining still something further at your next meeting, and for stopping again at the point of force. I have ventured to send to yourself and Monsieur de La Fayette a sketch of my ideas of what this act might contain, without endangering any dispute. But it is offered merely as a canvas for you to work on, if it be fit to work on at all. I know too little of the subject, and you know too much of it, to justify me in offering anything but a hint. . . . But after all, what excuse can I make, Sir, for the presumption? I have none but an unmeasurable love for your nation, and a painful anxiety lest despotism, after an unaccepted offer to bind its own hands, should seize you again with tenfold fury." [1]

The charter that Jefferson framed was as follows:

A Charter of Rights solemnly established by the King and Nation.

1. The States-General shall assemble, uncalled, on the first day of November annually, and shall remain together so long as they shall see cause. They shall regulate their own elections and proceedings, and until they shall ordain otherwise, their elections shall be in the forms observed in the present year, and shall be triennial.

---

[1] III, 45-6. June 3, 1789.

2. The States-General alone shall levy money on the nation and shall appropriate it.

3. Laws shall be made by the States-General only, with the consent of the King.

4. No person shall be restrained of his liberty, but by regular process from a court of justice, authorized by a general law (Except that a Noble may be imprisoned by order of a court of justice, on the prayer of twelve of his nearest relations). On complaint of an unlawful imprisonment, to any judge whatever, he shall have the prisoner immediately brought before him, and shall discharge him, if his imprisonment be unlawful. The officer, in whose custody the prisoner is, shall obey the orders of the judge; and both judge and officer shall be responsible, civilly and criminally, for a failure of duty herein.

5. The military shall be subordinate to the civil authority.

6. Printers shall be liable to legal prosecution for printing and publishing false facts, injurious to the party prosecuting; but they shall be under no other restraint.

7. All pecuniary privileges and exemptions, enjoyed by any description of persons, are abolished, and all debts, already contracted by the King, are hereby made the debts of the nation, and the faith thereof is pledged for their payment in due time.

9. Eighty millions of livres are now granted to the King, to be raised by loan and reimbursed by the nation; and the taxes heretofore paid shall continue to be paid to the end of the present year, and no longer.

10. The States-General shall now separate and meet again on the 1st day of November next.

Done, on behalf of the whole nation, by the King and their representatives in the States-General, at Versailles, this —— day of June, 1789.

Signed by the King and by every member individually, and in his presence."[1]

---

[1] III, 47-48.

But the Revolution was not to be solved in this easy way. The deputies wrangled on for several days longer over the question of organization. "The fate of the nation," writes Jefferson, June 17, "depends on the conduct of the King and his ministers; were they to side openly with the Commons, the revolution would be completed without a convulsion, by the establishment of a constitution, tolerably free, and in which the distinction of Noble and Commoner would be suppressed. But this is scarcely possible. The King is honest and wishes the good of his people; but the expediency of an hereditary aristocracy is too difficult a problem for him. On the contrary, his prejudices, his habits and his connections decide him in his heart to support it." The Queen and Princes are infatuated enough to hazard any measure, no matter how violent, to cut through the present difficulties, even civil war. But the ministry would prevent any such extreme. But the ministry itself does not inspire much confidence. "It is a tremendous cloud, indeed, which hovers over this nation, and he at the helm has neither the courage nor the skill necessary to weather it. Eloquence in a high degree, knowledge in matters of account and order, are distinguishing traits in his character. Ambition is his first passion, virtue his second. He has not discovered that sublime truth, that a bold, unequivocal virtue is the best handmaid even to ambition, and would carry him further, in the end, than the temporising, wavering policy he pursues. His judgment is not of the first order, scarcely even of the second, his resolution frail, and upon the whole, it is rare to meet an instance of a person so much below the reputation he has obtained."[1] The only hope lies in the Commons. "The Commons have in their chamber almost all the talents of the nation; they are firm and bold, yet moderate. There is indeed among them a number of very hot-headed members; but those of most influence are cool, temperate and sagacious. Every step of

---

[1] III, 52.

this House has been marked with caution and wisdom. The Noblesse, on the contrary are absolutely out of their senses. They are so furious they can seldom debate at all. They have few men of moderate talents and not one of great, in the majority. Their proceedings have been very injudicious. The Clergy are waiting to profit by every incident to secure themselves, and have no other object in view." [1]

Jefferson had a very high admiration for the policy of the Third Estate in those early discussions. They had shown, he thought, "through every stage of these transactions a coolness, wisdom, and resolution to set fire to the four corners of the kingdom and to perish with it themselves, rather than to relinquish an iota from their plan of a total change of government," [2] and he thought them perfectly capable of carrying out their well-conceived reforms. "While there are some men among them of very superior abilities, the mass possess such a degree of good sense as enables them to decide well. I have always been afraid their numbers might lead to confusion. Twelve hundred men in one room are too many. I have still that fear. Another apprehension is that a majority cannot be induced to adopt the trial by jury; and I consider that as the only anchor ever yet imagined by man, by which a government can be held to the principles of its constitution." [3]

But tempestuous times were ahead. Jefferson describes the events that led up to the storming of the Bastille, the prayer of the National Assembly ("a piece of masculine eloquence") to the King to order the removal of the troops which had been suspiciously massed about Paris and Versailles; the King's refusal and his remark that the deputies "might remove themselves if they pleased, to Noyons or Soissons," the dismissal of the Necker ministry, the falling of the King into the hands of men "the principal among

---

[1] III, 58. June 18, 1789.　　[2] Ibid. 69. July 11, 1789.
[3] Ibid. 71. July 11, 1789. There are "at least two thousand spectators attending their debates constantly." III, 62.

whom had been noted through their lives for the Turkish despotism of their characters," the attack upon the Bastille, and the murder of several prominent men, the sending of deputations from the States to the King, to which he gave only "dry and hard answers," the insistence of the Duc de Liancourt in telling the King what had really happened, how all these things gradually made an impression upon him and the court, the King's visit to the States, asking "their interposition to re-establish order," the appointment of Lafayette to be Commander-in-Chief of the Militia, the resignation of the new ministry and recall of Necker, and the visit of the King to Paris and his adoption of the tri-color cockade on the 17th of July. "About sixty thousand citizens of all forms and colors, armed with the muskets of the Bastille and Invalides, as far as they would go, the rest with pistols, swords, pikes, pruning hooks, scythes, etc., lined all the streets through which the procession passed, and, with the crowds of people in the streets, doors and windows saluted them [King and Assembly] every-where with cries of ' vive la nation,' but not a single ' vive le roy' was heard. The King stopped at the Hotel de Ville. There Monsieur Bailly presented and put into his hat the popular cockade, and addressed him. The King being unprepared and unable to answer, Bailly went to him, gathered from him some scraps of sentences, and made out an answer which he delivered to the audience as from the King. On their return the popular cries were ' vive le roy et la nation.' He was conducted by a Garde Bourgeoise to his palace at Versailles, and thus concluded such an *amende honorable* as no sovereign ever made and no people ever received."[1] Tranquillity was in a fair way to be re-stored, and popular police bodies were taking the place of the old organization. "But we cannot suppose this par-oxysm confined to Paris alone. The whole country must pass successively through it, and happy if they get through it as soon and as well as Paris has done."[2]

---

[1] III, 72-80. July 11, 1789.   [2] Ibid.

A striking light is thrown on the overheated, suspicious state of the public mind at this time by another extract from the same letter.

"I went yesterday to Versailles to satisfy myself what had passed there; for nothing can be believed but what one sees, or has from an eye-witness. They believe there still that three thousand people have fallen victims to the tumults of Paris. Mr. Short and myself have been every day among them, in order to be sure what was passing. We cannot find with certainty that anybody has been killed but the three before mentioned [Governor and Lieutenant-Governor of the Bastille and the Provost des Marchands], and those who fell in the assault or defense of the Bastille. How many of the garrison were killed nobody pretends to have ever heard. Of the assailants, accounts vary from six to six hundred. The most general belief is that there fell about thirty. There have been many reports of instantaneous executions by the mob on such of their body as they caught in acts of theft or robbery. Some of these may, perhaps, be true. There was a severity of honesty observed, of which no example has been known. Bags of money offered on various occasions through fear or guilt have been uniformly refused by the mobs. The churches are now occupied in singing '*De profundis*' and *Requiems* 'for the repose of the souls of the brave and valiant citizens who have sealed with their blood the liberty of the nation.'"

Though some difficulties were solved, others were not so easily. Jefferson hoped for no further outbreaks. "Still there is such a leaven of fermentation remaining in the body of the people that acts of violence are always possible, and are quite unpunishable; there being, as yet, no judicature which can venture to act in any case, however small or great. The country is becoming more calm. The embarrassments of the government for want of money are extreme. The loan of thirty millions, proposed by M. Necker, has not succeeded at all. No taxes are paid. A total stoppage of all payment to the creditors of the State is possible any moment. These form a great mass in the city as well as country, and among the lower class of people too, who have been used to carry the little savings of their service into the public funds upon life rents of five, ten, twenty guineas a year, and many of whom have no other dependence for daily subsistence. A prodigious number of servants are now also thrown out of employ by domestic reforms rendered necessary by the late events. Add to this the want of bread, which is extreme. For several days past a considerable proportion of the people have been without bread altogether; for though the new harvest is begun, there is neither water nor wind to grind the grain. For some days past the people have besieged the doors of the bakers, scrambled with one another for bread, collected in squads all over the city, and need only some slight incident to lead them to excesses which may end in nobody can tell what. The danger from the want of bread, however, which is the most imminent, will certainly lessen in a few days. What turn that may take which arises from the want of money, is difficult to be foreseen."[1]

Three weeks later he writes: " The danger of famine here has not ceased with a plentiful harvest. A new and unskilful administration has not got into the way of bringing regular supplies to the Capital. We are in danger of hourly insurrection for the want of bread, and an insurrection once begun for that cause, may associate itself with those discontented for other causes and produce incalculable events. But if the want of bread does not produce a commencement of disorder, I am of opinion the other discontents will be stifled, and a good and free constitution established without opposition."[2]

Soon after this Jefferson left for home, and the views of this eye-witness of the great drama ceased. Jefferson shows all through his correspondence that he favored moderation in the great crisis, though such moderation would effect a result neither one thing nor the other.

---

[1] III, 93-4. Aug. 27, 1789. [2] Ibid. III. Sept. 18, 1789.

Jefferson inclined strongly toward the so-called Patriotic Party. These men he thought possessed not only the inclination but the ability successfully to carry out the great reformation needed by France. Only they must be kept together. "It has been a misfortune," he says, "that the King and aristocracy together have not been able to make a sufficient resistance to keep the patriots in a compact body." In their differences of opinion lay their danger. When such differences became acute the leaders met at Jefferson's house on one occasion and discussed their disagreements. There were present Lafayette, Duport, Barnave, Alexandre La Meth, Blacon, Mounier, Maubourg, and Dagout. "They discussed together," he says, in a letter dated September 19, 1789, "their points of difference for six hours, and in the course of discussion agreed on mutual sacrifices. The effect of this agreement has been considerably defeated by the subsequent proceedings of the Assembly, but I do not know that it has been through any infidelity of the leaders to the compromise they had agreed on." This conference appears in Jefferson's Autobiography, composed thirty years later, in the following altered and glorified form: "The cloth being removed and wine set on the table after the American manner, the Marquis [de Lafayette] introduced the objects of the conference by summarily reminding them of the state of things in the Assembly, the course which the principles of the Constitution were taking, and the inevitable result, unless checked by more concord among the Patriots themselves. He observed that, although he also had his opinion, he was ready to sacrifice it to that of his brethren of the same cause; but that a common opinion must now be formed, or the Aristocracy would carry everything, and that whatever they should now agree on, he, at the head of the National force, would maintain. The discussions began at the hour of four, and were continued until ten o'clock in the evening, during which time I was a silent witness to a coolness and candor of argument unusual in the conflicts of political opinion; to a logical reasoning and chaste eloquence disfigured by no gaudy tinsel of rhetoric or declamation, and truly worthy of being placed in parallel with the finest dialogues of antiquity as handed to us by Xenophon, by Plato and Cicero. The result was that the King should have a suspensive veto on the laws, that the legislature should be composed of a single body only, and that to be chosen by the people. This Concordate decided the fate of the Constitution. The Patriots all rallied to the principles thus settled, carried every question agreeably to them, and reduced the Aristocracy to insignificance and impotence." [1]

Such a quotation as this shows the comparative value-lessness of the Autobiography in reference to the events of the Revolution. Written long after the whole drama was over, its ring is not as true as that of the letters.

This is shown in another instance. In his Autobiography Jefferson lays the whole responsibility of the Revolution upon the Queen. The King, he says, would willingly have acquiesced in any scheme of government upon which the reformers could agree. " But he had a Queen of absolute sway over his weak mind and timid virtue, and of a character the reverse of his in all points. This angel, as gaudily painted in the rhapsodies of Burke, with some smartness of fancy but no sound sense, was proud, disdainful of restraint, indignant of all obstacles to her will, eager in the pursuit of pleasure, and firm enough to hold to her desires or perish in their wreck. Her inordinate gambling and dissipations, with those of the Count d'Artois and others of her *clique*, had been a sensible item in the exhaustion of the treasury, which called into action the reforming hand of the nation; and her opposition to it, her inflexible perverseness and dauntless spirit, led herself to the guillotine, drew the King on with her, and plunged the world into crimes and calamities which will forever stain the

---

[1] Autobiography, I, 105.

pages of modern history. I have ever believed, that had there been no Queen, there would have been no revolution. No force would have been provoked, nor exercised. The King would have gone hand in hand with the wisdom of his sounder counsellors, who, guided by the increased lights of the age, wished only, with the same pace, to advance the principles of their social constitution. The deed which closed the mortal course of these sovereigns, I shall neither approve nor condemn. . . . I should not have voted with this portion of the legislature [the portion that decreed the death of Louis XVI]. I should have shut up the Queen in a convent, putting harm out of her power, and placed the King in his station, investing him with limited powers, which, I verily believe, he would have honestly exercised. In this way no void would have been created, courting the usurpation of a military adventurer, nor occasion given for those enormities which demoralized the nations of the world, and destroyed and is yet to destroy millions and millions of its inhabitants." [1]

So tremendous an estimate of the Queen is to be found nowhere in the contemporary letters of Jefferson. He says, indeed, in one place, " the queen weeps, but sins on," and in another, speaking of the reactionary intrigues before the Royal Session of June 23, that the Queen and the Princes are infatuated enough to hazard almost anything. [2] But these are almost the only references to the Queen, and are not weighty enough to make her the cause of the greatest revolution of modern times, a cause that might have had no effect if it might only have been lodged behind convent walls.

In short, Jefferson, before he left France, had no idea that a revolution of appalling violence was impending. In the outbreaks that had occurred before he left he saw no premonition of a most disastrous future. The murderers of Reveillon he denounced as " the most abandoned banditti of Paris," [3] and said that " never was a riot more unpro-

---

[1] I, 101-102.　　　[2] III, 51.　　　[3] Ibid. 26.

voked and unpitied." He spoke of Foulon as the victim of a " bloodthirsty spirit,"[1] but he thought that none of these outbreaks had any professed connection with the great national reformation that was in the making.

He sailed for home with the conviction that within a year one of the greatest of recorded revolutions would have been effected without bloodshed. And when the bloodshed began in grim earnest, he refused to see its significance, minimized its importance, and was reluctant to believe that a beautiful dream might become a hideous, repulsive monstrosity.

---

[1] III, 86.

GOUVERNEUR MORRIS ON THE FRENCH REVOLUTION.

MORRIS'S POLITICAL CREED.

Gouverneur Morris belonged by birth to that strong and influential class of landholders who had, by force of wealth, intellect and superior abilities for leadership, directed the colonial affairs of New York. His father and grandfather had both been men of eminence in the life of the colony, and from them he early acquired those wholesome ideas and sturdy habits of thought and action characteristic of a self-respecting gentry, uncorrupted from above, cherishing freedom as its fairest ornament and most vital possession, and entertaining a high conception of its obligations to society and the state.[1]

These families, possessing in large measure the wealth, education, talents and social authority of the colony, justified this position of commanding importance by their large public spirit and political sagacity. They were for the most part admirable types of manhood, well-intentioned, high-minded, deserving men of sterling worth. Fearless in the assertion of their rights as Englishmen, they were a most valuable element of vigor and energy in the colony, nourishing political freedom, encouraging education, strengthening the reign of law. Brought up in this circle, Morris while yet young became one of the leaders that swung New York into the revolutionary column, became the assistant and close friend of Washington, active in the war and influential in the convention that framed the Con-

---

[1] On the life of Gouverneur Morris see Roosevelt, Am. Statesmen Series, and Lodge, Historical and Political Essays.

stitution.   Fashioned by these various influences, his ideas
on politics and government had taken form in a political
creed that was simple, virile, distinctly conservative, yet
elastic, based upon experience and setting little store by
theory as an active agent in the construction and reconstruction of those institutions by which men seek to realize
the demands of life in common.

He was, in a certain sense, an opportunist in politics.
He believed that every nation should have that form of
government which was adapted to the nature of the people
and their historical development.   " Men," says he, " like
other animals, discover instinctively what is fit for them,
and thus government becomes the result of character,
manners and conditions."

The notion that the light of experience or reason could
reveal a single form of government, intrinsically the best,
and suited to men of all conditions, never occurred to
Morris, or if it did, certainly never found even a temporary
lodgment in his mind.   Government is not subject to
a priori decisions, universally applicable.   Of all human institutions it is precisely the one which is most contingent
upon ever-varying conditions.   This conception would
seem to be the only possible one, at once reasonable and
natural.   Yet it did not so appear to many ardent and
gifted minds of the closing eighteenth century, and by
holding it, Morris's view of the French Revolution was
determined.   When he heard Frenchmen talking of the
rights of man, he preferred to talk of the rights of Frenchmen, Englishmen, Americans.   When he found them desiring an American constitution with the exception of a king
instead of a president, he made the salient criticism that
they were leaving out of consideration that they had not
" American citizens to support that constitution."   " Whoever, therefore, desires," he said, " to apply in the practical
science of government those rules and forms which prevail
and succeed in a foreign country, must fall into the same
pedantry with our young scholars, just fresh from an uni-

versity, who would fain bring everything to a Roman standard. Different constitutions of government are necessary
to the different societies on the face of this planet. The
scientific tailor who would cut after Grecian or Chinese
models would not have many customers either in London
or Paris."[1]

Morris was a thorough republican in America because
he believed no other form of government would work as
well here. The materials for a monarchy or aristocracy
did not here exist. There were no gradations of rank,
no permanent, historic class distinctions in America which
are essential to any form of aristocratic government. Yet
his fondness for a republican government was very temperate. Seeing its qualities, he was not blind to its defects.
" In adopting a republican form of government," he says,
" I not only took it as a man does his wife, for better, for
worse, but what few men do with their wives, I took it
knowing all its bad qualities."

But for France he believed in a monarchy with its accompaniment of class distinctions, because monarchy was thoroughly rooted in the history of that country, in her social
and political institutions, in the sentiments of her people,
and its abrupt and complete destruction would violently
wrench the whole social fabric, the slow product of centuries of growth, dislocate all existing relations, and carry
in its train injustice, turbulence and anarchy. He saw no
magic in the word monarchy, no mystic spell in the word
republic. The cynical and contemptuous Morris would
never think of hurling such indiscriminate, wholesale an-
athemas against a particular class of men as came scorch-
ing from the flaming pen of the mild, humanitarian Jefferson, with his mammoths, kites and wolves in the guise of
kings. Morris might indeed find this or that king worthy
the mordant epithet, he did indeed criticise individual monarchs as freely and unsparingly as he did democratic mobs,

---

[1] Diary and Letters, edited by Anne Cary Morris, I, 114.

but it would be in every case because the character of the individual could be most accurately expressed in such terms, not because of his kingship. There was very little of the doctrinaire in him. It requires no violent effort of the imagination to see Jefferson a fanatic under favoring conditions. It would require such an effort to figure Morris to ourselves in that rôle.

Morris has left us harsher criticisms of the King of France than has Jefferson, but he certainly did not regard the destruction of the monarchy and the monarch with the same indifference; an indifference so great that it may perhaps be considered mildly joyous approval. No special form or scheme seemed to Morris for a moment the last word in the science of government. No man could see more clearly that every form has the defects of its qualities. Every kind yet discovered among men has its potently bad features. "The best is that which has the fewest faults, and the excellence of even that best depends more on its fitness for the nation where it is established than on intrinsic perfection." Circumstances, environment, the play of the active forces of the world are what give vitality and tone to every political principle.

Such, then, were his opinions on the general forms of government, flexible, contingent, conditional. Here there is no trace of the system-maker. In regard to the basis of all government, of whatever kind, his idea was equally clear and rational. That basis is property. The prosperity and power of a nation depend upon the amount of security given to it. Morris believed that in a republic, even more than elsewhere, property must be rendered impregnable behind entrenchments of legal rights and guarantees. Property not being secure, the cupidity of the masses is unchecked, lawlessness, violence, disregard of obligations may ensue, culminating in the weakening or overthrow of political institutions and the loosening or snapping asunder of the bonds that hold society together. "The engine," says he, "by which a giddy populace can be most easily brought to

do mischief is their hatred of the rich." This passage
shows his attitude toward democracy. Of pure democracy
never a word of praise, but only constant and deep-rooted
distrust. In our constitutional convention he advocated a
legislature consisting of two houses—a lower, democratic,
and an upper, aristocratic, elected for life,[1] which should
serve as a safeguard against the former. He told M. de
Lafayette, soon after reaching Paris, that he was opposed
to democracy "from regard to liberty." He urged the
French not to go too far in that direction in their new
constitution.[2] He thought Mr. Jefferson's ideas in many
respects "too democratical." Later in life, after he had returned to America, and having allied himself with the Federalists, with whom he naturally belonged, had seen that
party go down before the very force he dreaded and the very
leader whom he thought "too democratical," he expressed
the same sentiment, though oftener and louder. He speaks
of democracy, "that disease of which all republics have
perished except those which have been overturned by foreign force." Democracy is not a bad species of government, but it is "no government at all, but in fact the death
or dissolution of other systems, or the passage from one
kind of government to another." In Morris's belief, in
a purely democratic state the greed and envy of the poorer
classes would exercise a dismal sway. Hence he came to be
regarded in France as an aristocrat, and was taunted with
the same at home. Morris was above everything else outspoken—his critics said he was "indiscreet." He never
hesitated to express to the republican party of France his
perfect disbelief in the possibility or desirability of a successful realization of their doctrine. This of course was
unwelcome, however salutary it might have proved. Here
is to be found the cause of that description of him as a
restless and annoying busybody, the plague of the "good
party," pestering them with his hateful irony at the expense

[1] Letter of Madison to Sparks.   [2] Diary and Letters, I, 141.

of their enthusiasms, which disfigures Randall's Life of Jefferson. This appears in an even more irritating and unjustifiable way in the Life of Thomas Paine by Mr. Conway, whose genial biographical method seems to be the simple one of creating your hero by generating a suspicion that every one else is a rogue. Because Morris did not join in the crusade against kings, here so loudly verbal, in France so actual and literal, he was called a monarchy man in the Senate of the United States, and his rumored death in Paris at the hands of the mob announced with much serenity and complacency by the republican press of this country.[1]

Morris's political creed was essentially conservative. He had a marked aversion to breaking with the past, heedless of present conditions. History was to him the parent of political science. Experience and not pure reason was in his view the surest lamp unto the feet of men. "Those who will not trust the experience of history," he says, "are incapable of political knowledge." He was opposed to all violent changes. He had therefore the profoundest distrust of and contempt for those political fanatics who would leap into the unseen future to grasp at imaginary Utopias. Practical politics were to his mind no employment for dreamers. The wise statesman is not one who pursues vain philosophical abstractions, but one who tries patiently to form out of existing materials, honeycombed with defects, a state that shall be more perfect. Thus we shall see Morris having no sympathy with the showy and shallow generalizations of those philosophers who, as Burke said, "had never seen the state so much as in a picture."

---

[1] Such was Monroe's criticism when the question of his confirmation as Minister to France came up before the Senate. He is "a monarchy man and not suitable to be employed by this country, nor in France." King's Life and Correspondence of Rufus King, I, 421—a memorandum of Rufus King giving some of the objections to Morris raised in the Senate at the time of his appointment. Washington, though himself having confidence in Morris's qualifications for the difficult position, wrote him a fatherly letter containing a gentle warning against being too unconciliatory, and advised him to disarm opposition by careful conduct.

Morris loved freedom, he was "devotedly attached to the liberties of mankind," yet he regarded progress toward liberty as necessarily slow and as demanding restraint and sobriety from those who would enjoy it. Habits of political action are those most slowly acquired, must almost be bred into the race before they become safe supports of the state. Experience, experience alone is able to train men to an intelligent use of their rights. Morris thought that after France had once developed the principles of her new constitution, the lifetime of a generation would be required to render the practice familiar.

For the enjoyment of liberty we must first have morals. Without them it is but "an empty sound." Religion is favorable to morals. Its destruction loosens the bonds of duty, and "those of allegiance must ever be weak where there is a defect both of piety and morality." Whatever Morris's attitude towards morality and religion in the concrete may have been, he undoubtedly believed in them as eminently conservative social and political forces, and their subversion in France appeared to him, as it did to many other Americans, as of all portents the most menacing.[1]

Such, in brief, were some of Morris's general political beliefs. We have in them a key to many of his criticisms of the French Revolution.

Such opinions were not popular among many of the more

---

[1] One of the objections to Morris at the time of his appointment was that raised by Mr. Sherman of Connecticut, who was willing to "allow that he possesses a sprightly mind, a ready apprehension, and that he is capable of writing a good letter and forming a good draft," but who said that "with regard to his moral character," he considered him "an irreligious and profane man. He is no hypocrite and never pretended to have any religion. He makes religion the subject of ridicule and is profane in his conversation. I do not think the public have as much security from such men as from godly and honest men. It is a bad example to promote such men." Though they may prove all right it is hardly safe to trust them. "I feel no security that they will not do wrong in the future," even if they have not in the past. "General Arnold was an irreligious and profane man." King's Life and Correspondence of King, I, 420.

vocal reformers of France at this time. Morris appeared to many, both in France and America, as a false representative of the real ideas of his country, as lukewarm in a faith that demanded fervor, as a republican of the Venetian type, if indeed a republican at all, as an aristocrat without even the thinnest disguise. Thus the feeling arose that he was the determined opponent of the Revolution from the beginning and from principle, a suspicion to which much color was given by his social relations with the aristocratic circles in France, and which has found its way into the books. But this is only partly true. The personal attitude of Morris toward France at the beginning of the Revolution was that of a grateful citizen of a grateful sister nation. He considered France the "natural ally" of his country and he sincerely wished her well.[1] In a letter to the Comte de Moustier, then minister to this country, containing Morris's first allusions to the Revolution, he expresses "the wish, the ardent wish, that this great ferment may terminate not only to the good but to the glory of France. On the scenes which her great theatre now displays, the eyes of the universe are fixed with anxiety. The national honor is deeply interested in a successful issue."[2] Repeatedly does he reveal in his letters a thorough sympathy with her in her struggles for freedom and reform. Writing to President Washington, he says, "We have, I think, every reason to wish that the patriots [Lafayette and men of that class] may be successful. The generous wish which a free people must form to disseminate freedom, the grateful emotion which rejoices in the happiness of a benefactor, and a strong personal interest as well in the liberty as in the power of this country, all conspire to make us far from indifferent spectators. I say that we have an *interest* in the *liberty* of France. The leaders here are our friends; many of them have imbibed their principles in America, and all have been fired by our example. Their

---

[1] Morris. Diary and Letters, I, 27, 219.　　　[2] Ibid. 21.

opponents are by no means rejoiced at the success of our Revolution, and many of them are disposed to form connections of the strictest kind with Great Britain."[1]

Nor does this feeling vanish as the Revolution proceeds. In the summer of 1790 he "sincerely, nay, devoutly" wishes that the Constitution (in which, however, he does not believe, and which he declares is good for nothing) "may be productive of great and lasting good to France," and it is almost with the fervent sympathy of a Frenchman himself that he writes, as he contemplates the great events unrolling themselves before him, and the little men at the helm, with their vain and petty plans and their distressing incompetence: "·The present moment teems with great events. Would to God that, in a certain city which you have sometimes seen, there were great men established to meet with proper dignity the greatness of those incidents which will be hourly produced," and a moment later, "I deeply bemoan these things, for I love France sincerely."[2] Even at the close of the year 1792, when the entire fabric of the Old Régime had been destroyed, when the Royal family was in the hands of the Assembly, and the Assembly in the hands of the mob, when the social, moral and political demoralization of the country was complete, and when Morris sought in all this chaos for anything of which he could approve, his deep interest in and attachment to France were not shaken. He writes to Thomas Pinckney: "I wish much, very much, the happiness of this inconstant people. I love them. I feel grateful for their efforts in our cause, and I consider the establishment of a good constitution here as a principal means, under Divine Providence, of extending the blessings of freedom to the many millions of my fellow-men who groan in bondage on the Continent of Europe."[3]

This passage, like many others, shows that Morris was not the opponent of the principles of revolution in themselves,

---

[1] Diary and Letters, I, 68.   April 29, 1789.
[2] Ibid. I, 313-314.   [3] Ibid. II, 8.   Dec. 3, 1792.

that in the special case of France he believed that a revolution was desirable and even necessary, and that if only wisely conducted it might lead to useful and permanent improvement.[1] He believed that reform was demanded by the exigencies of the case. France indeed, as he soon thought, rushed forward in the new way too impetuously and too far, but he saw reason to hope that, seeing her error, she might in the future proceed more cautiously and more wisely. He clung to this hope as long as it seemed possible that affairs might take a better turn. Then he expressed repeatedly his sorrow that this splendid opportunity for introducing a better social and political order among men had been *lost* and perhaps *forever*.

It was then from no petty caste feeling, no illiberality of mind that Morris saw in the Revolution so much to doubt and censure. To the general aspiration of the French for freer life he instinctively responded. To the spirit of the national genius he was keenly alert. The French blood that flowed in his veins had preserved much of its light and racy Gallic quality. There is the same verve, the same sure insight and luminous conception and the same graphic presentation that distinguish the French. By the most characteristic qualities of his mind Morris was fitted to be a gifted, because an intelligent, critic of the French people at that great and critical time. To represent him as the smug patrician to whom the breath of freedom was a stench in the nostrils, as the blind and bigoted devotee of the *status quo* because under it he found himself quite well, as monarchy man and "high-flying aristocrat," because forsooth he did not share in their fulness the opinions of Jefferson or Paine, is to show oneself indisposed to give the evidence its true weight, or unable to appreciate the fact that along with a temperament that may be termed haughty, proud, aristocratic, may go great liberality of mind; that along with a marked personal preference for association

[1] Diary and Letters, I, 38, 303, 525.

with those who possess the graces and refinements of a privileged class, may go a breadth of view and sympathy that far transcends the class—surely a phenomenon sufficiently common in the history of republics that it need occasion no wonder or surprise.

FRANCE IN THE SPRING OF 1789.

Morris reached Paris the third of February, 1789. All eyes were then focused upon the coming States-General. The election campaign was at its height; the people, so long silent, were impatiently looking forward to the day when they should recover their rights of speech, and confidently expected the early inauguration of a new era, bright with useful reforms and fraught with the speedy abolition of odious abuses. The word "constitution" was upon the lips of every Frenchman and inflamed every mind. Hope had been awakened, and with buoyant enthusiasm looked undaunted into the difficult future. "Even voluptuousness itself arises from its couch of roses," writes Morris, early in February, "and looks anxiously abroad at the busy scene to which nothing can now be indifferent. . . . A spirit which has lain dormant for generations starts up and stares about, ignorant of the means of obtaining, but ardently desirous to possess the object, consequently active, energetic, easily led, but alas! easily, too easily misled. Such is the instinctive love of freedom which now boils in the bosom of your country, that respect for his sovereign, which forms the distinctive mark of a Frenchman, stimulates and fortifies, on the present occasion, those sentiments which have hitherto been deemed most hostile to monarchy. For Louis the Sixteenth has himself proclaimed from the throne a wish that every barrier should be thrown down which time or accident may have opposed to the general felicity of his people." [1]

Morris found on that side of the Atlantic a strong

---

[1] Diary and Letters, I, 21.

resemblance to what he had left on this—"a nation which exists in hopes, prospects and expectations, the reverence for ancient establishments gone, existing forms shaken to the foundation, and a new order of things about to take place in which, perhaps, even to the very names, all former institutions will be disregarded," a rather remarkable conjecture to hazard, thus early, when public opinion was still largely conservative, yet one which was destined to be fully realized later in the insane innovations of the *enragés*.[1]

Morris was astounded at the rapidity of the changes going on in France. Books on that country a half a dozen years old contained ideas no longer truly descriptive, furnished information no longer accurate or adequate.[2] Anglomania was raging. "Everything is à l'anglaise, and the desire to imitate the English prevails alike in the cut of a coat and the form of a constitution." Life in Paris moves so fast that calm reflection and mature deliberation become impossible. In this feverish atmosphere men are compelled to pronounce their definitive judgment on a given subject after a moment's hasty glance. The result is that public opinion, thus hurried, is likely to be unsound and insecure.[3]

The utter lack of thoughtful preparation on the part of the Government for the approaching events, the want of any definite programme, the absence of anything like statesmanship, filled Morris with amazement. "The Revolution that is carrying on in this country is a strange one," he writes; "a few people who have set it going look on with astonishment at their own work. The ministers contribute to the destruction of ministerial authority, without knowing either what they are doing or what to do. M. Necker, who

---

[1] That public opinion was less radical than is commonly supposed, see Morse Stephen's French Revolution and Lowell's "The Eve of the French Revolution," chapters on the *Cahiers*.

[2] Diary and Letters, I, 31. "Stay where you are a little while and when you come back you will hardly know your country." Letter to Marquis de la Luzerne, French ambassador at London, I, 35.   [3] Ibid. I, 57.

thinks he directs everything, is perhaps himself as much
an instrument as any of those which he makes use of."[1] Of
M. Necker he never had more than a mediocre opinion.
Meeting him for the first time, he observes, "He has the
look and manner of the counting-house, and, being dressed
in embroidered velvet, he contrasts strongly with his habili-
ments. His bow, his address, etc., say '*I* am the man.' . . .
If he is a really great man I am deceived. . . . If he is not
a laborious man I am also deceived."[2] He was cunning.[3]
He was excessively vain.[4] But he was not a man of great
ability.[5] With a ministry that was incompetent, vacillating
and short-sighted the outlook was not bright. Amid all
those in public life Morris discovered no one plainly marked
as the man of the times. "Gods," he exclaims, "what a
theatre this is for a first rate character."[6] He looks for
such a character and looks in vain. Years after he will consider it extraordinary that times so fruitful, so intense, so
pregnant, have brought forth no one to be their master.[7]

[1] Diary and Letters, I, 55.   [2] Ibid. I, 44-45.
[3] Ibid. I, 79.   [4] Ibid. I, 95.   [5] Ibid. I, 205.   [6] Ibid. I, 55-56.
[7] Ibid. II, 61. "It is a wonderful thing, sir, that four years of
convulsion among four and twenty millions of people has brought
forth no one, either in civil or military life, whose head would fit
the cap which fortune has woven." April 18, 1794.
Morris certainly never thought of Mirabeau as such a man. He
speaks of him only a few times, and then in terms highly depreciatory.
On the day of Mirabeau's funeral he wrote in his Diary: " The funeral
of Mirabeau (attended, it is said, by more than one hundred thousand persons, in solemn silence) has been an imposing spectacle.
It is a vast tribute paid to superior talents, but no great incitement
to virtuous deeds. Vices, both degrading and detestable, marked
this extraordinary creature. Completely prostitute, he sacrificed
everything to the moment. *Cupidus alieni, prodigus sui;* venal,
shameless, and yet greatly virtuous when pushed by a prevailing
impulse, but never truly virtuous, because never under the steady
control of reason nor the firm authority of principle, I have seen
this man in the short space of two years, hissed, honored, hated,
mourned. Enthusiasm has just now presented him gigantic; time
and reflection will shrink his stature. The busy idleness of the hour
must find some other object to execrate or to exalt. Such is man,
and particularly the Frenchman." I, 398. Later he calls him " one
of the most unprincipled scoundrels that ever lived." I, 502. And

In regard to the economic condition of the country Morris says but little. He finds agriculture in a very backward state. Much land lies fallow and much is but slovenly cultivated. Husbandry is a science but very little understood, yet were it understood, miracles might be performed. "If at the same time," he writes, "they should improve both their agriculture and constitution, it would be difficult to calculate the power of this nation. But the progress of the nation seems to be much greater in the fine arts than in the useful arts. This perhaps depends on a government oppressive to industry but favorable to genius."[1]

The aspect of Paris was ominous, misery there taking on its most intense forms. The people were suffering severely from cold.[2] Later as summer drew on famine set in. The great host of the unemployed increased daily,

---

still later he declares that "the price of his assistance was perfectly known for every measure." II, 254.

In Jefferson's contemporary writings there are hardly any references to Mirabeau—though in later years he apparently entertained his friends with descriptions fervid enough. "It is true, that if I had my choice," writes William Wirt, in 1806, "I would much rather have my son (as to mind) a Mirabeau than a Marshall—if such a prodigy as I have heard Mirabeau described by Mr. Jefferson, did ever really exist. For he spoke of him as uniting two distinct and perfect characters in himself, whenever he pleased;—the mere logician, with a mind apparently as-sterile and desolate as the sands of Arabia, but reasoning at such times with an Herculean force, which nothing could resist; at other times bursting forth with a flood of eloquence more sublime than Milton ever imputed to the Cherubim and Seraphim, and bearing all before him." Kennedy. Life of William Wirt, I, 137. Henry Clay told Randall that he had heard Jefferson speak in strong and glowing terms of Mirabeau's "matchless power over the minds of every class of men." Randall. Life of Jefferson, I, 527, note.   [1] Diary and Letters, I, 53.

[2] Writing to General Morris, his brother, he says: "I believe your apprehensions of the sufferings of people here from cold are not unfounded. But they have in that respect an advantage which you did not think of, viz., that they are stowed so close, and in such little cabins, that if they live through the first few months they have an atmosphere of their own about them. In effect, none of the beggars I have seen complain to me of cold. They all ask for means to get a morsel of bread, and show by their countenance that by bread they mean wine." I, 38.

and their demand for bread, ever growing louder and more
imperative, could only with the greatest difficulty be satisfied by extreme vigilance and attention on the part of the
government, a vigilance and attention rendered doubly difficult by the very intensity of the suffering they aimed to
allay.   All grain convoys must be guarded by the military
else they would never reach their destination, but would
be plundered on the way.   For weeks the grain supply
was maintained only by means of rigorous military protection.[1]

The most graphic portrayal of the state of French morals
at this time that we have from the pen of any American
is to be found in a letter written by Morris to Washington
in the latter part of April on the eve of the States-General.
"The materials for a revolution in this country are very
indifferent. Everybody agrees that there is an utter prostration of morals—but this general position can never convey
to the American mind the degree of depravity.   It is not
by any figure of rhetoric, or force of language, that the
idea can be communicated.   An hundred anecdotes and
an hundred thousand examples are required to show the
extreme rottenness of every member.   There are men and
women who are greatly and eminently virtuous.   I have
the pleasure to number many in my own acquaintance, but
they stand forward from a background deeply and darkly
shaded.   It is, however, from such crumbling matter that
the great edifice of freedom is to be erected here.   Perhaps,
like the stratum of rock which is spread under the whole
surface of their country, it may harden when exposed to
the air, but it seems quite as likely that it will fall and
crush the builders.   I own to you that I am not without
such apprehensions, for there is one fatal principle which
pervades all ranks.   It is a perfect indifference to the violation of all engagements.   Inconsistency is so mingled in
the blood, marrow, and very essence of this people, that

---

[1] Diary and Letters, I, 111.

when a man of high rank and importance laughs to-day at what he seriously asserted yesterday, it is considered as in the natural order of things. Consistency is the phenomenon. Judge then, what would be the value of an association should such a thing be proposed, and even adopted. The great mass of the people have no religion but the priests, no law but their superiors, no morals but their interest. These are the creatures who, led by drunken curates, are now in the highroad *à la Liberté*, and the first use they make of it is to form insurrections everywhere for the want of bread."[1] After several months' observation of the Parisian populace he writes that "Paris is perhaps as wicked a spot as exists." Here the blackest crimes, the most shameless corruption, the most flagrant misdeeds are fearfully common. "Incest, murder, bestiality, fraud, rapine, oppression, baseness, cruelty "—such are the crimes of which Morris accuses Paris, "and yet," says he, "this is the city which has stepped forward in the sacred cause of liberty."[2]

The radical and theoretical character of the current political thought, ready to embark with light heart upon the most venturesome experiments, found a determined opponent in Morris, who had been trained in the hard and unromantic school of practical politics. The literati sitting at ease in their quiet studies were spinning new political systems, attractive without doubt, yet suitable alone for men whose like had never yet been seen. Beholding the evils and deficiencies of the present form of government, they deduced therefrom the simple doctrine that everything would necessarily be better in proportion as it departed from existing institutions.[3] Such hopeless dilettantism had, in Morris's opinion, no rôle to play in the constructive work of statesmanship. Nor was this theoretical, speculative cast

---

[1] Diary and Letters, I, 68-69. See also I, 224, under date of Nov. 10, 1789. "Surely there never was a nation which verged farther towards anarchy. No law, no morals, no principles, no religion."
[2] Ibid. I, 200. Oct. 21, 1789.   [3] Ibid. I, 96, 198, 382.

of thought peculiar to the literati. It was characteristic of
the higher classes quite generally, who most imprudently
were playing with republicanism, only later content to cease
after being scorched themselves. For the present all heads
were buzzing with speculative ideas. "Republicanism,"
says Morris, in March, 1789, "is absolutely a moral in-
fluenza from which neither titles, places, nor even the
diadem can guard their possessor." In his view such ideas
of government were not at all suited to the condition and
character of the French people.

In the midst of this advanced society Morris was an
anomaly. Fresh from the newly founded republic across
the sea, to whose foundation he had himself contributed,
he was taunted here in Paris with being an aristocrat.
Madame de Tessé, Madame de Lafayette found his views
altogether too moderate. He wrote a friend that he had
the strangest employment possible. "A republican, and
just as it were emerged from one of the most republican
constitutions, I preach incessantly respect for the Prince,
attention to the rights of the nobility, and moderation, not
only in the object but in the pursuit of it."[1] This was the
burden of all his later advice to those active in the Revolution—moderation, respect for the established order. The
conservatism of his nature and training was thus early
aroused by the radical and dangerous theories about him,
as it was later to be confirmed by the violence of the deeds
to which they led. He steadily combated "the violence
and excess of those persons who, either inspired with an
enthusiastic love of freedom or prompted by sinister de-
signs, are disposed to drive everything to extremity."

Such was France as Morris found her in 1789. Reverence for existing institutions was gone, the very foundations of society had been sapped. A sodden, debased,
vicious populace; sentimental, romantic literati, whose ideas
came from study shelves and whose ignorance of the actual

---

[1] Diary and Letters, I, 27.

world was such as only closet scholars could pretend to, were crying loudly for liberty, which, like a phantom floating before them, they but dimly and imperfectly understood. Morris felt that such people were poor masters to build the edifice of freedom, for, in his view, their idea of freedom was superficial, their conceptions of society and the State inadequate or false or misshapen. Add to this the irresolution and wavering timidity of the ministry, dilly-dallying with half-measures; the populace of Paris, goaded on by hunger and ever ready to break forth into deeds of violence; the prévailing immorality, the levity and incompetence of the higher classes, and we have the picture of France at the outbreak of her Revolution, painted by a cool and far-seeing, and by no means hostile, American. Add further the condition of the army, the only remaining support of existing institutions, now that philosophy had deserted them, and the shadows of the picture deepen.[1] Popular loyalty had been undermined, and the army was an undisciplined, unreliable force, itself deeply infected with the new ideas which it might be asked to combat.

"All these things," says Morris, "in a nation not yet fitted by education and habit for the enjoyment of freedom, give me frequently suspicions that they will greatly overshoot their mark, if indeed they have not already done it."[2]

On July 1, 1789, two weeks before the storming of the Bastille, Morris writes to Jay that "Liberté is now the general cry and Autorité is a name, not a real existence."[3] M. Taine, in the first volume of his history, wrongly ascribes this to Morris's correspondence with Washington and gives it the date July 19.[4] It was, however, written July 1 in a letter to Jay. Manifestly Morris's criticism is much more striking if bearing the earlier date. To say of the government that it is in a state of dissolution a fortnight before the great popular insurrection which embodied

---

[1] Diary and Letters, I, 107, 108, 109, 115, 143. See also Sparks's Morris, II, 80.   [2] Ibid. I, 109. July 1, 1789.

[3] Ibid. I, 108. July 1, 1789.   [4] Taine. French Revolution, I, 38.

that dissolution occurred, and when it was as yet un-
dreamed of, differs widely from saying the same thing five
days after that event has taken place.

THE CONSTITUENT ASSEMBLY.—ITS CHARACTER.

On the fifth of May, 1789, the States-General were convened in the splendid Salle des Menus in the palace of Versailles, amid the pomp and display of royalty, the trappings
of a brilliant and doomed society. It was "the last gala
day of the old monarchy." Of all Morris's brilliant descriptions of revolutionary events none is more vivid than
that of this first session of the States-General. He says
that he reached Versailles early and at a little after eight
got into the hall. "I sit there in a cramped situation till
after twelve, during which time the different members are
brought in and placed, one 'bailliage' after the other.
When M. Necker comes in he is loudly and repeatedly
clapped, and so is the Duke of Orleans; also a Bishop who
has long lived in his diocese and practised there what his
profession enjoins. Another Bishop, who preached yesterday a sermon which I did not hear, is applauded, but
those near me say that this applause is unmerited. An old
man who refused to dress in the costume prescribed for
the Tiers, and who appears in his farmer's habit, receives
a long and loud plaudit. M. de Mirabeau is hissed, though
not loudly. The King at length arrives and takes his seat;
the Queen on his left, two steps lower than him. He
makes a short speech, and well spoken, or rather read.
The tone and manner have all the *fierté* which can be
expected or desired from the blood of the Bourbons. He
is interrupted in the reading by acclamations so warm and
of such lively affection that the tears start from my eyes in
spite of myself. The Queen weeps or seems to weep, but
not one voice is heard to wish her well. I would certainly
raise my voice if I were a Frenchman; but I have no right
to express a sentiment, and in vain solicit those who are

near me to do it. After the King has spoken he takes off
his hat, and when he puts it on again his nobles imitate his
example. Some of the Tiers do the same, but by degrees
they take them off again. The King then takes off his hat.
The Queen seems tó think it wrong, and a conversation
seems to pass in which the King tells her he chooses to do
it whether consistent or not consistent with the ceremonial;
but I could not swear to this, being too far distant to see
very distinctly, much less to hear. The nobles uncover
by degrees, so that, if the ceremonial requires these man-
œuvres, the troops are not yet properly drilled. After the
King's speech and the covering and uncoverings, the Garde
des Sceaux makes one much longer, but it is delivered in
a very ungraceful manner, and so indistinctly that nothing
can be judged of it by me—until it is in print. When he
has done M. Necker rises. He tries to play the orator, but
he plays it very ill. The audience salute him with a long,
loud plaudit. Animated by their approbation, he falls into
action and emphasis, but a bad accent and an ungraceful
manner destroy much of the effect which ought to follow
from a composition written by M. Necker and spoken by
M. Necker. He presently asks the King's leave to employ
a clerk, which, being granted, the clerk proceeds in the
lecture. It is very long. It contains much information and
many things very fine, but it is too long and has many
repetitions and too much compliment, and what the French
call *emphase.* The plaudits were loud, long and incessant.
These will convince the King and Queen of the national
sentiment, and tend to prevent the intrigue against the
present administration, at least for a while. After the speech
is over the King rises to depart, and receives a long and
affecting *Vive le Roi.* The Queen rises and, to my great
satisfaction, she hears for the first time in several months
the sound of *Vive la Reine.* She makes a low courtesy,
and this produces a louder acclamation, and that a lower
courtesy." [1]

---

[1] Diary and Letters, I, 75-76.

Such was the opening day of the Constituent Assembly, "the day which my heart has long awaited," as Louis the Sixteenth said in his address, thus voicing the thought uppermost in the mind of the nation. What was the character of this Assembly, called finally after such dreary and impatient waiting? Was it competent to discharge its important task, the thorough and permanent reformation of a great state? Morris's answer is decisively No! Neither its membership, nor its environment, nor its modes of procedure, nor the spirit which rules it, nor the external influences it obeys, inspire him with confidence. That political inexperience, that eloquent idealism, that ill-timed infatuation for philosophy and reason, whose presence in the nation he has already deplored, he finds dominant here in the Constituent Assembly. "There are some able men in the National Assembly," he writes, toward the end of July, 1789, "yet the best heads among them would not be injured by experience, and, unfortunately, there are a good number who, with much imagination, have little knowledge, judgment, or reflection. . . . They have all that romantic spirit and all those romantic ideas of government which, happily for America, we were cured of before it was too late."[1] Morris felt that such a species of thought might, perhaps, be adapted to the salons of the leisured great, serving there "as ingenious exercises for the mind," but that it could only grow rank and poisonous, transplanted to the national parliament. Here, in the face of the diseased body politic, he thought the practical knowledge of the statesman, not of the doctrinaire, was indispensable. Those who would cure such a society by exploits of the imagination, however daring, or of logic, however flawless, were not the ones for whom the crisis called. Yet

---

[1] Diary and Letters, I, 143. See also Sparks' edition, II, 127. "The greater part have adopted systematic reasonings in matters of commerce as in those of government; so that, disdaining attention to facts and deaf to the voice of experience, while others deliberate they decide, and are more constant in their opinions in proportion as they are less acquainted with the subject, which is natural enough."

of such a character were very many of those who had been
sent up to Versailles to prescribe for unhealthy France. It
is not difficult to understand why this was so, but none the
less was it a misfortune for France.

This same distrust of the Assembly is shown again in a
letter written to Washington in January of the following
year. "Your sentiments on the Revolution effecting here
I believe to be perfectly just," wrote Morris, " because they
perfectly accord with my own, and that is, you know, the
only standard which Heaven has given us by which to
judge. The King is in effect a prisoner at Paris, and obeys
entirely the National Assembly. This Assembly may be
divided into three parts. One, called the *aristocrats*, consists of the high clergy, the members of the law (not lawyers), and such of the nobility as think they ought to form
a separate order; another, which has no name, but which
consists of all sorts of people, really friends to a free government. The third is composed of what are called here
the *enragés*, that is, the *madmen*. These are the most
numerous, and are of that class which in America is known
by the name of pettifogging lawyers, together with a host
of curates, and many of those who, in all revolutions,
throng to the standard of change because they are not well.
This party, in close alliance with the populace, derives from
that circumstance very great authority. They have already
unhinged everything. . . . The torrent rushes on irresistible until it shall have wasted itself.

" The aristocrats are without a leader, and without any
plan or counsels as yet, but ready to throw themselves into
the arms of any one who shall offer. The middle party,
who mean well, have unfortunately acquired their ideas of
government from books, and are admirable fellows upon
paper; but as it happens, somewhat unfortunately, that the
men who live in the world are very different from those
who dwell in the heads of philosophers, it is not to be
wondered at if the systems taken out of books are fit for
nothing but to be put into books again. Marmontel is

the only man I have met with among their literati who seems truly to understand the subject."[1]

Great is Morris's scorn of this tendency to theorize upon everything, so widely prevalent; to solve pressing emergencies by appeals to books. He gives a case illustrating what he considers the rare fitness of the then rulers to conduct the affairs of the kingdom. There is a scarcity of bread which must be met in some way and immediately. Lafayette is alarmed about it and brings the matter up for discussion. Surely this is a question to be settled by practical common sense and business methods rather than by book lore. Yet the Duke de la Rochefoucauld, a man of prominence and influence, thinks to aid in meeting the difficulty by telling of some one "who has written an excellent book upon the commerce of grain."[2] Morris felt and continued to feel only the sincerest contempt for those theorists who, in Arthur Young's phrase, used to talk glibly about "making a constitution" as if it were "a pudding to be made by a receipt."[3]

But, if the equipment of these constitution-makers was vulnerable in so many points, could nothing be said in approval of the methods they adopted to enable them to form the new régime under which their aims were to be realized? But little, in Morris's view. The very structure of the Assembly itself, as well as the character of its internal regulations, were better fitted to thwart than to further its mission as a constitution-making body. He found the same objection that Jefferson did in its size. Containing nearly twelve hundred members, it was so large as to be unwieldy, demanding a hall so vast that conversational discussion became quite impossible. Nor was this all, for there were no closed sessions, but the galleries were thrown open to the public, who added a thousand more to the audience, and who themselves took an active part in the proceedings, applauding, hissing, or threatening the mem-

---

[1] Diary and Letters, I, 277-278.　　[2] Ibid. I, 156. Sept., 1789.
[3] Young's Travels in France. Bohn edition, 183.

bers. Furthermore, they neglected to adopt any distinct and tried method of parliamentary order. Of discussion proper there was little; only set speeches more or less elaborate. "They discuss nothing in the Assembly," says Morris. "One large half of the time is spent in hollowing and bawling—their manner of speaking. Those who intend to speak write their names on a tablet and are heard in the order that their names are written down, if the others will hear them,. which they often refuse to do, keeping up a continual uproar till the orator leaves the pulpit. Each man permitted to speak delivers the result of his lucubrations, so that the opposing parties fire off their cartridges, and it is a million to one if their missile arguments happen to meet. The arguments are usually printed; therefore there is as much attention paid to making them sound and look well, as to convey instruction or produce conviction. But there is another ceremony which the arguments go through, and which does not fail to affect the form, at least, and perhaps the substance. They are read beforehand in a small society of young men and women, and generally the fair friend of the speaker is one, or else the fair whom he means to make his friend, and the society very politely give their approbation, unless the lady who gives the tone to that circle chances to reprehend something, which is, of course, altered if not amended. Do not suppose I am playing the traveller. I have assisted at some of these readings, and will give you an anecdote from one of them. I was at Madame de Staël's, the daughter of M. Necker. She is a woman of wonderful wit, and above vulgar prejudices of every kind. Her house is a kind of Temple of Apollo, where the men of wit and fashion are collected twice a week at supper, and once at dinner, and sometimes more frequently. The Comte de Clermont-Tonnerre (one of their greatest orators) read to us a very pathetic oration, and the object was to show that, as penalties are the legal compensation for injuries and crimes, the man who is hanged, having by that event paid his debt to

society, ought not to be held in dishonor; and in like manner, he who has been condemned for seven years to be
flogged in the galleys should, when he has served out his
apprenticeship, be received again into good company as
if nothing had happened.   You smile; but observe that the
extreme to which the matter was carried the other way,
dishonoring thousands for the guilt of one, has so shocked
the public sentiment as to render this extreme fashionable.
The oration was very fine, very sentimental, very pathetic,
and the style harmonious. Shouts of applause and full
approbation. When this was pretty well over, I told him
that his speech was extremely eloquent but that his principles were not very solid. Universal surprise. A few
remarks changed the face of things. The position was
universally condemned, and he left the room. I need not
add that as yet it has never been delivered in the Assembly,
and yet it was of the kind which produces a decree by acclamation; for sometimes an orator gets up in the midst of
another deliberation, makes a fine discourse, and closes
with a good snug resolution, which is carried with a huzza.
Thus in considering a plan for a national bank proposed by
M. Necker, one of them took it into his head to move that
every member should give his silver buckles, which was
agreed to at once, and the honorable member laid his upon
the table, after which the business went on again. It is
difficult to guess whereabouts the flock will settle when
it flies so wild. . . ."[1]

---

[1] Diary and Letters, I, 278-279. Letter to Washington, Jan., 1790.
Samuel Breck, who happened to be in Paris during the month of
February, 1791, has left an interesting description of a session of the
National Assembly. "I had arrived late," he says, "and could
not get a place, so I had to wait on a rough stairway erected for
the occasion only and leading to the gallery. Here I was desired
to take a seat and be patient until some person should come out.
While thus stationed, I fell into a conversation with the soldiers
on guard, and chatted with them familiarly for a quarter of an
hour, so that when the door opened they good-naturedly admitted
me without asking for my card. When I entered I found myself
in the best place in the house, being just behind and above the

Such theatrical dilettantism was utterly repugnant to Morris's sense of the dignity and seriousness of the moment, and he was astonished to find it flourishing in the very midst of the Assembly. Men vested with the highest powers in the State and commissioned to provide for the present and future welfare of their country, were yet suscepti-

---

president and almost within reach of the far-famed Mirabeau. He was seated close by, acting as one of the four secretaries. The tribune, from which every speaker was obliged to address the house, was in front, and to crown my good fortune, there happened to arise just as I entered a most interesting discussion. The subject was this: The king's aunts having emigrated with the intention to go to Rome, had been arrested near the frontier and a notarial statement of the business was sent to the Assembly. The receipt of it occasioned a very animated debate, which commenced by the well-known Abbé Maurey rushing to the tribune, into which he entered after a scuffle with several other members who strove to keep him out. He had a huge muff, which he shook in the contest, while the president rang a bell to keep order. At length he put his foot on the threshold and darted in. The battle ceased and silence was restored. The abbé was on the side of the court. His oratory was fine and his talents of the first order. He condemned the arrest as irregular, because the princesses had passports. . . . As soon as he had left the tribune, Mirabeau arose in his place to reply. It was a privilege the acting secretaries had of addressing the house without going to the tribune. I heard him very distinctly on account of his being close by where I stood, yet his voice was husky and his articulation thick; in short, he spoke as if he had something in his mouth. Notwithstanding this, such was the clever arrangement of his words and the popularity of his theme that he was listened to with great attention. He was dressed in powdered hair and three curls were over each ear." Recollections of Samuel Breck, with passages from his Note-Books (1771-1862), edited by H. E. Scudder, pp. 167-168. For a description of the royal family at this time, whom Breck was enabled to see in their private chapel at mass, see Recollections, p. 169: "The king had a velvet suit and looked very like the impression on his coin. His body was in constant motion, rolling from side to side while he read his prayers. He was lusty and in good health. His brother, Monsieur, resembled him much, and his daughter, the Duchess d'Angoulême, now so ugly, was then a lovely-looking girl of about fourteen." Two other Americans of prominence were in France at various times during the Revolution, Joel Barlow and John Trumbull, but they have left only very scanty and disconnected records of what they saw.

The French Revolution.

ble to the most flippant influences. That they, battling as they were with the gravest crisis in their national history, should commit errors, great and irreparable perhaps, Morris could conceive; but to see them have hysterics, to see them in moments of tempestuous excitability so lose their self-control as to commit the most senseless and silly puerilities, was something for which he was not prepared. Yet he repeatedly saw gusts of violent emotion sweep over the National Assembly, leading to deeds which would have been ludicrous and grotesque had they not become deplorable when committed by the highest political body ever convened in the history of the nation.[1] After having watched the Assembly a year and a half, Morris writes that it has committed many blunders, which are not to be wondered at, " for they have taken genius instead of reason for their guide, adopted experiment instead of experience, and wander in the dark because they prefer lightning to light."

Nor was the environment of the Assembly such as to enable it to labor and debate in peace, the one absolutely essential condition for the success of any constitution-making body. Morris believed that all hope of self-poised deliberation and free discussion was lost to the Assembly when it moved to Paris, the 6th of October, 1789. The entry in his Diary for the next day is as follows: " If my calculations are not very erroneous, the Assemblée Nationale will soon feel the effects of their new position. There can be no question of the freedom of debate in a place so remarkable for order and decency as the city of Paris."[2]

---

[1] These displays of emotion in places little suitable for them occurred even in the financial reports of M. Necker. " His writings on finance teem with that sort of sensibility which makes the fortune of modern romances." I, 283. Other remarks of Morris on the National Assembly are in the same tenor. "It is impossible to imagine a more disorderly assembly. They neither reason, examine nor discuss. They clap those whom they approve and hiss those whom they disapprove." I, 197. In a letter to M. Necker years after, in 1803, he says: " On en lisait de fort beaux [discours] dans cette Assemblée, mais on n'y discutait rien." II, 434.   [2] Diary and Letters, I, 177.

Nor was there. The intimidations ·of Paris now began. Insurrections and popular outbreaks were organized from time to time whose object was to persuade the Assembly "by the gentle influence of the cord" to obey the people's behest.

At the close of the year 1790 Morris gives the situation as follows: "How will it all end? This unhappy country, bewildered in the pursuit of metaphysical whimsies, presents to one's moral view a mighty ruin. Like the remnants of ancient magnificence, we admire the architecture of the temple, while we detest the false god to whom it was dedicated. Daws and ravens and the birds of night now build their nests in its niches; the sovereign, humbled to the level of a beggar's pity, without resources, without authority, without a friend; the Assembly, at once a master and a slave—new in power, wild in theory, raw in practice, it engrosses all functions, though incapable of exercising any, and has taken from this fierce, ferocious people every restraint of religion and of respect. Here conjecture may wander through unbounded space. What sum of misery may be requisite to change popular will, calculation cannot determine. What circumstances may arise in the order of Divine will to give direction to that will, our sharpest vision cannot discover. What talents may be found to seize those circumstances to influence that will, and, above all, to moderate the power which it must confer, we are equally ignorant. One thing only seems to be tolerably ascertained, that the glorious opportunity is lost, and (for this time at least) the Revolution has failed."[1]

It is easy to understand Morris's antipathy toward such an assembly. No contrast could be more startling, more impressive than that of the body that had framed our constitution and that which was at work on one for France. In almost every respect they were at variance. Morris naturally compared our assembly, of which he had himself

---

[1] Diary and Letters, I, 359-360. Nov. 19, 1790.

been a member, manageable in numbers, full of sound and ripe political wisdom and sagacity, governed by well established modes of procedure, conducting its labors behind closed doors and in quiet, free from intimidation and threat, with the monster convention of France, where political inexperience, theory and idealism were such forces for derangement. This body, disorderly within and the victim of disorder without, acting under the influence of fear generated from the surrounding mob, or of contagious passion springing up uncontrolled and uncontrollable in its very midst, could only spend itself in confusion or folly; and knowing how difficult it had been to frame a constitution in the former, he might naturally enough despair of the efforts of the latter.

THE CONSTITUENT ASSEMBLY.—ITS WORK.

Holding such opinions of the character of the Constituent Assembly, Morris naturally felt no great assurance of a happy outcome of its labors. He believed that the Assembly was incapable, inadequate to its task. He considered the mental state of the nation shaken, distracted, unhealthy. He found that the American example had powerfully affected the attitude of French thought toward liberty, equality and constitutional popular government, yet he feared lest the French, lacking experience and poise, would seek to apply these new and seductive ideas in an arbitrary way with dangerous disregard of changed conditions.[1] He did not, however, allow his gloomy predispositions to color his judgment of the specific acts of the Assembly. I think it may truthfully be said that he looked at the laws which were enacted with an open and impartial mind, though he found most of them wanting. Independent in his criticism, gifted with keen insight into the motives that influence men and into the significance of their deeds, and guided by a conservative, but sound and ripe

---

[1] Diary and Letters, I, 39, 114.

political philosophy, he analyzes with great acumen some of the features of contemporary French history. He does not condemn invariably, as if by force of habit, or because of a lack of appreciative sympathy, and yet in the main his criticisms are condemnations.

The royal authority was attacked early in the Revolution, was gradually pillaged of most of its functions, and finally left weak and almost lifeless. The King was made a *roi fainéant*, seated upon an insignificant throne. By the constitution of 1791 he was deprived of all real power and became an inert figure-head. He was supposed to be the head of a parliamentary government, yet he could neither summon nor dissolve parliament nor take his ministers from it and in this manner figure in legislation. He had small power of appointment; civil, military, judicial, ecclesiastical and administrative positions all being filled by election. His veto was merely suspensive. He could neither declare war nor conclude peace. His highest and almost only functions were those of an intermediary clerk. Complete and sudden was the change that had come over the French monarchy.

In a monarchy so extenuated as this Morris had no faith. He believed that France needed a strong executive; that having been accustomed to it so long, she could not brusquely overthrow it without great danger to herself. He discovered that the reason for this restriction of royal authority to the discharge of mere formalities lay in the fact that the French had only known the evils of too powerful an executive, the disadvantages of one too weak being outside their experience. Their political education had been one-sided; their political knowledge was accordingly defective.

Now Morris was no stagnant conservative. He had no desire to see royal authority preserved intact as it was at the outbreak of the Revolution. He explicitly states that the character of the monarchy ought to be made more liberal and less arbitrary, and he was glad to believe that the King himself was of the same opinion. Restrictions were manifestly desirable, yet they should not be so sweeping as to result in the complete withdrawal of authority from the monarch. Morris was no reactionary, as he was also no radical. He believed in an executive, responsible indeed, yet strong. He saw the King gradually despoiled of all his power, and he believed that the only rescue from the ensuing anarchy lay in a partial return to this authority. He repeatedly urged his friends, Lafayette among others, to rally around the tottering throne. He assured them that the party of the King was the only one which could predominate without danger to the people. France is "used to be governed and must be governed."[1] In this desire to preserve authority for the King, Morris was not influenced by personal considerations. His criticisms of Louis XVI are indifferent, unflattering, at times harsh. "He is an honest man and wishes really to do good, but he has not either genius or education to show the way towards that good which he desires."[2] "His fears govern him absolutely. . . . He is a well-meaning man, but extremely weak, and probably these circumstances will in every event secure him from personal injury. An able man would not have fallen into his situation, but I think that no ability can now extricate him. He must float along on the current of events, being absolutely a cypher."[3] In January, 1790, Morris wrote to Washington as follows: " If the reigning prince were not the small-beer character he is, there can be but little doubt that, watching events and making tolerable use of them, he would regain his authority; but what will you have from a creature who, situated as he is, eats and drinks and sleeps well, and laughs, and is as merry a grig as lives? The idea that they will give him some money when he can economize, and that he will have no trouble in governing, contents him entirely. Poor man, he little thinks how unstable is his situation   He is be-

---

[1] Diary and Letters, I, 169.　　　　[2] Ibid. 114.
[3] Ibid. 142. See also 108.

loved, but it is not with the sort of love which a monarch should inspire; it is that kind of good-natured pity which one feels for a led captive. There is, besides, no possibility of serving him, for at the slightest show of opposition he gives up everything and every person."[1] It was for the office, not the man, that Morris argued.

Morris's belief in a strong executive was only deepened by the further decisions of the Constituent Assembly. It rejected the English and American form of a dual legislature, and decided that the national parliament should consist of a single chamber. Morris had sided with the Third Estate in believing that a constitution-making body should be unique. He thought that in forming their constitution it would be well to vote *par tête*, but that after its completion it would be better to vote *par ordre*. But when the Assembly had reduced the power of the King to a minimum, had arrogated most of the authority to itself and had declared that the permanent legislative form should be a single chamber, elected every two years, he considered that as travelling in the highroad to anarchy and that worst of all tyrannies, the despotism of a faction in a popular assembly.[2]

Morris further dissented from the legislation affecting the position of the nobility. At the outbreak of the Revolution, when royal authority was yet strong, he hoped it would come to the aid of the privileged orders, and believed that, should it so come, it might prevent their destruction.[3] He did not agree with Jefferson that it was desirable to annihilate all distinctions of order. "How far such views may be right respecting mankind in general is, I think, extremely problematical," says he, "but with respect to this nation I am sure it is wrong and cannot eventuate well."[4] Though moving daily in the most aristocratic

---

[1] Diary and Letters, I, 281. Later Morris refers to the "uncommon firmness in suffering" shown by Louis XVI, and laments that he has not "the talent for action." I, 572. Aug. 18, 1792.
[2] Ibid. 154. Sept. 13, 1789.   [3] Ibid. 100, 96.   [4] Ibid. 100.

circles of France, Morris's judgment of the French nobility was not thereby vitiated. He saw clearly the inherent weakness of the class, that though no longer possessing either "the force, the wealth or the talents" of the nation, it hugged its venerable privileges and "rather opposed pride than argument" to its assailants.[1] The nobles did not possess the ability of political leadership nor the practical shrewdness to know when it was necessary to yield. Without competent leaders, without well matured plans, they pursued a policy of sullen, unavailing obstruction, duplicity, selfishness, reactionary scheming. Morris early saw that unless they acquired a constitutional right to some of their privileges their days were numbered.[2] This they did not do, neglecting chances to win favor by assuming an open, candid attitude toward the other classes and the questions at issue, wrapping themselves up in their age-worn customs and usages, relying for support upon the royal authority, for success upon bold and clever stratagems— until it was too late. Yet Morris believed that they should be invested with a certain constitutional authority, that being "the only means of preserving any liberty for the people." Indeed, without such a provision the constitution itself could not probably stand. "If they have the good sense," says our critic, "to give the nobles, as such, some share in the national authority, that constitution will probably endure; but otherwise it will degenerate into a pure monarchy or become a vast republic. A democracy—can that last? I think not, I am sure not, unless the whole people are changed."[3] To confound the nobles entirely with the people he regarded as a "strange doctrine." Their destruction would involve "consequences most pernicious."

---

[1] Diary and Letters, I, 115. [2] Ibid. 38.

[3] Ibid. 116. Elsewhere speaking of the taking away of all political power from both King and nobles, Morris says that it would lead to tyranny either immediately or ultimately "as a consequence of the anarchy which would result from giving the wretched constitution of the Pennsylvania legislature to the Kingdom of France." I, 38.

He regarded the nobility as an institution of slow growth, with ramifications everywhere, the uprooting of which could do nothing but remove the sole protection of the people from the monarch or the monarch from the people, and thus prepare the way either for a complete despotism or complete anarchy. He would assign them a definite and useful rôle in the management of the State. He believed them capable of performing certain necessary and important governmental functions. But the temper of the Assembly and the people was hostile to any such step. Not only were they stripped of all the power they possessed, but even their titles, coats-of-arms and other distinctions were taken from them.

Morris's attitude toward this question, as toward that of royal authority, was not determined by personal sympathy or affiliations, but was the natural dictation of his general political creed. Though from the very beginning of his stay in France he moved chiefly in aristocratic circles and found there most of his friends, he was not thereby prejudiced in their favor. Nowhere does he manifest an admiration for the French nobility as such. His pages abound in illustrations of the flippancy and frivolity of the nobles. He criticises their policy during the critical months of May and June, 1789. He characterizes their pretensions as "absurd."[1] He finds among them "ridiculous notions of aristocratic folly."[2] Indeed, of certain members of the aristocracy whom he met in 1796 in Vienna he says: "The conversation of these gentlemen, who have the virtue and good fortune of their grandfathers to recommend them, leads me almost to forget the crimes of the French Revolution; and often the unforgiving temper and sanguinary wishes which they exhibit make me almost believe that the assertion of their enemies is true, viz., that it is success alone which has determined on whose side should be the crimes and on whose the misery."[3] He criticised the Court

---

[1] Diary and Letters, I, 383.   [2] Ibid. 398.   [3] Ibid. II, 220.

sharply, condemned the dismissal of the Necker ministry, which brought on the storming of the Bastille, as " a conspiracy against freedom." He thought that after what has happened, the Comte d'Artois, brother of the King, should be exiled from France.[1] Yet he held that despite its shortcomings the aristocracy could become a useful element in the State. And he was supported by the example of England, the only other free country of the time whose social development had been similar to that of France.

Morris was, then, opposed to the Revolution on this most fundamental question, that of the relations of the different classes toward each other. And as a thorough alteration and readjustment of these relations was one of the chief objects and results of the Revolution, this opposition is of vital importance. He was estranged from the Revolution by these radical changes. He dissented from its essential character.

On other matters subsidiary to these chief questions his opinions varied. On the subject of the church property his criticisms are few. He urged that it be obtained by the consent of the clergy, thus seeming to consent to some sort of confiscation, but upon a condition that manifestly rendered it impracticable. He did not believe in a State Church. He told some of his friends who were arguing for established religions, that " God is sufficiently powerful to do his own business without human aid, and that man should confine his care to the actions of his fellow-creatures, leaving to that Being to influence the thoughts as He may think proper."[2]

The Assembly abolished the provinces, the old historic territorial divisions of the country, and divided France up into eighty-three departments, nearly equal in size and population. After this Morris refers to France as " this (late) kingdom . . . . cast into a congeries of little democracies, not laid out according to the rivers and mountains, but with

---

[1] Diary and Letters, I, 129. July 15, 1789.   [2] Ibid. 302.

the square and compass, according to latitude and longitude," and he fears that as the provinces formerly had different laws and customs, and as under this new arrangement the "clippings and parings" of several provinces must fall together in some of the new divisions, "such fermenting matter must give them a kind of political colic."[1]

The establishment of municipalities, of which there were forty thousand, Morris finds radically wrong, and predicts that they will become the source of endless confusion and complications and great weakness, but he adds that nothing can now be done to remedy this state of things, for the people have been flattered with "such extravagant notions of liberty" that they must first be allowed to learn by experience the inadequacy and clumsiness of their ill-contrived, cumbersome institutions.[2] This prediction was abundantly verified by later experience, when the municipalities, becoming quite independent, split up the central authority into thousands of fractional morsels, so many sources of mutual opposition and obstruction.

Morris considered the abolition of the parliaments a necessary step. Their abolition was, he thought, a blow at tyranny and essential "to the establishment of freedom, justice and order."[3] He, however, denounced the decree stopping pensions—those given by the King to the Court and favorites—on the ground that it was a violation of the laws of property. He believed that when "privileges were abolished the road was opened for the destruction of all property," and in his view property, even in so doubtful a form, was not to be lightly tampered with.[4]

The Assembly was at work upon the Constitution during more than two years, from June 17, 1789, to September 3, 1791. For some time previous to its final completion the question was, would the King accept it, and, if so, would he accept it simply or would he seize the occasion to give expression to his personal opinions in regard to it? This

[1] Diary and Letters, I, 280.   [2] Ibid. 235, 267, 294.
[3] Ibid. 112, 215.   [4] Ibid. 236, 264-265.

question was much discussed in ministerial and governmental circles. At the suggestion of one of those who stood near the King, probably M. de Montmorin, then Secretary of State, Morris drew up a Speech and Observations, which should be delivered by the King before the Assembly on taking the oath. This paper was given to M. de Montmorin on the 27th of August, 1791, and returned to Morris on the 18th of October. Meanwhile the King took the oath without reservation or expression of opinion. Morris's brief, consequently, had no direct practical result, yet it remains an able and acute criticism of the Constitution. As it was intended for the public utterance of the King, Morris may have pronounced sentiments therein which he himself did not hold, but which he may have considered it expedient for the King to express, yet it is probably true that the writing reflects in substance his own opinions on the Constitution. It is worth while then to examine somewhat closely this critique.[1]

Before entering into this examination, "the eternal maxim of reason and justice, that all government ought to be instituted and exercised for the benefit of the people," is gladly and explicitly acknowledged, the identity of the interest of the King and that of the people is asserted, likewise the desirability of ministerial responsibility to the people through their representatives.

The inconvenience and inexpediency of joining the Declaration of the Rights of Man to the Constitution are indicated. If the Constitution secures these rights, whatever they may be, the Declaration is unnecessary, and if not, it would be useless and ineffectual. In either case there is a risk of contradictions and controversies. Cases of marked inconsistency between the affirmations of the Declaration of Rights and the exact provisions of the Constitution are pointed out. The first requisite of all is that the Constitution be in harmony with itself. If the different parts come

---

[1] Sparks' Morris, II, 490-512.

into antagonism with each other, serious misunderstandings and even irreconcilable difficulties may arise, nullifying or minimizing the benefits hoped for under the reformed régime.

Morris then proceeds to a detailed analysis of the political structure erected by the Constitution, and especially of the organization and distribution of the legislative, executive and judicial powers, whose thorough differentiation and separation are declared important.

Article I of the Constitution provides that the National Assembly, which is the legislative body, shall be permanent and composed of only one chamber, and that the King's veto shall be only suspensive, effective only for a given period. The criticism is made by Morris that a mere majority in a single chamber is thus given the entire legislative power of the nation and thus has complete control over its destinies; that the suspensive veto it not strong enough to oppose effectually any unwise misuse of this power; that should the Assembly attempt to encroach upon the executive power, such a veto would be but a weak weapon of defense in the hands of the latter, while no evils are to be apprehended from the absolute veto, which could not be used by the King to extend his own power, which the King would naturally not interpose to thwart legislation beneficial to the people, but which he would only employ to oppose attacks upon his constitutional authority.

Article II provides that the legislative body cannot be dissolved by the King; that the representatives of the nation are inviolable; that they can be arrested for a criminal deed, but can only be prosecuted upon the consent of the legislative body.

Morris says that this article therefore provides that the Assembly shall exist and the persons of the members be held sacred as long as a majority may think proper. A political body with such supreme power over its own existence may devise and execute plans hostile to the people or to the political authorities, with no resource left the latter to bring about a termination of their session and the punishment of the guilty save in a general insurrection or civil war. History assures us that absolute Assemblies may be as dangerous and as tyrannical as absolute monarchs.

Article III provides' that the legislative body shall have the right of police in the place of its sessions and in the district around to the extent which it shall itself determine upon. It shall have the right of disposing of the forces which by its own consent are quartered in the city when it shall be in session; and the executive power is forbidden to introduce any military forces within the distance of 60,000 yards from the Assembly, except by the demand or permission of the latter.

The criticism of this article is that by giving the Assembly such extensive command over military forces 'in the place of its sessions, power is thereby given the Assembly with which it can at once control the people and the King. Some future Assembly may, therefore, if it will, effect a *coup d'état* and assume larger powers than those delegated it by the Constitution. Means of resistance to such possible arbitrary proceedings would seem to be lacking both to the other State authorities and to the people as well.

Article IV provides that the ministers and other agents of the executive authority may be criminally prosecuted by the Assembly and that no other public authority may prosecute them. Thus, in Morris's view, should the Assembly be inclined to make encroachments upon ministerial and executive authority, the ministers in opposing it would have much to fear, whereas by submission they would be safe from prosecution from any other source.

Article V provides that the King may suspend administrative officials; that he shall thereu███ ███rm the Assembly of his act, and that the Assembly███ ███ove or confirm this suspension. Here again, says███ the authority of the Executive over its own agent███ ███ose who conduct the administration, is rendered███ ███ate to that of

the Assembly, executive power to the legislative. Here
again the ministers will be at the mercy of the Assembly
under circumstances of absolute dependence, and the administrators will seek rather to truckle to the Assembly,
to please those whom they have to fear, than to perform
their duty to the State.

By Article VI the judicial power in the last resort is given
to the Assembly, for an appeal may be taken from the
highest established court, the *Tribunal de Cassation*, in which
case the Assembly shall declare what the law is touching the
question at issue. The *Tribunal de Cassation* is therefore
obliged to settle the case in conformity with this decree.
Hence it is the Assembly which is really giving judgment.
"From hence it results," says Morris, "that the people
will no longer enjoy that security in their property and
possessions to which they are entitled; for it may happen
that many judgments of the *Tribunal de Cassation* will have
been submitted to before the case supposed in the article
[appeal] occurs, and that afterwards the Assembly may decree contradictorily to the tribunal, in which case the preceding judgments will doubtless be questioned. Moreover, as it is not to be supposed that a numerous Assembly
will consist of persons skilled in legal discussions, it may
happen that their explanatory decrees will affect the whole
system of jurisprudence. There is reason to fear also that
their decisions may be influenced by acts of intrigue or
other motives. The Assembly having reserved to itself
the sole right of accusing the judges for misconduct, timid
or corrupt judges will decide in favor of those who have
influence with the Assembly and against the poor and un-
protected."

By Article VII the right to make war and treaties of
peace is vested in the Assembly. In these matters the
King is merely an agent, and an agent of an inferior kind,
for he is not previously instructed, yet must act under the
constant uncertainty of being approved or disavowed. Yet
in Morris's view the King, by the very nature of his posi-

tion, permanent and overlooking everything, is better qualified to judge of foreign politics, their ever-shifting combinations and complications, thaft are persons taken from the
ordinary occupations of life.

Recapitulating then, it appears, says Morris, that the
legislative body has " the right to make laws and decide in
the last resort, both on the application and execution of
them; that they have the supreme right of war, peace and
treaties; that they have an existence dependent only on
their own will, power to protect themselves from the pursuit of justice, and the command of such force as they may
think proper; of course all power not already vested in them
is exposed to their assumption." A body possessed of such
vital and comprehensive powers may become dangerous
and despotic. Morris condemned the placing of such vast
authority, subject to such slight control, in a single group
of men.

In regard to the executive power the provisions of the
constitution were as follows:

Article I. To the King is delegated the care of watching
the external safety of the kingdom, to maintain its rights
and possessions. It belongs to the King to conclude and
sign with all foreign powers all treaties of peace, of alliance,
of commerce, and other conventions, which he shall judge
necessary to the welfare of the State, under the ratification
of the legislative body.

Morris contends that by this article the right of war,
peace and treaties being granted to the Assembly, the King
must act not only in subordination to their will, but
also in uncertainty as to what that will may be; that under
such an arrangement treaties of offense and defense, of commerce, of peace, become exceedingly difficult if not altogether impracticable; that so much power being given the
Assembly in the determination of these conventions, the
private, speculative, commercial or financial undertakings
of individual members may play a most dangerous and pernicious part in the determination of questions which should

be settled on strictly public grounds, as, for instance, in the case of the majority having judged a war necessary, there might yet be many of the majority who would wish to delay it that particular speculations in which they might be interested might be previously arranged; similar selfish motives might lead to a continuation of war, though the restoration of peace might be possible and desirable for the nation at large.

Article II. The King appoints two-thirds of the Rear Admirals, half of the Lieutenants-General, Field Marshals, Captains of Vessels, and Colonels of household troops; the third of Colonels and Lieutenant-Colonels, and the sixth of Lieutenants of vessels.

Thus under the new organization of the military force, only a few of the superior grades of officers are to be filled by royal appointment, the rest are to be filled by election for definite terms. An army so organized, in Morris's estimation, can only with the greatest difficulty be kept up to a strict discipline; but if even this were attained, the army would be only too likely to become a dangerous instrument in the hands of its chiefs. For if the chiefs do not feel a dependence on the King, they may more easily be led to fall in with the plans of some scheming general, and they will find less difficulty in winning over their troops to the execution of these plans, for an army which has lost respect for its Prince will not long retain it for a popular Assembly. It had been complained that one of the abuses of the ancient régime was that the command of the troops was given almost exclusively to an established order. This, however, says the critique, had its good side, for the commanders had every interest in supporting the constitution, and "if the ancient régime had been unexceptionable in other respects this part would have been eminently useful, for it is certainly wise to interest the army in supporting the constitution." Should a conspiracy ever be formed to subdue France by the arms of Frenchmen, the conspirators would much prefer to deal with officers of no property or

connection, because such men would the more readily follow those who could tempt them with great hopes and expectations; "whereas those who have property of their own
and whose relations and connections share in the administration, will not risk the advantages they possess in the
great game of revolutions."

Article III. Administrators are agents elected for a period
by the people, to exercise under the superintendence of the
King the administrative duties. The King has the right
of overruling acts of administrators of departments contrary to the laws or to orders issued to them, and can, in
case of obstinate disobedience, or if they compromise by
their acts the public safety or tranquillity, suspend them
from their offices. He shall inform the legislative body
thereof, and that body may remove or confirm the suspension.

This article relates to internal administration. It is conceded that administrators for strictly local concerns might
well be elected by the people of the locality for short periods.
Much local knowledge and minute attention will thus be
usefully employed and an industrious and honest administration be probably obtained. But when the execution of
the laws, the collection of taxes and the preservation of order
are given over to such bodies there is danger of inefficiency
and incompetence. For purposes of national administration
there must be administrators responsible to the nation as a
whole, not to particular localities. It should be in the
power of the central government to execute its will inde-
pendently without having to seek the co-operation of locally
elected boards or administrators. It should have effective
control of the entire internal national administrative machinery.

The judicial power of this new constitution is delegated
to judges elected by the people for definite periods. Here,
Morris says, a distinction should be made between inferior
and superior judges. The former may be appointed for
a limited period, but the latter should hold their offices

during good behavior. Their impartiality is of supreme importance to every member of society. It appears desirable from every point of view that they should not be named by popular election. Those who choose judges should not only have a just conception of the duty to be performed and of the talents requisite to the performance of them, but also an interest in making a good choice. There is every reason to doubt this being the case at popular elections. The elections may in large degree be governed by intrigue and corruption, and if intrigue and corruption succeed, first allegiance will be owed them on the part of the judges whom they place upon the bench.

A few general observations are now made upon the nature of the government which the situation of France and the character of French manners demand. A high-toned monarchy is considered the only government possible for France, demanded alike by the physical situation of the country and the history and genius of the people. But there must be a sufficient barrier erected against the royal authority. This is not to be sought solely in a single popular elective assembly. An hereditary Senate, whose members shall be great landholders, is advocated. It is by a just combination of the three (King, Senate, House of Deputies), where each having an absolute veto on the others, the particular interest of neither can prevail, that the general interest of the whole society will best be known and pursued, and France raised to that station of happiness and glory which nature seems to have intended for her. This form of government is no doubt open to objections, but human institutions mirror man, and it is vain to "seek perfections among imperfect beings."

The decree whereby the King is prevented from choosing his ministers from the Assembly ought to be repealed. It is desirable that those be appointed to carry out the purposes of the constitution who have proved themselves most ardent partisans in the national legislature.

Such are the criticisms which Morris would have the

King make upon the Constitution of 1791. They reveal his deep-rooted hostility to democracy; at the same time they reveal his insight into political affairs, his shrewdness and sagacity in the judgment of political institutions. For this constitution Morris had the most unfeigned contempt. He saw nothing in it but imperfections and impossibilities. He repeatedly declares it to be "ridiculous," "good for nothing."[1] It is a constitution without energy, without vitality, such that "the Almighty Himself could not make it succeed without creating a new species of man." Further, he says that the conviction is universal that it is inexecutable, and he adds what is certainly startling and ominous, that "the makers to a man condemn it."[2]

Though Morris had no faith in the constitution, though he condemned almost all of the legislation of the Constituent Assembly, considering it as a long series of huge political blunders, yet he saw the forces which were germinating beneath all these acts of presumption, audacity and inexperience, and which he believed would in time make for a renovated and improved political life and for increased national prosperity. Condemning the decisions of the Assembly concerning the constitution, he was not, however, blind to the value of much of its legislation as affecting the economic life of the nation. And here is an admirable illustration of his keen and discriminating critical ability. Here he is allied rather with Arthur Young than with Edmund Burke as a critic of the Revolution. In the very letter written to Washington, November 22nd, 1790, in which he bewails the condition of the country and cries out that one thing seems to be tolerably ascertained, namely, that "the glorious opportunity is lost and (for this time at least) revolution has failed," he discovers five reasons why increased national prosperity may be expected in the future. These are: (1) The abolition of those different rights and privileges formerly enjoyed by the provinces, which served

---

[1] Diary and Letters, I, 204, 238, 361, 440, 492, 508.
[2] Ibid. 457.

to keep them asunder and prevented their perfect fusion into a single unified nation, leaving within the State so many partially independent communities with varied forms and methods of taxation, and with unjust hindrances placed upon the free communication of commerce. (2) The abolition of feudal tyranny, by which the tenure of real property is simplified, the value reduced to money, and rent more clearly ascertained. (3) The extension of the circle of commerce to those vast possessions held by the Church in mortmain, and which were now thrown open to private individuals, whose greater enterprise would largely augment the wealth of the nation. (4) The destruction of a system of venal jurisprudence. (5) Above all, the promulgation and extension of those principles of liberty " which will, I hope, remain to cheer the heart and cherish a nobleness of soul when the metaphysical froth and vapor shall have been blown away." " The awe of that spirit," he continues, " which has been thus raised will, I trust, excite in those who may hereafter possess authority, a proper moderation in its exercise and induce them to give to this people a real constitution of government fitted to the natural, moral, social and political state of their country. How and when these events may be brought about I know not. But I think from the chaos of opinion and the conflict of its jarring elements a new order will at length arise, which, though in some degree the child of chance, may not be less productive of human happiness than the forethought provisions of human speculation." [1]

Morris saw the great dynamic force that was being generated by all these tremendous changes, and he felt that this immense energy, fast accumulating and coming to a head, would soon seek an outlet and, finding it, would bring about great and beneficial changes. And here again his insight into this great drama was keener and profounder than was Burke's. Burke thought at first that France

---

[1] Sparks' Morris, II, 118.

would be weakened by the Revolution. " France," says he, " is at this time in a political light to be considered as expunged out of the system of Europe. Whether she can ever appear in it again as a leading power is not easy to determine, but at present I consider France as not politically existing, and most assuredly it would take up much time to restore her to her former active existence." At this very moment Morris was writing with cooler brain and clearer vision. " In the midst, however, of all these confusions, what with confiscating the church property, selling the domains, curtailing pensions and destroying offices, but especially by that great liquidator of public debt, a paper currency, this nation is working its way to a new state of active energy which will, I think, be displayed as soon as a vigorous government shall establish itself." [1]

THE LEGISLATIVE ASSEMBLY.

The Constituent Assembly was dissolved September 30, 1791. The Constitution had been framed, accepted by the King, and promulgated. On October 1, 1791, the new Assembly, called the Legislative, came together and one of the most critical periods of the Revolution now began. Before its dissolution, a little less than a year later, the Assembly had launched decrees against the emigrants and the non-juring clergy, confiscating the property of the former and banishing the latter, had declared war and pronounced the country in danger. The constitutional party in the Assembly had gone down before the radical Left. Jacobinism had triumphed, Royalty had succumbed and had been led a prisoner to the Temple, and the Revolution had entered upon its most angry and gloomy phase. The Old Régime was already gone, the reign of the bourgeoisie was approaching its end, and the sway of the Parisian populace was about to begin.

During this period Morris seems to have played a partic-

---

[1] Diary and Letters, I, 383.

ularly active rôle. His opinions on current politics were
valued by the conservative party and his advice was often
sought by them. He was assured that he stood high in the
regard of the King and Queen.[1] He became actively im-
plicated in devising a plan of escape for them, and was
urged by the King to become the depository of his papers
and money, which he did.[2] He suggested plans to combat
the attacks of the republicans, dictated a philippic against
the *chef des républicains*, seized every occasion to urge the
formation of a good constitution,[3] and himself worked upon
one which might secure " the just rights of the nation under
the government of a real King."[4] He aided in seeking
to rescue the finances of the country.[5] So high was the
credit he enjoyed for political wisdom that, on one occasion, being absent in London, a friend sent his deputy to
him from Paris to consult with him upon the advisability
of taking a certain position in the Government.[6] He himself
was even proposed as Minister of Foreign Affairs for the
Kingdom of France.[7]

The flight of the King, frustrated at Varennes, had the
effect of checking a popular movement just setting toward
his support, occasioned by the excesses of the Constituent Assembly, but now turned aside into republican channels.[8] This was in June, 1791. The election campaign
for the Legislative Assembly was soon to open. So good
a weapon, unexpectedly falling into the hands of the extremists, was skillfully used by them. Morris found the
new Assembly deeply imbued with republican, or rather
democratical opinions.[9] As a body it was more incompetent than the Constituent, for all members of the former
Assembly were excluded from this, and thus political experience, so painfully acquired, was lightly sacrificed. The
Assembly began its labors by still further cheapening the

[1] Diary and Letters, I, 355, 467, 481, 495.   [2] Ibid. 557-561.
[3] Ibid. 468, 478.   [4] Ibid. 485, 486.   [5] Ibid. 467, 478.
[6] Ibid. 517. M. de Monciel.
[7] Ibid. 477. Proposed by M. de Molleville.
[8] Sparks' Morris, II, 137.   [9] Diary and Letters, I, 457.

dignity of the King by voting not to address him as " Sire "
or " Your Majesty." " Sire," said one eloquent Jacobin,
" signifies seigneur; it belonged to the feudal system which
has ceased to exist. As for the term ' Majesty' it should
only be employed in speaking of God and the people." To
be sure the vote was rescinded the very next day, yet the
act had vividly revealed the temper of the new Assembly.[1]

The Assembly, in so fevered a state of mind, spouting
forth such petty hostility toward royalty, could only be dealt
with in one way. It must not be provoked, its suspicions
must be allayed, if possible, irritation must be reduced
to a minimum. The party with which it tended to clash
must seek to divert its opposition by frankness and trust-
worthiness in its actions. It must avoid all appearances of
falseness and deception. It must not arouse the suspicion
that the countenance seen is but a mask behind which craft
and cunning are plotting.

Such should have been the candid attitude of royalty
toward the Assembly at this critical juncture. Morris
thought that the King and Queen should not only faith-
fully " march in the line of the Constitution, but should
not permit any person in their presence to jest on that
subject, much less seriously to blame the ministry or their
measures."[2] The unwise actions of the Court had already
compromised the throne on more than one occasion. Their
underhanded schemes would be more dangerous to themselves than the ill-will of their opponents—at least would
only much intensify the latter. If the Court persist in such
schemes they " bet a certainty against an uncertainty,"[3]
said Morris. Let it abjure all crooked method, if it seeks
its own salvation. It is not enough even that the ablest
and most honest men unite to save the kingdom. " The

---

[1] Mignet. History of Revolution, 115. Speech of Gaudet.
Morris, Diary and Letters, I, 461: " The members of the late
Assembly are all high-toned in their reprehension of this day's work
of their successors, which is too little respectful towards the King.
Are they indignant that any other should exceed them in marks
of indignity? "   [2] Diary and Letters, I, 531.   [3] Ibid. I, 474.

King and Queen must give them their full confidence,"
else it will all "answer to no purpose."[1] Yet of such an
heroic common-sense policy the Court, despite the pointed
lessons of recent years, was still incapable. The King,
honest himself and intent upon scrupulously observing his
oath to support the Constitution, was weak or unwise enough
to let those approach him and enjoy his intimacy whose
opposition to the new régime was openly avowed. The
Queen was yet more imprudent, and "the Court," says
Morris, "was involved in a spirit of paltry intrigue, unworthy of anything above the rank of footmen and chamber-
maids."[2] Every one had his or her little project, and
every little project had some abettors. Strong and manly
counsels frightened and repelled these fruitless intriguers.

Over against this unpopular court stood the Assembly,
more radical than its predecessor. This Assembly was
composed of a single chamber, and was under no control
save that of public opinion and of a newly-framed constitution, already widely condemned, and which had little more
force than a series of "paper maxims." The people were
becoming disappointed in the non-realization of the impossible prospects originally held out before them and were
under slight restraint. The Constitution was a clumsy
machine.

Morris believed that the only thing for the King to do
now was to wait until a revulsion of feeling should take
place. This governmental machine, becoming daily more
vexatious and troublesome, and the excesses of a radical
Legislature, would inevitably in the course of time reveal
the weakness of the new régime and bring about a reaction
in favor of royal authority. Such proved to be the case.
The very day after the passage of the decrees concerning
the manner of addressing the King they were rescinded, "as
they find the current of opinion in Paris to be against such
measures."[3] Early in October Morris says that the city

[1] Diary and Letters, I, 482.   [2] Sparks' Morris, II, 242.
[3] Diary and Letters, I, 461.   Oct. 6, 1791.

of Paris is becoming wonderfully fond of the King and has
a thorough contempt for the Assembly, " who are, in general, what used to be called in Philadelphia the blue stock-
ings." " At the theater the people cry out continually ' vive
le roi,' ' vive la reine,' ' vive la famille royale,' and when a
' patriot' tries to get up a counter movement by crying
' vive la nation' he is at once silenced."[1] This was the very
same people who were so bitter against him on his return
from the flight. They might easily become so again. Yet
for the moment the tide had turned. The Assembly, however, kept on committing new follies every day; the finances
went from bad to worse; the discontent became general and
would have broken out to the discomfiture of the Gironde
had it not been that the antipathy to the aristocrats was
still too strong, and also that no good opportunity presented itself.[2] The movement in favor of the King was
accelerated by these excesses of the Assembly, alienating
the support of the moderate men. Of this the hostile faction were well aware, and for this reason they found it advis-
able to drive everything to extremities out of the sheer
necessity of self-preservation. This the republican faction
proceeded to do. Morris says that they were led to those
extremely radical measures which finally culminated in the
declaration of war, by the fact that they saw their influence
waning with the people, and the popular desire constantly
increasing to return to a vigorous royal government, freed
from abuses, yet strong enough to restore stability and
order after the period of storm and stress through which
the country had for three years been passing.[3] This desire
for a return to peaceful and ordered life was, our critic says,
becoming every day more general. Yet the radicals, seeing
in this nothing but their own political death, threw themselves with desperate energy against a movement so threatening and sought to turn it back. To assure their own
political position a republic seemed better adapted than a

---

[1] Sparks' Morris, II, 147.   [2] Ibid. 153.   [3] Ibid. 162.

monarchy. Hence from the very opening of the Assembly a plan was formed among several of the members and others to overturn the Constitution which they had just sworn to observe, and to establish a republic in its place. " This arose," says Morris, " in part from the desire of placing themselves better than they could otherwise do, and in part from a conviction that the system could not last and that they would have no share in the administration under a pure monarchy."[1] The wisdom of these " new-fangled statesmen," as Morris calls them, was shown by the fact that Brissot, one of the leading Girondists and chairman of the Diplomatic Committee, actually proposed the cession of Dunkirk and Calais to England as pledges of the fidelity of France to the engagements she might make in a treaty of alliance to be concluded between the two countries.[2] Men so politically insane were capable of anything. They, the radicals, were unscrupulous, energetic and united. They were bold and were not embarrassed " by legal or constitutional niceties."[3] They would handle the postal service despotically. Every letter Morris received bore " evident marks of *patriotic* curiosity."[4] They would employ agents, as indeed had been done ever since the outbreak of the Revolution, to foment a spirit of revolt in other nations, to agitate against established authorities.[5] Genet was the one they were soon to send to the country in the far-off West, and what turmoil was the young man destined to raise! Such were their party tactics. Even against a ruler so palsied and impotent as Louis XVI they assumed the aggressive. Their object was to bring matters to a simple question, the choice between a monarchy and a republic, after having loaded the former with all possible odium. They seized every occasion to pass decrees which were popular but unconstitutional. If the King should exercise his right of veto he would be accused of " wishing a counter-revolution," whereupon an appeal would be made

---

[1] Sparks' Morris, II, 241, 242.   [2] Ibid. 162.   [3] Ibid. 196.
[4] Ibid. 151.   [5] Diary and Letters, I, 522.

to the people, the lower classes, over whom the extremists' influence was great. If the King should assent, his position would be rendered so much the more servile and intolerable; he would become so much the more helpless, his natural defenders and protectors fewer. Such was the policy of the Gironde, as Morris portrays it, and it was carried out to the letter.

The royal power finally went under in the war which the Assembly compelled it to proclaim. M. Taine maintains that this war, which was declared April 20, 1792, and which ravaged Europe till the downfall of Napoleon, was planned and caused by the Left of the Legislative Assembly, consisting mainly of Girondists, and says that if it may be ascribed to the efforts of any one man, that man was Brissot.[1]

Though Morris makes but few references to this, it is evident that he believed the Assembly to be the aggressor. "The Assembly," he says, "commits every day new follies, and if this unhappy country be not plunged anew into the horrors of despotism, it is not their fault. They have lately made a master stroke to that effect. They have resolved to attack their neighbors unless they disperse the assemblies of French emigrants who have taken refuge in their dominions."[2] This he regarded as a *pretext* for hostilities without itself being a distinct violation of the law of nations. This was in December, 1791. The war was formally declared the 20th of April, 1792. As early as July, 1790, Morris believed such a war inevitable, and that, too, for the very reason he assigned later, namely, the necessity by which the revolutionists would be driven to it as a means of self-preservation. But it was not till the end of 1791 that the agitation for it became general and emphatic. Then many elements other than this original one entered into the movement and gave it added impetus.

---

[1] Taine. French Revolution, II, 99.
[2] Sparks' Morris, II, 152.

The reasons for this are given in a letter to Washington, dated February 4, 1792. "Every member of the Ministry," he says, "is convinced that the Constitution is good for nothing, and, unfortunately, there are many of them so indiscreet as to disclose that opinion, when at the same time they declare their determination to support and execute it, which is, in fact, the only rational mode (which now remains) of pointing out its defects. It is unnecessary to tell you that some members of the National Assembly are in the pay of England, for that you will easily suppose. Brissot de Warville is said to be one of them, and indeed (whether from corrupt or other motives I know not) his conduct tends to injure his own country and benefit that of their ancient foes in a very eminent degree. The situation of their finances is such that every considerate person sees the impossibility of going on in the present way, and as a change of system after so many pompous declarations is not a little dangerous among people so wild and ungoverned, it has appeared to them that a war would furnish some plausible pretext for measures of a very decisive nature, in which state necessity will be urged in the teeth of policy, humanity and justice. Others consider a war as a means of obtaining for the government the eventual command of a disciplined military force, which may be used to restore order; in other words, to bring back despotism, and then they expect that the King will give the nation a constitution which they have neither the wisdom to form nor the virtue to adopt for themselves.

"Others, again, suppose that in case of a war there will be such a leaning from the King towards his brother, from the Queen towards the Emperor, from the nobility (the very few) who remain towards the mass of their brethren who have left the kingdom, that the bad success ultimately to arise from the opposition of undisciplined mobs to regular armies may be easily imputed to treasonable counsels, and the people be prevailed on to banish them altogether and set up a Federal Republic. Lastly, the aristocrats, burning with the lust of vengeance, most of them poor and all of them proud, hope that, supported by foreign armies, they shall be able to return victorious and re-establish that species of despotism most suited to their own cupidity. It happens, therefore, that the whole nation, though with different views, are desirous of war; for it is proper, in such general statements, to take in the spirit of the country, which has ever been warlike."[1]

Yet Morris did not believe France ready for it. He was never sanguine as to the outcome of the war. The odds, he thought, were far too great against her. If she were under a good government and at peace with England, then indeed she probably "could set Europe at defiance," but neither of these conditions existed. France, in his opinion, was no more fit for great exertion than a diseased man would be. "You have no idea, my dear sir, of a society so loosely organized," he says in a letter to Washington, December 27, 1791. "America at the worst of times was much better, because at least the criminal law was executed, not to mention the mildness of our manners. My letter predicting their present situation may, perhaps, have appeared like the wanderings of exaggerated fancy, but, believe me, they are within the coldest limits of truth. Their army is undisciplined to a degree you can hardly conceive. Already great numbers desert to what they expect will become the enemy. Their Garde Nationale, who have turned out as volunteers, are in many instances that corrupted scum of overgrown populations of which large cities purge themselves, and which, without constitution to support the fatigues, or courage to encounter the perils of war, have every vice and every disease which can render them the scourge of their friends and the scoff of their foes.

"The finances are deplorably bad. The discontent is general, but it does not break out, partly because the antip-

---

[1] Diary and Letters, I, 508-509.

athy to the aristocrats and the fear of their tyranny still operates, and partly because no safe opportunity offers. Every one is bewildered in his meditations as to the event, and, like a fleet at anchor in a fog, no one will set sail for fear of running foul. . . . The first success on either side will decide the opinions of a vast number who have, in fact, no opinion, but only the *virtuous* determination to adhere to the strongest party, and you may rely on it that if the enemy be tolerably successful, a person who shall visit this country two years hence will inquire with astonishment by what means a nation which in the year of 1788 was devoted to its kings, became in 1790 unanimous in throwing off their authority, and in 1792 as unanimous in submitting to it."[1] And later he says, "The war in which they are engaged furnishes a dreary prospect; there seems to be but one ground to hope for success, which is, that improbable things are those which usually happen."[2]

The condition of the army was indeed chaotic. The levies had been unsatisfactory, the recruits being raw, undisciplined and incompetent. But this was destined to melt away with the lapse of time and their growing experience. The opening campaign in the summer of 1792 was disastrous, but in the fall of that year the French were victorious and won the skirmish of Valmy, important in a moral, if not in a military, sense. Yet Morris was not inclined to believe this a sign of future successes. Writing September 22, 1792, he doubted if France would make as great efforts in the spring as she was then making. "The character of nations must be taken into consideration in all political questions, and that of France has ever been an enthusiastic inconstancy. They soon get tired of a thing. They adopt without examination and reject without sufficient cause."[3] The doubt was ill-founded. It was the next year that the Revolution, under the bold leadership of the Committee of

[1] Diary and Letters, I, 493-494.   [2] Ibid. 533. May 14, 1792.
[3] Ibid. Morris's prophecies in regard to military events were not as successful as his political predictions.

Public Safety, made its most gigantic exertions and won its most signal triumphs.

Early in 1791 Morris seems to have become convinced that France would be inevitably driven into the arms of despotism—a conviction that never left him afterward. He saw the State disorganized, society completely disjointed, and a confused and abnormal state of affairs generally, and he believed that out of this anarchy, despotism would sooner or later emerge to check it. "France," he says, "in on the highroad to despotism. They have made the common mistake that to enjoy liberty it is only necessary to destroy authority, and the common consequence results, viz. that the most ardent advocates for the Revolution begin now to wish and pray, and even cry out, for the establishment of despotic power as the only means of securing the lives and property of the people. This is terrible."[1]

The great mass of the people, he found, were already tired of the Revolution and would gladly accept pure despotism if it should give this security and were not accompanied with the return of their ancient oppressive institutions. Such was the state of the mind of France as the war impended.[2] "The best picture I can give of the French nation," says Morris, "is that of cattle before a thunderstorm."

Meanwhile the activity of the Jacobins constantly increased as they pushed on irresistibly to the 10th of August. The state of uncertainty and distress became daily more acute. In a second letter to Jefferson, written June 17, Morris says: "On the whole, sir, we stand on a vast volcano. We feel it tremble, we hear it roar, but how and when and where it will burst, and who may be destroyed by its eruptions, it is beyond the pen of mortal foresight to discover. . . . It is in contemplation to make a serious effort against that faction [the Jacobin] in favor of the Constitution, and M. de Lafayette will begin the

[1] May 14, 1792.
[2] Diary and Letters, I, 537-543. Letter to Jefferson, June 10, 1792.

attack. I own to you that I am not sanguine as to the success. . . . Thus while a great part of the nation is desirous of overturning the present government in order to restore the ancient form, and while another part, still more dangerous from position and numbers, are desirous of introducing the form of a federal republic, the moderate men, attacked on all sides, have to contend alone against an immense force. I cannot go on with the picture, for my heart bleeds when I reflect that the finest opportunity which ever presented itself for establishing the rights of mankind throughout the civilized world is perhaps lost, and forever."

Soon came the 20th of June, and the entry in Morris's diary for that day runs as follows: " There is a great movement in Paris and the guard is paraded. While I am writing the mob and the National Guards are marching and countermarching under my windows. I don't think they will come to blows. Dine with the Baron de Blome; after dinner we learn that the deputation of the Faubourgs has forced the unresisting guard, filled the château, and grossly insulted the King and Queen. His Majesty has put on the *bonnet rouge,* but he persists in refusing to sanction the decrees. ' This is neither the form in which it ought to be demanded of me, nor the moment to obtain it,' he calmly told the surging crowd of angry people who pressed upon him, almost to the point of suffocation. . . . The Constitution has this day, I think, given its last groan."[1]

Then came the 10th of August, and Morris wrote a few days later to Thomas Pinckney, our minister at London, in this vein: " We have had here within the last few days some serious scenes, at which I am not surprised, because I foresaw not only a struggle between the two corps which the Constitution had organized, viz., the executive, socalled, and the legislative, but I was convinced the latter would get the better. It is nevertheless a painful reflection that one of the finest countries in the world should be so

---

[1] Diary and Letters, I, 546.

cruelly torn to pieces. The storm which lately raged is a little subdued, but the winds must soon rise again, perhaps from the same quarter, perhaps from another; but that is of little consequence. A man attached to his fellow-men must see with distress the woes they suffer, but an American has a stronger sympathy with this country than any other observer, and nourished as he is in the bosom of liberty, he cannot but be deeply affected to see that in almost any event this struggle must terminate in despotism." [1]

THE NATIONAL CONVENTION.

The Convention met on the 20th of September, 1792. At its first session it decreed the abolition of the monarchy and declared France a republic.

From the first Morris had believed that the constitution, framed and adopted by the Constituent Assembly, being ill adapted to the France of the 18th century, possessed few elements of stability. He was not, then, surprised at its being overturned. "That," he says, "is a natural accident to a thing which was all sail and no ballast." [2]

This constitution had created an executive without power, who was, however, rendered responsible for events. It had lodged the entire power of the State in a single chamber of deputies who were under no control save that of public opinion, which was at that time a thing most variable. The populace, "a thing which, thank God," says Morris, "is unknown in America," intoxicated with the feeling of its own importance with which it had for three years been daily flattered, and disappointed in the non-realization of the golden prospects originally held out to it, was under slight restraint. [3] From these defects of the constitution and this uneasy state of the popular mind arose the revolution of the 10th of August and the following days. The executive

---

[1] Diary and Letters, I, 571-572.   [2] Ibid. 603.   [3] Ibid. 600.

fell inevitably into the power of the legislature, and this into the hands of such men as could influence the populace. The constitution plainly could not last. Yet the establishment of a republic was unexpected. It was no great national movement that brought it about, but simply popular pressure at Paris.

" Nothing new this day," so runs the entry for September 21, 1792, " except that the Convention has met and declared they will have no King in France." In writing the next day to Washington, Morris says, " You will have seen that the King is accused of high crimes and misdemeanors, but I verily believe that he wished sincerely for this nation the enjoyment of the utmost degree of liberty which the situation of circumstances will permit. What may be his fate God only knows, but history informs us that the passage of dethroned monarchs is short from the prison to the grave." The republic was proclaimed and the Year One began. Morris shows the different factions, Gironde and Mountain, trying to persuade the people that it and not the other is the author of the new government. The Republic came in quite suddenly and unexpectedly, but was apparently very popular. Though the people found themselves possessed of it " by a kind of magic, or at least a sleight of hand," they were nevertheless " as fond of it as if it were their own offspring." [1] Writing October 23, 1792, Morris says: " With respect to the present temper of the people of this country, I am clearly of opinion the decided effective majority is now for the Republic. What may be the temper and opinion six months hence no present sensible man would, I think, take upon him to declare, much less depend on the form of government which shall be presented by the Convention. If vigorous, it is very problematical whether the departments will adopt it, unless compelled by a sense of impending exterior danger; if feeble, it is (humanly speaking) impossible that it can control the effervescent temper of this people, and that appears suffi-

---

[1] Diary and Letters, I, 596.

ciently by the fate of the late constitution. Whether they
will be able to strike out that happy mean which secures
all the liberty which circumstances will admit of, combined
with all the energy which the same circumstances require;
whether they can establish an authority which does not
exist, as a substitute (and always a dangerous substitute)
for that respect which cannot be restored after so much
has been done to destroy it; whether, in crying down and
even ridiculing religion, they will be able, on the tottering
and uncertain base of metaphysic philosophy, to establish
a solid edifice of morals—these are questions which time
may solve." [1]

Morris's faith in the wisdom of Frenchmen had long
since vanished. Apparently the national character, which
might appeal to him in ordinary times, showed to little advantage in the stormy times of revolution. Ever since the
opening of the States-General he had seen the series of
political blunders lengthen day by day, increasing the general havoc rather than solving the great problem of a freer
and happier life for France. "Since I have been in this
country," he writes toward the close of 1792, "I have seen
the worship of many idols, and but little of the true God;
I have seen many of these idols broken, and some of them
beaten to dust. I have seen the late constitution, in one
short year, admired as a stupendous monument of human
wisdom and ridiculed as an egregious production of folly
and vice." [2]

From this time onward Morris regarded the different
measures taken in the Revolution as necessary ephemeral.[3]

---

[1] Diary and Letters, I, 598.   [2] Ibid. II, 7.   Dec. 3, 1792.
[3] "But I do not greatly indulge the flattering illusions of hope,
because I do not yet perceive that reformation of morals without
which liberty is but an empty sound. My heart has many sinister
bodings, and reason would strive in vain to dispel the gloom which
always thickens where she exerts her sway." II, 8. Again, comparing America and France, he says: "Such is the immense difference between a country which has morals and one which is
corrupted. The former has everything to hope, and the latter
everything to fear." II, 60.

He thought France must undergo many more shocks before finding order again.[1] " The character of France," he says, " has ever been an enthusiastic inconstancy. They soon get tired of a thing. They adopt without examination and reject without sufficient cause. They are now agog with their republic and may perhaps adopt some form of government with a huzza; but that they will adopt a good form, or, having adopted, adhere to it, is what I do not believe." [2]

Henceforth he chronicles events much less fully, and mainly as they may affect international complications about which, as Minister of the United States, he is obliged to keep his home government informed. His criticisms become less general and are concerned more with the details of diplomacy. Since the definite accession of the radicals to power in the autumn of 1792 he is thrown out of that close contact with those active in the Revolution which he had up to this time preserved, and cannot as heretofore " peep behind the scenes." He watches the little politicians play " their peddling parts " and pass on. He sees different parties fade away " like the shadows of a magic lantern." Everything is in a constant flux. Nothing is stable, nothing certain; everything changes from day to day. The Revolution increases in intensity. Waves of hatred break upon one party, sweeping it away, and fall back, only later to dash with redoubled force against another. " La roue immense," he writes, " à laquelle est attaché le sort de cet empire, écrase dans sa marche ceux qui l'ont fait mouvoir. Personne n'est assez forte pour l'arrêter quoique chacun se flatte de pouvoir la faire aller à son gré, mais ils se trompent tous." [3]

From the opening of the Convention the Jacobin Club raged as furiously against the new government as it had

---

[1] In 1795 he wrote Madame de Nadaillac: " Il me semble que votre malheureuse patrie doit subir encore plusieurs révolutions avant qu'on ne puisse compter sur un ordre quelconque." II, 85.
[2] Sparks' Morris, II, 230.   [3] Diary and Letters, II, 21.

against its predecessor. It now came to be a life and death struggle between the Girondists and the Jacobins. Morris notes that luckily for the Jacobins their leaders are "daring and determined," while those of their adversaries are many of them timid.[1] At first the majority has had rather the advantage, though frequently compelled by the Jacobins to decree what they do not wish. An event of immense national importance as well as decisive of the fate of the Gironde and the future supremacy of the Convention, was the trial of the King. "To a person less intimately acquainted than you are with the history of human affairs," Morris writes Jefferson, "it would seem strange that the mildest monarch who ever filled the French throne, one who is precipitated from it precisely because he would not adopt the harsh measures of his predecessors, a man whom none could charge with a criminal act, should be prosecuted as one of the most nefarious tyrants that ever disgraced the annals of human nature—that he, Louis XVI, should be prosecuted even to death. Yet such is the fact." Morris thought he would probably be condemned and for these reasons: (1) The majority of the Assembly, in order to preserve themselves, thought it necessary to dethrone the King, abolish monarchy and establish a republic. To do this it was necessary to throw all the odium they could upon the King and arouse the nation against him. This was easily accomplished. Having possession of his papers, they attained their object by garbling, suppressing and mutilating the evidence. They raised a terrible storm against the unhappy King, succeeded in sweeping him from the throne and brought in the republic. They were then in a difficult pass themselves. They did not know what to do with him. They feared to condemn him or to acquit him, but were impelled to destroy him whom they held captive. The Jacobin party were violently against the King, and Morris says that the monarchical and aristo-

---

[1] Diary and Letters, II, 9.

cratic parties also desired his death, believing "that such a catastrophe would shock the national feelings, awaken their hereditary attachment and turn into channels of loyalty the impetuous tide of opinion."[1] "Thus he has become," he adds, "the common object of hatred to all parties because he has never been the decided patron of any one." This is a startling view of the matter, but Morris was in a position to know.

The King was sentenced and beheaded on the 21st of January, 1793. Apropos of this, Morris wrote to Jefferson: "The late King of this country has been publicly executed. He died in a manner becoming his dignity. Mounting the scaffold, he expressed anew his forgiveness of those who persecuted him and a prayer that his deluded people might be benefited by his death. On the scaffold he attempted to speak, but the commanding officer, Santerre, ordered the drums to beat. The King made two unavailing efforts, but with the same bad success. The executioners threw him down and were in such haste as to let the axe fall before his neck was properly placed, so that he was mangled. . . . The greatest care was taken to prevent a concourse of people. This proves a conviction that the majority was not favorable to that severe measure. In fact the great mass of the people mourned the fate of their unhappy prince. I have seen grief such as for the untimely death of a beloved parent. Everything wears an appearance of solemnity which is awfully distressing."[2]

From now on life in Paris becomes more and more difficult and painful. Morris complains that it is impossible to act effectively with the ever shifting and varying parties. To stand well with any one of them would involve such a complete abdication of all moderation and diplomatic wisdom that it would be wrong. The reign of arbitrary will now becomes supreme. Morris, minister of a friendly nation, is arrested in the street and not allowed to pass the

---

[1] Diary and Letters, II, 10.   [2] Ibid. 31-32.

barrier of the town. Servants of the government attempt
to search his house for papers and persons who are sus-
pected with hiding there. He is insulted by the chairman
of the Diplomatic Committee. He protests, demands an
apology and receives one. But, as he writes, " The path
of life in Paris is no longer strewed with roses." Morris
was the only foreign minister to remain in Paris after the
10th of August. He writes a friend that the sky is becoming blacker and blacker. The prospect is dreadful. External dangers are threatening, but worst of all is the disorganized state of the internal government. " In short,"
says he, " the fragment of the present system is erected in
a quagmire." [1]

The Gironde is finally torn down by the violent Jacobins.
" The reason being," says Morris, " that they possess only
' parole energy.' " [2] Then the Reign of Terror begins.
October 18, 1793, Morris writes Washington: " The present
government is evidently a despotism both in principle and
practice. The Convention now consists of only a part of
those who were chosen to frame a constitution. These,
after putting under arrest their fellows, claim all power and
have delegated the greater part of it to a Committee of
Safety. You will observe that one of the ordinary measures of government is to send out commissioners with unlimited authority. They are invested with power to remove
officers chosen by the people and put others in their places.
This power as well as that of imprisoning on suspicion is
liberally exercised. The Revolutionary Tribunal, established here to judge on general principles, gives unbounded
scope to will. It is an emphatical phrase in fashion among
the patriots that terror is the order of the day." [3] This
Reign of Terror stands out vividly from the very few
references to it made by Morris. Writing of the September massacres he says that hundreds of the best people of
the country have been destroyed without form of trial and

---

[1] Diary and Letters, II, 37. Feb. 1793. [2] Sparks' Morris, II, 336.
[3] Diary and Letters, II, 53.

" their bodies thrown like dead dogs into the first hole that offered." [1] " I write," he adds, " from a place deserted by its former inhabitants, where in almost every countenance you can mark the traces of present woe and of dismal forebodings."

The entries in the famous diary become less and less frequent and less and less significant. Soon Morris's mission terminates and he proceeds slowly homeward, spending several years by the way in visiting his friends in the different countries of Europe.

---

[1] Diary and Letters, II, 15.

JAMES MONROE.

To the pessimist succeeded the optimist, to the critic the enthusiast. When the United States Government, greatly irritated, requested the recall of the troublesome Genet, France acceded, but asked in turn to be relieved of Morris. For reasons of policy the request was granted, though Washington took occasion to assure Morris of his continued confidence in him and his satisfaction with his conduct. Then was precipitated an episode famous in our diplomatic history. The appointment of Monroe, an ardent admirer of France and her Revolution, to the place left vacant by the withdrawal of Morris, intended as an act of conciliatory good will, speedily proved a most unhappy mistake, and became in the eyes of the Federalists the great scandal of the day. Into this unfortunate and tangled affair it is no part of our purpose to enter here. Monroe's mission to France is a part of our general political history and has been abundantly discussed by historians. Suffice it to say that he arrived in France soon after the fall of Robespierre, the Thermidorians being in the ascendant, and that, though known for his warm attachment to France, the Committee of Public Safety hesitated to receive him. He waited several days, making no headway. "Not another civilized nation upon earth," says Mr. Adams, " had a recognized representative in France at that time." [1] Monroe then, in great and just impatience, sought some other method of recognition. He applied directly to the Convention to appoint a date for his recep-

---

[1] Gilman's Monroe, 45.

tion. The Convention passed the necessary decree and named August 15, 1794, as the day of reception. Then occurred the famous "pageant," in the fever of which Monroe went so far to commit his country to obligations toward France which she did not desire. In a speech of great fervor he threw aside all reserve and pleased the ears of the Convention and no doubt expressed his own convictions. "Republics," he said, "should approach near to each other. In many respects they have all the same interest; but this is more especially the case with the American and French republics. Their governments are similar; they both cherish the same principles and rest on the same basis, the equal and unalienable rights of man. The recollection, too, of common dangers and difficulties will increase their harmony and cement their union. America had her day of oppression, difficulty and war; but her sons were virtuous and brave, and the storm which long clouded her political horizon has passed, and left them in the enjoyment of peace, liberty and independence. France, our ally and our friend, and who aided in the contest, has now embarked in the same noble career; and I am happy to add, that whilst the fortitude, magnanimity and heroic valor of her troops command the admiration and applause of the astonished world, the wisdom and firmness of her councils unite equally in securing the happiest result.

"America is not an unfeeling spectator of your affairs at this present crisis. I lay before you in the declarations of every department of our government—declarations which are founded in the affections of the citizens at large—the most decided proof of her sincere attachment to the liberty, prosperity and happiness of the French Republic."

The President of the Assembly, Merlin de Douai, responded with feeling and with a shrewd eye to the consequences. "The French people," he said, "have not forgotten that it is to the American people that they owe their initiation into the cause of liberty. It was in admiring the sublime insurrection of the American people against

Britain, once so haughty, but now so humbled; it was in themselves taking arms to second your courageous efforts, and in cementing your independence by the blood of our brave warriors, that the French people learned in their turn to break the scepter of tyranny, and to elevate the statue of Liberty on the wreck of a throne supported during fourteen centuries only by crimes and by corruption.

"How, then, should it happen that we should not be friends? Why should we not associate the mutual means of prosperity that our commerce and navigation offer to two peoples freed by each other? But it is not merely a diplomatic alliance; it is the sweetest, the most frank fraternity that must at the same time unite us, that, indeed, already unites us; and this union shall be forever indissoluble, as it will be forever the dread of tyrants, the safeguard of the liberty of the world, and the preserver of all the social and philanthropic virtues!

"In bringing to us, Citizen, the pledge of this union so dear to us, you could not fail to be received with the liveliest emotions. Five years ago, a usurper of the sovereignty of the people would have received you with the pride which alone belongs to vice, thinking it much to have given to the minister of a free people some tokens of an insolent protection. But to-day, the sovereign people themselves, by the organ of their faithful representatives, receive you; and you see the tenderness, the effusion of soul that accompanies this simple and touching ceremony! I am impatient to give you the fraternal embrace which I am ordered to give in the name of the French people. Come and receive it in the name of the American people, and let this spectacle complete the annihilation of an impious coalition of tyrants!"

Then Monroe stepped forward and received the embrace; the Convention ordered that the speeches of the day be printed in the two languages, "French and American," and that the flags of the two countries be displayed intertwined in the hall of the Convention, "in sign of the union and eternal fraternity of the two peoples."

John Quincy Adams was then in Europe entering upon his diplomatic career. He had already begun that monumental Diary, and one of his earliest entries is dated Amsterdam, January 18, 1795, and describes an official call that he made upon the " Representans du peuple Français." They talked about official business; then other subjects were touched upon,—Washington, Jay's Treaty, and so on. Finally they came to speak of Mr. Monroe's reception by the National Convention. " ' Parbleu,' said one, ' it was a scène attendrissante.' It was ' *une des plus fameuses séances* ' of the Convention. There were more than ten thousand persons present. ' He shed tears, he was so much affected. I saw him cry.' ' Oh! ' said another, ' c'était aussi bien de quoi faire pleurer.' " [1]

This bit of melodrama was ominous and the omen was fulfilled. Monroe was no cool and neutral diplomat. His actions were criticised by the home government, whom he criticised in turn. The trouble grew until he was recalled in 1796 in a fury that sought outlet in the publication of a pamphlet of five hundred pages, entitled " A View of the Conduct of the Executive," in which he printed his instructions, correspondence with the French and American Governments, and speeches. " It remains to this day, says Mr. Gilman, "a most extraordinary volume, full of entertaining and instructive lessons to young diplomatists." [2] It may be of interest to the diplomatist. It is of less, though

---

[1] Memoirs of John Quincy Adams, by C. F. Adams, I, 62.

[2] The " View " aroused the wrath of the Federalists, and counter pamphlets filled the air. Perhaps the most notable of these was one published anonymously by Alexander Hamilton. Scipio's Reflections on Monroe's View. Boston, 1798.

Monroe reached Paris, August 2, 1794. He took leave of the Directory, January 1, 1797. His recall was represented by the republicans as simply another of the treasonable machinations of the monarchy men. Elbridge Gerry, writing to Monroe, says, after speaking of the recall: " I am convinced that there has been a deep system, at home and abroad, to disgrace republicanism and republican officers, and that the late President has unfortunately confided too much in persons of this disposition." April 4, 1797. Some Letters of Elbridge Gerry, by W. C. Ford.

of some value to the student of the French Revolution. In the letters here published Monroe has much to say of the events taking place in France. They lack the discrimination of Jefferson, the insight and cool analytical quality of Morris. Uniformly favorable, they impress one with superficiality. There are none of those luminous descriptions of French conditions and French life that make the pages of his two predecessors so significant. They lack the larger view of things that Jefferson often had, however much he might be wedded to his idols, and they possess none of that racy, vivid, dramatic form that was the natural mode of expression with Morris. Yet, although of minor interest, they still merit some examination.[1]

In his first letter to the Secretary of State, dated August 10, 1794, Monroe says: " I heard at Havre of the crimes and execution of Robespierre, St. Just, Couthon and others of that party. . . . That Robespierre and his associates merited their fate is a position to which every one assents. It was proclaimed by the countenances and voices of all whom I met and conversed with from Havre to Paris. In the latter place where the oppression was heaviest, the people seem to be relieved from a burden which had become insupportable. It is generally agreed that, from the period of Danton's fall, Robespierre had amassed in his own hands all the powers of the government and controlled every department in all its operations. It was his spirit which ruled the Committee of Public Safety, the Convention, and the Revolutionary Tribunal. . . . Robespierre, therefore, had become omnipotent. It was his spirit which dictated every movement, and particularly the unceasing operation of the guillotine. Nor did a more bloody and merciless tyrant ever wield the rod of power. His acts of cruelty and oppression are perhaps without parallel in the annals of history. It is generally conceded, that for some

---

[1] I have used in the preparation of this chapter the Monroe Papers, preserved in the Library of the State Department in Washington, and the " View," published in Philadelphia, 1797.

months before his fall the list of prisoners was shown him
every evening, by the President of the Revolutionary Tribunal, and that he marked those who were to be the victims
of the succeeding day, and which was invariably executed.
Many whole families, those under the age of sixteen ex-
cepted, were cut off upon the imputation of conspiracies,
etc., but for the sole reason that some members had been
more friendly to Brissot, Danton, etc., or had expressed a
jealousy of his power. This oppression had, in fact,
gained to such a height that a convulsion became unavoid-
.able." . . .

" It may be asked: Is there any reason to hope that the
vicious operation of the guillotine will be hereafter suspended? May not factions rise again, contend with and
destroy each other as heretofore? To this I can only answer that the like is not apprehended here, at least to the
same extent; that the country from Havre to Paris, and
Paris itself, appears to enjoy perfect tranquillity; that the
same order is said to prevail in the armies, who have addressed the Convention applauding its conduct and rejoic-
ing at the downfall of the late conspirators." Still, he says,
until peace is established it is impossible to tell what may
happen. "But are not the people oppressed with taxes,"
he asks, "worn out by continual drafts to reinforce the
armies; do they discover no symptoms of increasing discontent with the reigning government, and of a desire
to relapse again under their former tyranny? . . . These
are great and important questions and to which my short
residence here will not permit me to give satisfactory answers. . . . At present I can only observe that I have
neither seen nor heard of any symptoms of discontent
showing itself among the people at large. The oppression
of Robespierre had indeed created an uneasiness, but which
disappeared with the cause. I never saw in the countenances of men more apparent content with the lot they enjoy
than has been shown everywhere since my arrival. In the
course of the last year the Convention recommended it to

the people, as the surest means of support for their armies, to increase the sphere of cultivation, and, from what I can learn, there never was more land under cultivation, nor was the country ever blessed with a more productive harvest.   Many fathers of families, and a great proportion of the young men, are sent to the frontiers, and it was feared it would be difficult to reap and secure it; but the women, the boys and the girls, even to tender age, have supplied their places.   I saw this with amazement upon my route from Havre to this place, and am told 'tis generally the case. The victories of their armies are celebrated with joy and festivity in every quarter, and scarce a day has latterly passed without witnessing a deputation to the Convention, and often from the poorest citizens, to throw into its coffers some voluntary contribution for the support of the war. These are not symptoms of disgust with the reigning government and of a desire to change it!"

Monroe thought that wisdom and moderation were winning the day over the violence of the Robespierrean régime and that the Revolution was drawing to a happy close. Writing a month later to the Secretary of State (September 15, 1794), he says: "Nothing of great importance has lately taken place in the public councils.   The remaining spirit of ancient party has, it is true, occasionally shown itself, but not with its former vigor; for it seems in a great measure to have withdrawn and to lurk in the bosoms of the more inveterate only.   Happily a different spirit, more congenial with the temper of the nation, and which inclines to humanity, to peace and concord, seems to pervade the mass of the Convention.   I think this latter will soon prevail so as not only to prevent, at least for the present, further enormities, but to heal, in some degree, the wounds which have already been inflicted."   As evidence of the growth of this spirit of moderation Monroe mentions the case of Barrère, Collot d'Herbois and Billaud Varennes, who were denounced in the Convention as having been supporters and encouragers of Robespierre.   The Convention, how-

ever, after having heard the long list of charges, dismissed
them with disdain, and even censured the accuser, Lecointre
de Versailles, as a disturber of the public peace. The
attacking party were now alarmed for their own safety,
thinking that the rejection of their motion showed the
invincible strength of the faction they had tried to pro-
scribe. But herein they showed themselves superficial
observers of the trend of events and opinions. They did
not perceive that there was a force in the Convention that
was making for peace, that was determined to curb the
passions of all violent factions. The accusers did not have
a majority of the, Convention, as has been seen. Neither
did the accused, as was shown by their defeat shortly after
in their effort to be re-elected to the Committee of Public
Safety. "I have mentioned this incident," says Monroe,
"because I deem it an important one, in the character of
the present moment; tending to prove the certainty with
which the Revolution progresses toward a happy close;
since the preponderance of those councils which are equally
distinguished for their wisdom, temperance and humanity,
continues to increase."

A letter dated October 16 is characterized by the same
serene optimism. "The councils of the Republic still continue to present to view an interesting but by no means
an alarming spectacle. Instances of animated debate, severe crimination, and even of vehement denunciation sometimes take place; but they have hitherto evaporated without
producing any serious effect. It is obvious that what is
called the Mountain party is rapidly on the decline, and
equally so that if the opposite one acts with wisdom and
moderation at the present crisis it will not only complete
its overthrow, but destroy the existence (if possible in
society) of all party whatever." True, there are violent
controversies still, but they are in a sense defensive rather
than offensive, that is, they are the attempts of men to ex-
culpate themselves of past enormities rather than to insti-
gate new. A molten mass doesn't cool off without convul-

sions; but nevertheless it cools. Again, at the opening of the next year, he expresses the same opinion.

" The operations of the government continue to progress in the same course they have done for some time past.... It has been the systematic effort of the administration to repair this waste [caused by the reign of terror] and heal the bleeding wounds of the country, and in this great progress has been made."[1] Not only have shackles been removed from commerce, but the Seventy-One have been liberated, Mr. Paine set free, the decree excluding nobles and foreigners from Paris and the seaports repealed. " These events have given satisfaction to the community at large." The last act, though apparently of comparatively little importance, has, notwithstanding, produced an excellent effect; " for as it breathes a spirit of humanity and on that account captivates all, so it has contributed, by passing in review many members of the ancient order of nobility (and who have not forgotten and never will forget old habits), to present before the public, and much to the credit of the Revolution, the strong and interesting contrast between the manly character of the French nation at the present day and the miserable effeminacy, foppery and decrepitude of former times."[2]

The tone of Monroe's letters did not change as time went by and he became presumably better acquainted with the conditions of the country and the character of those in power. He believed that the principles of the Revolution were rooted deep in the hearts of the people, who, come what might, would never be greatly swerved. From all that he had seen since his arrival he was convinced that as long as the majority of the Convention should remain true to the Revolution it would have the support of the people, and that even if that majority should turn false yet it would not be able to restore the ancient monarchy, though of course it could create great confusion and

---

[1] Letter to Secretary of State, Jan. 13, 1795.   [2] Ibid.

do much harm.   It was apparently a fundamental belief with
Monroe that the great mass of the French people were
true to the Revolution all through the shifting scenes of
wars and party strife; that they had supported the Convention, not because they approved everything it did, but
because they believed it to be faithful to the main object.
This confidence would continue as long as this loyalty
should last.

Nor did Monroe think that Frenchmen deserved the
reputation for turbulence, lawlessness, licentiousness, which
their actions during the past few years had won for them
in foreign countries.   " For it is unquestionably true," says
he, " that the great atrocities which have stained the different stages of the Revolution, and particularly the massacres
of the 2d and 3d September, 1792, and the invasion of the
Convention on the 31st May, 1793, which terminated in the
arrestation and destruction of the Girondine party, did not
proceed from a licentious commotion of the people.   On
the contrary, it is believed that many of the immediate
agents in the first were not inhabitants of Paris, but brought
from a considerable distance and some even from Italy,
put in motion by some secret cause not yet fully understood.   It is also affirmed that the great mass of the people
of Paris were ignorant of what was perpetrating at the time
of the transaction, and that those who knew of it were
struck with the same horror that we were when we heard
of it on the other side of the Atlantic."   Monroe then explains the 31st of May as a simple piece of finesse on the
part of Danton, Robespierre and others, who used a popular
movement that was perfectly legitimate for purposes quite
other than those the people had in mind.   The element of
popular turbulence and ferocity disappears largely in the
explanation.[1]

The outbreak of the 12th Germinal did not disturb our
ambassador's optimism.   The future, he thought, was for

---

[1] Letter to the Secretary of State, March 6, 1795.

the moderate party. Not even the famine, which was afflicting France at this time, seemed to him a probable source of political danger, however great might be the suffering it would occasion. "The distress of the people on account of the scarcity of bread has been like that of a besieged town," he writes. "They have been constantly upon allowance, and which was lately reduced to two ounces, and sometimes less per day. My family, which consists of fourteen persons, is allowed two pounds of bread per day. I mention this that you may have a just idea of the distress of others, and particularly the poor, for at a great expense, nearly forty dollars specie per barrel, I am supplied. The accounts which we have of the distress of the aged, the infirm and even of children are most afflicting; yet calmness and serenity are seen everywhere."[1]

The futile insurrection of the 20th of May, 1795, went to confirm Monroe in his opinions. The party of the Convention that suppressed this insurrection neither desired the return of royalty nor of the reign of terror. "Indeed," says Monroe, "this party has appeared to me to be, and so I have often represented it to you, as equally the enemy of the opposite extremes of royalty and anarchy; as resting upon the interest and wishes of the great mass of the French people, and who I have concluded . . . . are desirous of a free republican government, one which should be so organized as to guard against the pernicious consequences that always attend a degeneracy into either of these extremes . . . . Royalty, therefore, I consider at present as altogether out of the question. But that these convulsive shocks . . . . may produce some effect is probable. In my opinion they will produce a good one, for I am persuaded they will occasion, and upon the report of the Committee of Eleven, some very important changes in the Constitution of 1793, such as a division of the Legislature into two branches, with an organization of the execu-

---

[1] Letter to the Secretary of State, May 17, 1795.

tive and judiciary upon more independent principles than
that Constitution admits of; upon those principles indeed
which exist in the American constitutions and are well
understood there. Should this be the case, the republican
system will have a fair experiment here; and that it may be
the case must be the wish of all those who are the friends
of humanity everywhere." [1]

The new Constitution was finally completed and adopted.
Monroe pronounced it "infinitely preferable" to the one it
was to supersede. It would be, he thought, "a new bul-
wark in favor of republican government." Only one circumstance did he discover in connection with it that seemed
at all dark—the decree of the Two-Thirds—and upon this he
put as usual the best interpretation. " A motive for this was,"
he says, " the advantage the republic would gain from keeping in office many of those in whose hands depending
negotiations were, and who in other respects are acquainted
with the actual state of things. There may be, and doubtless are, other motives for this measure," but these he never
mentions. The Constitution was much better than the
preceding ones; much beyond what the past experience of
France might lead one to expect, and was an event of
more than national significance. It was to be tried under
very embarrassing conditions—foreign war, a party within
incessantly plotting its overthrow, a great derangement of
the finances of the country. The experiment could hardly
be called a fair one. If, however, it should succeed, and if
the republican system should be preserved despite such
great difficulties, the refutation would be complete of all
those arguments that have been thrown at men for ages
to prove the impracticability of such a government, especially in old countries.[2]

The insurrection of the 13th Vendémiaire is described in
one of his official dispatches. "A contest," says Monroe,
" in many respects the most interesting and critical that I

---

[1] Letter to Secretary of State, June 14, 1795.
[2] Ibid. Nov. 5, 1795.

have yet witnessed, and which promised, had the assailants succeeded, not perhaps essentially to impede or vary the direct course of the Revolution, but most probably to involve the nation in a civil war, open a new scene of carnage more frightful than any yet seen, and deluge the country by kindred arms with kindred blood." The insurrection was undoubtedly intended as a first step in the subversion of the Revolution and the restoration of the monarchy. But even if it had destroyed the Convention, royalty could not have been restored for any length of time, though the royalists might have come forward, the patriots lain quiet and the nation been greatly confounded. Monroe did not believe they could restore the throne. "You will observe," he says, "that my reasoning is founded upon a belief that the army is sound, that the great bulk of the citizens of Paris are so likewise, and that the farmers or cultivators in general, if not decidedly in favor of the Revolution, though in my opinion they are, are at least not against it, and which belief, though perhaps erroneous, is the result of an attentive observation of such facts and circumstances as have appeared to me to merit attention."

"But you will ask, if Paris is on the side of the Revolution, how happened it that such a force was formed there against the Convention whilst so small a one was marshalled on its side? . . . . But how happened it that so many of the disaffected were chosen into the electoral corps as to give the royalists a preponderance there? How could a people attached to the Revolution commit the care of it to those who were its foes, especially to such as, by their station and character, were universally known to be such? This touches a subject extremely interesting, for it leads to facts over which a veil has yet been thrown, but to which history will doubtless do justice, and in which case it will present to view a scene of horror in some respects perhaps not less frightful than that which was exhibited under the reign of terror. Behind the curtain, as it were, for it has made but little noise in several of the departments, the terrible scourge of terror has shifted hands and latterly been wielded by the royalists, who, beginning with the subaltern, and perhaps wicked agents of the former reign, had persecuted and murdered many of the soundest patriots and best of men. To such a height had this evil risen, and so general was the imputation of terrorism, that in certain quarters the patriots in general were not only discouraged, but in a great measure depressed. It is affirmed to be a fact by those who ought to know and who merit belief, that in some of those quarters, and even where the preponderance in point of numbers was greatly in their favor, none attended the primary assemblies, and that in others a few only attended and who took no part in the proceedings. This, therefore, will account why the royalists took the lead in those assemblies and why so many of them were chosen in the electoral corps.

"But by what strange vicissitude of affairs was this effect produced? How could it happen under an administration unfriendly to royalty?" Here is Monroe's answer: Terrorism, or what was then called so—persecution of the royalists had gone so far that it became absolutely necessary to end it. This the Thermidorians attempted after the overthrow of Robespierre. "But so nice was the subject upon which they had to act, and so delicate is the nerve of human sensibility, that it was impossible for the government under existing circumstances to moderate its rigor toward the royalists without giving, in a certain degree, encouragement to royalty. In this, therefore, it is to be presumed, the late event will produce a beneficial effect, for as the views of the royalists were completely unmasked and defeated, and which were always denied to exist until they were thus unmasked, it cannot otherwise than tend to open the eyes of the community in that respect and in the degree to repress the arrogant spirit of royalty." [1]

---

[1] Letter to the Secretary of State, Oct. 20, 1795.

Monroe feared that the transition from the Convention to the Directorate might be accompanied with more trouble and confusion. On the 27th of October, 1795, the Convention closed its career by declaring its powers at an end. Immediately thereupon the installation of the new government took place by the verification of the powers of the deputies and their distribution into two houses. Monroe was present and thus describes the event: " When I observe that the scene which was exhibited upon this great occasion resembled in many respects what we see daily acted on our side of the Atlantic in our national and State assemblies, you will have a better idea of the tranquillity which reigned throughout than I can otherwise describe. Nor shall I be accused of unbecoming partiality if I draw from the increasing similitude in their and our political institutions, which this Constitution and other proceedings furnish, the most favorable hopes of the future prosperity and welfare of this Republic." [1]

The outlook was, on the whole, most auspicious. The Directors were men of talent, integrity and devotion to the Revolution, a circumstance that seemed to Monroe to show the principles of those who chose them and to tend "essentially to give stability to the Revolution itself," and a few weeks later he was convinced that the new arrangements had been in the line of great improvements.

"Since the organization of the new government the character and deportment of all the departments are essentially improved. The legislative corps, in both its branches, exhibits, in the manner of discussion, a spectacle wonderfully impressive in its favor when compared with what was daily seen in the late Convention. And the executive departments begin to show an energy which grows out of the nice partition of their duties and the greater responsibility that belongs to each." [2]

The remaining letters of Monroe up to the time of his

---

[1] Letter to the Secretary of State, Nov. 5, 1795.
[2] Official Dispatch, Dec. 6, 1795.

departure from France in January, 1797, have very little interest for us in connection with the present study. They are mostly full of the bickerings and complications growing out of the Jay Treaty. He notices the bad condition of the finances, and mentions one or two attempts of the royalists to stir up trouble for their own peculiar purposes. This, however, seems to inspire him with no fear as to the stability of the government. There is no passage in Monroe's papers to show that he anticipated the breakdown of the Constitution, or the advent of a despot. Quite the contrary. " In the interior, too," he writes, " everything has assumed a new and more invigorating aspect than was shown before since the commencement of the Revolution. Great harmony prevails between the legislative corps and the executive, and a greater spirit of contentment is discerned by those who travel through France, among all ranks of people, than was seen at any time before since the beginning of that era. It is even said that a change is gradually making among those who were heretofore deemed the implacable foes of republican government, many of whom, now that they find they are protected in the rights of person and property, begin to lose much of their hatred to that form. In truth, prior to the establishment of the present Constitution, the people of France had little opportunity of judging correctly of the merits of the republican system. They judged of it by what they saw in the Revolution, for Europe exhibited no other example to their view; and estimating its merits by that standard, they saw in it nothing but a series of terrible and convulsive movements, which they dreaded even more than the tyranny that was lately overthrown. When, therefore, this circumstance is considered, and the improvement which the new government has introduced is properly appreciated, we immediately perceive the cause to which this change of sentiment in that class is to be ascribed." [1]

---

[1] Official Dispatch, July 24, 1796.

Monroe notes the astonishing victories of " Buonaparte " in Italy, but with little more emphasis than he bestows upon Jourdan and Moreau. He saw no political despot in the young man who was sending home statues and paintings from the south. He looked at everything with a strong republican bias, and his conviction that republicanism had come to stay in France seems to have remained unshaken.

In the address to the Directory, on presenting his letter of recall, he said: " In performing this act, many other considerations crowd themselves upon my mind. I was a witness to a revolution in my own country; I was deeply penetrated with its principles, which are the same with those of your Revolution; I saw, too, its difficulties, and remembering these and the important services rendered us by France upon that occasion, I have partaken with you in all the perilous and trying situations in which you have been placed.

" It was my fortune to arrive among you in a moment of complicated danger from within and from without; and it is with the most heartfelt satisfaction that, in taking my leave, I behold victory and the dawn of prosperity upon the point of realizing, under the auspices of a wise and excellent Constitution, all the great objects for which, in council and the field, you have so long and so nobly contended. The information which I shall carry to America of this state of your affairs will be received by my countrymen with the same joy and solicitude for its continuance that I now feel and declare for myself."

And the President of the Directory replied most happily that " the French Republic expects that the successors of Columbus, Raleigh and Penn, always proud of their liberty, will never forget that they owe it to France." [1]

---

[1] Dec. 30, 1796.

PART II.

OPINIONS OF AMERICANS AT HOME

FIRST MOVEMENTS OF PUBLIC OPINION.

"All political and civil revolutions," says De Tocqueville in one of the famous chapters of his famous book, "have been confined to a single country. The French Revolution had no country; one of its leading effects appeared to be to efface national boundaries from the map. It united and divided men in spite of law, traditions, characters, language; converted enemies into fellow-countrymen, and brothers into foes; or, rather, to speak more precisely, it created, far above particular nationalities, an intellectual country that was common to all, and in which every human creature could obtain rights of citizenship.

"No similar feature can be discovered in any other political revolution recorded in history. But it occurs in certain religious revolutions. Therefore, those who wish to examine the French Revolution by the light of analogy must compare it with religious revolutions."[1]

That the Revolution was at no time a purely local movement, that it refused to be compressed, but expanded as naturally as does a heated gas, is one of the platitudes of history. Crossing the Channel, crossing the Rhine, scaling the Alps and Pyrenees, the forces to which we give this name came down into the different countries of Europe to become factors of the first magnitude in their politics, both internal and external, for a long while to come. Nor did these forces affect merely those countries that lay in the immediate neighborhood of the land of their genesis. Thrown forth by the impulsion inherent in their very

---

[1] De Tocqueville. Old Régime, Ch. III.

nature, they found an ocean no more difficult to cross than the river Rhine, and a far-away, undeveloped country as ready for their play as the old complicated societies of Europe.

It was just as this stormy, tumultuous period was coming on that our new national government was being instituted. The conflict generated was one between the old and the new, the established order and an improved order that men hoped to establish, respect for the conservative restraints of the past and the demand for much wider freedom of the individual, and in the wars that soon broke out England and the allies stood for the one, France for the other. These different conceptions quickly found points of attachment in America. "Freedom and order," says John Quincy Adams, " were also the elementary principles of the parties in the American Union, and as they respectively predominated, each party sympathized with one or the other of the combatants. And thus the party movements in our own country became complicated with the sweeping hurricane of European politics and wars. The division was deeply seated in the cabinet of Washington. It separated his two principal advisers [Hamilton and Jefferson], and he endeavored without success to hold an even balance between them. It pervaded the councils of the Union, the two Houses of Congress, the Legislatures of the States, and the people throughout the land." [1]

But this division was not apparent at first; did not, indeed, at first exist.[2] The outbreak of the French Revolution was hailed in America with expressions of ardent

---

[1] J. Q. Adams. The Lives of James Madison and James Monroe, 1850, pp. 243-245.

[2] " In no part of the globe was this revolution contemplated with more interest than in America. The influence it would have on the affairs of the world was not then distinctly foreseen; and the philanthropist, without becoming a political partisan, rejoiced in the event. On this subject, therefore, there existed in the public mind but one sentiment." Marshall, Life of Washington, V, p. 186. See also J. Q. Adams, Lives of Madison and Monroe.

enthusiasm and lively sympathy, broken only here and there in widely isolated cases by some subdued utterance of distrust or doubt. France and America were united by a close friendship, born of a political alliance, and maintained by feelings of gratitude and by the interest awakened in both nations by years of intimate association with each other. During the latter part of the eighteenth century the influence exerted by each of these widely separated and widely different nations upon the other had been most marked. France had given to America her philosophy and her military aid. America had rendered the thought of revolution familiar to France, and stood forth herself as the successful living embodiment of certain great conceptions of liberty, equality and democratic government, to the attainment of which for themselves Frenchmen were more and more aspiring. They were interested in each other, and thus a condition favorable to proselytism was at hand.

That Frenchmen were influenced by America has been well and abundantly shown by Mr. Rosenthal in his " America and France." French memoirs are a witness to this with their many references to Franklin, who made America quite the fashion in the lively French capital, and to Jefferson, who was speedily recognized by the dilettante philosophers of Paris as a worthy member of the craft. The American revolution, in which Frenchmen had borne a part quite flattering to the national pride, was a frequent theme, and republican government seemed suffused with a peculiar light to these glowing readers of Rousseau. French newspapers also contained much matter relating to this country and bore witness to American influence. In 1789 one of them said of Washington that he might be considered, " without exaggeration or flattery, as superior to Curius, Fabricius, or any of the heroes *de l'age d'or de la république Romaine*," and this acute judgment was quoted in America with apparent satisfaction and gratitude.

Similarly, as the Revolution drew on, American news-

papers began to teem with articles on French subjects; the
House of Bourbon; the Parliaments; the evil influence of
women upon French politics; the everlasting mystery of
the Man of the Iron Mask; the meeting of the Notables in
1787. America naturally took a keen interest in the Revolution from the very beginning, looking upon it as destined
to spread abroad her own political and social ideals and
institutions. "Liberty," exclaimed the "Boston Gazette,"
when the news began to be wafted over here, "liberty will
have another feather in her cap. The seraphic contagion
was caught from Britain, it crossed the Atlantic to North
America, from whence the flame has been communicated to
France."[1] That a nation should rise from centuries of
unconditional slavery to a high order of freedom "on a
sudden, in the twinkling of an eye," is, says the same paper,
"an event to be contemplated with wonder,"[2] and it predicts
"that the ensuing winter will be the commencement of a
Golden Age."[3] Noticing the influence of French ideas
that was showing itself in local commotions in other parts
of Europe, the "Pennsylvania Packet" prints an article
under the caption of "Hildesheim; Third Spark from the
Sacred Fire."[4]

Quotations like these, which might be multiplied indefinitely, reveal the attitude of buoyant enthusiasm for the
French cause that was well nigh universal here during the
first years of the Revolution, and that with multitudes of
men could not be shaken by all the excesses and apparent
failures of the movement.[5]

---

[1] Boston Gazette, Sept. 7, 1789.   [2] Ibid. Sept. 28.
[3] Ibid. Nov. 30.   [4] Pennsylvania Packet, Nov. 27, 1789.
[5] "In its first stage but one sentiment respecting it prevailed, and
that was a belief, accompanied with an ardent wish, that it would
ameliorate the condition of France, extend the blessings of liberty
and promote the happiness of the human race." Marshall, Life
of Washington, V, 389.
This feeling showed itself in the verse of the day.

"Where'er the sunbeam gilds the rolling hour,
Wings the fleet gale, and blossoms in the flower,
May freedom's glorious reign o'er realms prevail,
Where Cook's bright fancy never spread the sail.

Not only did most Americans contemplate the Revolution with feelings of pleasure and pride as destined to
spread abroad their own ideas, but many of them eagerly
welcomed it as an ally in the propagation of doctrines in
which they believed but which had not yet won general
acceptance at home. Already the movement had swung
into being for the democratization of the country, which was
to be so powerfully re-inforced by Jefferson and to attain so
complete a triumph with Jackson. America might well be
the teacher of her elder sister in some respects, and these
men thought that she might equally well be her pupil in
others. That the soil was being rapidly prepared for those
French levelling principles which were later transplanted,
was abundantly shown in the uproar occasioned by the
etiquette and ceremonial that Washington chose to
throw about the presidency, and by the debates in the first
Congress on official titles. This democratic ideal, which
was so long of attainment, this incipient and vigorous distrust of everything not strictly popular in character, is
shown at its best in the pages of William Maclay, Democratic Senator from Pennsylvania, whose particular *bête
noir* was John Adams, who never hesitated to approve of
ceremonial and titles. Writing, September 18, 1789, he
says: " By this and yesterday's papers, France seems tra-
vailing in the birth of freedom. Her throes and pangs of

> Long may the laurel to the ermine yield,
> The stately palace to the fertile field,
> The fame of Burke in dark oblivion rust,
> His pen a meteor—and his page the dust."

" The Works in Verse and Prose of the Late Robert Treat Paine."
Boston, 1812, p. 77. From a poem read at the Harvard Commencement, July 25, 1792. Mr. Paine in after years spoke with
regret of his " stripling attempt to smite the pyramidal fame of
Burke."

The correspondence of Washington, Franklin, Jay, Maclay and
others attests still further this interest in the rising revolution.
See also R. H. Lee's Memoirs of the Life of Richard Henry Lee
and his correspondence, 2 vols., Philadelphia, 1825, II, 97. Letter
from Lee to Henry.

labor are violent. God give her a happy delivery! Royalty, nobility and vile pageantry, by which a few of the human race lord it over and tread on the necks of their fellow-mortals, seem likely to be demolished with their kindred Bastille, which is said to be laid in ashes. Ye gods! with what indignation do I review the late attempt of some creatures among us to revive this vile machinery! O Adams! Adams! what a wretch art thou!"[1]

Thus gratitude and the feelings of partisanship were calculated to inspire in Americans admiration of the French cause and devotion to it. Still, during the first three years

---

[1] Journal of William Maclay, 155.

It was even believed that the United States would draw material benefit from the commotions in France. The Wolcotts, for instance, both father and son, thought that French capital, feeling insecure at home, would seek extensive investment in our new national funds, consequently lowering the rate of interest the Government would have to pay. See Gibbs' Memoirs, I, 24, 33, 46. Madison thought that a new and desirable element would enter into our immigration—that many Frenchmen of the more cultivated and prosperous classes would be induced to take up permanent abode in America, now that cultivation and prosperity were such blots on their 'scutcheons at home. See Annals of Congress. Many such indeed did come, though only as refugees for the time being—Chateaubriand, Viscount de Noailles, Talleyrand, Rochefoucauld-Liancourt, Louis Philippe, Lafayette, Jr., and others. See Griswold, Republican Court, pp. 377-390. The presence of these strangers was in many ways desirable. They were high-bred gentlemen. "They brought to us the ideas and manners of a splendid though wrecked civilization and strange experiences worthy of wise suggestion." They offered "to the children of our wealthier families, in several instances, princes and nobles for teachers and associates." Griswold.

That the disturbances in France would play directly into the hands of the agents of American land companies seemed probable. Oliver Wolcott, writing to his father, observed: "In consequence of the Bill of Rights agreed to by the National Assembly, an association has been formed for settling a colony in the western country of the United States. About 100 Frenchmen have arrived with the national cockade in their hats, fully convinced that it is one of their natural rights to go into the woods of America and cut down trees for a living. I believe that my friend Barlow has been the principal agent in forming this association, and if it shall prove successful, it will be a great event and profitable for him." Gibbs, I, 46.

of the Revolution, though there could not have been for a moment any doubt as to where lay the sympathy of the country, there was no striking public manifestation of it. Every event that occurred in France was eagerly followed here. The description of scenes such as the opening of the States-General, the texts of speeches and laws and constitutions were printed often in full, and to judge from the space allotted to them were the most interesting topics of the day. Indeed, it was even believed that France, whose hand was but newly turned to constitution making, could yet reveal important secrets of the art to the far more experienced Americans.[1]

Events occurred, too, which seemed to keep the connection of the two countries vividly before the public mind. The debates on presidential titles in the first Congress have already been mentioned, debates that showed the emergence of that anxious distrust of all social badges which later became so aggressive, so formidable, preparing the way for the adoption of many revolutionary absurdities direct from France.[2] In favor of such titles stood stout John Adams. The Senate was willing but the House suspicious. Would not their introduction be but the beginning of the march back toward royalty? And did royalty come so well accredited out of the past experience of men that America could do no better than cheerfully to revive it and impose it upon the new, uncorrupted western world? Could not gentlemen observe the signs of the times? Were the nations of the earth to be seen embracing with increasing fondness the meaningless trumpery of an outworn form of government? Were they not rather showing a notable tendency to leave royalty somewhat in the lurch? Should America shamefully retreat from her rightful position of proud primacy in enlightened political institutions at the

---

[1] The example of the revolutionists was appealed to as a guide in the Constitutional Convention of Pennsylvania of 1790. Graydon Memoirs, 329.

[2] Annals of Congress. Newspapers of the day.

very moment when other nations were visibly preparing to range themselves alongside her? Many a democratic heart beat swiftly with indignation at the mere possibility. Here again we have the testimony of the watchful Maclay, a testimony more than personal—the testimony of a class. "It is worthy of remark," says this typical man of the people, "that about this time a spirit of reformation broke out in France which finally abolished all titles and every trace of the feudal system. Strange, indeed, that in that very country [America] where the flame of freedom had been kindled, an attempt should be made to introduce these absurdities and humiliating distinctions, which the hand of reason, aided by our example, was prostrating in the heart of Europe. I, however, will endeavor, as I have hitherto done, to use the resentment of the representatives to defeat Mr. Adams and others on the subject of titles."[1]

And again:

"Carrol of Carrolton edged near me in the Senate chamber and asked me if I had seen the King of France's speech and the acts of the 'Tiers États' by which the distinctions of the nobility were broken down. I told him I had, and I considered it by no means dishonorable to us that our efforts against titles were now seconded by the representative voice of twenty-four millions. A flash of joy lightened from his countenance. How fatal to our fame as lovers of liberty would it have been had we adopted the shackles of servility which enlightened nations are now rejecting with detestation!"[2]

Another of the early measures of the First Congress that served to interject foreign attachments into our domestic politics was the question of duties on tonnage brought forward in April, 1789. Should there be any discrimination made in the rates in favor of those countries having commercial treaties with us? These countries were France, Sweden, Holland and Prussia. On the other

---

[1] Maclay. Journal, 12-13. Memorandum, 1790.
[2] Ibid. 233. On the debates on titles see Hildreth, IV, 59-64.

hand, with England, which furnished by far the larger part of the tonnage employed in the American trade, we had no such treaty. Should we not discriminate in favor of France, our good ally, and against England, from whom we had suffered only ills material and spiritual? Would not such a measure be justly punitive? Would it not be provocative of better treatment in the future? Here at the very beginning of our national life the two leading countries of Europe were placed into that sharp contrast they were to maintain for American eyes for long years to come. Though hostility or friendship got no very remorseless or passionate utterance in this debate, the feeling of attraction or repulsion, later to become so marked, was there and was called into play. The alignment of American parties along the course of European attachments had begun. On the one hand there was the belief that discrimination against England would be disastrous to ourselves. We ought not to deprive ourselves of so great a convenience as British ships when we have so few of our own. On the other hand the feeling of resentment toward England and gratitude and affection for France influenced the judgment of many, as it did that of Jefferson, who wrote from Paris referring to the cordial relations existing between the French and Americans and objected to hazarding their continuation by any placing of the former " on a mere footing with the English." "When of two nations," he says, "the one has engaged herself in a ruinous war for us, has spent her blood and money to save us, has opened her bosom to us in peace, and received us almost on the footing of her own citizens, while the other has moved heaven, earth and hell to exterminate us in war, has insulted us in all her councils in peace, shut her doors to us in every port where her interests would admit it, libelled us in foreign nations, endeavored to poison them against the reception of our most precious commodities; to place these two nations on a footing is to give a great deal more to one than to the other if the maxim be true that to make unequal quantities equal, you must add more to one than the other. To say, in excuse, that gratitude is never to enter into the motives of national conduct is to revive a principle which has been buried for centuries, with its kindred principles of the lawfulness of assassination, poison and perjury, etc." [1]

The death of the Dauphin soon after reminded Americans anew of the debt they owed the monarch of France and called out a natural sympathy for him. The presentation of the key of the Bastille to Washington by Lafayette was an act of some conspicuousness at the time, interesting in itself, serving to confirm the popular favor in which the Revolution stood here by furnishing for public contemplation a striking sign of the triumph of liberty over despotism. It called forth a cordial letter of acknowledgment from Washington, and cemented in the popular mind the alliance between France and America by furnishing a concrete and picturesque illustration of the similarity of interests and aspirations which rendered such an alliance easy, natural and popular.

The announcement of the eulogies pronounced in Paris upon the occasion of Franklin's death aided still further in keeping France in the foreground of public thought by reminding Americans of that country where one of their own number had played so unique and so flattering a rôle. These accounts were published in the newspapers with evident pride. In Congress they were treated apparently as a matter of routine, not calling forth the great enthusiasm that the more sensitive " patriots " thought becoming. On Dec. 10, 1790, there was read in the Senate " a letter from Monsieur Beniere, President of the Commonalty of Paris, addressed to the President and Members of Congress of the United States, with twenty-six copies of a Civic Eulogy on Benjamin Franklin, pronounced the 21st day of July, 1790, in the name of the Commonalty of Paris, by Monsieur L'Abbé Fauchet." After the reading it was ordered that

---

[1] To Madison, Aug. 28, 1789, III, 99.

the letters and copies of the eulogy be sent to the House of Representatives.[1] Again was Maclay the victim of the moment. For John Adams had taken the occasion to launch forth certain sarcasms at the French and the whole matter was "received and transacted with a coldness and apathy" truly astonishing. The letter and pamphlets indeed were "sent down to the Representatives as if unworthy the attention of our body. I deliberated with myself whether I would not rise and claim one of the copies in right of my being a member. I would, however, only have got into a wrangle by so doing without working any change in my fellow-members. There might be others who indulged the same sentiments, but 'twas silence all."[2]

A. month later Congress received the decree of the National Assembly ordering mourning for Franklin for three days. And a letter from Siéyès accompanied it, clothed in all the warmth of Revolutionary phraseology. "The name of Benjamin Franklin," so runs the letter, "will be immortal in the records of freedom and philosophy; but it is more particularly dear to a country where, conducted by the most sublime mission, this venerable knew very soon to acquire an infinite number of friends and admirers, as well by the simplicity and sweetness of his manners, as by the purity of his principles, the extent of his knowledge, and the charms of his mind. . . .

"At last the hour of the French has arrived; we love to think that the citizens of the United States have not regarded with indifference our steps towards liberty. Twenty-six millions of men, breaking their chains, and seriously occupied in giving themselves a durable constitution, are not unworthy the esteem of a generous people who have preceded them in that noble career.

"We hope they will learn with interest the funeral homage which we have rendered to the Nestor of America. May this solemn act of fraternal friendship serve more and

---

[1] Annals of Congress, Senate, Dec. 10, 1790.
[2] Maclay, Journal, 350.

more to bind the tie which ought to unite two free nations. May the common enjoyment of liberty shed itself over the whole globe and become an indissoluble chain of connection among all the peoples of the earth. For ought they not to perceive that they will march more steadfastly and more certainly to their true happiness in understanding and loving each other than in being jealous and fighting?

"May the Congress of the United States and the National Assembly of France be the first to furnish this fine spectacle to the world! And may the individuals of the two nations connect themselves by a mutual affection worthy of the friendship which unites the two men, at this day most illustrious for their exertions for liberty—Washington and Lafayette!"[1]

Again did the Senate refuse to throw itself into a frenzy.

"A letter from the National Assembly of France on the death of Dr. Franklin was communicated from them and received with a coldness that was truly amazing. I cannot help painting to myself the disappointment that awaits the French patriots while their warm fancies are figuring the raptures that we will be thrown into on receipt of their letter and the information of the honors which they have bestowed on our countryman, and anticipating the complimentary echoes of our answers when we, cold as clay, care not a fig for them, Franklin, or freedom. Well, we deserve—what do we deserve? To be d——d!"[2]

Louis the Sixteenth's adoption of the constitution of '91, a letter from that monarch to Washington announcing the fact, a message from the latter to Congress calling forth replies from both Houses, could not help from keeping unrelaxed, if not from positively intensifying, the relations of the two powers. The Senate, indeed, in its reply, did little more than gratefully acknowledge the receipt of information so highly satisfactory, without passing judgment either expressly or by implication upon the document itself. The

[1] Annals of Congress, Jan., 1791.
[2] Maclay Journal, 379-380, Jan. 26, 1791.

House, however, praised the "wisdom and magnanimity" displayed in its formation and acceptance.[1]

It was in the course of the Mint and Coinage Debate of 1792 that the first references were made in Congress bearing directly upon French public affairs, and they show an inclination to that same pettiness and triviality so characteristic of much of the activity of French assemblies of the period. The bill provided that on one side of certain coins there should be a representation of the head of the President for the time being with his name and order in succession imprinted. To this there was objection on the part of some whose sagacity detected here another of the parts of the general scheme to lead the country back to monarchy. Consequently in alarm it was moved to amend by substituting for the President's head a figure "Emblematic of Liberty with an inscription of the word LIBERTY." "It would be viewed by the world as a stamp of royalty," said Mr. Page, of Virginia, in seconding the motion, and "would wound the feelings of many friends and gratify our enemies." Mr. Williamson, of North Carolina, likewise approved the change. "He thought the amendment consistent with Republican principles and therefore approved it." "Mr. Livermore of New Hampshire ridiculed with an uncommon degree of humor the idea that it could be of any consequence to the United States whether the head of Liberty were on their coins or not; the President was a very good emblem of Liberty, but what an emblematical figure might be he could not tell. A ghost had been said to be in the shape of the sound of a drum, and so might Liberty for aught he knew." Just how the impression of the President's head on our coins could imperil the liberty of the people he found great difficulty in imagining. Mr. Smith, of South Carolina, agreed with Mr. Livermore. The President represents the people of the United States. He may, therefore, with great propriety

---

[1] Annals of Congress, March, 1792.

represent them on their coins. Mr. Smith said he was surprised that a member who so much admired the French and their new constitution should be so averse to a practice they have established; the head of their King is, by their constitution, put upon the money. The amendment, however, was carried.[1]

There were a few men in this country, but only a few, who from the very beginning of the French Revolution looked at it askance. They were never caught by the sanguine enthusiasm that was all about them; their natural conservatism of temper led them to detect at once certain elements of weakness in the situation there that might possibly lead to disaster. Washington had early expressed a vague fear that the solution of the problem confronting Frenchmen would not be found as easy as they themselves were prone to think, though on the whole he seems to have regarded the rising Revolution as full of promise. Hamilton early caught what he thought was the false note in it all—the tendency to let the speculative faculty ride supreme. Gouverneur Morris, seeing the drama unroll before him, was decidedly skeptical. But they were almost the only ones who ventured the gentlest criticism in those opening years, with the exception of one whose incredulity and hostility were almost instinctive, and from the beginning unmistakably clear and strong, John Adams. Before Burke had ever sounded the alarm which brought the conservatism of the world rushing to defend itself, Adams had expressed a view of the probable outcome of the Revolution hardly less forceful. Writing to the same Dr. Price, who so aroused the wrath of Burke, and acknowledging the receipt of a copy of the sermon which was the immediate occasion of the latter's terrific onslaught, Adams said (April 19, 1790): "Accept my best thanks for your favor of February 1st and the excellent discourse that came with it. I love the zeal and spirit which dictated this dis-

---

[1] Annals of Congress, March. 1792.

course and admire the general sentiments of it. From the year 1760 to this hour, the whole scope of my life has been to support such principles and propagate such sentiments. No sacrifices of myself or my family, no dangers, no labors have been too much for me in this great cause. The Revolution in France could not, therefore, be indifferent to me, but I have learned by awful experience to rejoice with trembling. I know that encyclopedists and economists, Diderot and D'Alembert, Voltaire and Rousseau, have contributed to this great event more than Sidney, Locke or Hoadley, perhaps more than the American Revolution, and I own to you I know not what to make of a republic of thirty million atheists. . . . Too many Frenchmen, like too many Americans, pant for equality of persons and property. The impracticability of this God Almighty has decréed, and the advocates for liberty who attempt it will surely suffer for it." [1]

Such were the views of Adams, early conceived and resolutely held, of the sources and leaders of the Revolution. Adams, as his biographer says, "never relished the vague and fanciful speculations of the French school"; his mind had rather been "formed in the mould of the English writers," some of whom he names in the letter just quoted. [2]

There now began that breach in the friendship of Jefferson and Adams which, though deep, was only temporary, and which grew directly out of the French Revolution. Adams published in the course of 1790 a series of political papers called "Discourses on Davila" in the Gazette of the United States at Philadelphia. They grew out of the Revolution, whose principles, now gradually unfolding, were deeply abhorrent to Adams. Their immediate provocation was the publication by Condorcet of a pamphlet entitled "Quatre Lettres d'un Bourgeois de New-Haven, sur l'Unité de la Législation." Taking as his text "Davila's History of the Civil Wars in France in the 16th Century," Adams

---

[1] Life and Works of John Adams, IX, 563-564.
[2] Ibid. I, 454. Memoir by C. F. Adams.

proceeded to give his views again on government. His object was to show that powerful factions are the death of the State unless hemmed in by artifices of government to restricted spheres of activity. Though writing of the civil convulsions of France in the sixteenth century, of the ceaseless and disastrous quarrels of the Guises, the Montmorenci, the Condés, the Bourbons, he really has his eye constantly upon the passing phenomena of the Revolution, in which he sees a recurrence of causes and results similar to those observed by the Italian historian before him. Contemptuously rejecting Turgot's famous theorem, revived in Condorcet's pamphlet, of " all authority in one center and that center the nation," as a mystery more inscrutable than that of the Athanasian creed, he contends that as parties or factions animated by the fiercest rivalry are apparently inevitable in every state, government should be so organized as to preserve an equilibrium between these different forces, allowing neither to become predominant, for, if either should succeed, despotism would follow. Every passion should have its counterpoise. Provision should be made in the constitution for balancing party against party. This can be done by a system of checks and balances, such as that so skilfully devised by the framers of our own Constitution. It certainly is not desirable that the King should be all-powerful, a vast, undefined, resistless force in the State, in short, a despot. Nor is the despotism of an oligarchy any more attractive. The people should have a share in the government. But if they are " advised to aim at collecting the whole sovereignty in single national assemblies, as they are by the Duke de la Rochefoucauld and the Marquis of Condorcet; or at the abolition of the regal executive authority; or at the division of the executive power, as they are by a posthumous publication of the Abbé de Mably, they will fail of their desired liberty as surely as emulation and rivalry are founded in human nature and inseparable from civil affairs. It is not to flatter the passions of the people, to be sure, nor is it the way to obtain a present enthusiastic popularity to tell them that in a single Assembly they will act as arbitrarily and tyrannically as any despot, but it is a sacred truth, and as demonstrable as any proposition whatever, that a sovereignty in a single Assembly must necessarily, and will certainly be exercised by a majority as tyrannically as any sovereignty was ever exercised by kings or nobles. And if a balance of passions and interests is not scientifically concerted the present struggle in Europe will be little beneficial to mankind and produce nothing but another thousand years of feudal fanaticism under new and strange names."

" A Legislature in one Assembly," he says elsewhere in the Discourses, " can have no other termination than in civil dissension, feudal anarchy, or simple monarchy." In this, one of the fundamental tenets of the early revolutionists, Adams had not the slightest faith. Neither had he any in other parts of the government as shaped by the National Assembly. Asked by Talleyrand what he thought of the executive power in the new Constitution, he replied: " The King is Daniel in the lions' den; if he ever gets out alive it must be by miracle." Asked by the same person the same question in regard to a subsequent Constitution, his answer was suggested by another Biblical episode: " It is Shadrach, Meshech and Abednego in the fiery furnace. If they escape alive, it must be because fire will not burn."

Again Adams shows the same disdain for those who would abolish all distinctions. They, forsooth, would do not only the undesirable, but the impossible as well. " Alphonsus V," he says, " the astronomical King of Castile, has been accused of impiety for saying that, ' If at the time of the creation he had been called to the councils of the Divinity, he could have given some useful advice concerning the motions of the stars.' It is not probable that anything was intended by him more than a humorous sarcasm or a sneer of contempt at the Ptolemaic system, a projection of which he had before him. But if the National Assembly should have seriously in contemplation, and should resolve in earnest the total abolition of all distinctions and orders, it would be much more difficult to vindicate them from an accusation of impiety. God, in the constitution of nature, has ordained that every man shall have a disposition to emulation as well as imitation, and, consequently, a passion for distinction; and that all men shall not have equal means and opportunities of gratifying it. Shall we believe the National Assembly capable of resolving that no man shall have any desire of distinction, or that all men shall have equal means of gratifying it? Or that no man shall have any means of gratifying it? What, would. this be better than saying if we had been called to the councils of the celestials we could have given better advice in the constitution of human nature?" To the hopes and promises and systems that the philosophers are so enthusiastically pressing upon France, he says: "All this is enchanting. But amidst our enthusiasm there is great reason to pause and preserve our sobriety. . . . Amidst all their exultations, Americans and Frenchmen should remember that the perfectibility of man is only human and terrestrial perfectibility. Cold will still freeze, and fire will never cease to burn; disease and vice will continue to disorder, and death to terrify mankind."

"Property," says he, "must be secured or liberty cannot exist. But if unlimited or unbalanced power of disposing property be put into the hands of those who have no property, France will find.... the lamb committed to the custody of the wolf. In such a case all the pathetic exhortations and addresses of the National Assembly to the people to respect property will be regarded no more than the warbles of the songsters of the forest. The. great art of law-giving consists in balancing the poor against the rich in the Legislature, and in constituting the Legislature a perfect balance against the executive power, at the same time that no individual or party can become its rival."

Thus the Discourses ran on, appearing from time to

time in the columns of Fennos' paper, and giving great umbrage to the democrats throughout the country. These were surely not the views of a reformer hailing the revolution beyond the seas as the coming of a new dispensation among men. Adams himself later expressed his astonishment at having been able to write so dull and heavy a book especially when so little was to be gained thereby and so much to be lost.[1] To Jefferson the doctrines now preached by his renegade friend seemed big with hateful possibilities. There was a suspicion of monarchy lurking behind these vigorous phrases. Should Davila talk and all the world be šilent? Should monarchy come by default? Something must be done, or rather said. Jefferson didn't wish to say it himself, but he saw in Paine's "Rights of Man" the convenient and sufficient antidote, and consequently favored its republication in America.

The reprinting of Paine's pamphlet had an influence upon the estrangement of Adams and Jefferson and served to intensify the differing political principles for which they stood. One of the famous incidents of the day was the discovery of the part played by Jefferson in that republication. He himself explains it in a letter to Washington, May 8, 1791 (Philadelphia), the President being then absent on a tour through the Southern States. "The last week does not furnish one single public event worthy of com-

---

[1] "This dull, heavy volume still excites the wonder of its author; first, that he could find amidst the constant scenes of business and dissipation in which he was enveloped, time to write it; secondly, that he had the courage to oppose and publish his own opinions to the universal opinion of America, and, indeed, of all mankind. Not one man in America then believed him. He knew not and has not heard of one since who then believed him. The work, however, operated powerfully to destroy his popularity. It was urged as full proof that he was an advocate for monarchy and laboring to introduce a hereditary president in America." Works, VI, 227.

The discourses are to be found in the sixth volume of Adams' Works, pp. 223-403, enriched by a series of sharp, pugnacious and triumphant foot-notes made as late as 1812-13 by Adams in his private copy, showing from the history of France between 1790 and 1813 how good a prophet he was.

municating to you; so that I have only to say 'all is well.'
Paine's answer to Burke's pamphlet begins to produce
some squibs in our public papers. In Fennos' paper they
are Burkites, in others they are Painites. One of Fennos'
was evidently from the author of the *Discourses on Davila.*
I am afraid the indiscretion of a printer has committed me
with my friend Mr. Adams, for whom, as one of the most
honest and disinterested men alive, I have a cordial esteem,
increased by long habits of concurrence in opinion in the
days of his republicanism and even since his apostasy to
hereditary monarchy and nobility; though we differ, we
differ as friends should do. Beckley had the only copy of
Paine's pamphlet and lent it to me, desiring, when I should
have read it, that I should send it to a Mr. I. B. Smith, who
had asked it for his brother to reprint it. Being an utter
stranger to I. B. Smith, both by sight and character, I wrote
a note to explain to him why I (a stranger to him) sent him
a pamphlet, namely, that Mr. Beckley had desired it, and, to
take off a little of the dryness of the note, I added that I was
glad to find that it was to be reprinted; that something
would at length be publicly said against the political heresies which had lately sprung up among us, and that I did
not doubt our citizens would rally around the standard of
Common Sense.

"That I had in my view the Discourses on Davila, which
had filled Fennos' paper for a twelve-month without contradiction, is certain; but nothing was ever further from
my thoughts than to become myself the contradictor before
the public. To my great astonishment, however, when the
pamphlet came out the printer had prefixed my note to
it without having given me the most distant hint of it. Mr.
Adams will unquestionably take to himself the charge of
political heresy, as conscious of his own views of drawing
the present government to the form of the English Constitution, and I fear will consider me as meaning to injure
him in the public eye. I learn that some Anglomen have
censured it in another point of view, as a sanction of Paine's

principles tends to give offence to the British Government. Their real fear, however, is that this popular and republican pamphlet, taking wonderfully, is likely at a single stroke to wipe out all the unconstitutional doctrines which their bell-wether Davila has been preaching for a twelve-month.

"I certainly never made a secret of my being anti-monarchical and anti-aristocratical; but I am sincerely mortified to be thus brought forward on the public stage, where, to remain, to advance or to retire, will be equally against my love of silence and quiet and my abhorrence of dispute." [1]

Jefferson thoroughly approved of Paine's pamphlet; Adams as thoroughly detested it, as is shown in the following quotations:

"Paine's pamphlet," Jefferson writes to Short, "has been published and read with general applause here. . . . The Tory paper, Fennos', rarely admits anything which defends the present form of government in opposition to his desire of subverting it to make way for a King, Lords and Commons. There are high names here in favor of the doctrine, but these publications have drawn forth pretty generally expressions of the public sentiment on this subject, and I thank God, they are to a man firm as a rock in their republicanism."

A note appended to the above after the word "names" was as follows:

"Adams, Jay, Hamilton, Knox, and many of the Cincinnati. The second says nothing; the third is open. Both are dangerous. They pant after a union with England, as the power which is to support their projects, and are most determined anti-Gallicans. It is prognosticated that our republic is to end with the President's life, but I believe they will find themselves all head and no body." [2]

---

[1] Jefferson's Works, III, 257.
[2] Quoted by Randall, II, 12, from Tucker's Jefferson.

He wrote to Paine himself:

" I am glad you did not come away till you had written your ' Rights of Man.' That has been much read here with avidity and pleasure. A writer under the signature Publicola has attacked it. A host of champions entered the arena immediately in your defence. The discussion excited the public attention, recalled it to the ' Defence of the American Constitution' and the ' Discourses on Davila,' which it had kindly passed over without censure in the moment, and very general expressions of their sense have been now drawn forth; and I thank God that they appear firm in their republicanism, notwithstanding the contrary hopes and assertions of a sect here, high in name, but small in numbers. These had flattered themselves that the silence of the people under the ' Defence' and ' Davila ' was a symptom of their conversion to the doctrine of King, Lords and Commons. They are checked at least by your pamphlet, and the people confirmed in their good old faith." [1]

That Adams disapproved the pamphlet may be shown with equal explicitness. Lear says in a letter to Washington (Philadelphia, May 8, 1791): " I had myself an opportunity of hearing Mr. Adams' sentiments on it one day soon after the first copies of it arrived in this place. I was at the Vice-President's house, and while there Dr. and Mrs. Rush came in. The conversation turned upon the book, and Dr. Rush asked the Vice-President what he thought of it. After a little hesitation, he laid his hand upon his breast and said in a very solemn manner, ' I detest that book and its tendency from the bottom of my heart.'" [2]

Maclay, in his journal, gives another reference to Adams' attitude toward the pamphlets of the period. "This is a day of no business," he says, "in the Senate. Before the House formed, Mr. Adams, our Vice-President, came to where I was sitting and told how many late pamphlets he

---

[1] July 29, 1791.
[2] Washington's Writings, Sparks' ed., X, 162 note.

had received from England; how the subject of the French Revolution agitated the English politics; that for his part he despised them all but the production of Mr. Burke, and this same Mr. Burke despised the French Revolution. Bravo, Mr. Adams! I did not need this trait of your character to know you."[1]

The republication of Paine's pamphlet brought another contestant upon the field " to complicate the action." John Quincy Adams, a young lawyer of twenty-four, waiting for clients, employed his leisure in writing a series of articles exposing the weaknesses and fallacies of Paine's argument. They were first published in the Columbian Centinel over the signature of " Publicola." Attracting attention both at home and abroad, they were reprinted in New York, Philadelphia and London. The high quality of these youthful essays is shown by the fact that they were very generally attributed to John Adams. " They were not his, however," says Charles Francis Adams, " excepting so far as the son might have imbibed with his growth the principles which animated the father through life." They were written " without any communication with his father."[2]

In these papers Adams, after stating the leading doctrines in Paine's work, seeks to show how false and untenable they are. He denies that " whatever a whole nation chooses to do it has a right to do," maintaining that on the contrary " nations, no less than individuals, are subject to the eternal and immutable laws of justice and morality." Paine's doctrine, he declares, threatens every man in his inalienable rights, and " would lead in practice to a hideous despotism, concealed under the parti-colored garments of democracy."[3] Out of this controversy over the very fun-

---

[1] Maclay, Journal, p. 249. Maclay speaks of Adams' " nobilimania," of which he is never cured, into which he constantly relapses, p. 349.

[2] Adams. Life of John Adams, I, 454-455.

[3] Josiah Quincy. Memoir of the Life of John Quincy Adams, p. 9. These articles called forth praise from those high in station.

damental principles of government, of which the Discourses
on Davila, Paine's Rights of Man, essays of Publicola and
others were episodes, came a very marked widening in the
party lines of the United States.[1]

Thus the cleft was beginning to appear which was later
to become so wide and deep, rending the previous unanimity of enthusiasm and approval. That unanimity was indeed first threatened when the main lines of the new French
Constitution became known. Some who had thought deeply
upon the science of government felt that the doom of
that Constitution was sealed in its very provisions. John
Adams, as we have seen, was foremost among these. "The
Constitution is but an experiment," he said, "and must
and will be altered. I know it to be impossible that France
should be long governed by it. If the sovereignty is to

"The Viscount de Noailles called on me," writes John Adams
to his wife. "He seems to despair of liberty in France and
has lost apparently all hopes of ever living in France. He was
very critical in his enquiries concerning the letters which were
printed as mine in England. I told him candidly that I did not
write them, and as frankly in confidence, who did. He says they
made a great impression upon the people of England. That he
heard Mr. Windham and Mr. Fox speak of them as the best thing
that had been written, and as one of the best pieces, both of reasoning and style, they had ever read." Letters of John Adams to
his Wife. Edited by Charles Francis Adams, II, 130.

[1] "Those principles" [of the Adamses], says Charles Francis
Adams, "were widely remote from the doctrines of Paine. They
seemed to Mr. Jefferson like adding fuel to the funeral pile of
liberty; and the whole force of his friends was soon concentrated
to resist their progress. The Adamses, on the other hand, deny-
ing the justice of this imputation, regarded Mr. Jefferson's support
of Paine as bordering too closely upon social disintegration and
favoring a mere popular tyranny. Thus came about the joining
of that issue upon fundamental principles in America which must
ever take place under all forms of free government, so long as
human society shall remain what it is. The conservative and the
democratic republic may be considered as the general types which
have from that day to this marshalled the respective divisions of
the people of the United States in opposition to each other when
not affected by disturbing influences from without." Life of John
Adams, I, 455. On the question whether Jefferson was guilty of
duplicity in this episode see Ibid. I, 618-619, and Randall, Life of
Jefferson. III, 7-10, note.

reside in one Assembly, the King, princes of the blood
and principal quality will govern it at their pleasure as long
as they can agree; when they differ they will go to war and
act over again all the tragedies of Valois, Bourbons, Lor-
raines, Guises and Colignis two hundred years ago."[1]
Jay was similarly distrustful.[2] Gouverneur Morris had no
idea it would last. Joel Barlow, now an extreme Revolu-
tionist, didn't think it could or should endure—it was only
a half-way measure, useful as such. About this time he
wrote his "Advice to the Privileged Orders" and "Conspiracy of Kings," which were influences of some importance
in bringing about the second revolution. But the great
mass of the American people no doubt thought very favorably of the new Constitution. They did not question it
minutely. They were not critics handling the scalpel
of keen analysis. The plain, blunt facts of the case they
perceived, and they did not stop to think of the remote con-
tingencies. France, hitherto an absolute monarchy, had become a constitutional government, as any one could see.
This was auspicious, and sufficient matter for gratulation.
Aaron Burr, writing to Mrs. Burr, said: "From an attentive perusal of the French Constitution, and a careful examination of the proceedings, I am a warm admirer of the
essential parts of the plan of government which they have
instituted and of the talents and disinterestedness of the
members of the National Assembly."[3] Apparently this
was the general attitude of public opinion at this time.
Thus, though Hamilton might doubt, and Jay distrust,
and Adams scathingly denounce, though the Senate might
on occasion show a slight indifference to affairs beyond the
sea, though a cleft might threaten to sunder sentiment in
twain, yet it was a scarcely perceptible seam after all, and
even that appeared about to be closed in the fervid heat of
the closing months of 1792 and the opening ones of 1793.

---

[1] Adams, Works, IX, 563-4, April 19, 1790.
[2] Correspondence and Public Papers of John Jay, IV, 200-202.
[3] Davis, Memoirs of Aaron Burr, I, 312, Dec. 15, 1791.

AN EXTRAORDINARY YEAR.

Though Americans had been interested in the Revolution from the very outset for a variety of reasons, it was only toward the close of the year 1792 that this interest was publicly manifested. But when the monarchy was completely overthrown and the Republic proclaimed, all America was thrilled. From this time on the movements of the French armies were followed with great excitement, and when, toward the close of this year, the Republic had so far asserted itself as to have driven back the invaders, the Revolution seemed so far accomplished as to demand a public manifestation of joy on the part of the Americans. Then began a year utterly without parallel, so far as I am aware, in the history of this country. American citizens gave themselves up to the most extraordinary series of celebrations in honor of the achievements of another country which in no way directly concerned them and did not need directly to affect them. The news of the retreat of the allies reached this country about the middle of December. At once the celebrations began. One was held in Baltimore, the first of which I find any record, on the 20th of December, when "a numerous and respectable company of gentlemen, Friends of the Rights of Man," as the report runs, met at "Mr. Grant's fountain inn for the purpose of celebrating the late triumph of liberty over despotism in France," and who, "after partaking of an excellent dinner," drank fifteen republican toasts.[1] In its next issue the National Gazette said that it was desirable "that the other capitals on this continent should imitate Baltimore in her convivial meetings to celebrate the glorious successes of France over the despotic combination."[2] The imitation began forthwith; had, indeed, already begun, for in New York, December 27th, bells had been rung, a liberty pole erected, surmounted by a crimson Phrygian cap, and the

---

[1] National Gazette, Dec. 26, 1792.   [2] Ibid. Dec. 29, 1792.

Tammany Society had held a most enthusiastic banquet in the wigwam. At this celebration several patriotic songs were sung. Here is one " hastily composed":

> " By hell inspir'd with brutal rage,
> Austria and Prussia both engage,
>   To crush fair freedom's flame;
> But the intrepid sons of France
> Have led them such a glorious dance
>   They've turned their backs for shame.
>
> May Heaven continue still to bless
> The arms of freedom with success,
>   Till tyrants are no more;
> And still as Gallia's sons shall fly
> From victory to victory,
>   We'll, shouting, cry Encore! " [1]

In Boston there were already signs prophetic of the coming of the French frenzy. The mind of the editor of the Independent Chronicle was beginning to glow. He speaks of " the uncommon joy and satisfaction with which a free people have received the highly animating information" of the French victories. In continuing the narration of that " brilliant chain of successes," he finds his pleasure " ineffable." [2] The editor of the Centinel waited " on the rack of impatience for further accounts" of the victories of the French,[3] and when the further accounts were forthcoming announcing the retreat of the Prussians, he noted that " joy was visible on the countenance of every citizen, which expressed itself in cordial congratulations on the event." [4] A week later there appeared the following curious notice:

" ☞ As the French citizens have rendered essential services to the establishment of Liberty and Independence in America in the former conflict with Great Britain, Quere —Whether a return of the compliment might not be enjoyed by a convivial dinner at which every French or

---

[1] Columbian Centinel, Jan. 9, 1793.
[2] Independent Chronicle, Jan. 17, 1793.
[3] Columbian Centinel, Dec. 19, 1792.   [4] Ibid. Dec. 29, 1792.

American freeman might have an opportunity of wishing his friend joy upon the success of the arms of Liberty and Equality.

"Those gentlemen who are desirous of attending upon the occasion are requested to leave their names at Col. Coleman's, on or before the next Tuesday, that matters may be properly regulated."[1]

A few days later the following card appeared in the Boston Gazette (Jan. 21, 1793):

"CIVIC FEAST.

A number of Citizens, anxious to celebrate the success of our Allies, the French, in their present glorious struggles for Liberty and Equality, and that every member of the community should partake in the general joy, have agreed to provide an Ox, with suitable Liquors, on Thursday, the 24th inst., being the day appointed for the Civic Feast. A subscription for this purpose is still open at Colonel Coleman's, State Street. Tickets for the Civic Feast may be procured at Citizen Brooks."[2]

This was the beginning of the Civic Feast held in Boston, January 24, 1793, an event long famous in the annals of that town. It may serve well enough as the type of an almost interminable series of such festivals, and was marked by no greater extravagance, though perhaps by more elaborateness, than others. The enthusiastic descriptions of this famous French frolic in the Boston papers of the day produce a strange and unreal impression upon one whose first impulse is to think of the New England temperament as self-contained, sober and sedate as becometh the descendants of those sturdy, though rather forbidding, men who first sought the bleak and gloomy shores of Massachusetts in the dead of winter.

The plans for the celebration grew as men thought about it. Soon the Inspector of Police felt called upon to issue a

---

[1] Columbian Centinel, Jan. 5, 1793.
[2] Boston Gazette, Jan. 21, 1793.

public card—he entered fully into the spirit of the day appointed for the Civic Feast—far was he from wishing to diminish the happiness of the people—on the contrary his happiness and theirs were quite synonymous—but fireworks are dangerous and he would therefore issue certain orders regarding their use.[1] In its next issue the Centinel published the following strain, under the caption "The Festive Season":

> "A Nation's born—Let Freemen, loud,
> Thus echo to the skies.
> Success to Gallia's New-Born Sons!
> Columbia's free Allies."

Further it announced that "as a prologue to the festive scenes of the week a number of citizens dined together at the Coffee House on Monday last," where the first toast given was "Universal Liberty and Equality," and the last, "May Tyranny, Despotism and Usurpation with their concomitants, be forever blotted from the Records of Man and securely deposited in the Archives of that Region, prepared by the Deity for the reception of Every Evil Work."[1]

Then came the great 24th.

This Civic Festival was ushered in by a salute of cannon from the castle in the harbor.[3] At eleven o'clock the feature of the day, the great-procession, started, led by two citizens mounted on horseback and waving civic flags; then Citizen Waters, the Marshal; then the band; then citizens, eight and eight; then twelve citizens in white frocks with cleavers, knives, steels and other implements; then a roasted ox ornamented with ribbons and with gilded horns. From the right horn was displayed the Republican flag of

---

[1] Columbian Centinel, Jan. 19, 1793.   [2] Ibid. Jan. 23, 1793.
[3] On the Boston Civic Feast see Columbian Centinel, Independent Chronicle, Boston Gazette, issues for the last week in January, 1793. Also Thomas' Reminiscences of the Last Sixty-five Years, I, 19-20; Wm. Sullivan, Familiar Letters, 76-77; Wm. H. Sumner's History of East Boston, 262-264 (account quoted nearly verbatim from the Williams Journal of Daily Occurrences on Noddles Island); also Memorial History of Boston, III, 203-4; IV, 10-11.

France and from the left that of the United States, and in front a board on the end of a spit bore the inscription in large gold letters, "Peace Offering to Liberty and Equality." After the ox came citizens eight deep. Then a cart bearing eight hundred loaves of bread and drawn by six horses, "suitably decorated," followed by a huge hogshead of punch and another cart heaped high with bread and another hogshead heaped high with punch. The procession moved through the town, saluting the houses of the Governor, the Lieutenant-Governor, the Consul of France, drawing up finally in State Street, having named Liberty Square by the way, where a liberty pole sixty feet high had just been erected. The ox, which had been roasted on Copp's Hill, and the bread and punch were served on tables in State Street, the line extending from the Old State House to near Kilby Street. A correspondent of a local paper was so moved by the power of this curious scene in State Street in cold midwinter that he wished for the pen of Burke that he might worthily describe it. This is very interesting, considering what Burke would probably have said. "While the streets, houses, yea, even the chimney-tops," he says, "were covered with male spectators, the balconies and middle stories of the houses exhibited bevies of our amiable and beautiful women, who, by their smiles and approbation, cast a pleasing lustre over the festive scenes." And to impress on the tender minds of the rising generation the precepts of that glorious period, every child was presented with a civic cake bearing the words Liberty and Equality. "To the feeling heart the sight of these little ones, thus feasted, was extremely gratifying," says the editor of the Columbian Centinel.

At two o'clock another procession moved from the State House to Faneuil Hall, where a great banquet was held, Citizen Samuel Adams presiding. The Hall was elaborately decorated. At the west end, over the head of the president, rose an obelisk, having in front the figure of Liberty, her left hand supporting her insignia and her right displaying "The Rights of Man." Under her feet lay broken in a hundred pieces the badges of Civil and Ecclesiastical Despotism—a crown, sceptre, mitre and chains. Over her head a descending cherub presented in its right hand a wreath as the Reward of Virtue, and in its left the Palm of Peace. Over the whole there was an Eye supposed to be the benign Eye of Providence, which appeared to view with approbation the scene below. The French and American flags were everywhere, and many were the mottoes and inscriptions to Liberty and Equality, to Justice and to Peace. So fervid was the feeling aroused by the incidents of the day that "amidst other displays of urbanity" a purse was raised for the release of the prisoners in the town jail; "the doors of the prison house were thrown open, and those who had long been immured therein were invited to join their festive brethren and again breathe the air of Liberty."

In the evening the State House was illuminated, while throughout the town there were fireworks and bonfires, and it was considered matter for gratulation that though "the utmost hilarity and frolick" were exhibited throughout the day, not a single accident happened that could "give pain to the heart of sensibility."[1]

These celebrations were not local; they occurred in the South, in the North, in the Middle States; Philadelphia saw scores of them. Nor were they limited to the cities, the capitals of this continent, as Freneau was pleased to call them. The cities did but give the word and set the tone

---

[1] "The descendants of the Puritans seem to have borrowed the temperament of the French as well as their symbols," says a recent writer. "Cloudless was the outlook for humanity as the flowing bumpers were drained on that auspicious day. A bad omen was not to be tolerated; the resources of exegesis must make it a good one. When a balloon refused to bear heavenward a scroll proclaiming Liberty and Equality, it was happily suggested that, as the denizens of the air needed not these precious watchwords, they had graciously remained to bless the inhabitants of the earth." Memorial History of Boston, IV, 13. Article by J. P. Quincy on Social Life in Boston.

for similar demonstrations in the towns of which they were the natural foci. Some of these were semi-religious in character, as, for instance, one held in Plymouth, Massachusetts, on the 24th of January, a contemporary description of which is a vivid revelation of the state of the popular mind. "The serene and beautiful morning of the 24th," so runs the description, "was ushered in by a discharge of fifteen cannon. At ten o'clock the inhabitants repaired to the Meeting-House to hear an address which the Rev. Dr. Robbins was requested to deliver upon the occasion. A well adapted Prayer and Hymn of Praise preceded the Address, which, though composed in haste, was sensible, animated and eloquent. A brief but connected sketch of the principles and leading events of the French Revolution led the people to understand *wherefore they had come together*, while every one was delighted with the happy eloquence of the speaker, and cordially united with him' in adopting the sublime and striking language of the Prophet Daniel, ' Blessed be the name of God forever and ever: for wisdom and might are his and he changeth the times and seasons. *He removeth Kings.*' After the address, Billings' Independence was sung by a select choir, who performed their parts with energies suited to the subject. ' Down with these earthly Kings,' thundered the majestic bass. ' No King but God,' was the sublime response." After the church service there was a parade through the town, during which, "at proper intervals, an Ode to Liberty, which Citizen J. Croswell composed in a moment of happy inspiration, was repeatedly sung. . . . The company retired seasonably in the afternoon, satisfied with themselves, with each other and with their country. A cheerful ball closed the enjoyment of this agreeable day."[1]

Similar celebrations are mentioned in Medford, Dorchester, Portsmouth, Providence, Roxbury, Cambridge, Princeton.[2] In Watertown a Civic Feast was held at which

---

[1] Columbian Centinel, Jan. 30, 1793.
[2] Ibid. Feb. 2, 6, 9, 1793; Independent Chronicle, Feb. 14, 1793.

one hundred villagers, "after having laid a basis of *solids*
amid the effusions of cheerful Bacchus," proceeded to give
fifteen exciting toasts.[1]

In Charleston a "grand civic pageant" took place January 11, 1793, in honor of the French, and so great was the
public enthusiasm that on the eve of that day the bells of
St. Michael's were rung and a salute of guns was fired by
the artillery. The same honors were repeated the next
morning, and in the course of the day a procession paraded
the streets, headed by the Governor of the State, the Chief
Justice, the French consul in "full costume," the orator of
the day, the Rev. Mr. Coste, Judges, Chancellors, Speaker
of the House and other public officers. In passing before
the French Protestant Church, the Consul, as an expiation
for the persecution of Louis XIV against the Church,
halted the procession, took off his hat and saluted it with
the national colors. Arrived safely within St. Philip's
Church, "the place appointed for the religious exercises of
the day," the Rev. Mr. Coste delivered an "animated oration," the Te Deum was sung, and the service was closed
by the singing of the "Hymne de Marsellais," to an organ
accompaniment. In the afternoon there was a grand fête
at Williams' Coffee House, two hundred and fifty persons
taking part. "This day of real fraternizing ended har-
moniously."[2]

In Savannah a celebration was held January 24th, at
which "an oration that would have done honor to the
greatest orators of ancient Greece and Rome was delivered
upon this glorious occasion to a crowded audience by
Joseph Clay, junr., Esq."[3] In Norfolk, Va., the people,
exulting over the French victories over Brunswick, and
"being deeply impressed with an anxious solicitude for the
general happiness of mankind, have agreed to have a Ball
on Friday the 8th, as a testimonial of our gratitude to a

---

[1] Columbian Centinel, Jan. 30, 1793.
[2] Fraser, Reminiscences of Charleston, 40-41.
[3] Dunlap's Daily Advertiser, Feb. 27, 1793.

nation that greatly contributed to the independence and
happiness of America and are now contending for the
establishment of their own." Among the subscribers were
Arthur Lee and Richard Henry Lee. Similar festivities
were held in Fredericksburg, Petersburg and other places.[1]

In Philadelphia joy was unconfined. "We have just
received the glorious news of the Prussian army being
obliged to retreat, and hope it will be followed by some
proper catastrophe on them," writes Jefferson from that city,
December 15. "The news has given wry faces to our
monocrats here, but sincere joy to the great body of our
citizens. It arrived only in the afternoon of yesterday, and
the bells were rung and some illuminations took place in
the evening."[2] Public attention had already been turned
in Philadelphia to the French Revolution the preceding
summer. King Louis was popular, both because he had
once aided us and seemed now disposed to gratify the
wishes of his own people. He was publicly toasted at the
4th of July celebration, 1792. The 14th of July was celebrated too. The shipping along the river front was gaily
decorated with flags. There was a dinner at Oeller's, at
which toasts complimentary to the French King and people
were drunk.[3] The first celebration after the announcement
of the French victories and in their honor was held at
Oeller's, January 1, 1793. Hodgkinson, the comedian, sang
a patriotic song. Those present organized the Société Française des Amis de l'Egalité. Other celebrations in honor
of the Republic were held on the 6th of February—date of
the Franco-American alliance—one at the City Tavern, at
which Governor Mifflin, the French Minister, De Ternant,
and the French Consul General, De la Forest, and the
officers of the city militia, were present. "At the head of
the table stood a pike bearing the cap of liberty and the
French and American flags entwined, surmounted by a dove

[1] Dunlap's Daily Advertiser, Jan. 31, 1793; Feb. 7, 1793.
[2] Jefferson's Works, III, 494.
[3] Scharf & Westcott, History of Philadelphia, I, 469.

bearing the olive branch. After the drinking of toasts, singing of songs, etc., the officers, with the band, proceeded to the house of the French Minister, where the band played ' Ça ira ' and ' Yankee Doodle.' " [1]

Nor were these celebrations merely temporary. They were but the dashings of the first wave of the French Revolution upon our shores. Another and a greater swept over the land with the coming of the new French Minister, Genet. It is no part of the present thesis to trace the official career, the amazing performances of this amazing young diplomat. Genet, who precipitated one of the most famous incidents in our diplomatic history, was a member of one of the notable families of France. His father had been connected with the ministry of foreign affairs for forty-five years. One of his sisters was Madame Campan, so intimate with the royal family; another was the beautiful Madame Angine, mother-in-law of Marshal Ney. As a boy he was intellectually precocious. At the age of twelve he translated the History of Eric XIV into the Swedish language, appending historical remarks of his own. For this he received high praise and a gold medal. He was an excellent linguist, a member of many of the most distinguished learned societies in Europe. He was still under thirty years of age; was a man of fine presence and polished manners, entertaining in conversation. From his early youth he had served the State, first as secretary to the eldest brother of Louis XVI, then as attaché to the embassies of Berlin, Vienna, London and St. Petersburg. He was in Russia at the outbreak of the Revolution. When Louis XVI was dethroned the Empress ordered him to leave her dominions. Genet indignantly protested, thereby greatly endearing himself to the triumphant faction at home, who at once appointed him minister to the young republic beyond the seas.[2]

Genet came here an ardent, impulsive, eloquent young

---

[1] Scharf & Westcott, I, 472-3; Gazette of the United States, Feb. 9, 1793.   [2] Biographie Universelle.

Frenchman, aflame with the ideals of the Girondists, whose messenger he was, ideals that scorned all the world's tradition and wont, recking little of national boundaries and habits, a universal gospel, announcing the salvation of the world of politics. His career here was short, sharp and decisive. He went off with a great report. Disorder, most admired disorder, was the result of his ministrations to the American people. Great was the ferment and the uproar that arose all about him. France had just declared war against England, and Genet came to embroil us in the trouble. From the beginning he acted rather as one of the rulers of the country than simply as a delegate to it, a blunder that brought one fatality after another in its train. With a total misconception of his own position, and an equal misconception of the character of those to whom he was accredited, all the elements of trouble were at hand. With his pert and bouncing attitude toward our government, his blustering arrogance, turning· quickly into hysteria when met with the slightest rebuff, this man of sound and fury, for such he soon proved himself to be, quickly effected international difficulties for the young nation he came to visit that taxed all the abilities of a very able administration. He concerns us here, not primarily in this capacity of diplomat, but as one who, sweeping through the country from Charleston northward, imparted to multitudes of men his own heated enthusiasm for the French cause, or, by force of repulsion, abhorrence of everything for which he stood. Greeted everywhere with very great favor, his picturesque course kindled joy in the hearts of the republicans and wrath in those of the federalists.[1]

Genet did not land in Philadelphia, but at Charleston, a

---

[1] At first he apparently impressed every one quite favorably. James Iredell wrote to Mrs. Iredell from Baltimore (May 16, 1793): " I waited on the new French Minister here in company with many other gentlemen, and was very much pleased with him, as were, I believe, all the rest. He is a very handsome man, with a fine open countenance and pleasing, unaffected manners." McRee's *Life and Correspondence of James Iredell*, II, 386.

point most distant from the seat of government. Charleston was just in the mood to give him a most cordial welcome. A movement was already on foot there for the solemn abolition of the use "of all aristocratical terms of distinction and respect," a movement that, according to the National Gazette, had the support of "a very large number of reputable names."[1] "In a State where sansculottism had already made much progress, the animating presence of the Parisian Missionary was all that could be wanted," exclaimed derisive William Cobbett, who had already begun to make merry with the rising sect of "Jacobins."[2] Genet, greatly stimulated, no doubt, by the cordiality of the greeting in which many of those in high official station had joined, proceeded to play the sovereign. He caused privateers, manned mostly by Americans, to be fitted out; issued letters of marque and reprisal to American citizens, and took the extraordinary step of authorizing the French consuls throughout the country to act as judges of admiralty in the trial and condemnation of all prizes that might be brought into American ports. After having remained about ten days in Charleston, this "Sansculotte Corps Diplomatique"[3] marched off to Philadelphia. There it had been resolved a fortnight before his arrival to give him a splendid reception. The republicans seized the occasion to strike with terror the "cowardly conservatives, anglomen and monarchists."[4] Genet is coming. He should be properly received, writes a correspondent to the National Gazette, "And may we not hope that the true republicans of this country will hoist the three-colored flag, the emblem of patriotism; and to complete the spectacle, that our fair Pennsylvanians will decorate their elegant persons and adorn their hair with patriotic ribbands on the occasion."[5]

---

[1] National Gazette, March 23, 1793.
[2] Cobbett, Hist. of Am. Jacobins in Wm. Playfair's Hist. of Jacobinism, p. 10.
On public opinion in Charleston see also Fraser, Reminiscences, 39.   [3] Cobbett.   [4] Griswold, Republican Court, 348.
[5] National Gazette, April 10, 1793.

As a preparation for this great event, Philadelphians were regaled with the sight of a French man-of-war, L'Ambuscade, which came sailing up the river the second day of May, saluting and being saluted by multitudes of people and by the gaily decorated vessels along the wharves. This ship seemed herself the very personification of the new militant republic, so bedight was she with republican emblems. The figures on bow and stern wore caps of liberty; the fore-topgallant mast was also crowned with one. Her quarter galleries were decorated with gilded anchors bearing the *bonnet rouge.* From the top of her foremast floated a warning banner, " Enemies of equality, reform or tremble "; from the mainmast, " Freemen, behold, we are your friends and brethren," and from the mizzenmast, " We are armed to defend the rights of man." [1]

Genet left Charleston, April 19. At once the societies of Philadelphia began preparing drafts of addresses to him and laying schemes for " elegant " dinners in his honor. On May 15 the National Gazette announced that several hours before his arrival three cannon would be fired from the frigate L'Ambuscade, so that the citizens might have ample time to go out and meet him at Gray's Ferry. On the 16th Genet arrived, overflowing with gratitude for the manifestations of interest and enthusiasm with which he had been overwhelmed ever since leaving Charleston. " On his way hither both farmers and merchants readily offered him their flour and other articles of provision at a lower price than they would dispose of them to the agents of any other nation. This article of flour alone amounts to more than 600,000 barrels." [2]

Crowds flocked out from every avenue to meet him. A town meeting was called to congratulate him on his arrival. At this meeting a committee of seven citizens was appointed to draw up an address of welcome. The committee consisted of men prominent in Philadelphia life—

---

[1] National Gazette, May 4, 1793; Griswold, Republican Court, 348.
[2] National Gazette, May 18, 1793.

David Rittenhouse, J. D. Sergeant, Dr. Hutchinson, A. J. Dallas, Peter S. Duponceau and Charles Biddle.[1] This was reported at a general meeting of citizens next evening and accepted, and a committee of thirty appointed to present the same to Genet. The committee accordingly repaired to the City Tavern, two by two, followed by an immense concourse of citizens walking in procession.[2]

The character of this address, which indeed is only typical of others, is shown by the following extract:

" For such reasons, sir, we have been naturally led to contemplate the struggles of France with a fraternal eye, sympathizing in all her calamities, and exulting in all her successes; but there is another interest, the interest of freedom and equality, which adds to the force of our affections and renders the cause of France important to every republic and dear to all the human race.

" Be assured, therefore, that justly regarding the cultivation of republican principles as the best security for the permanancy of our own popular governments, we rest our favorite hopes at this momentous crisis on the conduct of the French; and earnestly giving to the national exertions our wishes and our prayers, we cannot resist the pleasing hope that, although America is not a party in the existing war, she may still be able in a state of peace to demonstrate the sincerity of her friendship by affording every useful assistance to the citizens of her sister republic."

Genet, very much touched, delivered an extempore reply. " He observed that he was not an orator, and should not at any time affect the language of eloquence; that even, however, in uttering the genuine and spontaneous sentiments of his heart on an occasion so interesting and so flattering, he experienced some embarrassment arising from his defective acquaintance with the language in which he was about to speak, but this defect he was certain freemen

---

[1] Charles Biddle, Autobiography, 251; Pennypacker, Historical and Biographical Sketches, 86. [2] National Gazette, May 18, 1793.

would excuse. . . . He then adverted to the address and acknowledged in the most pathetic expressions the sense which he and his fellow-citizens must entertain in finding so noble an avowal of the principles of the Revolution in France." . . . "France," continued M. Genet, "is surrounded with difficulties, but her cause is meritorious; it is the cause of mankind and must prevail. With respect to you, I will declare openly and freely, for the minister of a republic should have no secrets, no intrigue, that from the remote situation of America and other circumstances, she does not expect that America should become a party in the war, but remembering that she has already combated for your liberties and, if it was necessary and she had the power, would cheerfully again enlist in your cause, we hope, and everything I hear and see assures me our hope will be realized, that her citizens will be treated as brothers in danger and distress. Under this impression, my feelings at this moment are inexpressible, and when I transmit your address to my fellow-citizens in France they will consider this day as one of the happiest of their infant Republic." "It is impossible to describe with adequate energy," says the National Gazette, "the scene that succeeded." Tremendous were the shouts and salutations. Genet was compelled to address the citizens in the streets, which he did "in a few but emphatic sentences."[1]

On the same day a committee appointed by the German Republican Society of Philadelphia waited on the new Minister with another address, to which he replied, expressing the conviction that Germany would "yet be free." Numerous other addresses were presented calling forth similar responses.

The republicans were in high glee over the warmth of the popular feeling thus shown for France. All this and much more that was to come occurred after the proclamation of neutrality had gone forth from the President's hand

---

[1] National Gazette, May 22, 1793.

(April 22) and was scarcely consonant with an impartial attitude toward the contending parties. But the republicans did not like this proclamation and were glad enough of the chance to express their opinion of it in a pointed manner; glad enough to minimize its effects if possible.

Madison, writing from Orange early in May, had expressed the most anxious desire that the reception of Genet might testify what he believed to be the real affections of the people. "It is the more desirable, as a seasonable plum after the bitter pills which it seems must be administered."[1] He hoped Genet would not be misled into supposing this country indifferent, as he surely would if he took either "the fashionable cant of the cities" or the "cold caution of the Government" for the real sense of the public.[2] A few days later (June 19) he wrote in this strain: "I regret extremely the position into which the President has been thrown. The unpopular cause of Anglomany is openly laying claim to him. . . . The proclamation was, in truth, a most unfortunate error. It wounds the national honor by seeming to disregard the stipulated duties to France. It wounds the popular feelings by a seeming indifference to the cause of liberty. And it seems to violate the forms and spirit of the Constitution by making the Executive Magistrate the organ of the disposition, the duty, and the interest of the nation, in relation to war and peace —subjects appropriated to other departments of the Government. It is mortifying to the real friends of the President that his fame and his influence should have been unnecessarily made to depend in any degree on political events in a foreign quarter of the Globe; and particularly so that he should have anything to apprehend from the success of liberty in another country, since he owes his preeminence to the success of it in his own. If France triumphs, the ill-fated proclamation will be a mill-stone, which would sink any other character, and will force a struggle even on his."

---

[1] Letters of James Madison, I, 578.   [2] Ibid. I, 579-580.

Jefferson's attitude was similar. He began to talk about the "manly neutrality," which was the one we ought to have adopted, instead of this pusillanimous one that threatened to be "a mere English neutrality." Our proceedings "towards the conspirators against human liberty, and the asserters of it," were "unjustifiable in principle, in interest, and in respect to the wishes of our constituents." The result was that the people, not seeing the Government express their mind, "were coming forward to express it themselves."[1]

This was precisely what they were doing. The President might proclaim neutrality and firmly force it upon the different departments of the Government. The conservative merchants of Philadelphia—three hundred of the principal ones—might rally about him approving the proclamation and promising to observe it strictly themselves and to "discountenance in the most pointed manner any contrary disposition in others." But in vain. With leaders feeling as did Jefferson and Madison, as Genet drew on from Charleston, there was apparently no power to check the popular enthusiasm. We have seen how it first expressed itself—through numerous addresses. Then the opposition press began to teem with articles of the most glowing description. "The genuine display of affection for the cause of France has once more abashed aristocracy and hailed equality triumphant," writes "An Old Soldier" to one of the Philadelphia papers. "The bosoms of many hundred freemen beat high with affectionate transport, their souls caught the celestial fire of struggling liberty, and in the enthusiasm of emotion they communicated their feelings to the worthy and amiable representative of the French nation. . . . Proclamations, unsanctioned by preceding laws, and processions of merchants, are equally indifferent to freemen when opposed to the national dictates of the head and the warm impulses of the heart. Thanks to our

---

[1] Jefferson's Works, III, 557, 562.

God, *sovereignty* still resides WITH THE PEOPLE, and that neither proclamations nor *royal demeanor and state* can prevent them from exercising it. Of this the independent freemen of this metropolis gave a striking example in the reception of M. Genet." It is an insult to put France on a plane with other countries. " Still it must not be imagined that my voice is for war. If we really could help France war would be our *duty*, our *security*, but our assistance may best be rendered in peace." [1]

" Mirabeau " wrote in great gratitude to Genet: " America is indebted to France for her present portion of liberty; nay, more, she must look up to her for its preservation; for so incorporate is their fate that they must rise or set together. If the oak is prostrated by the blast, the ivy which has entwined itself around it must participate in the ruin. Should France be subjugated by the confederated tyrants, woe unto America, for if a direct attack should not be made by them upon her liberties, the seductive power of corruption may make them pass away like a meteor."

Two days after his arrival the banquets began. The first one was at Oeller's. There were a hundred covers. The Minister and his family were there, Ternant, La Forest, the captain and officers of L'Ambuscade, and some of the State officials. Fifteen toasts were drunk. An " elegant " ode was read. The " Marseillaise hymn " was sung " with great taste and spirit " by Citizen Bournonville, the whole company joining in the chorus. Citizen Genet, at the request of the society, gave a song " replete with truly patriotic and republican sentiments," delivered " with great energy and judgment." The table was decorated with the tree and cap of liberty and the French and American flags. After the last toast had been drunk the cap of liberty was placed on the head of Citizen Genet and then travelled from head to head around the table, " each wearer enlivening the scene with a patriotic sentiment." These tokens of liberty

---

[1] National Gazette, May 22, 1793.

and American and French fraternity were delivered to the officers and mariners of L'Ambuscade, "who promised to defend them till death."[1]

The whole atmosphere of these celebrations was heated, overcharged, smacking of the cafés of Paris. Citizen Bompard, commander of L'Ambuscade, gave a dinner on board his vessel at which Governor Mifflin and Generals Knox and Stewart were present. They drank the usual toasts, and as they were about to leave, the boatswain, Dupont, addressed them in the name of his messmates in a speech "replete with feeling." "You see before you your good friends the French. Several of us have shed their blood to establish your liberty and independence; we are willing if necessary to shed the last drop of what remains for the maintaining that freedom which like you we have acquired. We are still your good friends and brethren, and if you should again want our assistance, we shall always be ready to give you proofs of our attachment." The Governor answered this "artless and energetic" speech by expressing his most sincere wishes for the happiness of the French nation and the success of the privateer L'Ambuscade.[2]

The 4th of July was celebrated in much the same way, more as a French than an American holiday. The 14th of July was duly observed. The officers of the second regiment of Philadelphia militia assembled at Weed's Ferry to commemorate the overthrow of the Bastille. Governor Mifflin and Genet were invited. The cannon discharged 85 rounds in honor of the 85 departments of France. Among the toasts were these: The Fourteenth of July; may it be a Sabbath in the calendar of freedom, and a Jubilee to the European world! The Tenth of August; may the freemen who offered up their lives on the altar of Liberty be ever remembered as martyrs and canonized as saints! May the Bastilles of despotism, throughout the earth, be crum-

---

[1] National Gazette, May 25, 1793.   [2] Ibid. June 1, 1793.

bled into dust and the Phoenix of Freedom grow out of the ashes! May the sister republics of France and America be as incorporate as light and heat; and the man who endeavors to disunite them be viewed as the Arnold of his country! May honor and probity be the principles by which the connections of free nations shall be determined; and no Machiavellian commentaries explain the text of treaties! The Treaty of Alliance with France; may those who attempt to evade or violate the political obligations and faith of our country be considered as traitors and consigned to infamy! May the succeeding generation wonder that such beings as Kings were ever permitted to exist![1] It was probably at this dinner that the head of a pig was severed from its body, and being recognized as an emblem of the murdered King of France, was carried round to the guests. "Each one placing the cap of liberty upon his head, pronounced the word 'tyrant'! and proceeded to mangle with his knife the head of the luckless creature doomed to be served for so unworthy a company."[2]

A month later enthusiasm broke out in New York as one day a French fleet was seen entering the waters of the Hudson. Everywhere was the tricolor, men even wearing it on their watch-chains. To add to the excitement Genet arrived from Philadelphia. The march northward still remained triumphal. Here as everywhere he was met by delegations—a committee had gone out to meet him at Paulus Hook—here as everywhere he was presented with congratulatory addresses—here as everywhere there were firing of cannon, ringing of bells, and eating of elaborate dinners. All this was the more convincing evidence of the popularity of his cause since he had already been made to feel the displeasure and opposition of the Government.[3]

---

[1] National Gazette, July 17, 1793.

[2] Thompson Westcott, in Westcott & Scharf, I, 474. See also Griswold, Rep. Court, p. 350; Cobbett, Hist. of Am. Jac., p. 26; Lamb, History of New York, II, 392.

[3] Lamb, Hist. of City of New York, II, 393.

" Thus rolled Genet's time away, in a variety of such non-sensical, stupid, unmeaning, childish entertainments as were never thought or heard of till Frenchmen took it into their heads to gabble about liberty," growled fiery William Cobbett.[1]

These demonstrations and the attention he received from important individuals, as Gov. Moultrie in South Carolina, Gov. Mifflin in Pennsylvania, Gov. Clinton in New York, turned Genet's head, raised his effrontery to the breaking point. On the occasion of his official presentation to Washington he took offence at a bust of Louis XVI. It was an insult to his government, by whom the execution of the King had been ordered, this recognition of " Capet and his family."[2] Invited to dine on the 4th of July with the Cincinnati, he returned a very polite answer but mentioned he " could not sit at table with the Count de Noailles."[3] The Count, although he had served in our war and was a member of the society, was manifestly no proper person to dine with, for was he not tainted with aristocracy?

But soon the story changed. The collapse came through the privateers which Genet had fitted out and which came sailing back into American harbors with their booty and their international complications. The attitude of the Government was firm and hostile. Fierce and arrogant and blustering was Genet, disposed to act in a rather high-handed manner with this stiff-necked and perverse administration. " Your account of Genet is dreadful," writes Madison to Jefferson in great alarm. " He must be brought right if possible. His folly will otherwise do mischief which no wisdom can repair."[4] And we find Jefferson, who two months before was saying of Genet's mission that it was " impossible for anything to be more affec-

---

[1] Hist. of American Jacobinism, 15.
[2] Griswold, Republican Court, 350; Scharf & Westcott, Hist. of Phila., I, 473-4.
[3] Biddle, Autobiography, 253.   [4] Madison's Letters, I, 586.

tionate, more magnanimous. . . . In short, he offers everything and asks nothing," now writing Gouverneur Morris that M. Genet had in the short time of his residence with us developed "a character and conduct so unexpected and so extraordinary as to place us in the most distressing dilemma, between our regard for his nation, which is constant and sincere, and a regard for our laws, the authority of which must be maintained; for the peace of our country, which the executive magistrate is charged to preserve; for its honor offended in the person of that magistrate; and for its character, grossly traduced in the conversations and letters of this gentleman." To carry out his will Genet finally threatened to appeal to the people. He had over-reached himself—though even then there were newspapers that so far forgot their duty as to support him. Soon he was recalled and this mortifying episode was closed.

Genet's life in Philadelphia gave such an extraordinary *élan* to the extreme republican principles, was so successful in winning extravagant and indiscriminating applause for everything French, and widespread imitation here, that his opponents welcomed anything as an aid in overcoming him. Even the yellow fever plague that broke out that summer was considered in the line of punishment for having wandered so far from the true God. "Can it ever be forgotten," exclaims Graydon, who lived through all this, "what a racket was made with the Citizen Genet? The most enthusiastic homage was too cold to welcome his arrival; and his being the first minister of the infant republic was dwelt upon as a most endearing circumstance. What hugging and tugging! What addressing and caressing! What mountebanking and chanting, with liberty caps and the other wretched trumpery of sansculotte foolery. . . . Such was the state of parties in the summer of 1793, when the metropolis of Pennsylvania, then resounding with un-hallowed orgies at the dismal butcheries in France, was visited with a calamity which had much the appearance which heaven sometimes sends to purify the heart "—yellow

fever.[1] Nor was this craze without its element of danger
to the State, in the opinion of many.

Referring to the excitement which prevailed in Philadelphia in 1793-4, John Adams, in a letter to Thomas Jefferson
written many years afterward, said: "You certainly never
felt the terrorism excited by Genet in 1793 when ten thousand people in the streets of Philadelphia day after day
threatened to drag Washington out of his house and effect
a revolution in the government or compel it to declare war
in favor of the French Revolution and against England.
The coolest, the firmest minds even among the Quakers in
Philadelphia have given their opinions to me that nothing
but the yellow fever which removed Dr. Hutchinson and
Jonathan Dickinson Sergeant from this world, could have
saved the United States from a fatal revolution of government."

Such then were some of those numberless celebrations
of which the papers of that day are full, celebrations that
were conducted in an atmosphere which was highly favorable to hysteria. It would be difficult to color too highly
the picture of the enthusiasm for the cause of France that
found expression in this country in 1793 and 1794, stimulated and intensified, no doubt, though by no means caused
by the ebullient Genet. It was the real French frenzy.
There was much talk of the Rights of Man, of hydras and
despots and cleansing of Augean stables. Every supposed
lover of liberty, from Cato to William Tell and Thomas
Paine, was toasted at a hundred convivial boards. Many
were the wishes expressed in the toasts at these banquets,
which are an illuminating historical evidence, that "the
rays of liberty might penetrate with the rapidity of light
the remotest corners of the earth," that "the reign of
philosophy might succeed to that of superstition and only
end with time," that the thrones of tyrants might be
"changed into guillotines, and the heads of all those who
refuse to acknowledge the sovereignty of the people be

---

[1] Graydon's Memoirs, 335.

levelled"; that "the fair of America and France might give birth to none but Brutuses and Scaevolas"; that "the Amazon Kate," who was no other than Catharine of Russia, might "live to see the rights of man prevail throughout her empire"; that the banners of freedom might soon wave not only over Vienna, Berlin, and Warsaw, but also over remote Ispahan and heathen Constantinople. Wherever liberty might be espied in any guise whatever, thither turned the thoughts of the feasters. They rose to toast "Stanislas, Chief Citizen of Poland"; "George Washington, the Father of Freedom; Lafayette, Freedom's Darling Son; Thomas Paine, the Clarion of Freedom"; "the Republic of Genoa"; "The Mountain: may tyranny be chained at its foot and may the light of liberty from its summit cheer and illuminate the whole world." One wished that "hereditary folly" might "be hereditary with hereditary rank." Another hoped that "The Gallo-Columbian fraternity of freemen" might be as durable as the ocean that divided those two favored lands; another longed to see a revolutionary tribunal in Great Britain to "give lessons of Liberty to her King, examples of Justice to her Ministry, and Honesty to her corrupt Legislature." The broadest idealism was apparent in some. An altruistic Bostonian arose in 1795 to drink to "All Mankind." Another, proposing a similar toast—to "The Great Family of Mankind," added, "May the distinction of nation and language be lost in the association of freedom and of friendship till the inhabitants of the various sections of the globe be distinguished only by their virtues and their talents," and another expressed his hope that the time would soon come when the Rights of Man should be recognized as "the supreme law of every land and their separate fraternities be absorbed in one great democratic society comprehending the human race."

The enthusiasm of Americans could not exhaust itself in one round of festivities. Repeatedly during this and succeeding years right down to 1797, when our troubles with

France broke out under John Adams, they came together in honor of their " magnanimous allies " and to drink
to those radiant abstractions to which men were so fond
of drinking in those days.   They celebrated Washington's
birthday, often apparently with less attention to Washington than to the French.   February 6th, the date of the
formation of the Franco-American alliance; May 1st, St.
Tammany's day; the anniversary of Bunker Hill; the 4th
of July; the 14th of July; the 10th of August; the 22d of
September, these latter days of no direct significance to
America, though of the greatest in the calendar of France;
Thanksgiving day, and the anniversary of the surrender of
Yorktown were often celebrated and in a thoroughly
French style.[1]

DEMOCRATIC SOCIETIES.

Suddenly this great popular ferment produced something
new and unexpected, and ominous in the political life of
the young republic, of which she was destined to have more
than one disquieting experience in the future.   Secret
political organizations made their appearance.   The swift-
ness of the rise and spread of Democratic Societies in this
country is a striking witness to the turmoil and passion of
that moment, a turmoil and passion from which they
seemed to emerge spontaneously, and which they in turn
plentifully re-inforced.   No one can read very far into the
history of these years without seeing unmistakably the
fervor and the virulence, the consternation, the exultation,
the vague fear, the positive and sharply defined hatred

---

[1] The following are a few of the numberless references to such
events in the papers of the day: Bache's Aurora, March 4, July 31,
August 13 and 15, 1793; February 8 and 12, 1794; February 9, 1795.
Independent Chronicle, July 25, August 2 and 15, 1793; January 23,
March 20, May 19, July 17, August 18, 1794; February 25, April 9,
20, 30, September 24, 1795; March 7, July 7, 1796. American Daily
Advertiser, February 14, May 5, 1794; February 9, 1797. Boston
Gazette, August 19, 1793. Columbian Centinel, July 16, 1794. Fed-
eral Orrery, June 15, 1795; September 26, October 20, 1796.

aroused by these new institutions among different classes of Americans. They added immensely to the bitterness of party strife. Fierce of utterance themselves, they called forth equal fierceness of opposition. They fostered certain tendencies that needed no such encouragement, a willingness to borrow joy or trouble from the fate of others, a disposition to mix in affairs not one's own. They lived a noisy life and after awhile subsided, having exerted a doubtful influence and leaving behind them an unpleasant memory. It is well to enquire briefly into the character and purposes of societies that in their day created so much stir.

A few days after Genet's arrival in Philadelphia, "The Democratic Society of Pennsylvania" was organized in that city. The reasons for its creation, its temper, and a certain temper of the times may best be seen in "The Principles, Articles, and Regulations" which were drawn up and adopted May 30, 1793, and which were printed in the papers all over the country.[1] These "Principles, Articles and Regulations" are:

"The RIGHTS OF MAN, the genuine objects of Society, and the legitimate principles of Government, have been clearly developed by the successive revolutions of America and France. Those events have withdrawn the veil which concealed the dignity and the happiness of the human race, and have taught us, no longer dazzled with adventitious splendor, or awed by antiquated usurpation, to erect the temple of LIBERTY on the ruins of *palaces* and *thrones*.

"At this propitious period, when the nature of freedom and equality is thus practically displayed, and when their value (best understood by those who have paid the price of acquiring them) is universally acknowledged, the patriotic mind will naturally be solicitous, by every proper precaution, to preserve and perpetuate the blessings which Providence hath bestowed upon our country; for, in review-

---

[1] The one quoted here is "The National Gazette," July 17, 1793. The document may be found in part, together with the accompanying circular, in Dallas's Life of Dallas, pp. 56-58.

ing the history of nations, we find occasion to lament, that
the vigilance of the people has been too easily absorbed in
victory; and that the prize which has been achieved by the
wisdom and valor of one generation, has too often been lost
by the ignorance and supineness of another.

"With a view, therefore, to cultivate a just knowledge of
rational liberty, to facilitate the enjoyment and exercise of
our civil rights, and to transmit, unimpaired, to posterity,
the glorious inheritance of a *free republican government*, the
DEMOCRATIC SOCIETY of Pennsylvania is constituted and
established. Unfettered by *religious* or *national* distinctions,
unbiassed by party, and unmoved by ambition, this institution embraces the interest and invites the support of every
virtuous citizen. The public good is indeed its sole object,
and we think that the best means are pursued for obtaining
it, when we recognize the following as the fundamental
principles of our organization:

I. THAT the people have the inherent and exclusive right
and power of making and altering forms of government;
and that for regulating and protecting our social interests, a
REPUBLICAN GOVERNMENT is the most natural and beneficial form, which the wisdom of man has devised.

II. THAT the republican constitutions of the UNITED
STATES and of the STATE of PENNSYLVANIA, being framed
and established by the people, it is our duty, as good citizens, to support them. And in order effectually to do so,
it is likewise the duty of every freeman to regard with
attention, and to discuss without fear, the conduct of the
public servants, in every department of government.

III. THAT in considering the administration of public
affairs, men and measures should be estimated according
to their intrinsic merits; and therefore, regardless of party
spirit or political connection, it is the duty of every citizen,
by making the general welfare the rule of his conduct, to
aid and approve those men and measures, which have an
influence in promoting the prosperity of the commonwealth.

IV. THAT in the choice of persons to fill the offices of

government, it is essential to the existence of a free republic, that every citizen should act according to his own judgment, and therefore any attempt to corrupt or delude the people in exercising the rights of suffrage, either by promising the favor of one candidate or traducing the character of another, is an offence equally injurious to moral rectitude and civil liberty.

V. THAT the *People of Pennsylvania* form but one indivisible community, whose political rights and interests, whose national honor and prosperity, must, in degree and duration, be forever the same; and, therefore, it is the duty of every free man, and shall be the endeavor of the Democratic Society, to remove the prejudices, to conciliate the affections, to enlighten the understanding, and to promote the happiness of all our fellow citizens."

Such are the official principles—not very ominous, not very exciting. Then follows the constitution. The society is to be co-extensive with the State, but for the convenience of members there shall be chapters or "meetings," as they are called, in each county that chooses to adopt the constitution. A member admitted in any "meeting" is a member of the Society at large and may attend any of the meetings wherever held. Members are admitted by majority vote after having been proposed a suitable length of time. Provision is made for officers and their election. The most important of these seems to be the "Corresponding Committee" of five members, whose duty is to correspond "with the various meetings of the Societies, and with all other Societies that may be established on similar principles, in any other of the United States."

Now the platitudes cease and the real motive of the Society is revealed in the "Circular Letter ordered to be sent to the Counties," which follows:

"Fellow Citizen:

We have the pleasure to communicate to you a copy of the constitution of the Democratic Society, in hopes, that after a candid consideration of its principles and objects, you may be induced to promote its adoption in the county of which you are an inhabitant.

"Every mind capable of reflection must perceive that the present crisis in the politics of nations is peculiarly interesting to America. The European confederacy, transcendent in power, and unparalleled in iniquity, menaces the very existence of freedom. Already its baneful operation may be traced in the tyrannical destruction of the constitution, and the rapacious partition of the territory of Poland; and should the glorious efforts of France be eventually defeated, we have reason to presume, that, for the consummation of monarchical ambition, and the security of its establishments, this country, the only remaining depository of liberty, will not long be permitted to enjoy in peace the honors of an independent, and the happiness of a republican government.

"Nor are the dangers arising from a foreign source the only causes, at this time, of apprehension and solicitude. The seeds of luxury appear to have taken root in our domestic soil; and the jealous eye of patriotism already regards the spirit of freedom and equality as eclipsed by the pride of wealth, and the arrogance of power.

"This general view of our situation has led to the institution of 'The Democratic Society.' A constant circulation of useful information, and a liberal communication of republican sentiments, were thought to be the best antidotes to any political poison with which the vital principles of civil liberty might be attacked; for, by such means, a fraternal confidence will be established among the citizens; every symptom of innovation will be studiously marked; and a standard will be erected to which, in danger or distress, the friends of liberty may successfully resort.

"To obtain these objects then, and to cultivate on all occasions the love of peace, order, and harmony; an attachment to the constitutions and a respect to the laws of our country, will be the aim of 'The Democratic Society.'

Party and personal considerations are excluded from a system of this nature; for in the language of the articles under which we are united, men and measures will only be estimated according to their intrinsic merits, and their influence in promoting the prosperity of the state.

"From you, citizen, we hope to derive essential aid, in extending the Society and maintaining its general principles. We request therefore an early attention to the subject, and solicit a constant correspondence."[1]

In the "Declaration" sent out by "The Massachusetts Constitutional Society," soon formed in Boston, we discover still further the animus of these new organizations:

"Under a Constitution which expressly provides '*That the people have a right in an orderly and peaceable manner to assemble and consult upon the common good,*' there can be no necessity for an apology to the public for an Association of a number of citizens to promote and cherish the social virtues, the love of their country and a respect for its Laws and Constitutions; nor can it be derogatory to Freemen *in America* to declare their attachment to *Universal Liberty* and openly to profess a sacred regard to the great principles of *Natural Equality.*"

After having set up a government, citizens ought not to resign it into the hands of agents—whither does this tend but toward despotism? We conceive "that it is the right and duty of every Freeman, to watch with the vigilance of a faithful centinel the conduct of those to whom is intrusted the administration of Government, that they pass not the sacred barriers of the Constitution."

"Predicated on these principles the members of this Association have united and agreed to meet in whole, or in such parts as may be expedient, to converse together for the purpose of gaining and communicating information on the affairs of their country; to express with decency and

---

[1] The constitution, circular and other explanatory papers were first drafted by Alexander James Dallas. See Life and Writings of Alexander James Dallas by his son, George Mifflin Dallas, 55-56.

firmness, their sentiments respecting the measures adopted by their Delegates, and to offer their opinions with candor on matters of political concernment.

"As Freemen we publicly declare that we adore the cause of Liberty, wherever it may be in exertion; and our wishes and our prayers are frequently engaged against the Despots of the Earth.

"We are persuaded that the present struggles of the French People are directed to the subversion of Aristocracy and Despotism, and to the lasting improvement and happiness of the human race, as they are founded on the *Equal Rights of Men*.

"With such objects in view and on these principles, the particular *form* of administering their government in detail, we consider, at *present*, unessential. But on the accomplishment of the great objects of their Revolution, depends not only the future happiness and prosperity of Frenchmen, but in our opinion of the *whole World of Mankind*. Their success will put an effectual check to the progress of despotic ambition, while the failure of so great and gallant a nation would encourage the Despots of the earth to aspire to the hope of extinguishing the spirit of Liberty perhaps in every other part of the globe. When, in addition to this, we recollect the generous assistance, which the French nation afforded us, in the day of our distress and danger, we cannot but wish that the Great Ruler of the universe had placed it within our power to reciprocate their friendship, by aiding them in the establishment of that Liberty, for which they are now bleeding with so much firmness and magnanimity." [1]

The reasons then that led Americans to form their first secret political societies were suspicion of the government, envy of those in power, ardent and excited attachment to France, ill-concealed hatred of England as the arch-despot —a hatred that in some of the constitutions was openly and

---

[1] Boston Gazette, Jan. 20, 1794; Independent Chronicle, Jan. 16, 1794.

bitterly expressed, as in that of the Democratic Society of Chittenden County, Vermont.[1]

The invitation sent out by the Philadelphia Society for the formation of affiliated societies met with a quick response. These new democratic organizations sprang up in almost every part of the Union, all proclaiming the same purpose of sleepless vigilance of the Government, a determination to rescue the people from its oppression or corruption, to maintain the Rights of Man undimmed, all marked by the same warmth of feeling for our " magnanimous ally," and from all there issued great clouds of circulars and addresses couched in the current political vernacular of France. In the newspapers of the day I have seen mention of societies in Charleston, Baltimore, Philadelphia, New York, Boston, Portland; in Pinckney (S. C.), in Lexington, Paris, Georgetown, Danville, Kentucky; in Wythe County, Virginia; Washington and Lancaster, Pennsylvania; Newcastle, Delaware; Chittenden, Bennington, Addison, Rutland and Cumberland counties, Vermont, and these certainly were but a small number of those in existence from Maine to Georgia.[2] Their ideas and feelings were almost wholly French, their chief aim was to propagate extreme democratic doctrines. The society at Charleston even went so far as to petition the Jacobin Club in

---

[1] Spooner's Vermont Journal, April 21, 1794.

[2] The certificate of membership in these societies ran as follows:

"To all other societies established on principles of *Liberty, Equality, Union, Patriotic Virtue and Perseverance;* We, the members of the Republican Society of Baltimore, certify and declare to all Republican or Democratic societies, and to all Republicans individually, that citizen ———— hath been admitted and now is a member of our society, and that, from his warm zeal to promote Republican principles and the rights of humanity, we have granted him this our certificate (which he has signed in the margin) and do recommend him to all Republicans, that they may receive him with fraternity, which we offer to all those who may come to us with similar credentials. In witness whereof, etc." Harper's Cyclopedia of United States History, 382. The seal of the Baltimore society was composed of a figure of Liberty, with pileus, Phrygian cap and fasces, with the name of the society.

Paris for the honor of adoption. The request met with some opposition on the ground that Americans did not deserve such a favor, as they had not yet shed their blood in the cause of France. The Americans, however, found a friend in Collot d'Herbois, who urged that the bestowal of the desired honor would "have a tendency to induce the Americans to discharge their obligations." This argument won the day and the petition was granted.[1]

These clubs at once threw themselves into the current of American politics, stirring up the mud generally. They filled the land with the noise of criticism. Attacking most of the measures of the Government and pretending to speak in the name of "the people," they added an uproar to our political life, disproportionate, probably, to the real weight of their numbers.

At their meetings resolutions galore were adopted and their publication "by the Republican Printers throughout the country" demanded and obtained. These resolutions have their own significance. The Philadelphia Society resolved "That we view with inexpressible horror the cruel and unjust war carried on by the combined powers of Europe against the republic of France," and that "we ought to resist to the utmost of our power all attempts to alienate our affections from France and detach us from

---

[1] The following is a quotation from a French paper printed in the Independent Chronicle, March 17, 1794, reporting a session of the Paris Jacobin Club of October, 1793:

"The Republican Society in Charleston, in Carolina, one of the United States of America, demanded of the Jacobin Club its adoption.

Hautier.—We have spilt our blood for the establishment of America, and think that the Americans ought to do the same for us before we grant them adoption.

A Citizen.—Before engaging them to intermeddle with our war it is necessary to understand one another, to come to an agreement with them. I do not see then a more efficacious way for the previous reunion than the adoption of their society.

Collot d'Herbois.—We should not neglect the advantages which may arise from this request. I conclude that we agree to this adoption. Resolved."

her alliance." [1] This was long after Washington's Proclamation of Neutrality. The Charleston Society writes to
the brethren that be in Philadelphia as follows: "In contemplating the present situation of our country, we antici-
pate with uncommon satisfaction, the benefits which will be
rendered to her by the formation of societies in different
parts of the Union, upon the same principles and having
the same views of the Democratic Society of Philadelphia,"
and adds, "Although we cannot but lament as men the
amazing want of Republicanism, which now forms a conspicuous trait in the characters composing the highest
offices in the Federal Government; although we observe
with indignation that aristocratic pride and mistaken ambition have for some time past been gaining daily ground
among us; yet we hope fully that from the steady, spirited,
and persevering virtue of a few, the whole will be brought
once again to think and to act as becomes the character of
a free people; and that from a just reflection a conviction
in their minds shall arise to prove that the true happiness of
a nation consists in a simple purity of manners, which will
always lead them to prefer honor, even with poverty, to
the splendor of riches and titles obtained by sacrificing public honor and national faith and virtue." [2] Later this same
Charleston Society "contemplating the daring outrages
and diabolical machinations of the British Court, and the
evil intrigues now practised by her agents and emissaries,
to undertake and destroy the liberty and happiness of
America; and holding it just and laudable to call the attention of our fellow citizens to the alarming situation of
public affairs, do hereby submit to their consideration the
sense entertained of these important circumstances, and
resolved as follows:

Resolved, That it is the peculiar privilege of the citizens
of the United States, to meet at all times and on all occasions peaceably to pursue the best means for obtaining and

---

[1] Bache's General Advertiser, Jan. 13, 1794.
[2] Ibid. April 3, 1794.

preserving the public happiness and freely to investigate or censure or approve the conduct of all persons in public employment, and to submit their opinions to the sense of the community.

Resolved, That this Society view with indignation the conduct of certain members of Congress, one of these a representative from Charleston district; being convinced from the whole tenor of their actions and debates in Congress, they are possessed of the basest and most dangerous principles; that far from being republicans they are indifferent to the repeated insults offered the American flag, and the repeated depredations committed on the property of the citizens of America; that in addition to such insults and depredations, the detention of the western posts, contrary to express treaty; supplies to the Indians, our deadly foes; the treaty devised and concluded by the British government, to set the Algerines upon our commerce, are to them but trifles, when compared to the prosperity of the funds in which, by their infamous speculations, they are become deeply interested.

Resolved, That it is our opinion that war is inevitable; we cannot therefore be too early in making preparations; we therefore recommend that such other forts should without delay be erected, as will secure this State from depredations and insult; and that it is the duty of all good republican citizens to provide themselves as speedily as possible with such implements of war as may be necessary for their defence.

Resolved, That proclamations are intended only as promulgations of laws constitutionally enacted, to inform the citizens, who, in consequence of the attention necessary to their various occupations, may require such information; or, proclamations may with propriety be made to give warning of the approach of any public calamity, or to announce to the people the day and place of any public act; but when any person or set of men in office, instead of announcing only the laws of the land, attempt by proclamation to declare his or their own will or determination as the sovereign rule, binding on the people, the judges, and the courts of justice; such an exercise of power is unconstitutional, tyrannical, arbitrary, and in the highest degree dangerous, an usurpation of authority of the most despotic nature, and a direct attack upon the liberties of the people.

Resolved, That all public officers are appointed under the Constitution, their political creator and ruler, and they are but the servants of the public.

Resolved, That treaties solemnly made with nations which act with sincere friendship and preserve zealously their faith towards us, ought to be inviolably adhered to and guarded from infraction at every risque; that the cause of France is our own; that our interest, liberty and public happiness are involved in her fate; that we are bound to support her by every tye of principle and gratitude as well as a principle of self-preservation; that for any man or set of men, either in private or public and particularly those to whom the welfare of our community is intrusted, to advocate doctrines and principles derogatory to the cause of France, or her commerce with America, or in support of the base measures of the combined despots of Europe, particularly Great Britain, is a convincing manifestation of sentiments treacherous and hostile to the interest of the United States, and well deserves the severest censure from all true republican citizens of America."[1]

Many of the matters upon which these societies resolved were of purely local importance, but most of them concerned more or less directly our foreign relations, and into these they sought to introduce strong French partisanship. One society resolved in favor of governmental protection of infant manufactures;[2] many in favor of the navigation of the Mississippi;[3] many against the excise laws. But first and most unanimously they declared against Washington's policy of neutrality. Government " by proclamation " was widely denounced as a most portentous usurpation. Some

---

[1] Independent Chronicle, April 18, 1794.
[2] Boston Gazette, May 26, 1794.   [3] Minerva, April 17, 1794.

of these societies did not claim that we ought to take part in the war on the side of France, yet they at the same time denounced the President's policy as base ingratitude. Here, then, just at the first critical juncture of our foreign relations, were numbers of energetic and noisy associations all over the land doing their best directly or indirectly to foil, impede or overthrow the only policy that wisdom could recommend. The vehemence of their criticism of this policy— of the Proclamation and all that grew out of. it—the Jay mission in particular—grew apace. Their activity tended to break up all neutrality, to drive us into an alliance with France, if with any one, and to assume a hostile attitude toward England.

The New York Society, a few days after Mr. Jay's departure, proceeded to smite that gentleman in an address to the people. "We take pleasure in avowing that we are lovers of the French nation; that we esteem their cause as our own. We most firmly believe that he who is an enemy to the French revolution cannot be a firm republican; and therefore, though he may be a good citizen in other respects, ought not to be intrusted with the guidance of any part of the machine of government." A Pennsylvania Society declared that the President had no right to proclaim this country neutral—that came only within the competence of the legislature; it even denied that neutrality was the duty or true interest of the United States and loudly denounced the mission to England and the envoy himself because of "his high standing in the community." "The Revolution of France," it was said, " had sufficiently proved that generals may be taken from the ranks, and ministers of state from the obscurity of the most remote village. Is our president, like the grand sultan of Constantinople, shut up in his appartment and unacquainted with all talents and capacities but those of the seraskier or mufti who happens to be about him?"[1]

---

[1] The Life and Writings of John Jay, by his son, William Jay. 2 vols., New York, 1833. On Democratic Societies see I, 315-321. See also Independent Chronicle, May 19, 1794, for bitter denunciation of Jay's appointment by one of these societies.

Fierce was the wrath of the Democratic Society in Wythe County, Virginia, at various things that were happening. This soon found vent in an "Address to the People of the United States," which ran as follows:

"Fellow Citizens:

"It is a right of the people peaceably to assemble and deliberate; it is a right of the people to publish their sentiments. These rights we exercise and esteem invaluable.

"A war raging in Europe, a war of tyrants against liberty, cannot be unfelt by the people of the United States; it has roused our feelings. We have rejoiced when victory followed the standards of liberty. When despots were successful we have experienced the deepest anxiety. We have lamented that our good wishes were the only aid we could give the French.

"Among the different powers combined against the rights of man we have marked the British nation, the champion of despotism. With indignation we have heard their insolent dictates to the small neutral powers of Europe, to join in the subjugation of France. With sorrow we have seen every principle of liberty, hitherto retained by the people of Britain, violated by its present corrupt government and their most virtuous inhabitants transported to foreign lands or going into voluntary exile. But we hope these things will ultimately produce good and that there is still a latent spark, which by excessive friction, will kindle to a flame and will consume the rotten edifice of the British government, on the ruins of which another may arise, the basis whereof shall be justice, liberty and equality.

"While with anxious expectation we contemplate the affairs of Europe, it will be criminal to forget our own country. A session of Congress having just passed, the first in which the people were equally represented, it is a fit time to take a retrospective view of the proceedings of government. We have watched each motion of those in power, but are sorry we cannot exclaim 'well done, thou good and faithful servant.' We have seen the nation in-

sulted, our rights violated, our commerce ruined—and what
has been the conduct of government? Under the corrupt
influence of the paper system, it has uniformly crouched to
Britain; while, on the contrary, our allies, the French, to
whom we owe our political existence, have been treated
unfriendly; denied any advantages from their treaties with
us; their Minister abused; and those individuals among us,
who desired to aid their arms, prosecuted as traitors—blush
Americans for the conduct of your government.

"Citizens! Shall we Americans who have kindled the
spark of liberty stand aloof and see it extinguished when
burning a bright flame in France, which hath caught it
from us? Do you not see if despots prevail, you must
have a despot like the rest of the nations. If all tyrants
unite against free people, should not all free people unite
against tyrants? Yes! Let us unite with France and stand
or fall together.

"We lament that a man who hath so long possessed the
public confidence, as the head of the executive department
hath possessed it, should put it to so severe a trial as he
hath by a late appointment. The constitution hath been
trampled on, and your rights have no security.

"Citizens! What is despotism? Is it not a union of
executive, legislative and judicial authorities in the same
hands? This union then has been effected. Your chief-
justice has been appointed to an executive office, by the
head of that branch of government: In that capacity he is
to make *Treaties.* Those *treaties* are your *supreme law,*
and of this *supreme law* he is *supreme judge!!* What has
become of your constitution and liberties?

"Fellow Citizens!

"We hope the misconduct of the executive may have
proceeded from bad advice; but we can only look to the
immediate cause of the mischief. To us it seems a radical
change of measures is necessary. How shall this be effected? Citizens! It is to be effected by a change of men.
Deny the continuance of your confidence to such members

of the legislative body as have an interest distinct from that of the people. To trust yourselves to stockholders, what is it, but like the Romans, to deliver the poor debtor to his creditor, as his absolute property. To trust yourselves to speculators, what is it but to commit the lamb to the wolf to be devoured.

"It was recommended by the conventions of some of the states, so to amend the constitution, as to incapacitate any man to serve as president more than eight years successively. Consider well this experiment. 'Tis probably the most certain way to purge the different departments and produce a new state of things.

"Believe us, fellow-citizens, the public welfare is our only motive." [1]

Such then were the methods of these secret organizations that arose so quickly and spread so rapidly throughout the Union. They aimed to rescue the free institutions of the land, to safeguard the Rights of Man. How these were threatened it would be difficult to see, or in what mysterious manner they were to be saved by little organized cliques. Though really representing but a part of the community, and surely in many sections but a small part, they loudly pretended to be the voice of the people. When their right to be considered the authoritative organ of public opinion was questioned, they drew themselves up solemnly and reaffirmed that they were. For instance, when the editor of one of the papers suggested, under the title "Great Cry and Little Wool," that the Democratic Society of Chittenden County, which published addresses twelve columns long, consisted of only twelve members, the impressive reply came from out the heart of the hills, "We are eighty-four citizens of the County of Chittenden, and State of Vermont, amongst whom are eight members of the Legislature —*all* the General Officers of the County—the High Sheriff —the *majority* of the Bench—and *all* the Bar, except two,

---

[1] Independent Chronicle, Aug. 11, 1794.

whom prudence has as yet prevented asking for admission." [1]
It was elsewhere asserted that its members were "as
respectable characters as the vicinity can produce." [2]

The effect produced by these societies was soon evident.
The fierceness of the opposition was equal to the vehemence
of the societies themselves. "It is well known here, writes
Oliver Wolcott from Philadelphia, that these popular societies speak the sentiments of certain demagogues, and that
the clubs consist of hot-headed, ignorant, or wicked men,
devoted entirely to the views of France." [3] Patrick Henry
wrote that, although a Democrat himself, he did not like
the Democratic Societies. [4] Fisher Ames, speaking of a
recent meeting of the Boston club in Faneuil Hall, said:
"This is bold and everything really shows the fixed purpose of their leaders to go to desperate lengths. It is a
pleasant thing for the yeomanry to see their own government taken out of their hands and themselves cipherized
by a rabble formed into a club. Thus Boston may play
Paris, and rule the State," [5] and later he said that, though
right-minded men despised these clubs, still it was not safe
to make light of your enemy. "They poison every spring;
they whisper lies to every gale; they are everywhere, always
acting like Old Nick and his imps. Such foes are to be
feared as well as despised. They wait in silence for occasions, and when they occur, out they come and carry their
points. They will be as busy as Macbeth's witches at the
election, and all agree that the event is very doubtful." [6]

Others dubbed them "demoniacal" clubs instead of
democratical, and "nurseries of sedition." [7] Unbounded was
the hatred of the Federalists for these annoying intruders. [8]
That these clubs were a turbulent and troublesome element

---

[1] Independent Chronicle, March 2, 1795.
[2] Vermont Gazette, Feb. 13, 1795.   [3] Gibbs, Memoirs, I, 134.
[4] William Wirt Henry, Life, Correspondence and Speeches of
Patrick Henry, II, 551.
[5] Fisher Ames' Works, edited by Seth Ames, I, 146-147.
[6] Ibid. I, 148.   [7] Gibbs, Memoirs, I, 179.
[8] Morison, Life of Jeremiah Smith, pp. 61-64.

in our politics cannot be gainsaid. Such was their tireless
persistence that William Cobbett ventured " to say without
running the risk of contradiction, that more enmity to the
General Government was excited in the space of six months
by the barefaced correspondencies and resolves of these
clubs, than was excited against the colonial government at
the time of the Declaration of Independence," [1] but then
William Cobbett would venture to assert almost anything
against the Democrats. This animosity finally found dangerous utterance in the Whiskey Insurrection of 1794.
Washington himself believed that the rebellion in Pennsylvania had been fomented largely by the Democratic clubs—
largely in order to impair his own influence and embarrass
the administration, and in his message to Congress that year
he denounced them as " certain self-created societies," that
had "assumed the tone of condemnation " of the Government's measures, hoping "by a more formal concert" to
defeat their operation.[2]

Great was the joy of the Federalists at this denunciation
of the odious clubs, coming from so weighty a source.
Eagerly did they seize the words as weapons with which to
work their destruction. Jeremiah Smith, writing from
Congress, said that the President's speech was very popular
with the friends of the Government, that it was too applicable to the Democratic clubs to admit of any doubt. " We
smile and they pout. Let their mortification be increased
tenfold." [3] In the Senate it was easy to secure an answer
to the President's message in which the societies were denounced in the same words. In the lower House, however,
the Democrats made a stand and dragged the debate
through several days. Mr. Giles, who was one of their
leading spokesmen, said "that when he saw or thought he
saw the House of Representatives about to erect itself into

---

[1] History of the American Jacobins, 1796, 23.
[2] Annals of Congress, Nov. 19, 1794, and sequiter for the significant debate that grew out of this remark in the President's speech.
[3] Morison, Life of Jeremiah Smith, p. 65.

an office of censorship, he could not sit silent." He quib-
bled with the plain meaning of the words " self-created,"
saying that " there was not an individual in America who
might not come under the charge of being a member of
some one or other self-created society "—religious, political,
philosophical, as the case might be. " The Baptists and
Methodists, for example, might be termed self-created
societies." And how about the Cincinnati? It would be
well for Congress to studiously refrain from all legislation
aiming to restrict public opinion directly or indirectly. If
these societies are unlawful—let the law take its course—
no further laws are necessary. If they are not unlawful,
further legislation is unwise and inexpedient. Mr. Smith
(of South Carolina) said that " he was a friend to the freedom of the press, but would any one compare a regular
town-meeting, where deliberations were cool and unruffled,
to these societies, to the nocturnal meetings of individuals,
after they have dined, where they shut their doors, pass
votes in secret, and admit no members into their societies
but those of their own choosing." Mr. Tracy believed in
answering them. To be sure whenever a subject of that
kind was brought up " there were certain gentlemen in that
House, who shook their backs, like a sore-backed horse,
and cried out ' The Liberties of the people.' " But as for
him, he thought that the declaration of the House would
discourage these societies " by uniting all men of sense
against them." Mr. Christie said that he was sorry to see
men attempting to " saddle a public odium on some of the
best citizens of the State which he represented." He mentioned the Republican Society of Baltimore, which he
affirmed consisted of gentlemen—men who were superior
to any censure that Congress might seek to throw upon
them. Indeed, they were " a band of patriots, not the
fair-weather patriots of the present day, but the patriots of
seventy-five." They should be rather praised, for at the
very beginning of the late insurrection they offered to go
and help suppress it.

Mr. Sedgwick approved the condemnation. It "would have a tendency to plunge these societies into contempt and to sink them still farther into abhorrence and detestation." He pronounced them to be illicit combinations. "Will the American people perversely propose to shoulder and bolster up these despised and repenting societies which are now tumbling into dust and contempt. Their conduct differed as far from a fair and honorable investigation as Christ and Belial. They were men prowling in the dark. . . . From Portland in Maine to the other end of the Continent, have they ever approved of one single act?"

The House finally adopted a milder form of reference to these societies and the incident was closed as far as Congress was concerned.[1]

The official displeasure of the President was a heavy blow to the societies, but they endeavored to hold their ground. Society after society passed long resolutions showing that it had disapproved any disobedience of the law—that it had not favored, but had censured the Insurrection. But they denounced any attempts to muzzle men. The Independent Chronicle at first assumed an attitude of cold scorn of all assailants of the Societies. "What a continual yelping and barking are our Swindlers, Aristocrats, Refugees and British Agents making at the Constitutional Societies. But how gratifying must it be to the friends of Constitutional Government to observe these societies proceeding in the paths of patriotic virtue with a composure and dignity which become men engaged in such important and timely service. Thus have we seen a noble mastiff proceeding on his way, without deigning even to cast a look upon the impotent and noisy puppies at his heels."[2]

The Republican Society of Baltimore, noticing the denunciation of the President, took occasion to say in its address of defence that it had from the beginning disapproved the Insurrection, and then it asked if " dungeons and

---

[1] See Annals of Congress, Nov. 1794.
[2] Independent Chronicle, Sept. 18, 1794.

chains and death" await the man who would "dare to express disapprobation which he felt respecting the measures
of government."[1] The Democratic Society of New York,
in an address five columns long, also defended the right
of these organizations to exist. "Free investigation"
is threatened. These societies may well serve as guardians
of liberty. "How has it happened that Athens and Sparta,
once the celebrated seats of Liberty, once the boast of philosophers, the pride of Greece, and the envy of mankind,
have fallen the devoted victims of Otterman Tyranny."[2]

But whistle as much as they might, their courage was
gone and their prestige had been affected. Their discomfiture was still further augmented by letters which Monroe
was sending home, severely criticising the Jacobin clubs
of France. The societies did not immediately pass into
obscurity. Indeed, new ones were formed here and there
even after this episode. But henceforth they were less
visible, less audible, less important.

The significance of these societies for us, in this investigation, lies in the fact that they were hotly enthusiastic for
the French Revolution, both in its aspect as a body of general principles, capable of general adoption, and as a concrete attempt of a single country to alter and improve its
national life. These societies approved all that was happening in France. They furnished the medium through
which multitudes looked at these strange and exciting
phenomena. They shaped one kind of public opinion.

Nor is it necessary for us to adopt the attitude of the Federalists toward them. They were not composed of simply
the restless and discontented and noisy elements of the
population. Many eminent men belonged. In Philadelphia David Rittenhouse and Charles Biddle and James
Hutchinson and Alexander James Dallas and Jonathan D.
Sergeant and P. S. Duponceau, men of ability and high
standing in the community, were members. James Sullivan,

---

[1] Independent Chronicle, Jan. 15, 1795.   [2] Ibid. Jan. 29, 1795.

later Governor, belonged to the Boston society. But there
is reason to believe that many of these were swept in by
the first gust of popular enthusiasm, and that as the more
violent party got the upper hand they either withdrew or
slipped into a corner.[1]

The Democratic clubs were thus a means of holding a
large part of public opinion in favor of the French Revolution, notwithstanding all its distressing horrors. They
were also the means of intensifying in a high degree the
opposition of its opponents. They were also the agents
who introduced in this country many of the doctrines and
many of the follies that were having so astonishing a vogue
in France.

LEVELLING PRINCIPLES.

It was at this time that French levelling principles also
came surging in upon American politics and social life.
The National Gazette· published, over the *nom de plume*
Mirabeau, an article entitled "Forerunners of Monarchy
and Aristocracy in the United States," which was widely
quoted in other papers. These forerunners, as detected by
the observing Mirabeau, were:

1. The titles of Excellency, Honorable and Esquire, "all
of which are of monarchical· origin and are absurd in a
republic."

2. Levees!

3. Keeping the birthdays of the servants of the public.
"Mr. Paine says very justly that it is dangerous for a people to believe that any one man or set of men are necessary

---

[1] Charles Biddle says in his Autobiography (p. 254): "In July
[1793] I went to Long Branch and lodged at Col. Green's with a
number of my Federal friends, who, upon my first arriving at the
shore, congratulated me on my having the *honor* of being elected
Vice-President of the Democratic Society; however, finding it was
a subject I did not like, they soon dropped it."
Sullivan, finding reason to disapprove of the extreme views of
the Boston Society, took occasion publicly to erase his name from
their books. Amory, Life of Sullivan, I, 275.

to the safety or happiness of a country, and keeping the birthdays of individuals has a tendency to create such an opinion."

4. Establishing a ceremonial distance between the officers of the government and the people. "It is to make the creature greater than the Creator. It is to repeat the folly and crime of idolatry."

5. Parade of every kind in the officers of government, such as "pompous carriages, splendid feasts and tawdry gowns. These baubles are an insult to the understanding of a free people."

6. "Looking up to the heads of the departments and praising or blaming them for the good or evil things which flow from the government."

7. High salaries to the officers of government. "These are necessary in monarchical or aristocratical governments, where men must be bribed by dinners and presents to do their duty, but in a republic they are unnecessary." . . . "Above all, it is highly monarchical and aristocratical for the officers of government to spend their salaries only in feasting one another. It draws a dangerous line between the rulers and the ruled of a free country. It institutes at once a *privileged order* of men. An office creates no change in the mind or body of a man, and the moment he separates himself from his constituents by a fastidious distance he should be displaced."

8. Profligacy in the officers of government, "whether it manifests itself in swearing, drunkenness, debauchery or a want of justice in the payment of debts. These are all royal and noble vices and should never be tolerated in the rulers of a republic."

9. "An opinion that the care of the State should be the exclusive business of the officers of the government." Mechanics, parsons, and doctors have a perfect right to point out abuses in government.

10. An irredeemable debt.

"It is to be hoped that the citizens of the United States

will guard their infant republic from all the forerunners of
monarchy which have been mentioned. . . . When the
mind becomes familiar with the trappings of royalty and
aristocracy, the transition to monarchy and tyranny is inevitable."[1]

Such was the warning of the penetrating "Mirabeau."
"Condorcet" was of a similar mind, approved the diag-
nosis of "Mirabeau," and probed even deeper. "The
assumption of the titles of office by the officers of government in social life." Lo! is not there yet another "fore-
runner," asks he. It is a "vain display of superiority" and
"designates a little and frivolous mind" and shows "a disposition for distinction and inequality." . . . "In the social
communication between man and man the officers of government are no more than citizens." Another danger is the
"Secret Deliberation of the Senate." "The spirit of a
Venetian Senate suits not as yet the meridian of the United
States; neither does the conduct of a *conclave* or a *divan*
comport with the feelings of Americans."[2]

"Siéyès" has something to add in the next issue, and
"Cornelia" writes commending the remarks of her predecessors: "They are but too just," says she, "but they have
not struck the evil at its root." This she proceeds to do.

It is well known what an influence women exert over
men. All history is the proof thereof. That we direct the
fashions is incontrovertible. Now there are fashions in
opinions as well as dress. "Am I not just in the inference
that we form your political characters; that we can hold out
liberty or slavery to you." . . . "Let us fashion men to
virtue, but not to the *servility* and *adulation* of royalty."[3]

This is one series out of the mass of silly, stupid, imbecile
rant in which the papers of that day abound. But this is
only the beginning of the story. Articles breathing forth
French levelling principles in all their queer, grotesque

---

[1] National Gazette, Dec. 12, 1792. [2] Ibid. Dec. 15, 1792.
[3] Ibid. Dec. 26, 1792.

varieties followed thick and fast, crowding each other in the public prints.

"Diogenes" "does not *beg leave*, but demands the *inherent right* of a free and independent citizen to write, and caused to be published" in the American Daily Advertiser the following "impartial and republican" sentiments: "When I attend the courts of justice the tympana of my ears are greeted with the lordly sounds contained in petitions, etc., of ' To the Worshipful Mayor,' ' His Honor the Judge,' etc. When in the State Legislature, of ' His Excellency the Governor,' etc. When in the National Legislature, of ' His Excellency the President of the United States,' ' The Honorable Member who spoke last,'" etc. " These diabolical terms," says Diogenes, " whether in humble imitation of royalty or the tottering remains of a dying aristocracy, are surely repugnant to the divine principles of a republican government. View the pride of nations, the great focus of human refinement, the central and glorious spot which gave the first genuine birth to the rights of man—I mean France. And let us, as I hope it is not yet too late, take from her a republican lesson. There we find republicanism in the most elevated degree of pure and uncontaminated perfection. Instead of the ridiculous epithets of Sir, Mr., Esquire, Worshipful, Reverend, Right Reverend, Honorable, Excellency, etc., which are all contrary to the principles of a republican government and despicable to every citizen who thinks for himself, we find the social and soul-warming term Citizen applied even to the first servant of the people in that sublime nation."[1] Let us go and do likewise. The title Reverend is painful to other sensitive souls. " To give the title *Reverend* to *any man, be he who he may*, is not only anti-republican but absolutely blasphemous," writes a correspondent to a Boston paper. " Reverend only belongs to the Supreme Being, we read,

---

[1] Quoted from American Daily Advertiser in National Gazette, Dec. 26, 1792.

'holy and reverend is His name '—no more of your reverends among poor, frail mortals."[1] And another says: "Neither the Patriarchs, Prophets, Evangelists or Apostles ever assumed this sacred title. We do not read of the Revs. Aaron, Jeremiah or Isaiah, or the reverend body of the Disciples."[2] Another resents the use of the term with equal energy, though for a different reason. Did it not originate "in papal Europe, where the clergy were little better than a kind of inquisitorial aides-de-camp to civil despotism?"[3] And the title "Esquire," says Editor Freneau, is "not tenable upon the fair ground of republican equality." "It encourages that worldly vanity so much reprobated by the Apostle." Men tilted their lances even against the apparently inoffensive title "Mr." and with the approval of no less a man than Thomas Jefferson, who, on the occasion of the debate on presidential titles in the First Congress, had expressed the hope that the terms of Excellency, Honor, Worship, Esquire, would disappear forever from among us with the triumph of the Lower House in that controversy, and that that of Mr. would follow them,[4] and they were urged to adopt as a substitute the "social and soul-warming term Citizen." This was to some extent achieved during these hysterical months of 1793. Men addressed each other as Citizen So-and-so. They were so introduced at banquets and so described in the papers. The New York Democratic Society provided by its constitution that the term citizen should be prefixed to the designation of all its officers; that thus instead of the "aristocratic address" of Mr. Chairman, the republican appellation, Citizen Chairman, should be used. This society gave a public dinner on the 4th of July, and faithful to their freshly-imported principles, toasted the President of the United States as "Citizen George Washington" without any indication of

---

[1] Quoted from Boston Gazette in National Gazette, Jan. 16, 1793.
[2] Independent Chronicle, Oct. 31, 1793.
[3] National Gazette, Feb. 27, 1793. [4] Jefferson's Works, III, 89.

his position in the country or any allusion to his public services.[1]

Men and women still married, but even here dominant Paris set the mode, as is shown in such announcements as these, which were quite frequent for a while in the columns of the newspapers:

" Married.

" By Citizen Thatcher, Citizen Frederick W. Geyer, Jr., to Citess Rebecca, daughter to Citizen Nathan Frazer."

" On Thursday evening last, by Citizen Lathrop, Citizen Jonathan Wild, to Citess Mary, daughter to Citizen Samuel Ridgway."[2] To a paragraph announcing the marriage at Watertown of Mr. James Symes to Miss Sally Harback, the following couplet was appended:

" A virtuous lady he has got,
And Citizen Elliot tied the knot."[3]

Of course such a queer, outlandish custom called forth infinite facetiousness from the Federalists. " Cit and Citess is to come instead of Gaffer and Gammer, Goodey and Gooden, Mr. and Mrs., I suppose," observes sarcastic John Adams.[4] The Gazette of the United States remarks that " while Liberty and Equality, Paine and the Rights of Man are all the rage to the Eastward," it is pleasant to know that the brethren of the South are not far behind, that in addressing their sable fellow-creatures they say: " Citizen Caesar, or Citizen Pompey, clean my boots," and the auctioneer cries " twenty pounds for Citizen Alexander—who bids more?"[5]

Americans found a difficulty in the use of the term, which their French cousins escaped, in adapting it to the needs of women. Should the masculine be " citizen " and the feminine " citess "? Or should the latter be " civess "? Or. why not not call the men " cits " and the women " citi-

---

[1] Life and Writings of John Jay, by William Jay, I, 315-321.
[2] Boston Gazette, Jan. 21, 1793.
[3] Columbian Centinel, Feb. 2, 1793.
[4] Letters to Mrs. Adams, II, 123.
[5] Gazette of the United States, Feb. 2, 1793.

zens "?[1] Reviewing the controversy, some mocking Federalist showed that even the title citizen wasn't at all satisfactory.   In Rome it was not understood to imply equality; there were nobles, patricians and plebeians, all of whom were citizens; further it could not be applied to even all republicans; for instance, recent immigrants.   Some one had suggested the word brother as a better mode of address; but this was open to objections, for we should thereby lose a word useful for designating a dear relative.   And it would also have to be admitted that that title could not well " be applied to more than one-half of the species."   To the writer the term " biped " seemed more adequate and satisfactory.   " This title is perfectly simple; it fits people of every country; it is male or female; it is not of aristocratic origin, and while it accords with truth, it cannot bear the suspicion of flattery."[2]   But despite all onslaughts of sarcasm this distinctly French invention enjoyed a considerable popularity here.   People who would adopt it would not be likely to be especially sensitive to ridicule.

Another writer objected to the existence of the Phi Beta Kappa and other societies at Harvard. The present era, he says, seems to be one of general reformation in the political world. There are certain reformations that may well be made in the literary republic. The " P. B. K. is an infringement of the natural rights of society," inimical to the " principles of liberty and·equality."   " For three years classmates live in harmony. When lo! just as they have become ripe for friendship and have entered their last year, the demon of discord exerts her sway and lets loose the spirit of faction and party."[3]

---

[1] Columbian Centinel, March 16, 1793, contains the following:

" Citess.

" No citess to my name I'll have, says Kate,
Tho' Boston lads about it so much prate;
I've asked its meaning and our Tom, the clown,
Says, *darn it*, 't means ' a Woman of the Town.' "

[2] Gazette of the United States, Feb. 6, 1793.
[3] Columbian Centinel, May 15, 1793.

These are but a few illustrations of that mass of weak, dull, inane fribbling which was served up to the patient readers of that day twice a week or oftener. How such a wretched, scrubby growth could have sprung up from American soil it is difficult to understand. Numberless examples might be given showing the same supersensitive, trivial, maudlin state of mind prevailing among a large section of the American public as prevailed in France and which was derived mainly from France.

Evidences of royalty were attacked, whether in the form of public buildings or names of streets. A medallion, inclosing a bas-relief of George II surmounted by a crown, which had been permitted to remain on the eastern front of Christ Church, Philadelphia, was removed by the vestry in obedience to intimations published in Bache's Advertiser to the effect that if they did not take it down themselves it might be done for them. The reason given was that to the certain knowledge of the Democratic Society "it had a tendency to keep young and virtuous men from attending public worship."

Streets were rebaptized. A square in Boston which reminded of royalty was henceforth to be called Liberty Square.[1] An alley in the same town called Royal Exchange Alley was rechristened with much formality and came out of the operation as Equality Lane. The corporation of the city of New York changed the name of Queen Street to that of Pearl, Crown to that of Liberty. In vain did Noah Webster suggest satirically that if any name were to be changed "this vile aristocratical name New York" should be, so redolent with royalty. In vain did he ask what was to become of Kings County and Queens and Orange. "Nay, what will become of the people named King? Alas for the liberties of such people!" It boots little to get rid of one or two royal names while others

---

[1] Boston Gazette, Jan. 28, 1793; Bache's General Advertiser, Feb. 1, 1793.

remain to plague and taint the community.[1] To sarcasm the democrats were quite impervious.

The Democratic clubs, whose activity we have noted in other matters, also played an important part in introducing French levelling principles in revolutionary vernacular. It was through them that the word "democrat" was ushered into our politics, a term regarded with abhorrence and loathing by the Federalists as most odious French spawn, disliked and repudiated even by Jefferson and the more moderate republicans as a bantling for which they did not wish to be held responsible. Through them, and through the opposition they aroused, other new terms came rushing into our political life, whose origin they themselves betray. Anarchists, aristocrats, mobocrats, monocrats, Jacobins, clubbists, Anglomen, Gallomen were soon flowing readily from the pens of the newspaper men, adding vigor, if not dignity, to our political discussion. We read of "acts of incivism," "breaches of civism." Mirabeau, Condorcet, Siéyès, Republica, Ça ira, became popular as *noms de plume.* The day of badges and buttons was foreshadowed in the coming of cockades—the tricolor direct from France, and the black, later adopted by the partisans of England.[2]

Thus not only did Americans express their approval of the French Revolution by eagerly adopting its modes of thought, its characteristic phrases, but by adopting its other modes of expression as well, its songs, its dances, its cockades, its clubs, its destruction of the reminders of royalty. Thus imitation, the sincerest form of flattery, shows how the admiration of a large section of the American people for everything French extended even into trivial details.

John R. Watson, then a boy in Philadelphia, lived

---

[1] Minerva, April 19, 1794.

[2] Wansey, who travelled in this country in the summer of 1794, wrote as follows: "At least one out of ten that I met in the streets was a French person, wearing the tricolored cockade, the men with it in their hats, the women on their breasts." Henry Wansey. An Excursion to the United States of North America in the Summer of 1794, p. 175.

through all this and has left us the valuable evidence of a contemporary in a graphic passage in his Annals of Philadelphia in the Olden Time.[1] The mania was so high that it had caught the children. " I remember," he says, " with what joy we ran to the wharves at the report of the cannon to see the arrivals of French prizes; we were so pleased to see the British Union down! When we met French officers or marines in the streets we would cry Vive la république! Although most of us understood no French, we had caught many national airs, and the streets by day and night resounded with the songs of boys such as these: ' Allons, enfans de la patrie, le jour de gloire est arrivé' and ' Dansons le carmagnole, vive le sang, vive le sang' and ' Ça ira, Ça ira.' Several verses of each of these and others were thus sung. All of us put on the national cockade. . . . I remember several boyish processions, and on one occasion girls dressed in white, and in French tricolored ribbons, formed a procession, too. There was a great Liberty pole with a red cap at the top erected " near the French minister's house in what is now Girard Square, " and there I and a hundred others taking hold of hands and forming a ring round the same, made triumphant leapings, singing the national airs [of France]. . . . I remember that among the grave and elderly men who gave the impulse and prompted the revellings was a burly, gouty old gentleman, Blair McClenahan (famed in the democratic ranks of that day), and with him and the white misses at our head we marched down the middle of the dusty street, and when arrived opposite to Mr. Hammond's [the English Minister] there were several signs of disrespect manifested to his house. All the facts of that day, as I now contemplate them, as among the earliest impressions of my youth, seem something like the remembrance of a splendid dream. I hope never to see such an enthusiasm for any foreigners again, however merited. It was a time when, as it now

---

[1] I, 180.

seems to me, Philadelphia boys had usurped the attributes of manhood; and men who should have chastened us had themselves become very puerile."[1]

CONTEMPORARY LITERATURE AS AN EVIDENCE.

We may still further discover the intensity of this interest in the Revolution by an examination of what must pass as the American literature of the period, both prose and poetry. No doubt, judged by any sound canons, much of the prose of that day must be relegated to the windy limbo of bombast, and much of the poetry must be dubbed as

---

[1] Nor did the desire for change and imitation stop here apparently. Samuel Breck says in his Recollections that "a gang of atheists opened a temple in Philadelphia in 1796 or '97, which they dedicated to Reason, so that, throwing off entirely the Christian creed, they took Tom Paine and Robespierre's Goddess of Reason and such like for their idol. This effort was associated with a licentious newspaper called 'The Temple of Reason.' I am happy to say that public opinion soon after put the whole down." Recollections of Samuel Breck, ed. by H. E. Scudder, 118. I have been unable to ascertain the exact value of this passage. The looseness of statement, the confusion of conception, as shown in connecting Robespierre with the worship of the Goddess of Reason, seem to mark it as one of those evidences of religious bigotry which the Federalists showed in such consummate perfection, especially when the French Revolution could be brought into the argument. It may, on the other hand, reveal a direct and conscious imitation on the part of some of the Democrats of the religious thought and attitude of the revolutionists. That the disposition to change things, even the most fundamental and most impregnable, was fostered by the Revolution, is shown not only in the ways mentioned in the text, but also by the curious attempt of a Philadelphia scholar to alter the language—that it might no longer be English, but "American." The author states in his preface that as the present era seems to be one of great changes and improvements, and refers to France as illustration, we might well perfect that most important instrument—language— which in this case he proposes to do by inventing a few new characters, inverting some of the old and adopting altered modes of spelling. William Thornton. Cadmus, or a treatise on the elements of written language. Philadelphia, 1793. There is a copy of this curious thesis in the Congressional Library in Washington.

simply poor prose decked out in the rags of doggerel, but
however grievous their sins of form might be, still they
served the men of that time as literature, and expressed
the thoughts that were in the air in a manner that was generally acceptable. The French Revolution, with its stirring
ideas and its striking episodes, naturally enough called forth
a literature all its own in this country as in others. As
it evoked a controversial literature in England, of which
prominent examples are Burke's Reflections and Mackin-
tosh's Vindiciae Gallicae and Paine's Rights of Man, so here
it impelled the Adamses to write their Discourses on Davila and Essays of Publicola, while Noah Webster reviewed
the Revolution in a widely read pamphlet, and Joel Barlow
helped in the shaping of events by his various writings.
As there it fired the eloquent Doctor Price and other liberal
clergymen, so here it was at first glorified in numberless
fervid sermons and later denounced in numberless others.
As there it caught the enthusiasm and inflamed the fancy
of Wordsworth and Coleridge, so here it thrilled and fascinated and repelled, flowering forth in much metrical, if
not poetical, effort. As France invaded our politics she
also invaded our literature. Poems began to appear in
abundance, whose titles are significant. " On seeing a
Print exhibiting the Ruins of the Bastille,"[1] " July the
Fourteenth,"[2] Man shall be Free," " The Decree of the
Sun, or France Regenerated,"[3] " Sonnet to General Lafayette," " Lines to Thomas Paine," " Lines on the Death of '
Louis XVI," " The American's Prayer for France," " Ode
to Liberty," " Ode to Equality," " The Progress of Freedom,"[4] " Fayette in Prison, or Misfortunes of the Great—

---

[1] Posthumous Works of Ann Eliza Bleecker, N. Y., 1793, pp.
329-332, 353-355.
[2] Michael Forrest, " Travels through America." A poem. Philadelphia, 1793, p. 50.
[3] The Decree of the Sun; or, France Regenerated. A poem in
three cantos. The first offering of a youthful muse. Boston, 8vo,
pp. 21.
[4] The Poetical and Miscellaneous Works of James Elliott, Greenfield, 1798.

a Modern Tragedy,"[1] "The Conspiracy of Kings," by Joel
Barlow, "Ode on the Death of Charlotte Corday," "Guil-
lotina, or the Annual Song of the Tenth Muse,"[2] "Aristocracy, an Epic Poem,"[3] the "Jacobiniad,"[4] "Epitaph for
Robespierre whenever he dies,"[5] "The Lament of Washington" [on Lafayette's imprisonment].[6]

Americans appreciated the fact that they were living in
an astonishing year. This is shown in an ode on Mount
Vernon by Col. David Humphreys,[7] and by another poet
of the time of some little note, Josias Lyndon Arnold, who
wrote humorously under the title

THANKSGIVING, Nov. 26, 1789.

"In future times, when wonder-mongers pry,
And search old records with a curious eye,
They'll stand *amaz'd*, that in a *single year*
So many *wonders* on the page appear.
That—men of feeling, tyrant custom brav'd,
And gave relief to Africans enslav'd;
Taught the white world that men of sable skin
Had souls as white and pure as their's within.
That Frenchmen burst thro' slav'ry's iron cage,
And rose to greatness on the human stage;
That first Columbia saw the glorious hour
That rais'd her credit, as she rose in power;
And when—miraculous event indeed!
A *Day of Thanks Rhode Island State* decreed."[8]

Poets, commemorating the 4th of July or other patriotic
days, almost invariably turned their eyes to France before
bringing their lays to a close. A poem addressed to the
members of the Cincinnati of New York on the 4th of July,
1793, is a type of these.

"Bend your eyes toward that shore
Where Bellona's thunders roar;
There your Gallic brethren see
Struggling, bleeding to be free.
'Oh! unite your prayers that they
May soon announce their natal day."[9]

---

[1] By "A Gentleman of Massachusetts," Worcester, 1802, pp. 40.
[2] Lemuel Hopkins, Connecticut Courant, Jan. 1, 1796. Echo, p.
220.   [3] Philadelphia, 1795, 8vo, pp. 16.
[4] Federal Orrery, Dec. 1794 and Jan. 1795.
[5] Ibid. Nov. 24, 1794.   [6] Wm. Bradford.
[7] American Poems, Litchfield, 1793, pp. 123-125.
[8] Josias Lyndon Arnold. Poems. Providence, 1792, p. 107.
[9] Posthumous Works of Ann Eliza Bleecker, pp. 351-353.

As a rule most of the fugitive stanzas of that day commemorating the various events of the Revolution were
serious affairs indeed, most seriously intended, but now and
then some mocker, upon whom the stress of events sat
lightly, to whom the great movement seemed rather like
roaring melodrama dashed with strong elements of comedy,
would relieve the monotony by jesting. Such strains were
rare, but they fall most welcome upon the ear that is tired
of the din of extravagant enthusiasm or narrow and bitter
denunciation.[1]

There might be a few who would mock and jeer, but there
were more who were all aglow with enthusiasm as they
beheld the Revolution, and whose pens rushed to extol,
denouncing all who opposed or ridiculed or stood indifferent. Conspicuous among these were Hugh Henry
Brackenridge, Philip Freneau and Joel Barlow. Brackenridge, a graduate of Princeton in the same class with
Freneau and Madison, drifted into the Alleganies and became prominent in the Whiskey Insurrection. His political
aspirations and attachments were strongly democratic. He
was a very popular orator and was enamored of the French
Revolution.[2] His expansive enthusiasm and rapturous
rhetoric made him very tempting game for the sarcastic
and derisive Federalists.

Freneau, of far greater literary gift, was descended from
an old Huguenot family which had been driven from France
by the revocation of the Edict of Nantes. He became a

---

[1] See J. L. Arnold, Poems, 1792, 70-76. Also Royal Tyler's
Convivial Song for the 4th of July, 1799, at Windsor, Vt., in Hemenway's Poets and Poetry of Vermont, p. 7.

[2] His son, H. M. Brackenridge, says of him: He was "an enthusiast in the cause of France, and, from his high temperament,
incapable of pursuing anything in moderation. . . . He wrote with
the pungency and force of a Junius, and spoke with the inspired eloquence of a Henry; it is therefore not to be wondered at that he
became a formidable politician. He purchased types and press,
and set up a young man as editor of a paper, which he previously
named the 'Tree of Liberty,' with a motto from Scripture—
'And the leaves of the tree shall be for the healing of the nation.'"
Recollections of the West, p. 82.

journalist, and, supported by Jefferson, published a paper
that was a stench in the nostrils of the Federalists, so radical and so vituperative was it. The files of this paper, the
National Gazette, present a vivid picture of the blind and
turbulent enthusiasm of masses of Americans for things
French. In it Freneau caused the publication, in 1793, of
a series of "Probationary Odes by Jonathan Pindar, Esq.,
a cousin of Peter's and candidate for the post of Poet-Lau-
reate." These odes, probably written by Freneau himself,
were chiefly lampoons on the principal members of the
Government—Adams, Knox and Hamilton.[1] The first
was addressed "To all the Great Folks in a Lump," the
second "To Atlas," meaning Hamilton, the third "To a
Select Body of Great Men," meaning the Senate, the fourth
"To a Would Be Great Man," Adams.

> " Daddy Vice, Daddy Vice,
>   One may see in a trice
> The drift of your fine publication;
>   As sure as a gun
>   The thing was just done
> To secure you a PRETTY HIGH station.
>
>   When you tell us of *kings*
>   And such pretty things
> Good mercy! how brilliant your page is!
>   So bright is each line
>   I vow you'll shine
> Like—a glow worm to all future ages.
>
>   On Davila's page,
>   Your discourses so sage,
> Democratical numskulls bepuzzle
>   With arguments tough
>   As white leather or buff,
> The republican Bull Dogs to muzzle.
>
>   'Tis labor in vain,
>   Your senses to strain,
> Our brains any longer to muddle;
>   Like Colossus you stride
>   O'er our noddles so wide
> We look up like frogs in a puddle."[2]

---

[1] They began to appear about the first of June and ran for twelve
or fifteen numbers.

[2] Duyckinck, Cyclopaedia of American Literature, I, 330.

This "ode" is typical of the others. They all grew out of the ferment occasioned in our politics just at this time by the intrusion of the French Revolution.

The resistless influence of that movement is shown much more strikingly in the case of another American, Joel Barlow. Barlow, a classmate of Noah Webster at Yale, played a peculiar part in the history of this period. He was one of those cosmopolitan patriots of whom Paine and Clootz were other examples, representatives of mankind in general, eager to spring to the demolition of abuses, no matter whom those abuses really concerned. Barlow was Connecticut born and one of the little literary circle there which was, withal, quite a credit to the times. In 1788 he went to Europe as the representative of a business venture and did not return for fifteen years. It is interesting to see this Connecticut Yankee, whose natural tendencies and affiliations were all conservative in this country, become the French visionary, completely saturated with the optimistic theories prevailing there. Throwing himself impetuously and confidently into the great convulsions of the time, he soon won for himself a great reputation as a political pamphleteer. Living now in London, now in Paris, and finding his associates among those who were clamoring for change, he soon became an ultra radical. The next few years were marked by great literary activity on his part. Plunging into the conflict raging about him, he added his share to it by poems, pamphlets and addresses, denouncing the most essential and characteristic features of the existing régime. He was a member of the Constitutional Society of London and was recognized throughout Europe as one of the leading exponents of the republican idea.[1] Among other things, he wrote "The Conspiracy of Kings," a political satire in poetical form; "Advice to the Privileged Orders in the Several States of Europe, resulting from the Necessity and Propriety of a General Revolution

---

[1] Todd, Life of Joel Barlow.

in the Principle of Government," the most extensive and probably the best of his prose writings; " A Letter to the National Convention of France, on the Defects in the Constitution of 1791, and the Extent of the Amendments which ought to be Applied," and lastly, " A Letter to the People of Piedmont on the advantages of the French Revolution and the Necessity of Adopting its principles in Italy."

"The Conspiracy of Kings, A poem addressed to the Inhabitants of Europe from another quarter of the World," was a very bitter attack upon the sovereigns of England, Holland, Naples, Sweden and the German States, who had just formed a coalition against France. " The poem is of the kind called satire; attempts to catch the tone of Juvenal; aims to be very exasperating, even appalling; somehow succeeds in being only abusive; emits mere howls of metrical vituperation," says a recent critic.[1]

> Appealing to Eternal Truth and bidding,
> " People and priests and courts and kings attend,"
> And listen to " the untainted voice that no dissuasion awes;
> That fears no frown and seeks no blind applause,"
> Which is " borne on western gales from that far shore,
> Where justice reigns and tyrants tread no more "—
> He launches forth this fearful bolt:
> "Think not, ye knaves, whom meanness styles the Great—
> Drones of the Church and harpies of the State—
> Ye, whose curst sires, for blood and plunder fam'd,
> Sultans or kings or czars, or emp'rors nam'd,
> Taught the deluded world their claims to own,
> And raised the crested reptiles to a throne.—
> Ye, who pretend to your dark host was given
> The lamp of life, the mystic keys of heaven;
> Whose impious arts, with magic spells began,
> When shades of ign'rance veil'd the race of man.
>
> Think not I come to croak with omen'd yell
> The dire damnations of your future hell.
>
> I know your crusted souls!
>
> Oh, Burke, degenerate slave, with grief and shame
> The Muse indignant must repeat thy name.
> Strange man, declare, since at creation's birth,
> From crumbling chaos sprang this heaven and earth;

---

[1] Moses Coit Tyler. Three Men of Letters, 171.

Since wrecks and outcast relics still remain,
Whirl'd ceaseless round confusion's dreary reign,
Declare, from all these fragments, whence you stole
That genius wild, that monstrous mass of soul?

And didst thou hope, by thy infuriate quill,
To rouse mankind the blood of realms to spill?
Then to restore, on death devoted plains,
Their scourge to tyrants, and to man his chains?
To swell their souls with thy own bigot rage
And blot the glories of so bright an age?

'Tis Rank, Distinction, all the hell that springs
From those prolific monsters, Courts and Kings;
These are the vampires nurs'd on nature's spoils.

Of these no more. From Orders, Slaves and Kings
To thee, O MAN, my heart rebounding springs;
Behold th' ascending bliss that waits your call—
Heaven's own bequest, the heritage of all.

Freedom at last, with reason in her train
Extends o'er earth her everlasting reign.
See Gallia's sons, so late the tyrant's sport,
Machines in war and sycophants at court,
Start into men, expand their well-taught mind,
Lords of themselves and leaders of mankind." [1]

"The Conspiracy of Kings" was very popular with the liberals in England. It was brief enough to be caught up by the newspapers and was quickly spread throughout the realm, capturing the favor of the Whigs and the bitter hatred of the Tories.

A more important work, however, was his "Advice to the Privileged Orders," a volume of political essays, attacking the feudal system, arraigning abuses in Church and State. Chapters on the Feudal System, the Church, the Military, the Administration of Justice, the System of Revenue and Public Expenditure, the Means of Subsistence, Literature and Science and Art, War and Peace, make up the volume. [2] It attacked primogeniture, ridiculed many of

---

[1] The Political Writings of Joel Barlow, N. Y., 1796, pp. 237-258.
[2] Published in two parts. The first part appeared in London in 1792.

the absurdities and anomalies and intricacies of English law, condemned capital punishment, and denounced lotteries and tontines, then so popular. " It is safe to say," writes Mr. Todd, " that no political work of the day created so wide an interest or was so extensively read."[1] Fox eulogized it formally in the House of Commons. The British Government commanded its suppression, proscribed its author and then seized upon his private papers as those of a suspicious person. Barlow fled in hiding from the British officials. " Mr. Burke often makes honorable mention of you in Parliament," wrote Mrs. Barlow. " Sometimes he calls you a prophet—the prophet Joel."[2] Mr. Jefferson wrote the author acknowledging a copy of the work, " Be assured that your endeavors to bring the trans-Atlantic world into the road of reason, are not without their effect here. Some here are disposed to move retrograde, and to take their stand in the rear of Europe, now advancing to the high ground of natural right; but of all this your friend Mr. Baldwin gives you information, and doubtless paints to you the indignation with which the heresies of some people here fill us."[3]

In some ways the most interesting and instructive of these products of Barlow's pen is his " Letter to the National Convention of France, on the defects of the Constitution of 1791, and the extent of the amendments which ought to be applied."[4] This letter, dated London, September 16, 1792, is an *exposé* of the vices of the constitution that had been framed after so much exertion by the National Assembly. It has the true Revolutionary ring. The optimism, the audacity, the phraseology are racy of the soil from which they sprang. Tradition sits but lightly upon this young reformer from beyond the seas; innovation, wide-spread and fundamental, has no terrors for him.

---

[1] Todd, Life of Barlow, 89.　　　　　　　　　　[2] Ibid. 89.
[3] Jefferson's Works, III. 451, June 20, 1792.
[4] Contained in The Political Writings of Joel Barlow, 1796, 160 seq.

The 10th of August has occurred. Plainly something will soon happen in France. Barlow, observing, makes suggestions. Far is it from his thoughts to account for the extraordinary step he is taking in addressing the Legislature of a foreign state—he a private citizen of a country not at all concerned. " My intentions require no apology," he says in the opening of his letter, " I demand to be heard as a right. Your cause is that of human nature at large; you are the representatives of mankind; and though I am not literally one of your constituents, yet I must be bound by your decrees. My happiness will be seriously affected by your deliberations; and in them I have an interest which nothing can destroy. I not only consider all mankind as forming but one great family, and therefore bound by a natural sympathy to regard each other's happiness as making part of their own; but I contemplate the French nation at this moment as standing in the place of the whole. You have stepped forward with a gigantic stride to an enterprize which involves the interest of every surrounding nation; and what you began as justice to yourselves, you are called upon to finish as a duty to the human race." The solution found by the Constituent Assembly for the woes of France, Barlow holds in light esteem. Indeed monarchy, absolute or limited, is no solution at all but simply the postponement of it. He considers it remarkable that that Assembly, beginning " with the open simplicity of a rational republic," should immediately have plunged " into all the labyrinths of royalty," that so great a part of the Constitution should be an attempt to " reconcile these two discordant theories," remarkable that the King's flight should have had " so little effect in opening the eyes of so enlightened a people as the French." At no period of the Revolution have the affairs of state gone on more smoothly or more effectively than during the suspension of the King's powers from the time of his return to the final adoption of the constitution in September. The experiment that France has made during the last year with limited monarchy has been of value only in that it has taught convincingly a new doctrine "that kings can do no good." Barlow supposes that France is done with monarchy, that she will soon formally abolish it. Her own history is eloquent enough with the evils of kingly government—its cost, the weakness or the wickedness of the monarchs (which is the ordinary rule). Barlow rejects peremptorily the idea, sometimes brought forward, that certain peoples may not be fit for liberty. In regard to this every people is its own best judge. He even says that government by a line of kings, even supposing them always good and able, would not be the best government. "If the Algerines or the Hindoos were to shake off the yoke of despotism, and adopt ideas of equal liberty, they would that moment be in a condition to frame a better government for themselves, than could be framed for them by the most learned statesmen in the world." Instance "the great Mr. Locke" and South Carolina. It is therefore to be supposed that monarchy is already condemned in France. But there are many vices in the constitution, not apparently connected with the King, yet which have their origin in regal ideas. It is necessary "to purify the whole code of these vices and to purge human nature from their effects."

Barlow would suggest, therefore, that, in re-opening the question so badly answered by the Constituent Assembly, and in the more perfect reconstruction now about to be made, "the undisguised reason in all things" should be "preferred to the cloak of imposition."

Should this be done the National Church would no longer be maintained. Those err who advocate the payment of the Catholic clergy from the national purse on the ground that property, formerly supposed to belong to the Church, has been declared by the Constituent Assembly to belong to the nation, and that some equivalent is due from the nation in return. The Church signifies nothing "but a mode of worship; and to prove that a mode can be the proprietor of lands requires a subtility of logic that I shall not attempt to refute." The Church as an hierarchy

is but a prop to monarchy and they should both be buried
"in the same grave." Religion will not thereby suffer.
Religion is "a natural propensity of the mind, as respira-
tion of the lungs." "If this be true there can be no danger of its being lost; and I can see no more reason for
making laws to regulate the impression of the Deity upon
the soul, than there would be to regulate the action of light
upon the eye."

In regard to constitutional laws and ordinary laws there
is, indeed, a difference. But we should not attach a sacred-
ness to the former that will stand in the way of progress.
It was an act of arrogance on the part of the Constituent
Assembly to suppose that they had framed a constitution
that would require no amending for a number of years.
Our predecessors cannot frame a better government for us
than we for ourselves. That would suppose them "to have
known our condition by prophecy better than we know it
by experience." It was ridiculous for the Constituent
Assembly to suppose that by throwing artificial and arbitrary barriers about the constitution, they could "prevent
the people from exercising the irresistible right of innovation." There should, of course, be a gulf between constitutional and ordinary laws, but the gulf shouldn't be so
very deep or impassable. The way of amending the constitution should be made easy and expeditious. Barlow
would propose that every annual national assembly should
have power to *propose*, and the next succeeding one to
adopt and *ratify* any amendments it might think proper.
"But it should always be done under this restriction, that
the articles to be proposed by any one assembly should be
agreed to and published to the people in every department
within the first six months of the session of that assembly."
The people would therefore have time to reflect.

Barlow recommends that population be made the only
basis of representation; to make territory or property a
qualification, as did the Constituent Assembly, is absurd.
Every independent man should be declared an active citi-

zen. The period of majority should be placed as early as twenty years. " Every individual ought to be rendered as independent of every other individual as possible; and at the same time as dependent as possible on the whole community." Now "of all individuals those who are selected to be the organs of the people, in making and executing the laws, should feel this dependence in the strongest degree." Frequency of elections is therefore desirable. Barlow advocates that they be held annually. " I know of no office, in any department of state, that need be held for more than one year, without a new election. Most men who give in to this idea with respect to the legislature, are accustomed to make an exception with regard to the executive and particularly with regard to that part which is called the judiciary. I am aware of all the arguments that are usually brought in support of these exceptions; but they appear to me of little weight, in comparison to those in favor of universal annual elections. Power always was, and always must be a dangerous thing." The people therefore should keep that which they must necessarily delegate well in hand. Barlow also recommends the periodical exclusion of legislators, executives, judges, and magistrates of every description from the offices they have been holding, that they may the more feel their dependence upon the people, and that thus thousands of men versed in public affairs may from time to time be sent into the departments, serving as a leaven, furnishing a stimulus to political ambition, teaching the art of government—an art, then, that every one will soon acquire. " Every man of ordinary ability would be not only capable of watching over his own rights, but of exercising any of the functions by which the public safety is secured. For whatever there is in the art of government, whether legislative or executive, above the capacities of the ordinary class of what are called well-informed men, is superfluous and destructive and ought to be laid aside."

There should be no difference between governors and

governed. Salaries should, for this reason, be small. Public officers should not indulge in pomp. This is un-republican, an insult to the understanding. As to the relation of the representative to his constituents, there are those who hold that once chosen he is no longer to be considered as representing the people of the particular department sending him, but of the country as a whole, and that therefore during his term he is not accountable to his constituents. Barlow urges, however, that if the constituents should become dissatisfied at any time with the conduct of their representative, they should have the right to recall him and elect another in his place. "This will tend to maintain a proper relation," he says, "between the representative and the people, and a due dependence of the former upon the latter. Besides, when a man has lost the confidence of his fellow citizens of the department, he is no longer their representative; and when he ceases to be their's, he cannot in any sense be the representative of the nation; since it is not pretended that he can derive any authority, but through his own constituents."

Barlow then denounces imprisonment for debt. He advises the Assembly to take up the whole question of punishments for crime and make what alterations and revisions commend themselves. "In the glooms of meditation on the miseries of civilized life, I have been almost led to adopt this conclusion, that society itself is the cause of all crimes; and as such it has no right to punish them at all. But, without indulging the severity of this unqualified assertion, we may venture to say that every punishment is a new crime; though it may not in all cases be so great as would follow from omitting to punish." It is to be hoped, at any rate, that punishment by death will be abolished.

Barlow urges that more attention be given to public instruction in the laws. It is but half the duty of the legislator to make good laws. He must also see to it "that every person in the state shall perfectly understand them. The barbarous maxim of jurisprudence *That ignorance of the*

law is no excuse to the offender, is an insolent apology for
tyranny, and ought never to disgrace the policy of a
rational government.   I think therefore it would do honor
to your constitution and serve as a stimulus to your legislators and to your magistrates, in the great duty of instruction, to declare *That knowledge is the foundation of obedience,
and that laws shall have no authority but where they are understood.*"

Barlow denounces State Lotteries and hopes that France
will cease to have any.   He also denounces the possession
of colonies and hopes France will also cease to have them.
" As yours is the first nation in the world, that has solemnly
renounced the horrid business of conquest, you ought to
proceed one step further and declare that you will have no
more to do with colonies.   This is but a necessary consequence of your former renunciation.   For colonies are an
appendage of conquest; and to claim a right to the one
would be claiming a perpetual or reiterated right to the
other."   France should set the example to the world of declaring her colonies absolutely free and independent states,
and of inviting them to form governments of their own.

Barlow also advises against the maintenance of a standing
army—which the Constituent Assembly had seemed unwill-
ing to abolish.   " A standing military force is the worst
resource that can be found for the defense of a free republic.
In this case the strength of the army is the weakness of
the nation."

Such were Barlow's suggestions to the French at that
critical moment, such was his conception of their situation
a week before the republic was declared.   In closing he
said: " If I have said anything from which a useful reflection shall be drawn, I shall feel myself happy in having
rendered some service to the most glorious cause that ever
engaged the attention of mankind."

Thomas Paine praised this letter in the Convention,
November 7, 1792.   On the 27th of the same month Barlow himself appeared before the bar of the Assembly to

deliver the congratulations of the Constitutional Society of London, and was greeted with tremendous applause; and in February of the following year he was made a citizen of France, an honor conferred upon only two of his compatriots, Washington and Hamilton.

This letter is its own best commentary. That a man trained in the sturdy but unromantic democracy of Connecticut, and tempered by a long and painful war, which arose out of a nice sense of constitutional right and a strong respect for the authority of tradition and historic usage, should have become an ardent romanticist in politics, venturesome to a degree, ready to sacrifice the strong though imperfect achievements of time for the sake of greater ideal perfection in a sphere where his own experience might have shown him that idealism could only slowly enter at best, is a striking witness to that strength of appeal, that power of fascination which the forces that we call the Revolution had in so rare a degree for ardent, aspiring, generous-minded men. The Revolution owes many of its darkest passages to the fairest qualities of human nature, a fact, however, which unfortunately does not decrease their darkness.[1]

---

[1] Barlow also wrote and had published in 1792 " The Confederacy of Kings against the Freedom of the World, being Free Thoughts upon the present State of French Politics; a Vindication of the National Assembly in suspending Louis XVI; Conjectures on the Movements of the Confederate Armies; and their Influence in reinstating the King and establishing a constitution by force." In " Three Letters addressed to the Right Hon. Edmund Burke," he attempted to hold Burke up to the " execration of posterity."

Even the excesses of later years occasioned little diminution of Barlow's admiration for the Revolution. In a letter written in 1798, he says: " Whoever will give himself the trouble of obtaining a competent knowledge of the French Revolution, so as to be able to judge it with intelligence and weigh the infinite complication of difficulties and incentives to ungovernable passions that have lain in the way of its leaders, must indeed be shocked at their follies and their faults; but he will find more occasion to ask why they have committed so few, than why they have committed so many." Todd, 168.

But the eulogists of the Revolution soon ran foul of those who opposed and criticised, and whose pens were as slashing as their own. Among those who hewed and hacked away at those whom they were pleased to call our Jacobins, were Robert Treat Paine and the so-called Hartford Wits. The former enjoyed quite an unusual reputation for talent and brilliancy from the time of his college days. Eagerly did he satirize the Jacobins in various poems delivered at Harvard Commencements or published in the Federal Orrery. His first poem mentioning the Revolution, however, was laudatory. This was delivered in July, 1792, when he took his A. B. degree. Being assigned an English poem he chose for his theme "The Nature and Progress of Liberty," than which none could have been more popular. He opened with an apostrophe to the subject of his thought:

> "Hail, sacred Liberty, divinely fair!
> Columbia's great palladium, Gallia's prayer!
> From heaven descend to free this fettered globe;
> Unclasp the helmet and adorn the robe.
> May struggling France her ancient freedom gain;
> May Europe's sword oppose her rights in vain."

Then he gave a lunge at Burke:

> "Where'er the sunbeam gilds the rolling hour,
> Wings the fleet gale, and blossoms in the flower;
> May Freedom's glorious reign o'er realms prevail,
> Where Cook's bright fancy never spread the sail.
> Long may the laurel to the ermine yield,
> The stately palace to the fertile field;
> The fame of Burke in dark oblivion rust,
> His pen a meteor—and his page the dust." [1]

But three years later when he was taking his Master's degree and was assigned the delivery of a poem he lashed the Jacobins by showing their ignoble origin:

---

[1] The Works in Verse and Prose of the late Robert Treat Paine, Jun., Esq., with Notes. Preceded by a Biographical Sketch by Charles Prentiss. Boston. 1812.

" Envy, that fiend who haunts the great and good,
  Not Cato shunned, nor Hercules subdued.
  On Fame's wide field, where'er a covert lies,
  The rustling serpent to the thicket flies;
  The foe of Glory, Merit is her prey,
  The dunce she leaves, to plod his drowsy way.
  Of birth amphibious, and of Protean skill,
  This green-eyed monster changes shape at will;
  Like snakes of smaller breed, she sheds her skin,
  Strips off the *serpent* and turns JACOBIN." [1]

In the fall of 1794 Paine began the publication of a semi-
weekly newspaper called " The Federal Orrery." In December of that year and the opening months of the succeeding
year he published a series of papers, entitled " Remarks on
the Jacobiniad," in which an imaginary poem was reviewed
and made the means of satirical skits on the prominent Republicans of Boston. These papers probably came from
the pen of the Rev. J. S. J. Gardiner, assistant rector of
Trinity Church, though we believe that has not been defi-
nitely proven. The satire was coarse, but none the less
was it satire. The Federalists greeted its appearance with
enthusiasm. " I admire the Jacobiniad," said Fisher Ames.
" The wit is keen, and who can deny its application." [2] " The

---

[1] The Invention of Letters. Works, xl-xlii. President Willard,
of Harvard, had struck out these lines from Paine's poem, as also
similar ones from the poem of Prentiss, Paine's friend, fearing they
would give offence to Gov. Sam. Adams, himself the leading
Jacobin of New England. Paine, however, delivered the lines, and
two years later, in his Phi Beta Kappa poem, he scored the Democratic Clubs severely. " When the erased lines were spoken, a
little hissing was heard, which was soon drowned by repeated, loud
rounds of applause." Prentiss, Introduction to Paine's Works.
See also The Ruling Passion. Phi Beta Kappa poem. Harvard,
July 20, 1797. Paine's Works, p. 188. It was in The Invention of
Letters that occurred the famous apostrophe to Washington,
beginning " Could Faustus live." Mr. W. W. Story, speaking of
the literature of the period, says: " The Della Cruscan school then
reigned supreme in America, and even in England the influence of
the Lake poets was very limited. Poetry was prose gone mad. . . .
In America there was no native poet whose reputation was superior
to that of Robert Treat Paine, and I have often heard my father
speak of the tremendous applause with which these lines addressed
to Washington . . . were received as he delivered them at the Commencement of Harvard, in the year 1795." Story. Life and Letters
of Joseph Story, I, 108.   [2] Ames, Works, I, 165.

Boston poets are formidable and would be guillotined, if the Robespierres whom they expose had the power." [1] But the Democrats attacked the author of the Jacobiniad in return.[2] "The leaders of the Jacobin faction were sorely galled by this battery of ridicule. This drew upon him the summary vengeance of a mob who attacked the house of Major Wallach, with whom he lodged, who gallantly defended his castle against the unprincipled banditti and compelled them to retire," is the ponderous description given by Paine's biographer of this little Boston epic. Paine also had a private encounter with the son of one of the men whom his satire had rendered sensitive. Gardiner was flayed in the columns of the Chronicle and Gazette.

As good an example as may be given of Paine's lampoons is one he wrote *à propos* of the celebration held in Boston by the Democrats, September 21, 1795, in honor of the French Republic, by means of a procession and a dinner in Faneuil Hall:

"Song of Liberty and Equality. Which ought to have been sung in Faneuil Hall on the 21st, the Birthday of the French Republic; and ought to be sung on the Birthday of all other Republics, whether male or female, that may hereafter be born.

TUNE, BLACK SLOVEN.

Ye sons of equality, freedom and fun
Come rouse at the sound of the gun—the gun:
Awake from your stupor—for feasting prepare.
With Sansculotte stomach let every one meet
Like bears o'er a carcass, to *fight* and to *eat*—
    Freely we'll share
      Whate'er stands before us,
      While Freedom's the chorus—Huzza.

'Tis three years, this moment, since Freedom, by chance,
Was safely delivered of France—of France;
And the cub is well grown, for so tender an age.
Be sure her *complexion* is hardly so good—
'Tis thought that her mother was longing for blood:
    For, when in a rage
      She's rather uncivil,
      Cuts throats like the devil—Huzza." [3]

---

[1] Ames, Works, I, 163.
[2] Independent Chronicle, April 30, 1795 and May 21, 1795.
[3] Quoted by Buckingham. Specimens of Newspaper Literature, II, 239.

Most vigorous opponents of all were the Hartford Wits, Hopkins, Humphrey, Alsop, Dwight. Hopkins wrote an epitaph on Robespierre:

> "Which in some proper time to come
> We hope will grace his mournful tomb."

After denouncing Robespierre unsparingly and interpreting his career as simply giving the opportunity—

> "To prove, with Danton, which of right
> Should have in Hell the highest seat,
> An atheist or a hypocrite?"

he closes—

> "May Heaven our favorite planet bear
> Far, far from Gallia's blazing star;
> Ye lights of Europe, shun its course,
> Or order yields to lawless force,
> As though a random comet hurled,
> Should dash at once and melt the world." [1]

"The Echo" is a title given to a series of parodies or burlesques on the newspaper articles, the speeches, addresses, and proclamations of the day that were written in so hysterical and swollen a manner. The contributors to "The Echo" resolved to make these productions ridiculous by simply outdoing them. They aimed to rid the country of the abominable literary style so much in vogue, to exorcise the excessively declamatory and rhetorical elements by means of sarcasm and caricature. [2] They also aimed at the same time to laugh into obscurity the Democrats whose minds, so inflated with the new French vaporings, seemed inevitably to seek expression in the most sounding rhodomontade. What began then as a cheerful, exhilarating exercise in the caricature of a noisy newspaper style, soon rose to the shrillest pitch of bitter political controversy.

---

[1] Dr. Lemuel Hopkins in The Poets of Connecticut. Edited by Rev. Charles W. Everest, p. 56. See also p. 55, poem on "Poland."

[2] On the evil influences of the French Revolution upon the literary taste of this country, see Samuel L. Knapp's Lectures on American Literature, 176.

With the exception of a few lines written by Dr. Mason
F. Cogswell and Elihu B. Smith, and parts of one or two
numbers, the entire work was the production of Richard
Alsop and Theodore Dwight.[1]   The authors usually quoted
from some paper and then appended their parody. The
following example will show their method, and at the same
time throw some light upon the influence of the Revolution
here.

" Echo XII.   From the Diary of April 13, 1793.
Messrs. Printers:—

" It is grating to the feelings of the friends of Liberty, to
hear dastardly base men, protected by the mild laws of a
plentiful Republican Country, come forward in public company, among a free, enlightened, and generous people,
whose country heretofore flowed with the blood of Warren,
Montgomery, and the rest of Heroes and American Wor-
thies, who gloriously fell in opposing the unlawful rights
of a King; I say, shall the refuse of the human species, the
enemies of man (I mean the friends and advocates of kings
and despots) dare stigmatize the French nation, in the hearing of American patriots, with the cruel epithets of murderers, assassins, madmen, regicides and the like, for decap-
itating Louis XVI. Do these ignorant, prejudiced wretches
not remember that the French nation's moderation and
partiality to Louis exceeded everything that could in reason
be expected from a people emerging from the vilest state of
slavery (in which they had been kept for ages past by king-
craft and priest-craft united) to the pinnacle of importance
and power; have they not sufficiently proved their attachment to him, by erasing from their memories the remembrance of their late bondage and past grievances under a
brood of kings, and confirming him in the regal power?

---

[1] Everest, Poets of Connecticut, p. 94, note.
The numbers appeared from time to time in different papers—
American Mercury and Connecticut Courant—were widely copied
throughout the country and, in 1807, were collected into a single
volume called " The Echo, Printed at the Porcupine Press by
Pasquin Petronius."

In forming their constitution have they not given him sufficient authority and support? Have they not made the crown hereditary in his family, if they would prove themselves worthy? Was there anything necessary for the honor and dignity of the king of a free people (if such can exist under the king) but was granted him? How has he requited them for their predilection in his favor? Did he not break the solemn oaths he had taken, and sacred vows he had made to be faithful to the nation, and govern it agreeably to the constitution he had accepted? Did he not openly despise the love of the nation for him, in attempting repeatedly to fly to the enemy? Did he not support the emigrant princes (rather devils) and their army, composed of a species of beings not far distant from the brute creation, raised in the principalities of despots, with an intent to enter France with fire and sword? Patience would fail me, indignant horror would overwhelm me, and the callous heart of a Hessian . . . would shudder to enumerate all the arts, plots, hypocrisies, perjuries, murders, conspiracies, etc., etc., that Louis and his base adherents have been guilty of, to effect a counter revolution in favor of despotism, which he well knew could not be done without the effusion of blood," and so on at length.—G. Or no Friend to Kings.

To which came back the following echo from the banks of the Connecticut:

HARTFORD, *May* 6th, 1793.

How dire, how grating to that lawless clan,
Who build up freedom on a lawless plan,
To hear each day a pack of dastards base—
Mere water-gruel of the human race—
In this our land, where freedom sprung to birth,
The fairest portion of the spacious earth;
Where, in strange union, Law and Peace we meet,
And full-fed Plenty waddling thro' the street;
I say—how dire to see this rascal throng,
With all the pride of self-importance strong,
Come into company among such free,
Such bold, enlightened, generous folks as we,
Whose bleeding country pour'd a purple flood,
And blush'd with Warren's and Montgomery's blood;

With other chiefs whom I've forgot by name,
Tho' doubtless numbered on the rolls of fame.
Shall this vile refuse, this ungodly clan,
The foes of every *native right of man*—
The right of doing whatso'er he list,
By secret stratagem or force of fist—
I say, shall these thus impudently dare,
Pour their vile scandals in a patriot ear,
And call the French a pack of cruel dogs,
Murderers, assassins, regicides or rogues;
Merely because by soft compassion led,
They've taken off their hapless monarch's head;
From all his woes a kind release have given,
And sent him up an extra post to heaven—
To tell their Maker *they* intend to go
Where all are *equal* in the world below.
Do not these wretches know that generous nation
The French, exceed all men in moderation,
And that they lately have become, 'tis plain,
E'en to a proverb, gentle and humane?
'Tis true such instances we seldom find,
In this degeneracy of human kind,
Such virtue as transcends whate'er I thought,
That pious people ever could have wrought.
What generous feelings in their bosoms glow!
How prompt to soothe the pangs of royal woe!
Have they not proved, 'mid every trying scene,
Their love most strong for Louis and his Queen?
First, in forgetting what a brood of kings,
Old Despotism had fledg'd beneath her wings;
Then in depriving him of legal sway,
Lest he should take *French leave* and scud away;
Next in confining him with so much care,
From the rude peltings of external air;
And lastly, what I deem by far the best,
Of love and loyalty the happy test,
In cutting off his head to save his life
From scenes of woe, of horror and of strife;
And thus, by *certain means*, to keep away
Old age, that mournful period of decay."

One of the most striking figures in this war of opinions
about the French Revolution was William Cobbett, the
Englishman who came to this country in 1792, bringing
with him, as the event proved, a stinging pen. At first he
taught school in Philadelphia, soon publishing a French
grammar that was greatly successful at the time and that
proved to be a book of more than ephemeral character.

But he soon got caught in the hot controversies that were agitating Philadelphia and began to lash the Democrats under the name of Peter Porcupine.[1] His attitude toward the Revolutionists is well epitomized in his remark that there was something preposterous in the idea of a "club of distracted monsieurs" giving liberty to the world. The principles of the Revolutionists were "anarchical" and "blasphemous," as much opposed to true liberty as hell is to heaven. The very names of his pamphlets reveal the vehemence and acrimony of this abusive and trenchant polemic—"A Bone to Gnaw for the Democrats," "A Little Plain English," The "Censor,"[2] "The Bloody Buoy, thrown out as a Warning to the Political Pilots of all Nations; or a faithful relation of a multitude of acts of horrid barbarity, such as the eye never witnessed, the tongue expressed, or the imagination conceived, until the commencement of the French Revolution." Besides these and scores of other pamphlets on current events, Cobbett wrote a history of American Jacobinism, an extreme and bitter arraignment. He was greatly applauded by the party he aided, but bitterly hated by the democrats, who fell to calling him Mr. Hedgehog—The Pork Patriot; then other things, most scurrilous, such as "a celebrated manufacturer of lies," a "retailer of filth," a "pestiferous animal," a "fugitive felon," a "man with a talent at lies and Billingsgate." This, says one writer, "will convince Peter that I know him well, and that I have only disclosed a part of the truth."[3] Whether it

---

[1] The best biography of Cobbett is by Edward Smith, London, 1878, 2 vols. At the end of the second volume there is an excellent bibliography of Cobbett's writings. His works were collected and published in 8 volumes, London, 1801, entitled Porcupine's Works. There are also sketches of Cobbett in Sir Henry Lytton Bulwer's Historical Sketches; Thorold Rogers' Historical Gleanings; and in Spencer T. Hall's Biographical Sketches of Remarkable People. See also Harper's Monthly, IV.

[2] "The Censor, a work by Peter Porcupine, administers his monthly corrective to our disorganizers. The author is said to be an Englishman, who has kept school in this city." Chauncey Goodrich to Oliver Wolcott. Gibbs' Memoirs.

[3] In Bache's Aurora.

does this or not, it at any rate shows in high relief the libellous character of most of the newspaper discussions of that time.[1]

SUNDRY SIDE-LIGHTS.

The absorbing nature of the interest in the Revolution is shown in many other ways, in almost as many, in fact, as men have for expressing their thoughts and emotions. On all hands men fell to discussing the merits and, later, the

---

[1] For further references to the Revolution in the literature of the day see—

George Richards. The Declaration of Independence. A Poem, accompanied by Odes, Songs, etc., adapted to the Day. By a Citizen of Boston. Boston, 1793.

Michael Forrest. Travels through America. A Poem. Philadelphia, 1793.

Bleecker. The Posthumous Works of Ann Eliza Bleecker in prose and verse. To which is added a collection of essays, prose and poetical, by Margaretta V. Faugeres. New York, 1793.

Elihu B. Smith. American Poems, selected and original. Litchfield, 1793.

The Decree of the Sun, or France Regenerated. A Poem in three cantos. The first offering of a youthful Muse. Boston.

Aristocracy, an Epic Poem. Philadelphia, 1795.

Story. Liberty. A poem. Delivered on the 4th of July, 1795, by The Stranger [Isaac Story]. Newburyport, 1795.

Freneau. Poems written between 1768 and 1794 by Philip Freneau. Monmouth, 1795.

Monarchy. A Parody on the Eclogue of Pope, 1795.

Crawford. The Progress of Liberty. A Pindaric Ode by Charles Crawford. Philadelphia, 1796.

Prentiss. A Collection of Fugitive Essays in Prose and Verse by Charles Prentiss. Leominster, 1797.

Arnold. Poems by the late Josias Lyndon Arnold, Esq. Providence, 1797.

Elliot. The Poetical and Miscellaneous Works of James Elliot. Greenfield, 1798.

Fayette in Prison, or Misfortunes of the Great. A modern tragedy, by a gentleman of Massachusetts. Worcester, 1802.

Humphreys. The Miscellaneous Works of David Humphreys. New York, 1804.

"The Echo," 1807.

Davis. Poems by Richard B. Davis. New York, 1807.

Everest. Poets of Connecticut, 1829.

shortcomings of that strangely contradictory movement. Its promised glories were quickly caught up by our Fourth of July orators, who seemed to feel intuitively the additional lustre they imparted to a day already very lustrous. " It is now acknowledged," said John Lathrop, Jr., to the town authorities of Boston, " as a fact in political biography, that Liberty descended from heaven on the Fourth of July, 1776. . . . The mighty blow resounded through the universe. . . . The deep-rooted thrones of aged monarchies were shaken to their centers." [1]   Other speakers, too, deduced the whole commotion from our Declaration of Independence, as did Mr. George Richards, in a speech at Portsmouth, New Hampshire: " Neither have the effects of our independence been less perceptible in Europe than visible in America.   It was a spark from the altar flame of liberty on this side of the Atlantic, which alighted on the pinnacle of despotism in France and reduced the immense fabric to ashes in the twinkling of an eye." [2] John Phillips delivered a speech in Boston so popular that for a long time the newspapers continued to publish extracts from it.   Deriving the initial cause of the Revolution from the French soldiers who had served in our war, and who, on returning home, viewed with fresh horror the despotism there prevailing, or, as the orator said, who " perceived the tree of liberty profusely watered with their blood; its foliage spreading, yet yielding them no shelter; its fruit blooming and mellowing in luxuriance, yet, denied the delicious taste," exciting "no passion but despair," he proceeded in this vein: " The fervid spirit which glowed within them soon pervaded their country and threatened destruction to their government.   On the first favorable contingency the enthusiastic energies of reviving Freedom burst the cerements which had confined it for two thousand years, and the Gothic fabric of feudal absurdity, with all its pompous pageants, colossal pillars and prescriptive bulwarks, the wonder and veneration of ages, was instantly

---

[1] Loring, Hundred Boston Orators, 255-256.
[2] Mr. Richards' Oration on Independence, July 4, 1795.

leveled with the dust. . . . An astonished world viewed with awful admiration the stupendous wreck. They beheld with pleasing exultation the fair fabric of Freedom rising in simple proportion and majestic grace upon the mighty ruin. The gloomy horrors of despotism fled before the splendid effulgence of the sun of liberty. The potent rays of science pierced the mist of ignorance and error; republican visions were realized and the reign of reason appeared to commence its splendid progress. . . . But the whirlwind of discord threatened to raze the fabric from its foundation. The lowering clouds of contention hung around and darkened the horizon." [1] This note of regret, of disappointment, of hope deferred became more pronounced as the months went by. William Smith, a member of Congress, and an orator of repute, expressed this feeling in an address to his constituents in Charleston, South Carolina: "Through the wondrous meanderings of her stupendous revolution, how have we rejoiced to see her combating and crushing the hydra of her ancient despotism. How have we mourned to see the brilliant prospect oft o'erclouded and the hydra of popular tyranny springing up in its place. . . . In tracing the rise and progress of this astonishing revolution the humane American must wish to draw a veil over the mournful scenes which have tarnished so bright an epoch of modern history. But have not even they their use? Will they not impress on our minds more forcibly than all the precepts of moralists the dire effects of the prostration of religion, government and law? . . . At the recital of such atrocities human nature stands confounded. Should they be hereafter recorded by the faithful historian, Liberty, appalled, will turn from them with horror, and outraged Humanity, in tears, will snatch the crimsoned page from the polluted volume." [2]

---

[1] Loring, Hundred Boston Orators, 248-249.
[2] An Oration delivered in St. Philip's Church, before the Inhabitants of Charleston, South Carolina, on the Fourth of July, 1796, by William Smith, M. C. See also Loring, Hundred Boston Orators, 279-280, Speech by John Lowell.

But there were those who thought differently of this matter. "Citizen" Brackenridge, one of the militant democrats of the West, delivered a Fourth of July oration in Pittsburg, extenuating the violence of the revolutionists. "Shall we blame the intemperature of the exertions?" he asked. "Was there ever enthusiasm without intemperature? And was there ever a great effect without enthusiasm? Thy principles, O Liberty! are not violent and cruel; but in the desperation of thy effort against tyranny it is not always possible to keep within the limits of the vengeance necessary to defence. Do we accuse the air or the bastile of the mountain when the rock is burst and the town engulfed? The air of itself is mild and scarcely wafts a feather from its place. But, restrained and imprisoned, the yielding and placid element becomes indignant and tears the globe before it."[1]

The French Revolution became a topic to be discussed in state papers. It invaded the messages and proclamations of several of our governors. John Hancock spoke of it in his Thanksgiving proclamation of '93.[2] Governor Chittenden of Vermont wrote his Fast Day and Thanksgiving proclamations in a similar vein.[3] But towering above all others in enthusiastic expression of his admiration for France, more constant than all in his thought upon her extraordinary Revolution, was Samuel Adams, recognized leader of the Republicans of New England, Lieutenant-Governor of Massachusetts from 1789 to 1794, and Governor from that year to 1797. Adams, whose scent for liberty was so keen, had from the beginning looked at the Revolution with the most sanguine expectations. He gladly presided at the banquet in Faneuil Hall on the day of the famous Civic Feast, January 24, 1793, and on other similar occasions he was ever ready to propose toasts ex-

---

[1] National Gazette, July 27, 1793. See also other speeches in the same paper, July 24 and Aug. 16, 1793.
[2] Columbian Centinel, Oct. 9, 1793.
[3] Vermont Journal, April 1 and Nov. 11, 1793.

haling undiminished devotion to the cause.[1]   During these years there is hardly any document from his hand that does not reveal a decided sympathy with the French Revolution.[2] In his speech before the Legislature, January 17, 1794, he enters into a disquisition upon Liberty and Equality, quotes Montesquieu upon these subjects, and says: " The Republic of France have also adopted the same principle and laid it as the foundation of their constitution.   That nation, having for many ages groaned under the exercise of the pretended right claimed by their Kings and Nobles, until their very feelings as men were become torpid, at length suddenly awoke from their long slumber, abolished the usurpation and placed every man upon the footing of equal rights."[3] In his Fast Day proclamation he urged the citizens of Massachusetts, among other things, to implore God on that day " to inspire our friends and allies, the Republic of France, with a spirit of wisdom and true religion, that firmly relying on the strength of His Almighty arm, they may still go on prosperously, till their arduous conflict for a government of their own, founded on the just and equal rights of men, shall be finally crowned with success."[4]

If we seek still further evidence of this interest we may

---

[1] 14th of July celebration, Boston, 1794; 22nd of September celebration, Boston, 1795.

[2] Wells, Life and Public Services of Samuel Adams, III., 329, note.

[3] Independent Chronicle, Jan. 20, 1794. The Legislature in its reply echoed the same sentiments. Independent Chronicle, Feb. 20, 1794.

[4] Independent Chronicle, March 6, 1794. For further illustrations see Boston Gazette, June 2, 1794; Independent Chronicle, Jan. 19 and Oct. 19, 1795; Federal Orrery, Oct. 17, 1796.

Adams' letters breathe the same spirit.   See Wells, III., 319 and 321.   Even after Genet's impudence had run mad, Adams wrote him as follows (Oct. 22, 1793): " I am thoroughly convinced that your heart is animated with the same zeal for the interests of our country as for your own; and I have much pleasure in seeing that you firmly hope that a public discussion will insure to your conduct the approbation of all reasonable men, and will cover with shame those who, yielding to the force of prejudice, have so successfully aimed calumnies and outrageous charges at you.   I hope sincerely that your official residence in the United States may render you personally happy; and am already convinced that it cannot but be use-

examine the newspapers, we may run over the advertise-
ments of the booksellers for a clue as to what men were
reading, and the answer is decisive. The French news
fills more columns in the papers of the day, I think it is
safe to say, than does the American. Among the books
that were widely advertised and evidently widely read were
Mirabeau's Speeches, Cordorcet's Life of Turgot, Letters
from Paris in 1791 and 1792, with a Representation of the
Capture of Louis XVI at Varennes, 2 vols., Dumouriez's
Memoirs, Comparative Display of Different Opinions of the
French Revolution, Williams' Letters from the 28th of July
to the Establishment of the Constitution of 1795, Calendrier
Républicain, so well received that the editor determined
to bring it out every year—the one then advertised was for
the Year V, Robespierre's Reports, Rabaut's History of the
French Revolution, translations of the different French
constitutions, Paine's Rights of Man, Barlow's Conspiracy
of Kings and Advice to the Privileged Orders, Osgood's
Political Sermon (Citizen de Novion's in reply), Heroic
Actions of the French Republicans, Prière Républicaine,
Morality of the Sans Culottes or Republican Gospel, Bou-
quier's Report on National Schools, Gregoire's Report on
the Means of Completing the National Library.[1]

A study of the history of the American theater will but
confirm the impression already made. The stage became
political and democratic. The high wave of feeling that
broke over the country in 1793 dashed over it too, and with
many amusing consequences. Prigmore, a wandering
player, took occasion to introduce politics into the comedy
" Jenny Jumps," thereby giving great offense to the Federalists, who objected to paying for his rabid democracy
and who vented their spleen in remarks of dubious compliment as to his abilities as an actor.[2] Hodgkinson, one of

---

ful to the universal cause of liberty and the rights of man." Wells,
III., 321. This was written more than two months after Genet had
threatened to appeal from the President to the people.

[1] All these are advertised in the Aurora.

[2] Seilhamer, History of the American Theater, III., 68.

the best known and most popular actors of the day, brought endless trouble upon himself by getting tangled up in the turbulent discussions of the street. Once, coming on the stage as Captain Flash in " Miss in Her Teens," he wore an English costume, which indeed the part required, but some of the vigilant defenders of the cause of France among the " fierce democracie " of Tammany Hall hissed him and ordered him to take it off. Instead of ignoring the demand or simply appealing to the requirements of the play whereby an English officer is not unnaturally made to wear an English uniform in an English comedy, he had the happy thought to say that he represented a coward and a bully, whereby the French faction was appeased, but the English thrown into high dudgeon. Then, to make a bad matter worse, he wrote to the Daily Advertiser, professing to give the exact words of his speech, and later published a card in which he endeavored still further " to soften his unfortunate phraseology," thus rearing up a great crop of enemies on every hand.[1]

Theaters, like individuals, came to range themselves more or less along the line of the familiar divisions. The Boston Theater depended largely for its patronage upon the Federalists, with the result that it sought to satisfy their tastes. Consequently a new theater, called the Haymarket, was built avowedly to cater to the Republicans. Divided patronage threatened both, and the expedients to which both resorted to maintain themselves are edifying and instructive.[2]

Within, also, the French enthusiasts made themselves heard. They demanded of managers that the " truly harmonic " and " republican tune " of *Ça ira* be played at the performances, and this was often done. Was it not, forsooth, the French Yankee Doodle?[3] Often did the audi-

---

[1] Dunlap. A History of the American Theater, p. 111. For a somewhat similar case see Seilhamer, III., 332-3.

[2] Seilhamer, III., 332-3. See also Priest, Travels in the United States of America, 165-166. The Boston Haymarket Theater was built in 1796 at the corner of Tremont and Boylston streets.

[3] Independent Chronicle, Jan. 30, Feb. 10, Feb. 13, 1794.

toriums resound with the warlike stanzas of the Marseillaise, often did they ring with such shouts as "Vivent les Français!" "Vivent les Américains!"[1]

The names of the plays advertised in the papers are significant. "Tammany," one of the earliest American operas, and one that enjoyed great popularity, was a work political in character, and pronouncedly republican, and seemed to Dunlap, the historian of the American Theater, and a Federalist in politics, as "a melange of bombast," seasoned high "with spices hot from Paris," swelling "with rhodomontade." While it was admitted that the opera was received with unbounded applause, it was said with a sneer that the audience was made up of "the poorer classes of mechanics and clerks."[2]

Helvetic Liberty, or the Lass of the Lakes; Liberty Restored; The Demolition of the Bastile; Tyranny Suppressed; Louis XVI, were other plays that were on the rude and shaky American stage of this period and that show the temper of the time.

And if we seek still further to know this temper, we find the present thesis confirmed by the descriptions of travelers, of Priest, Wansey, and notably of Larochefoucauld-Liancourt.[3] Larochefoucauld traveled leisurely all over the country, everywhere compelled to talk European politics,

---

[1] Dunlap, p. 106.

[2] Seilhamer, III., 85-86. Mrs. Holton, a sister of Mrs. Siddons, was the author of the book of this opera. James Hewitt, who had been the leader of the orchestra for many years, wrote the music. Mrs. Holton arrived in New York in the winter of 1793-4 and " at once became the bard of the American Democracy." She wrote an ode on the recapture of Toulon, which was read at the celebration of that event in New York and for which she won the thanks of the Democratic Society. She interested the Tammany Society in the production of her opera, after which indeed it was named. "This was the first important attempt at the composition of operatic music in America." Richard Bingham Davis, a young New York poet, then in his 23rd year, wrote a prologue.

[3] Priest, Travels in the United States of America, 1793-1797. Wansey, An Excursion to the United States of North America in the Summer of 1794. Larochefoucauld-Liancourt, Travels through the United States, 1795-1797.

everywhere hearing the same expressions of warm attachment to France, except now and then in the large centers' where commercial interests seemed to him to vitiate men's judgments. Stopping near Pottsgrove, Penn., in the early part of 1795, he had this experience: "The good people of the inn inquired with much eagerness for news from France. My friend told them that it would be obliged to sustain another and more dreadful campaign. 'How, a still more dreadful than the preceding campaign!' they exclaimed—'notwithstanding the English were beaten last year?' 'There are many other enemies,' replied my friend, 'Russians, Austrians.' 'Aye, aye,' said the good people, 'all those who do not like liberty; but the French will nevertheless triumph, if it please God, over all the f—.' These are the sentiments and such is the language of most Americans; and indeed this must be the opinion of all who are not acquainted with the crimes attending our revolution; and even they who are so, very justly impute them to the various factions, and carefully distinguish and separate them from the cause of liberty. The principles and conduct of the coalesced powers are treated with the same degree of indignation as those of the terrorists."[1]

Public opinion farther northward was the same. From Saratoga he writes: "Good wishes for the success of the French, a detestation of their crimes, and decided hatred against the English, form here the universal sentiments, as they do in general throughout the United States."[2] From Virginia: "You hear in Virginia the same language expressive of attachment to France, of hatred and especially of distrust in regard to England, and of affection for M. de la Fayette, which you meet with in every other part of the United States that is not situated in the immediate vicinity of great towns and places absorbed in mercantile speculations."[3] From Massachusetts: "The general temper of the

---

[1] Travels, I., 41.   [2] Ibid., II., 74-75.
[3] Ibid., III., 130. On the hatred of England and the part played by French agents in keeping it alive, see Priest, pp. 56-57.

people here, as in the other parts of the country which I
'have traversed, is that of respect for the president, attachment to the constitution, aversion to war, and an ardently
favorable disposition toward the French."[1]

Naturally a movement that so riveted the attention of the
fathers produced a due effect upon the sons. Young colle-
gians eagerly scanned the ground for suggestions for their
forensic efforts. We have seen how Robert Treat Paine
and his friend Prentiss let no academic function slip by
without an expression of their youthful views upon the great
and exciting topic. They were but the more conspicuous
representatives of a class. Debates or orations were delivered at Brown, Dartmouth, Yale, and Harvard upon the
fruitful theme. The venerable Ashbel Green attended the
Commencement at Harvard in 1791 and noted in his diary
that the best oration was one on the French Revolution,
spoken by a candidate for the master's degree.[2] And the
next year the eighth number on the programme was "A
French Conference. Upon the Comparative Importance of
the American, French and Polish Revolutions to Mankind.
By Messers. Thomas Danforth, John Gorham, and Brad-
street Story," and in the afternoon the exercises began with
"An English Oration. Upon the Progress of Reason, etc.,
concluding with some remarks upon the French Revolution. By Mr. George Blake." The editor of the Columbian Centinel announced that he should publish this and
two or three other "performances of the day," that his
absent readers might taste "in a small degree, of the sentimental banquet we enjoyed."[3] Apparently some of these
anniversary utterances were marked by the same violence
and dogmatism characteristic of those heard every day in
the newspapers and the streets, for the college authorities
endeavored to restrict the freedom of speech on these occa-

---

[1] Ibid., III., 411. See also I., 55, 120; III., 250, 274-275, 397-398,
411, 488-489, 607-609; IV., 320-321.
[2] Life of Ashbel Green, p. 234.
[3] Columbian Centinel, July 21, 1792.

sions, which the young men, however, found adequate means of evading.[1] They, too, must have their turn.

THE GROWING OPPOSITION AND ITS REASONS.

It was the introduction into America of just these follies that have been described in the foregoing pages, of this spirit of noisy criticism of everything American and indiscriminate approval of everything French, that, coupled with the famous Genet incident and the President's firm stand on neutrality, caused many men to pause and consider what this Revolution really was, to examine its course and nature with greater care. Enthusiasm waned perceptibly. The conservative elements of society, at first quite as fascinated as the others by the rich promise of the new movement, now generally rallied in opposition. The number of its hostile critics now increased greatly. The Revolution had had opponents here from the very beginning, as we have seen, notably the Adamses, John and John Quincy, who had published the Discourses on Davila and the Essays of Publicola. A cleft in the unanimity of enthusiasm for France had begun to show itself with the adoption of the first French constitution, which was criticised by many of our ablest political thinkers. But now the opposition became more outspoken and more general. Men opposed the Revolution on the grounds of its violence, its hostility to religion, its attention to matters of trivial importance, its encouragement of the baneful spirit of faction, its doctrine of complete equality.

Most of the violence down to the execution of Louis XVI. was criticised but lightly here. This does not mean that there was any suppression of the news, but that whatever turbulence had occurred was regarded merely as the friction natural to times of change. The riots of June 20th were mildly condemned by a paper that was soon to defend with vigor all excesses, however extreme, the National Gazette, but condemned because, as the editor thought,

---

[1] Willard, Personal Memoirs, I., 329.

the French themselves abhorred them.' The 10th of August and the September massacres stunned a good many Americans, who began for the first time to view with some disfavor a movement that could produce such horrors.' With the dethronement of the King and his subsequent execution, however, came a sharp precipitation of public opinion. Toward Louis XVI. Americans naturally felt well disposed, and even affectionately grateful, and his execution and that of the Queen a few months later, created much indignation and inspired much horror. Boston celebrated its great civic fête the days after the King's death, and many, when they heard of the latter event, regretted their participation in the former. The gilded horns of the famous ox were taken down from the top of the liberty pole and buried, and henceforth Boston was more sober.

This execution of Louis XVI., toward whom Americans felt so kindly, horrified very many of them. " When will these savages be, satiated with blood?" exclaimed John Adams.' Oliver Wolcott, Sr., wrote to Oliver Wolcott, Jr., that he experienced heartfelt sorrow at the murder of Louis, for such he believed it might properly be called—" an event, it is true, which might have been expected, for whenever a people go so far as to imprison their prince, they will never again trust him, but will destroy him." ' Similar was the opinion of the son.' Chauncey Goodrich of Connecticut declared it " a wanton act of barbarity, disgraceful even to a Paris mob."' Patrick Henry, a republican *par excellence*,

---

' National Gazette, Sept. 8, 1792. On the other hand, radical and optimistic Joel Barlow, who was in France at this time, said in a letter dated June 25th: " You will hear frightful stories about the riots at the Tuileries on the 20th. You must believe but little. There was no violence committed. The visit to the king by armed citizens was undoubtedly contrary to law, but the existence of a king is contrary to another law of a higher origin." Todd, Life and Letters of Joel Barlow, 96.

' Columbian Centinel, Dec. 1, 1792. Life and Correspondence of Rufus King, I., 430. Washington's Writings, by W. C. Ford, XII., 202-203. Gibbs' Memoirs, I., 81-85.

' John Adams, Life and Works, II., 160.

' Gibbs' Memoirs, I., 91.   ' I., 90.   ' I., 90.

was loud in reprobating the execution of the King.' One paper declared, " The account of the decapitation of Louis XVI. appears to affect every American with grief and horror as an act of wanton cruelty, justified by no existing necessity," and it predicted that France herself would soon repent;' another, that the death sentence was an "unjust and iniquitous judgment,"' and that " the cruel and unjust assassination of the late unfortunate monarch must stamp indelible infamy on the transactions of that ferocious party who at present sway a many-headed power in the Gallic nation."' Washington disapproved,' and so did Jay,' and so did Fisher Ames.' But the condemnation of this act of the revolutionists was by no means unanimous here. The more devoted of the republicans either openly defended it or sought some way of extenuating it, softening its significance. "Whether the execution of Louis XVI. was politic or impolitic," said the Vermont Gazette, "we shall not at present decide, but the general fact that the French people have the right to choose whatever form of government they please admits of no doubt."' The " Aurora" published an Elegy on the Death of Louis XVI., moderate in tenor. France, to be sure, had suffered much from kings, but dragging Louis from his throne should be enough to atone for this.

" This lesson, Frenchmen, from Columbia learn,
To smart th' oppressor's hand, but not consume;
.   .   .   .
Frenchmen, be cautious in your growing work,
Nor blast your journal with th' increasing blot,—
Behind *one* fault, 'tis found, vast numbers lurk
Unseen, till crowding, they dilate the spot!"'

' Conway's Randolph, 153.
' Spooner's Vermont Journal, April 8, 1793.
' Gazette of United States, March 20, 1793.
' Gazette of United States, April 13, 1793.
' Ford's Washington, May 6, 1793, xii., 288-89.
' Jay's Life and Correspondence, IV., 200-202.
' Fisher Ames' Works, edited by Seth Ames, II., 33.
' Vermont Gazette, July 12, 1793. Also Boston Gazette, May 13, 1793.   ' General Advertiser and Aurora, March 26, 1793.

But others went much further. The National Gazette illustrates extremely well the facility with which many of our newspapers of the pronouncedly democratic class adapted themselves to the exigencies of shifting situations and even sought to exploit them for partisan purposes. In September, 1792, it condemned the project of dethroning Louis XVI. as uncalled for, violent, repulsive to the cooler heads,[1] but a fortnight later it began to hedge, saying that time would probably show that the King had acted "the political hypocrite."[2] "The king's trial," it said later, "will soon unveil his real character to the world,"[3] and in another month this paper's adaptation to the situation was complete. It saw its bearing upon home affairs and began to publish articles excusing the execution and then even defending it. "The general concern that seems to agitate the citizens of the United States at the accounts of the traitorous and perjured Louis XVI., the inveterate enemy of the people, having lost his head, is a convincing proof of a strong remaining attachment to royalty in this country," says the first of these articles in the new style. "Let any man recollect the conduct of Louis Capet, his many heinous sins, his flight after having taken an oath to be faithful to the nation, the impediments he constantly threw in the way of the revolution and the aid he afforded to the enemies of France, and lastly, his treason and reiterated instances of hypocrisy—I say when a man considers these things, let him reflect if Louis merits our tears or compassion. On the other hand let him revolve in mind the fate of those victims sacrificed in the Champs de Mars by royalty and Lafayette [between twelve and fifteen hundred this paper says were killed]; also the fate of those patriots who fell on the 10th of August and the 1200 defenders of liberty maimed and massacred at Frankfort—these, and not the momentary fate of a perjured king, should be causes for exciting the sigh of sympathy from the breasts of real republicans."[4] In the next issue comes

---

[1] National Gazette, September 26, 1792.   [2] October 10, 1792.
[3] February 20, 1793.   [4] March 20, 1793.

sarcasm at the expense of those who sympathize with the fate of Louis. The "American Royalists" are embarrassed how to show their grief: "whether by muffling all the bells for at least twelve months; by dressing as mourners—in which case they must wait till *the court* leads the way; or by burning the 693 members voting for death in effigy."[1] In the succeeding issues come defenses thick and fast,[2] then low abuse. An article appeared entitled "Louis Capet has lost his Caput." "From my use of a pun it may be seen that I think lightly of his fate. I certainly do. It affects me no more than the execution of another malefactor."[3] The charge that Americans showed ingratitude by joining in exultation at the fall of a benefactor was indignantly repelled. There was a time when General Arnold was entitled to the praise and gratitude of Americans, but when his true character became known, were they still bound to honor and revere him?[4] Are we, out of gratitude, to support a man in wrongdoing? Nothing could be more abhorrent to the moral sense.[5] True, he made a treaty of alliance with us, but that is no occasion for gratitude, for in all this he was utterly irresponsible, "he knew not what he was about."[6] Far from being abashed by the tales of crime that came rolling in, the editor affirms that the most recent accounts from France are "extremely satisfactory to every true American-citizen." "Since the Roman republic, nothing in point of dignity or resolution can be compared to the magnanimity of our Gallic friends,"[7] and "Equality," writing to the paper, declared that the justice of the judgment of Louis had not been exceeded "since the days of Moses, that great legislator."[8] Other papers were equally eager to defend or extenuate the execution of the King.[9]

---

[1] National Gazette, March 23, 1793.
[2] April 17, 20; May 11, 15; June 8, 1793.   [4] April 20, 1793.
[3] February 20, 1793.   [5] May 11, 1793.
[6] May 1, 1793.   [7] May 1, 1793.   [8] June 15, 1793.
[9] Boston Gazette, American Daily Advertiser.

There were cases enough of vulgar insult, too. The incident at a Philadelphia banquet, where the head of a pig, representing Louis XVI., was passed around and mangled by the feasters, has already been mentioned.[1] William Cobbett testifies to the following, in his usual free and easy style: "Never was the memory of any man so cruelly insulted as that of this mild and humane monarch. He was guillotined in effigy, in the capital of the Union, twenty or thirty times every day, during one whole winter and part of the summer. Men, women and children flocked to the tragical exhibition, and not a single paragraph appeared in the papers to shame them from it."[2]

Half-way between Chester and Wilmington was an inn where the stage usually stopped. The innkeeper at this time had a sign painted, representing a decapitated female, the head lying by the side of the bleeding trunk, underneath which was the inscription, "The guillotined Queen of France."[3] This, however, was too much for the public, who compelled its alteration.

The truth is that there were large numbers of Americans willing to defend almost every excess which the Revolutionists might see fit to commit. Nor were they by any means simply the low, disorderly, irresponsible elements of the population who went to this extreme. Jefferson, whose letters from France had showed great faith in the good intentions of the King, was moved to simply one or two cool allusions when he heard of his death: "We have just received here the news of the decapitation of the King of France. Should the present foment in Europe not produce republics everywhere, it will at least soften the monarchical governments by rendering monarchs amenable to punishment like other criminals, and doing away that rages of insolence and oppression, the inviolability of the king's person. We, I hope, shall adhere to our republican gov-

---

[1] P. 183.   [2] Hist. of Am. Jac. 26, 27.
[3] Larochefoucauld, Travels, III., 488, 489.

ernment, and keep it to its original principles by narrowly watching it."[1]

Madison, another Republican leader, wrote in a similar vein to Jefferson: "The sympathy with the fate of Louis has found its way pretty generally into the mass of our citizens, but relating merely to the man, and not to the monarch, and being derived from the spurious accounts in the papers of his innocence, and the bloodthirstiness of his enemies. I have not found a single instance in which a fair statement of the case has not new-modelled the sentiment. 'If he was a traitor he ought to be punished as well as another man.' This has been the language of so many plain men to me that I am persuaded it will be found to express the universal sentiment whenever the truth shall be made known."[2]

Thus there were those who would defend the excesses of the Revolution as well as those who would attack them. And this continued to the end. The execution of the King, an act very conspicuous in itself, precipitated public opinion. Were men willing to defend the violence therein shown, or not? If they could view without disapproval, or even with approbation, the execution of one to whom they owed so much as the King, they would have no difficulty in accommodating themselves to the fate of others in whom they had no direct personal interest. And this proved to be the case. The execution of the Girondists, of the Queen, the Reign of Terror, were attacked and defended generally along the lines already so deeply drawn by the execution of our benefactor. John Adams might continue his vigorous broadsides; Fisher Ames might express his deep abhorrence of the Revolution, of "its despotism by the mob or the military from the first," "its hypocrisy of morals to the last";[3] he might say that if others could find "in the scenes that pass there or in the principles or agents that direct them, proper subjects for amiable names, and sources of joy and hope in the pros-

---

[1] Jefferson's Works, III., 527, March 18, 1793.
[2] Letters of James Madison, I., 577.   [3] Ames' Works, II., 71-88.

pect," he had nothing to say, it was an amusement which it was not his intention either to disturb or to partake of. He might add that whatever political improvements might be hoped for, economically, industrially, France presented only a wide field of waste and desolation. " Capital, which used to be food for manufactures, is become their fuel. What once nourished industry now lights the fires of civil war and quickens the progress of destruction. France is like a ship with a fine cargo burning to the water's edge."[1] Hamilton might indignantly resent the assertion made by republicans that there was no more spilling of innocent blood in the French than in our own Revolution and might vehemently deny the justice of any comparison between the two—the difference being no less great " than that between liberty and licentiousness."[2] But these men by no means represented the only point of view, even among the educated.   There were those who sincerely believed and stoutly maintained that our own liberties were bound up inextricably with those of France, and that these were fearfully menaced by all the potentates of Europe; that any excesses France might commit were pardoned by the fundamental and supreme right of self-defense.   Men by no means blood-thirsty held this view.   The mild, large-minded Gallatin was of this class.   " As to the present cause of France," he writes, "although I think that they have been guilty of many excesses, that they have many men amongst them who are greedy of power for themselves and not of liberty for the nation, and that in the present temper they are not likely to have a very good government within any short time, yet I firmly believe their cause to be that of mankind against tyrants, and at all events that no foreign nation has a right to dictate a government to them.   So far I think we are interested in their success; and as to our political situation, they are certainly the only real allies we have yet

---

[1] Ames' Works, II., 33.
[2] Hamilton's Writings, Lodge, VIII., 302-303.

had." [1] And a few months later: " France at present offers
a spectacle unheard of at any other period. Enthusiasm
there produces an energy equally terrible and sublime. All
those virtues which depend upon social or family affections,
all those amiable weaknesses which our natural feelings
teach us to love or respect, have disappeared before the
stronger, the only, at present, powerful passion, the *Amor
Patriae.* I must confess my soul is not enough steeled not
sometimes to shrink at the dreadful executions which have
restored at least apparent internal tranquillity to that republic. Yet, upon the whole, as long as the combined despots
press upon every frontier and employ every engine to destroy and distress the interior parts, I think they and they
alone are answerable for every act of severity or injustice,
for every excess, nay, for every crime, which either of the
contending parties in France may have committed." [2] And
Jefferson could write to Mr. Short, reproving him in a most
paternal fashion for the extreme warmth with which he had
censured the proceedings of the Jacobins. Jefferson mentioned the attempt of the " Patriots," to which class he
thought the latter belonged, to retain an hereditary executive in the reformed state. " The experiment failed completely, and would have brought on the re-establishment of
despotism had it been pursued. The Jacobins knew this,
and that the expunging of that office was of absolute necessity. And the nation was with them in opinion," Jefferson
proceeds to say, " for, however they might have been formerly for the constitution framed by the first assembly, they
were come over from their hope in it and were now generally
Jacobins. In the struggle which was necessary, many
guilty persons fell without the forms of trial, and with them
some innocent. These I deplore as much as anybody, and
shall deplore some of them to the day of my death. But I
deplore them as I should have done had they fallen in battle.
It was necessary to use the arm of the people, a machine not

---

[1] Life of Albert Gallatin, by Henry Adams, Aug. 25, 1793, 103-104.
[2] Adams, Life of Gallatin, 110.

quite so blind as balls and bombs, but blind to a certain degree. A few of their cordial friends met at their hands the fate of enemies. But time and truth will rescue and embalm their memories, while their posterity will be enjoying that very liberty for which they would never have hesitated to offer up their lives. The liberty of the whole earth was depending on the issue of the contest, and was ever such a prize won with so little innocent blood? My own affections have been deeply wounded by some of the martyrs to this cause, but rather than that it should have failed I would have seen half the earth desolated; were there but an Adam and an Eve left in every country, and left free, it would be better than as it now is. I have expressed to you my sentiments because they are really those of ninety-nine in a hundred of our citizens. . . . You have been wounded by the sufferings of your friends and have by this circumstance been hurried into a temper of mind which would be extremely disrelished if known to your countrymen. . . . I know your republicanism to be pure, and that it is no decay of that which has embittered you against its votaries in France, but too great a sensibility at the partial evil with which its object has been accomplished there." [1]

The misfortunes of another, Lafayette, were followed with far more sympathetic interest here than were those of the King. As soon as it began to be rumored about that he was in trouble, Americans hastened to offer him a home in this country if he would only come. Soon formal addresses to him found their way into the papers, and soon toasts breathing the sentiment of loyalty and commiseration were proposed at the banquets then all the rage. Americans, boisterously praising the French Republic, were in somewhat of a dilemma in praising one who was opposed to that Republic and whose acts seemed to smack of treachery to his country. But the dilemma was generally ignored, a contradiction more or less being allowed men living in

---

[1] Jefferson to Short, Jan. 3, 1793, III., 501-503.

such tumultuous and chaotic times. The following toast betrays this half-disturbed state of mind: " Our Friend and Brother, Lafayette. May a generous nation forgive his errors (if any) and receive him to her bosom." [1] But most of them revealed no consciousness of any wrongdoing on Lafayette's part. " The unfortunate but patriotic Lafayette! May he outlive his enemies and return in triumph to the arms of his enraptured and enlightened countrymen." [2] " The Marquis de La Fayette! May the gloom of a despot's prison be soon exchanged for the embraces of his father Washington, in the land of freedom." [3] " The Marquis de la Fayette! Released from his dungeon, may the swiftest gale of the Atlantic waft him to the embraces of a grateful nation," [4] were sentiments voiced at various dinners. He was extolled in a poem read at a Harvard celebration. The Columbian Centinel declared that it was unfortunate for him that the castle of Spandau was not situated as near Philadelphia as the Bastille was to Paris, for, were it only so situated, the free-born sons of Columbia would glory in effecting the liberation of their hero. [5]

Everywhere Americans speak of De la Fayette " with tears in their eyes," writes the traveller Larochefoucauld, whose opportunities for knowing were excellent. " May he come, said a man to us this morning who was riding on horseback by the side of our carriage—may the Marquis come, we will make him rich. It is through him that France made us free; never shall we be able to do so much for him as he has done for us." [6] And later he says that " to cherish and commiserate Fayette seems to be a sort of religious duty in this country," [7] while there are numbers of honest souls

---

[1] Gazette of the United States, March 20, 1793.
[2] Bache's General Advertiser, March 4, 1793; see also ibid. July 31, 1793.
[3] Federal Orrery, Feb. 25, 1796; see also ibid. April 21, 1796.
[4] Independent Chronicle, July 7, 1796.
[5] Columbian Centinel, May 29, 1793.
[6] Larochefoucauld-Liancourt. Travels through the United States, II, 53.   [7] Ibid. III, 250.

everywhere to be found "who declare that a general tax imposed for the sole purpose of raising for him a considerable property would be paid with the greatest cheerfulness throughout the whole extent of America." [1]

Washington could do nothing for the release of his friend except to make a personal entreaty of the rulers of Austria and Prussia, for we did not yet have any official diplomatic intercourse with them. He directed Jefferson to instruct Morris to "neglect no favorable opportunity of expressing informally the sentiments and wishes of this country." [2] That Morris did what he could is shown by his Diary. [3]

Washington's interest in Lafayette gave rise to one of the most famous poems of the day. William Bradford, once seeing him weep at mention of Olmütz, went home and composed "The Lament of Washington," a poem that immediately attained a great popularity and was everywhere recited and sung:

> "As beside his cheerful fire,
> Midst his happy family,
> Sat a venerable sire,
> Tears were starting in his eye,
> Selfish blessings were forgot,
> Whilst he thought on Fayette's lot,
> Once so happy in our plains,
> Now in poverty and chains.
>
> . . . .
>
> Courage, Child of Washington!
> Though thy fate disastrous seems,
> *We* have seen the setting sun
> Rise and burn with brighter beams.
> Thy country soon shall break thy chain
> And take thee to her arms again." [4]

---

[1] Ibid. III, 397-398.
[2] Washington's Writings. Ford's edition, March 13, 1793.
[3] Morris. Diary and Letters, passim. For the services rendered the Lafayettes by this country see Tuckerman's Life of General Lafayette, II, 105, 142, 219, and Mme. de Lasteyrie's Life of Madame de Lafayette, 260-262, 313, 317-322.
[4] Bradford's verses "were sometimes sung to a plaintive air, composed on the execution of Marie Antoinette, which was current in

Thus we see that Americans felt most keenly the meaning of the violence of the Revolution. Some were willing to go to all lengths in defending it as an unfortunate necessity, while others condemned it in the most relentless rhetoric. It made men give an account to themselves of this swift and strange movement. And though some remained loyal defenders to the end, others, like Thomas McKean, were startled back from the path they were treading by the shock of the King's execution. "It is true," writes McKean twenty years later to John Adams, "I was a friend of the revolution in France, from the assembly of the Notables until the King was decapitated, which I deemed not only a very atrocious but a most absurd act. After the limited monarchy was abolished I remained in a kind of apathy with regard to the leaders of the different parties, until I clearly perceived *that* nation was incapable at *that* time of being ruled by a popular government; and when the *few*, and afterward an individual, assumed a despotic sway over them, I thought them in a situation better than under the government of a mob, for I would prefer any kind of government to such a state, even tyranny to anarchy."[1] Such was also

---

Philadelphia after that melancholy tragedy." Griswold, Republican Court, 393.

In 1795 Lafayette's son, George Washington Lafayette, came to this country, where he remained for nearly two years. Washington withdrew him from public notice, for which he was vigorously criticised by the democrats as showing gross inhospitality toward the son of a great benefactor. "It was circulated among these devils," writes Jeremiah Smith, "that the President took no notice of the lad, because he loved the British and hated the French." Morison: Life of Jeremiah Smith, 98. See also Lodge's Cabot, 88. Young Lafayette while here assumed the name of Motier and lived in seclusion near New York. Reasons of state prevented Washington, as President, from entertaining emigrants, but as soon as he became a private citizen he welcomed many of his old companions in arms to Mt. Vernon. He also bade Lafayette, Jr., to make his home with him until his return to France, which he did. See Custis, Recollections and Private Memoirs, 448-449. On Washington's attitude toward Lafayette's imprisonment see also Griswold, Republican Court, 390-392, and Sullivan, Familiar Letters, 107.   [1] Life and Works of John Adams, X, 14.

the effect of this "second" revolution upon John Jay,[1] who had approved the "first." As the Revolution proceeded, its increasing violence increased the number of its hostile critics here.[2]

Another feature of the Revolution that looked most doubtful to American eyes was the open hostility to religion. John Adams wrote, in 1790, that he knew not "what to make of a republic of thirty million atheists."[3] Patrick Henry, who thought that even deism was "but another name for vice and depravity," was bound to look with disfavor upon a certain class of revolutionary deeds.[4] Many Americans during the 18th century feared the influence of the skeptical French philosophy of the day, and when the Revolution came, giving, as it seemed to do, an official utterance to that philosophy, they were all the more alarmed.[5] This, too, was a very important consideration with Hamilton, as is shown in the fragment already referred to, in which he criticised the Revolution with extreme severity. Reviewing the successive steps in the audacious attack of the eighteenth century upon Christianity, until irreligion, "no longer confined to the closets of conceited sophists, nor to the haunts of wealthy nobles, has more or less displayed its hideous front among all classes," he adds: "A league has at length been cemented between the apostles and disciples of irreligion and anarchy. Religion and government have both been stigmatized as abuses; as unwarrantable restraints upon the freedom of man; as causes of the corruption of his nature, intrinsically good," and the upshot of his argument

---

[1] Correspondence and Public Papers of John Jay, IV., 200-201.
[2] See also Trumbull's Autobiography, 170.
[3] Works, IX, 563. Letter to Dr. Price, April 19, 1790.
[4] Wm. Wirt Henry. Life, Correspondence and Speeches of Patrick Henry, II, 570.
[5] Timothy Dwight. Sermons. 2 vols. Edinburgh, 1828. On Dwight as a champion of Christianity against the assaults of freethinkers, especially those begotten in France in the 18th century, see Tyler, Three Men of Letters, 109-116. Dwight published in 1788 "The Triumph of Infidelity," a satire; in reality a defense of the Christian faith and even Christian orthodoxy.

is that such maxims, once firmly lodged in men's minds, naturally, inevitably, produce a French Revolution.[1]

Similar considerations also exerted a great influence upon Noah Webster's thought and found expression in his writings. In 1793 Webster had become the editor of a new daily paper in New York, the Minerva, founded for the express purpose of combating the French faction under Genet. He had previously written, under the name Candor, in the "Courant," in a vein favorable to the French, but a conversation with Genet, whom he happened to meet at a dinner in New York, completely changed his views.[2] Henceforth he was a severe, though on the whole discriminating critic of the Revolution. In the next year he worked over his various newspaper comments on the Revolution into a pamphlet of some seventy pages.[3] Upon the title-page he asserts his marked preference for the old-fashioned philosophy of Cicero, which said that religion ought never to be despised; that the foundations of the state ought to be laid in religious institutions, to the "latest French fashion" of philosophy, which declares that "religion in no country is founded in truth" and that "death is an everlasting sleep." Webster maintains that the French, far from being the true liberals they claim to be, are in reality the most implacable persecutors of opinion, and he goes on to argue that the Revolution is necessarily fatal to morality, that by removing all religious restraints it has increased violence, which will in time "decivilize" the people, and is indeed fast doing so, as is shown in the September massacres, the war against Lyons and Toulon, and the actions of the Revolutionary Tribunal.

The conservative press of the country published accounts of the speeches and measures directed against the religious institutions of France, which were widely copied and un-

---

[1] Lodge. Hamilton's Works, VII, 374-377.
[2] Scudder. Life of Noah Webster, 130.
[3] Noah Webster. The Revolution in France considered in Respect to its Progress and Effects. New York, 1794.

doubtedly influential. The Gazette of the United States, for instance, printed an extract from a speech delivered in the Convention by M. Dupont, which aroused the suspicion or wrath of many Americans, for whom this side of the Revolution had no attractions.

" What! [he exclaims] monarchies are extirpated, thrones are overturned, and sceptres are broken to pieces, kings are no more; yet the *altars of God remain.* Shame to the enlightened spirit of Frenchmen! Will you permit still to exist these ignominious monuments of our ignorance and weakness? You have freed your country from the bondage of execrable tyrants; rescue them also from the *infamous* dominion of *superstition* that enslaves and shackles the mind. *Nature and reason—these* ought to be the gods of man—these are *my* gods. Kings and priests are leagued in *one cursed* design—and the cursed instrument of the latter is *eternal fire.* Let others tremble at this terrific bugbear. As for me, I despise it; as for myself, I here honestly confess to this Assembly I am an atheist." [1] This called forth many vigorous comments.

Later, the New York Herald, the weekly edition of the Minerva, called the attention of its readers to " one of the most extraordinary publications ever circulated in America, entitled CHRISTIANITY UNVEILED." " Certain men in this country," says the editor, " espouse not French politics merely, but French *infidelity,* and openly avow their hopes and wishes to see the religion of our country eradicated and the system of *reason* established here as in France." The book under consideration was a translation from the French of Boulanger and claimed to be an examination of the principles and effects of the Christian religion. " It is much of a piece," says the editor, " with many other books which our modern democratic patriots are reprinting and circulating with great industry and with the professed design of undermining Christianity for the purpose of establishing Reason in its place." He then gives the following extracts:

---

[1] Gazette of the United States, March 13, 1793.

"The only morality taught by Christians is the enthusiastic, impracticable, contradictory and uncertain morality contained in the Gospel. This is calculated only to degrade the mind, to render virtue odious, to form abject slaves, to break the spring of the soul; or if it is sown in warm and active minds, to produce turbulent fanatics, capable of shaking the foundations of society."

"Proud of the protection of Jehovah, the Hebrews marched forth to victory. Heaven authorized in them knavery and cruelty."

"Does it [the Christian religion] render mankind better? Alas! it arms them against each other, renders them intolerant, and forces them to butcher their brethren."

The editor says he would not have published these extracts except to show the depravity of a sect among us.[1]

Later he notices one of the articles of the new French Declaration of Rights, to the effect that men should do to others what they wish others to do to them. This he says may be considered curious. "This would raise our surprise as an unusual effort of human wisdom had it not been a maxim or precept in the mouth of every Christian man, woman and child for nearly eighteen centuries. Very fortunate is it, indeed, that the Golden Rule has received the sanction of the French Convention. It may have a good effect upon our Democrats."[2]

It was with the accusations of irreligion that the American defenders of France had the greatest difficulty. There was indeed a faction here to which these attacks of the French were not repugnant, but pleasing, were even sympathetic, and many anti-Christian pamphlets were published at this time. But the majority of the admirers of France were rather thrown on the defensive by this phase of the Revolution, and sought to soften the appearance of harshness and injustice in French proceedings and to palliate, extenuate, explain away. Speaking of Dupont's utterance in the National Assembly, quoted above, the National Ga-

---

[1] New York Herald, March 17, 1795.   [2] Oct. 21, 1795.

zette said that while he could declare himself an atheist without harm and even with plaudits, he would have been roundly hissed had he declared himself an aristocrat. " But after all, what does it prove except that an aristocrat is a more dangerous animal than either a deist or an atheist. The aristocrat oppresses the moral and physical faculties of men, the deist or atheist oppresses nobody." His opinions are his own, and " ask not the aid of cruel and rich priests." He is not the one who sets up stakes and fires religious animosity. France does not wish to be under the despotism of cruel and crafty priests, and who can blame her![1] Later, this same paper approves the suppression of the ringing of church bells, and hopes this will be imitated here. In cities it is " one of the most prominent nuisances." " The hateful knell, which was congenial to the gloomy habits of monks and such beings . . . can by no means be acceptable to a busy and industrious laity; and many there are who are hurried from the bed of sickness to the grave in consequence of this superstitious abomination."[2]

Others, instead of approving, attempted to show that the charge of irreligion was unfounded. The Aurora quotes Art. 7 of the French Constitution: " The right of peaceful assemblies and the free exercise of all religious worship can not be forbidden." Is not this enough to refute the charge so lightly made?[3] Other attempts of a similar nature were made by other papers.[4] These men, hard pressed during the first few years of the Revolution, leaped with exultation when Robespierre brought on his new religion. Eagerly did they seize his speech on the Supreme Being as a refutation of the charge of irreligion that had so often been brought against the Revolution. Henceforth their opponents must look about for some other accusation. " The publications of Robespierre, who is now the organ of the Republic, prove that the French are influenced by the purest

---

[1] National Gazette, March 27, 1793.   [2] March 30, 1793.
[3] Aurora, Feb. 18, 1794.
[4] Independent Chronicle, March 6, 1794.

motives. That they have a just sense of the SUPREME
BEING and are led to adopt the wisest and most orthodox
principles of any nation in Europe." England, on the
other hand, is a disgrace to religion, and its ministers and
priests are become lawless banditti to invade the thoughts
and tyrannize over the consciences of men.[1] Accounts are
given of the grand festival to the Supreme Being. "Yet
this is the nation that is accused of atheism and irreligion."[1]
Indeed, how gross a calumny thrown on this band of republicans by their enemies! It is only "the desperate effort of
men who sicken at their prosperity."[1]

But while there were those who defended the religious
policy of the Revolutionists, there were others, ardent be-
lievers in the movement, upholders of it against all comers,
who seemed to feel that in this one particular the French
were going astray. Most conspicuous among these was
Governor Samuel Adams, who, in his Fast Day proclamation in 1794, gave as one of the reasons for such a day that
among other things we might implore God "to inspire
our friends and allies, the Republic of France, with a spirit
of wisdom and true religion; that firmly relying on the
strength of His Almighty arm, they may still go on prosperously till their arduous conflict for a government of their
own, founded on the just and equal rights of men, shall be
finally crowned with success; and above all, to cause the
religion of Jesus Christ in its true spirit to spread far and
wide till the whole earth shall be filled with His glory."[1]

Like every other organ of public opinion at that time, the
pulpits fell to discussing the merits and defects of the Revolution. And in the attitude that the preachers took we see
the same diversity, the same varied interpretation as elsewhere. Many were repelled by the lawlessness and impiety
that characterized it, the one seeming to occasion the other
and to reinforce it. Men made their reputations as pulpit

---

[1] Independent Chronicle, July 24, 1794.
[1] Independent Chronicle, Aug. 4, 1794. For further remarks on
Robespierre and religion see Ind. Chr., Aug. 7, Aug. 11, Sept. 4.
[1] Independent Chronicle, March 6, 1794.

orators by reason of their utterances on this subject. Thus the first thing which brought the Rev. David Osgood, A. M., pastor of the Congregational Church in Medford, prominently before the public was a political sermon delivered on Thanksgiving Day, 1794, in which he denounced the excesses of the Revolution, and especially the pernicious Genet and "certain self-created societies." The discourse passed through several editions within a few months. From this time on Osgood was greatly admired and applauded by the Federalists, of whose principles he was a stout and able defender.[1] Consequently he was instantaneously attacked by the opposition, who denounced this "inquisitorial ecclesiastic" as densely ignorant and as favoring monarchy.[2] And the "Citoyen de Novion," who was no other than James Sullivan, later Governor of Massachusetts, came forward to vanquish the presumptuous parson in an energetic lay sermon entitled "The Altar of Baal Thrown Down, or the French Nation Defended against the Pulpit Slander of David Osgood, A. M."

But all Thanksgiving sermons were not of the same tenor as Parson Osgood's. The pastor of the church in Rowley, Mass., Ebenezer Bradford, declared in 1795 that "No event in the course of Divine Providence, except the enjoyment of the Gospel, can be estimated more highly or rationally demand more gratitude from an American than the late successes of the French nation."[3]

---

[1] Sprague. Annals of the American Pulpit, II, 76. See also Morison. Life of Jeremiah Smith, 67-68. " By the way, we are all hugely pleased with Parson Osgood's Thanksgiving sermon and swear . . . that he was inspired. If the virtuous members of Congress (meaning those of our party) had the power to confer degrees, he would instantly be daubed over with titles. . . . It is proposed to print an edition in this city [Phila.] . . . What is very unusual, it has been published entire in a newspaper in this city, and, I believe, read by many people who were never in the whole course of their lives in the inside of a church."

[2] Independent Chronicle, Jan. 15, 1795. Friends to the Clergy and Enemies to Ecclesiastic Presumption were much in evidence for several weeks in the columns of the Chronicle rebutting Osgood.

[3] Thanksgiving sermon, 1795, on "The Nature and Manner of giving Thanks to God, illustrated." I have examined a score or

Another ground of hostility to the Revolution was the character of some of its doctrines, which were unacceptable to many conservative Americans, particularly the doctrine of equality.   Of course it was just this doctrine more than any other that won it friends here; it was just this sentiment that appealed so strongly to numbers of Americans, plunging them into the extraordinary excesses of enthusiasm and imitation which have already been described. But as this doctrine came to stand forth more sharply and conspicuously as one of the great aspirations of the Revolution, as its most significant and striking issue, it operated no less distinctly as a force of repulsion.   Many men could view with pleasure a reformation in France along very liberal lines, would have been glad indeed to see a constitutional form of government replace permanently the arbitrary government of the Old Régime.   But with Rousseau, despite their own Declaration of Independence, they

---

more of these political sermons, delivered mostly in 1794 and 1795. They reveal the same points of view and the same dogmatism as most of the other utterances of the time, differing from them only in the Biblical character of many of the phrases and in many curious and entertaining examples of exegesis. One of the fairest and sanest of them is that delivered by Jedediah Morse in Charlestown, Feb. 19, 1795, on " The Present Situation of other Nations of the World Contrasted with Our Own."

One who enjoyed a very high, reputation as a pulpit orator at this time was William Linn, pastor of a Dutch Reformed Church in New York. At the beginning he was a warm partisan of the French Revolution, as was shown in a sermon preached before the Tammany Society on the Fourth of July, 1791, in which he plunged into a glorification of the movement and a denunciation of its opponents, especially Edmund Burke (" The British orator, though he sublimely rave, he raves in vain.   No force of genius, no brilliancy of fancy, and no ornament of language can support his wretched cause. . . . The Revolution in France is great, is astonishing, is glorious "). Even as late as 1794 he published a series of sermons on The Signs of the Times, the delivery of which created much opposition, as well as much enthusiasm, by reason of their approval of the Revolution. A few years later, however, he denounced it, having been alienated by the infidelity and anarchy that seemed to grow out of it. Duyckinck: Cyclopaedia of American Literature, I, 326-327.

would not for a moment parley. Equal they believed men
should be before the law, and that was all. Equality, as it
seemed to be regarded in France, they considered arrant
nonsense, just as completely and emphatically contradicted
by nature as its apostles held it to be affirmed. This was
one of the points in Hamilton's indictment of the Revolution. Wise and good men, he says, took the lead in reveal-
ing to the world the odious character of the old despotism,
in showing forth the advantages to be expected from a
more moderate government, in which the individual should
enjoy a greater liberty, should have a freer room for the
play of his own ambitions. Then came the "fanatics in
political science," who have since exaggerated and per-
verted their doctrines. "Theories of government unsuited
to the nature of man, miscalculating the force of his passions, disregarding the lessons of experimental wisdom,
have been projected and recommended. These have everywhere attracted sectaries, and everywhere the fabric of
government has been in different degrees undermined."[1]
Gouverneur Morris lashed this doctrine with his most in-
cisive and mordant sarcasm. "What folly is it," exclaimed
caustic Chauncey Goodrich of Connecticut, "that has set
the whole world agog to be all equal to French barbers!"
"It must have its run, and the anti-feds will catch at it to aid
their mischievous purposes. I believe it is not best to let
it pass without remark, and before long the authors of
entire equality will show the world the danger of their wild
rant."[2] "By the law of nature," wrote John Adams in contempt of this doctrine, "all men are men and not angels—
men and not lions—men and not whales—men and not
eagles—that is, they are all of the same species. And this
is the most that the equality of nature amounts to. But man
differs by nature from man almost as much as man from
beast. The equality of nature is moral and political only
and means that all men are independent. But a physical

---

[1] Lodge's Hamilton, VII, 374-377.
[2] Gibbs' Memoirs, I., 88. Goodrich to Wolcott, Feb. 17, 1793.

inequality, an intellectual inequality of the most serious kind is established unchangeably by the Author of nature; and society has a right to establish any other inequalities it may judge necessary for its good."[1]

Thus the doctrine of equality as preached so fervently by the fiery French, was a hard and impossible teaching for many Americans of the eighteenth century.

As the Revolution proceeded and the fierce rivalry of the different factions increased in intensity, many Americans became alarmed lest the spirit of faction and discord should leap beyond all restraints here. That this was the inevitable issue of the principles proclaimed in France seemed to be shown by her daily history. That those ardent admirers of hers in this country, with their constant laudation and attempted introduction of French principles, would bring along the demon goddess herself, was the sincere fear of many of the ablest men of the time. It was against the spirit of faction that the Hartford Wits directed many of their most malignant shafts. It was against this unlovely disturber of the peace that Robert Treat Paine hurled his coarse but pungent sarcasms, and Noah Webster wrote the famous pamphlet to which I have already referred and for which the men of his way of thinking were sincerely grateful.[2] "The most important truth suggested by the foregoing remarks is," says Webster at the close of his pamphlet, "that party spirit is the source of faction, and faction is death to the existing government." This is the principal danger to which our government is exposed. "Americans! be not deluded. In seeking liberty France has gone beyond

---

[1] Life of John Adams, by J. Q. Adams, Lippincott, 1871, II, 185-189; Letter to Mrs. Adams, December 19, 1793.

[2] Wolcott, Jr., to Noah Webster. Gibbs, I, 134, May 3, 1794: "I acknowledge your favor of the 20th of April, with the enclosed pamphlet, which I have perused with much satisfaction. It is precisely the thing which I have long wished to be furnished, and will eminently serve to fix the public opinion on national principles and to tranquillize those passions which have threatened the peace of this country."

her. You, my countrymen, if you love liberty, adhere to
your constitution of government. The moment you quit
that sheet-anchor you are afloat among the surges of passion
and the rocks of error, threatened every moment with ship-
wreck. Heaven grant that while Europe is agitated with
a violent tempest in which palaces are shaken and thrones
tottering to their base, the republican government of America, in which liberty and the rights of man are embarked,
fortunately anchored at an immense distance on the margin
of the gale, may be enabled to ride out the storm and land
us safely on the shores of peace and political tranquillity." [1]
The fervor of this exordium shows the strength of the anxiety behind it. It is impossible to read the utterances of the
day without having borne in upon you in a hundred ways
the fact that very many Americans regarded the so-called
French principles as utterly subversive of all social and
political order, and the further fact that they could find no
terms fierce enough with which to properly denounce those
who were seeking to introduce those methods here. Jeremiah Smith gives evidence of this. "I am sorry," he writes,
"that French politics gain ground with you. They are my
utter abhorrence. I almost hate the name of a Frenchman.
They have opened some leaves in the volume of human
nature that I never believed were in the book. They have
done the cause of liberty an irreparable injury. I do not
wish them success. Their principles are hostile to all government, even ours, which is certainly the best." [2] George
Cabot declared that French principles would "destroy us
as a society"; that they were "more to be dreaded in a
moral view than a thousand yellow fevers in a physical." [3]
Wolcott, Sr., wrote to Wolcott, Jr., expressing the hope
that France would not get possession of New Orleans, for
"there is no nation in the universe whose neighborhood we

[1] Webster, The Revolution in France, 71-72.
[2] Morison. Life of Jeremiah Smith, 61-62, Feb. 12, 1794.
[3] Lodge. Life and Letters of George Cabot, 78, March 10, 1794.

ought equally to detest,"[1] and the son, responding cordially
to the parental thought, declared without hesitation that
he had "rather know that the United States were to be
erased from existence than infected with the French principles,"[2] a remark as wise and moderate as that wherein
Jefferson expressed a readiness to see the entire population
of every country wiped out, reserving, however, one Adam
and one Eve, if thereby the precious boon of liberty might
be preserved. Wisdom and moderation were apparently
rare among either Jews or Gentiles at that troublous time.[3]

And another reason why many Americans turned from
the Revolution was "its despicable attention to trifles."
These are the words of Noah Webster, and they form one
of the three capital charges in his arraignment. He can-

---

[1] Gibbs. Memoirs, I, 132.
[2] Gibbs. Memoirs, I, 133-134; also I, 136.
[3] This tendency to ascribe all our noisy party broils to the
French is shown still further by a curious pamphlet called "The
Jacobin Looking Glass," and published anonymously by "A Friend
to Rational Liberty" (Worcester, 1795). The author attempts to
trace the history of the opposition to the Government (synonymous
in his view with "faction") from the Revolution down through the
Whiskey Insurrection. Opening with a truly startling statement.
"Fellow-citizens, I am averse to contention, especially in politicks,"
he proceeds to belabor the democrats. They were men who, when
the Government was founded, didn't get offices, consequently
"their noses" were "put out of joint." . . . "In this situation did
the sons of faction remain, like the poor invalid at the pool waiting for the troubling of the waters, when in came the angel and that
angel was Genet. This evil genius quickly troubled the waters,
and in they leaped, like Cerberus in the Styx, to quench their
thirst with blood and charge their tongues with poison." . . .
"Now you hear of nothing but *constitutional* and *democratick societies.*
From New Hampshire to Georgia the Genetines lay the eggs and
hatch sedition." If they could have their way, says this rather
typical pamphleteer, the guillotine would be an ordinary sight in
America, "of which every one not of their party would soon feel
the effects." . . . Now, Americans, beware of these men. "Give
them but power and see the effect. America, that peaceful habi-
tation of man, would soon be drenched with the blood of her
favorite sons. War is their element and peace their bane. But,
my friends, keep aloof from such men; beware of those tooting
gentry, who disturb the abodes of domestick happiness with their
midnight omens."

didly admits that much of the violence of the Revolution
may be attributed to the opposititon of despotic powers
whose aims are unjustifiable. " But there are some proceedings of the present convention," says he, " which admit
of no excuse but a political insanity, a wild enthusiasm,
violent and irregular, which magnifies a mole-hill into a
mountain, and mistakes a shadow for a giant." " The convention," he adds, " in their zeal for equalizing men have,
with all their exalted reason, condescended to the puerilities
of legislating even upon names." That they should abolish
titles of distinction along with the privileges of the different
orders was natural, but such titles as " Monsieur" and
" Madame " are literally terms of equality, not of distinction.
Yet these titles, which, in Webster's words, had " no more
connection with Government than the chattering of birds,"
became the subject of grave legislative discussion, and their
use was officially forbidden. " The cause of the French
nation," says he, " is the noblest ever undertaken by men;
it was necessary; it was just," and as long as the legislators
of France confined themselves to the correction of real
evils they were admirable, " the most respectable of reformers," but when they stooped to legislate upon trifles
they became contemptible. " What shall we say," he adds,
" to the legislature of a great nation waging a serious war
with mere names, pictures, dress, and statues? Is this also
necessary to the support of liberty? There is something
in this part of the legislative proceedings that unites the
littleness of boys with the barbarity of Goths."[1]

CONCLUSION.

But the opposition, though growing in numbers, in clear-
ness of perception and in precision of purpose, was very,
very far from silencing the enthusiasm for France which
had burst forth with a spontaneity testifying to the frank
honesty of the motives behind it, and which was to burst

---

[1] Webster. The Revolution in France, 39.

forth again and again in the months that were to come.
Into the details of these later events we do not need to
enter with the same fulness of treatment meted out to the
former. They add little that is new either in the way of
description or explanation. Suffice it to say that no occasion for expressing interest in the welfare of France slipped
by without calling forth the expression. There was the
debate on Madison's Resolutions in the Congress of 1794,
in which the national antipathy to Great Britain, the national fondness for France, were arrayed as party forces.
These two countries were pitted against each other in the
debate. It was urged that the resolutions ought to pass as
an expression of our gratitude to France for her timely
aid in critical days gone by. To which it was retorted that
generosity and gratitude were more at home in heaven than
on earth; that though they might be discovered now and
then determining the relations of individuals, they were
rarely decisive in those of nation with nation. Furthermore, had not confession been made in the French convention that the assistance had been rendered not so much
out of love to us as out of hatred of England and a desire
to humiliate a proud and dangerous rival. The similarity
of principles and institutions was urged as a reason for
drawing the two republics together. This similarity did not
appear so evident to others. . "The French republic was
one and indivisible; ours consisted of sovereign states,
having extensive and important local jurisdictions and a
diversity of laws and interests. Federalism was treason in
France; consolidation was treason here. The French executive was plural, and their legislature a single body—
arrangements counter to the practice of almost all the states
and to the provisions of the Federal Constitution. Was
every part of the United States in a condition to extend the
idea of equality to the same length it had been carried in
France? Might not the conflagrations, the bloody scenes
of St. Domingo be exhibited in that case on our own
peaceful shores?" "The French were a brave, generous,

enlightened nation," said one speaker. "They had performed the most brilliant achievements recorded in history. They had broken the chains of despotism, had obliterated hierarchical and feudal tyranny, and had exercised the power belonging to all nations of establishing a government of . their own." They deserved to be happy under it, and would to God they might be. But if any parallel was to be drawn between our government and that of any nation of Europe, it was "the British constitution which presented the most numuerous points of resemblance." This association of the American government with that of Great Britain was very offensive to members of the House, several of whom exclaimed against it. "It is enough for us," said one of them, "that the French Constitution has liberty for its basis." The French and American governments agree in the fundamental principles of the consent of the people and equality of rights, while the fundamental principle of the British government is coercion, and its object a monopoly of rights. Whatever similarity there may be is one of form merely. Another said that if he had any prejudices they certainly were not in favor of England, but rather of the people with whom she was at war. "I can never forget that probably by them we exist as a nation. France is the place of my fathers' sepulchres. No man more ardently wishes liberty and happiness to the French nation. No man, it is but just to add, more sincerely laments that spasm of patriotism which now convulses the body politic of France and greatly hazards the cause of freedom. But we ought not to suffer a torrent of feeling to sweep us from our post. We are neither Britons nor Frenchmen, but Americans, the representatives of Americans, the guardians of their interests."[1]

In other debates in this and succeeding years the Revolution made itself felt either in a half-suppressed way or openly. Immigration becoming much greater than ever

---

[1] Quotations are from Hildreth's account of the debates, IV, 459-475.

before, a new naturalization law was brought forward at the close of the year 1794. Both Federalists and Democrats were willing to make naturalization more difficult, the former because of their fear of foreign democrats, the latter because of their fear of foreign aristocrats. One of the provisions of the law was that a citizen of a foreign state seeking naturalization here must not only renounce allegiance to the foreign state, but if he bore any title of nobility, must renounce that also. The Federalists then enquired sarcastically, why require the renunciation of a .mere title which had no privileges attached? Why not, said Dexter of Massachusetts, require the new citizen to renounce his membership in the Jacobin Club should he happen to be a member? Why not require him to renounce the Pope? "Is not priestcraft quite as dangerous as aristocracy?" On the other hand it was retorted that titles of nobility were mere names, and that if a man were not willing to sacrifice that much for the inestimable boon of becoming a citizen of the United States he was not worthy of it. The Democrats carried the day and the introduction of titles in America was again defeated.

References were made to the Revolution on other occasions, when the question of the San Domingo refugees was before Congress, and especially when discussion raged for months over the Jay Treaty. And again in 1795, when a communication was laid before it from the members of the Committee of Public Safety respecting the new metric system of weights and measures and urging our adoption of it. The Senate ordered the printing of three hundred copies of the communication for the use of the members.[1] Here the matter was dropped; no further notice was ever taken of it. The Federalists pronounced the documents extremely curious, as showing very clearly how sanguine the French were in their hopes of remodeling everything in these States, and expressed their joy that the proposition had not

---

[1] Annals of Congress, Jan. 8 and 9, 1795.

come a year earlier, when most probably an earnest attempt
would have been made to "frenchify" our customs in one
more particular.[1]

The attempts of the French in the art of constitution-
making also commanded the interested attention of the
Americans. The first constitution they had, as a rule, approved, as we have seen. It created a constitutional monarchy where formerly had been an absolute one. The
short-lived Constitution of '93 was printed in full in many
of the papers and much commented upon. "You will in
this outline," wrote Oliver Wolcott, "see that the poor
Frenchmen have much to suffer before they settle their
affairs. An executive with seven heads, a judiciary chosen
by the people at large, and a right reserved to each citizen
to propose new or the repeal of existing laws, will produce
more friction than can easily be overcome. Yet in this
country men are sworn to praise this plan in derogation of
our own Constitution. May God preserve us from the
effects of such fanaticism."[2] Indeed, this was quite true.
Among other excellencies of the new document the avoid-
ance of a single executive was mentioned, for does not that
lead naturally to despotism?[3] But it was the Constitution
of '95 that enjoyed the greatest favor here. Indeed, by this
time Frenchmen were showing a tendency to learn from
experience, and once more our own exeperience seemed to
be counting for something with them.

The republican journals hailed the new instrument of
government with extravagant praise. The Aurora declared
that it secured to the French every great feature of democracy which the warmest republican could wish, and expressed the hope that it would put the seal of perpetuity
upon the work of the Revolution. It also added that it was
free from many of the defects which were becoming daily
more and more apparent in our Federal Constitution.[4] The

---

[1] Peter Porcupine's Works, II, 229. [2] Gibbs. Memoirs, I, 92.
[3] Vermont Gazette, Nov. 15, 1793. Quotation from New York
Journal. [4] Bache's General Advertiser and Aurora, Aug. 27, 1795.

Independent Chronicle pronounced it "a most beautiful monument of political architecture,"[1] "the noblest work, the best guarded against the abuse of power, and in all respects the freest national government in the world,"[2] "the most perfect model" ever adopted by any nation. "It comprehends all the beauties and excellences of our own in their full lustre. But it avoids its defects."[1] "Study it, ye Americans, it may become necessary to new-model your own."[3] Even the Federalists seemed disposed to approve. The Federal Orrery called attention to points of resemblance to our Constitution and to two great abuses in French government that would be corrected, the sharp separation of the executive, legislative and judicial departments, in place of their former consolidation, and the erection of a second chamber to serve as a check on the hitherto unlimited sovereignty of the Lower House. True, the executive is its weak point. It ought not to be shared by the legislature, nor ought it to be plural; but this latter needs "no antidote but experience."[4] And Noah Webster mentioned in the Minerva with evident pleasure the fact that Boissy d'Anglas, in a report preliminary to the new constitution, had called John Adams, the author of the Defense of the Constitutions, a book loathed by the Democrats, *one of the greatest modern writers on government.*[5]

And so the great Revolution swept on, admired and denounced with fervor by observers three thousand miles away. With every new series of republican victories in France came a new series of dinners in America extolling the same.[5] There was the same enthusiasm, the same radiant outlook, the same ardor for the republican cause. But there were new elements as well. France, having been reborn a

---

[1] Independent Chronicle, Sept. 7, 1795.
[2] Oct. 22, 1795.　　　　　　　　　　　　　[3] Sept. 3, 1795.
[4] Federal Orrery, Aug. 20 and Aug. 24, 1795.
[5] Minerva, Nov. 4, 1795.
[5] Independent Chronicle, April 20, 1795, Oct. 15, 1795, July 7 and 11, 1796. Federal Orrery, June 15, July 16 and 20, and Sept. 24, 1795, Oct. 20, 1796.

republic, begot one of her own in turn, the Batavian, whose advent was duly celebrated. "The bells have rung this morning a merry peal of joy," writes James Sullivan from Portsmouth, N. H., to his friend, Governor Samuel Adams; "salutes have been fired from the artillery, and the gentlemen of the town are repairing to a civic feast, served up at the town hall, to celebrate the revolution in the Netherlands, and the accession of an important republic to the true interests of mankind. I shall partake of this feast among my old friends and acquaintances with a cheerful readiness, and leave you to conjecture the degree of happiness which I shall possess."[1] Henceforth there were toasts to "Our Sister Republics, France and Holland," to "The Triune Republic of America, France and Holland,"[2] and there was much talk about this globe becoming "one universal republic."

Again the dissenters brought forth their favorite weapon of ridicule. They organized mock celebrations, aiming to parody the tendency of the republicans to range the wide world for subjects for their thought, and at these mock celebrations mock toasts were drunk to "The King of Corsica," to "The Memory of Caligula and his Consular Horse," to "The Dey of Algiers and Success to Piracy," to "Judge Green of Bermuda," to "The South Sea Bubble," to "Sterling Despotism throughout the World," to "Our Noble Selves."[3]

There was another scene in Congress. The two great republics exchanged flags. The convention had voted to have the French and American colors suspended intertwined in their assembly hall, and Monroe had taken it upon himself to send them ours in the name of the American people. In return the Committee of Public Safety ordered the French flag to be sent to the Congress of the United States. It was presented to Washington on New

[1] Amory, Life of James Sullivan, I, 299-300.
[2] Federal Orrery, June 15 and July 6, 1795.
[3] Minerva, June 20, 1795.

Year's Day, 1796, by the French ambassador. The President delivered an unusually fervid speech of thanks, rendered so, perhaps, by the desire to allay our growing troubles with France.[1] Transmitted to Congress, it was voted to deposit the flag in the "archives" of the nation, and not in view as the French no doubt intended it should be. A week later the French minister wrote a letter of complaint to the Secretary of State that the flag had been so "shut up," and said that this disposal of it would be regarded by his countrymen as a mark of indifference or contempt, and demanded that it be released from its dungeon and displayed in the House of Representatives. But Timothy Pickering was then Secretary of State, a man little disposed to lend himself to the exaltation of the French Revolution in any form. The flag remained shut up.[2]

But the time for enthusiasm for France was well-nigh spent. Diplomatic difficulties were fast leading toward a rupture. France was disposed to deal summarily with this ungrateful republic, so fair of speech, so wanting in action. The neutrality proclamation had been a severe blow. The Jay treaty was another cause of estrangement. On our side Monroe was censured by the home Government for compromising his country too much with the French. He was recalled, and Charles C. Pinckney was appointed his successor, but was formally notified that neither he nor any other minister would be received from the United States until the grievances of which France complained were redressed, and it was hinted that neutral commerce might be treated rather differently in the future. The problem was rapidly being compounded with which doughty John Adams was to wrestle mightily, into a discussion of which it is no purpose of ours to enter.

But in that summer of 1796 there was a momentary revival of methods that had for some time been left in abeyance. The French minister, Adet, like his more famous

---

[1] Wait's State Papers and Publick Documents of the United States, II, 95-97.   [2] William Sullivan, Familiar Letters, 103.

predecessor, Genet, resorted to rhetoric and opened direct communication with the people. He issued the famous " cockade " proclamation, calling upon all Frenchmen resident in America to wear the tri-colored cockade, " the symbol of a liberty, the fruit of eight years' toils and five years' victories." To this call not only the exiles, but many Americans also, who wished thus to testify to their devotion to the French cause, responded. Soon in another manifesto he called upon the American people to fulfil their treaty obligations like men of honor. " When Europe rose up against the republic at its birth and menaced it with all the horrors of famine," runs this product of true revolutionary diplomacy, " when on every side the French could not calculate on any but enemies, their thoughts turned toward America, and a sweet sentiment then mingled itself with those proud feelings which the presence of danger and the desire of repelling it produced in their hearts. In America they saw friends. Those who went to brave tempests and death upon the ocean forgot all dangers in order to indulge the hope of visiting that American continent, where, for the first time, the French colors had been displayed in favor of liberty. Under the guarantee of the law of nations, under the protecting shade of a solemn treaty, they expected to find in the ports of the United States an asylum as sure as at home; they thought, if I may use the expression, there to find a second country. The French government thought as they did. Oh, hope worthy of a faithful people, how hast thou been deceived! So far from offering the French the succors which friendship might have given without compromitting itself, the American government in this respect violated the obligation of treaties."

Then follows a list of these alleged violations from 1793 down. Then the announcement of the suspension of diplomatic relations "until the government should return to sentiments and measures more conformable to the interests of the alliance and the sworn friendship between the two nations." Then comes a most harrowing appeal to Americans, by all the memories of their glorious struggles in common against the hated Britons, to recall the government to itself. "Alas! the soldiers who fell under the sword of the Britons are not yet reduced to dust; the laborer in turning up his fields still draws from the bosom of the earth their whitened bones, while the plowman, with tears of tenderness and gratitude, still recollects that his fields, now covered with rich harvests, have been moistened with French blood; while everything around the inhabitants of this country animates them to speak of the tyranny of Great Britain and of the generosity of Frenchmen. . . . O Americans! covered with noble scars! O! you who have so often flown to death and to victory with French soldiers! . . . Let your government return to itself and you will still find in Frenchmen faithful friends and generous allies!"

This remarkable appeal was understood to be an effort to influence the Presidential election of 1796 in favor of Jefferson. A "French President," exclaimed the Federalists, is what our republicans would give us. This is what the French Revolution, mixing in our affairs, will lead us to.

It is not surprising, in view of all these extraordinary evidences of enthusiasm for a foreign people with which the preceding pages abound, that Washington should warn the American people most earnestly in his Farewell Address against "permanent, inveterate antipathies against particular nations and passionate attachments for others," and should say "that such an attachment of a small or weak towards a great and powerful nation dooms the former to be the satellite of the latter"; that "against the insidious wiles of foreign influence the jealousy of a free people ought to be *constantly* awake, since history and experience prove that foreign influence is one of the most baneful foes of republican government."

Thus the two nations were drifting apart into open hostility and that bond of sympathetic attachment was about to be snapped asunder because America did not wish to apologize for her Neutrality Proclamation and her Jay

Treaty and all that grew out of them; because she, whose
chief boast was her independence, did not wish to become
a " poor little twinkling star " hiding its head " at the rays
of the *Grande République Française.*" [1]   Finally the gross
insults of the Directory heaped upon our commissioners
dried up at once the fountains of admiration and devotion
that had flowed so freely in the past and turned friendship
into enmity.   But the issue henceforth was to be a different
one.   The question was no longer one of the French Revolution as a movement apart by itself, a movement to be
admired or denounced according to one's taste.   It was one
of national pride and resentment and determination.   And
into this new question we will not go.

Meanwhile, certain stray items were finding their way
into the papers, faintly foreshadowing a new chapter in the
history of the world.   The army of Italy was doing wonderful things, so wonderful that the citizens of New York
must needs have a banquet and celebrate.   " General Buonaparte and the victorious army of Italy!   May their successes at the gates of Rome be extended to the Tagus," was
a sentiment that called forth nine cheers.[2]   The Independent Chronicle pronounced Bonaparte's letters to his army
" beautiful " and his proclamations as " written in the style
of Hannibal."   It declared that he stood " at this awful
crisis in the exalted attitude of a conqueror dispensing justice and the blessings of liberty to a prostrate and admiring
world "; and soon it was announcing that the most celebrated statues which once embellished republican Athens
and republican Rome would at last " quit the seat of superstition and return to the capitol of a free republic." [3]

The French Revolution was for several years, strangely
enough, the great dominant fact in American political life.
It furnished issues, watchwords and leaders, and was an
important agent in determining the alignment and construction of parties.   That our foreign policy should be

---

[1] Cobbett. Works, IV, 268.   [2] Federal Orrery.
[3] Independent Chronicle, Aug. 22, Aug. 25, Dec. 19, 1796.

determined largely by foreign politics is easily understood. As one of the family of nations, we were inevitably drawn into the family broils. And this would naturally react upon the local politics. But this general fact does not at all explain the remarkable intensity of the interest in the Revolution that prevailed in America between 1789 and 1797, when estrangement from France gave it a rough check, though by no means a death-blow. Why was it that a revolution three thousand miles away pervaded every phase of American life, its politics, its literature, its pulpit utterances, its plays, its forms of social intercourse, developing here its own fanaticism and its own puerilities? Why were the destinies of the French Republic a source of such constant and intimate concern to multitudes of Americans, who seemed to regard French victories as their own, French customs as worthy of immediate and unfeigned imitation? Why did they reveal the same irritability and sensitiveness of mind that were in many cases so absurd and in many so little self-respecting? Why was it, too, that there was here a party of staunch and bitter conservatives, who became more and more staunch and more and more bitter, as the revolution in a foreign land went on; who regarded the whole movement as unhallowed and born of evil; while through all this acrimonious war of opinions, toward which no one in all the land was indifferent, there were heard notes of broadest idealism which sounded to many, no doubt, as strangely out of place, but which were freighted with the future?

De Tocqueville's remark recurs to mind. If we would study the French Revolution in the light of analogy we must compare it with religious rather than with other political revolutions. Religious revolutions, growing out of general abstract ideas, ideas that hold as true of the people of one country as of those of another, the relations of the individual toward his God and toward his fellow-men, have spread over wide areas, ignoring political or geographical lines of demarcation; and the more abstract their teachings the more widely have they spread. Similarly, the French Revolution, growing out of and embodying general political ideas, held to be as applicable to one people as another, dealing with the citizen in the abstract, proclaiming his general privileges and duties in reference to political affairs, the Rights of Man in short, had the same power of fascination, of universal appeal, as the movements inspired by Mohammed or by Luther.

"It was by thus divesting itself of all that was peculiar to one race or time, and by reverting to natural principles of social order and government, that it became intelligible to all and susceptible of simultaneous imitation in a hundred different places.

"By seeming to tend rather to the regeneration of the human race than to the reform of France alone, it roused passions such as the most violent political revolutions have been incapable of awakening. It inspired proselytism and gave birth to propagandism, and hence assumed that quasi-religious character which so terrified those who saw it, or, rather, became a sort of new religion, imperfect it is true, without God, worship, or future life, but still able, like Islamism, to cover the earth with its soldiers, its apostles, and its martyrs."

The remark of the brilliant French writer is both striking and true. One of the most broadly patent characteristics of the Revolution was its cosmopolitanism, shown both by its principles, many of which were general, fundamental, international, and by the fact that it rallied about it in every country devoted and enthusiastic defenders who were captivated by its message of help and hope. Nowhere is this general feature of the Revolution, as a universal faith, a temper of mind, a way of looking at things, shown in higher relief than in America, for here was a country that had thrown off almost all the mediaeval incumbrances or anomalies that gave to the Revolution in Europe its immediate provocation and its tremendous impetus. Yet this country, where life was, on the whole, simple, natural, marked by few abuses, where political rights were widely diffused and the political sense ingrained, was, unexpectedly enough, moved through and through by a revolution that was a-making far away.

Thus the general programme and promise of the Revolution were such as would naturally appeal to Americans. But there were other and special reasons that explain the fervor of their passion. First, there was the natural fondness of Americans for Frenchmen, which had its historic justification. The sentiment of gratitude to a nation that had aided us in our dire necessity was deeply lodged in the hearts of the American people. Regarding this matter dispassionately, nothing could be more natural than the enthusiasm that had its tap-root in such a sentiment, and in ordinary times and within proper limits nothing could be more honorable or more healthy. Most of the utterances of these years bear witness to the vitality and power of this belief, that to France we owed a debt of appreciation that could never be paid. The Federalists might endeavor to show that the French had had their own purposes in that alliance, and that they were not the unselfish, chivalrous, lofty persons represented by the popular legend. But the great mass of the American people instinctively rejected this unflattering view of the motives of our allies and it never made much impression. Was not the rare, deep friendship of Washington and Lafayette typical of the relations of the two nations? Did not that reveal far more convincingly than any ingenious and subtle arguments of soured partisans, the real motives that had led Frenchmen to pour out their blood and spend their treasure in a far-off wilderness? In whatever part of America the Duke de Larochefoucauld might happen to be he was instantly made to feel the high esteem in which his countrymen were held. To be sure, he met men enough everywhere who expressed a deep abhorrence of the crimes of the Revolution, deplored the death of Louis, denounced Robespierre and his associates as "the banditti of France," yet who, minimizing these repellent features, expressed a warm attachment to that nation. "If an American were to fight against a Frenchman, that would be like fighting against his father," was a sentiment once addressed to him and repeated in other forms not infrequently.

This generous feeling of national gratitude was only heightened by another, the feeling of rankling resentment against Great Britain, which stood forth now as the worst enemy of our best friend. The old feeling, which had perhaps been dying down a little since the peace, blazed up once more, nor did England do aught to allay it. In a war between that country and France, what anti-federalist could doubt where justice lay and where sympathy should be shown? He argued that the former was at the head of a desperate coalition, pledged to stamp out free government in a land whose people were striving for it, and did not Americans have enough reason to know that George III. was an old tyrant anyway? No wonder, then, that when these two tremendous passions were inflamed to a quivering heat and thrown into the ordinary party strife of the day, that party strife should become mad and hysterical. All the more resplendent, consequently, was the statesmanship of Washington in dealing with so embarrassing a situation.

Other considerations, too, fanned the flame. Were not the French making the first practical and effective assertion of democratic principles in Europe? Were not their interests identical with ours? Leaving all talk of duty aside, did not mere consistency, mere loyalty to our own most cherished principles, demand that we approve those who had aided us to become free and who were now struggling to become so themselves? The Federalists might deny that there was any similarity between the two revolutions; but did their denial establish the fact? Did not all the world know, did not Frenchmen themselves proclaim, that they had lighted their torches at our altars? Were they not doing precisely what we had done, aiming at their own elevation, believing that greater liberty means richer personal development. Was not—and here the vision widened and became more entrancing—was not the Old World, as a whole, simply following the example of the New; had not a political millennium commenced whose sway was to be universal; and were not the gallant French the ones destined to bring this sublime achievement to pass? The truth is that the imagination of the American people had been mightily aroused and was working under the stress of ideas of extraordinary and overwhelming power.[1] And this explains, as it also condones to some extent, many of the absurdities and puerilities that have been described above.

There was, of course, another side to all this. The Federalists felt no affinity with the hydras, the mammoths and kites upon whom the Republicans so often poured out the vials of unspeakable scorn. They were no apologists for despotism. "Some men were Federalists," says Col. Higginson, "because they were high-minded; others because they were narrow-minded"; and in this neat description of their character we have a key to their position on many public questions. At the outset they, like all other Americans, hailed the Revolution as a bow of promise, but for them the bow soon disappeared, swallowed up in the lowering darkness of the gathering night, while for the Republicans it did not so speedily vanish. It was not simply a question as to who favored liberty and who did not. Each side believed that American liberty was at stake, and that it alone was its defender. The Republicans believed either that the monarchs of Europe, having crushed out liberty there, as they would if they should conquer France, would then proceed to stamp it out here, so hateful would the sight of it be to them anywhere and so dangerous; or that a defeat in Europe meant at least a rebuff here, for they held that the Federalists would go to any reactionary length in exploiting such a catastrophe, for had not their high pontiff, Jefferson, declared in terms unequivocal that the country

---

[1] See Freneau's Hymn to Liberty, delivered at Monmouth, 1795. Duyckinck: Cyclopaedia of American Literature, I, 331.

was "galloping fast into monarchy," driven thither by the odious "monocrats"? The Federalists, on the other hand, came to believe sincerely that only by combating French principles could American liberties be preserved; that liberty, as proclaimed by Frenchmen, with all its miserable trumpery of clubs and poles and red caps, was but a delusion and a sham. The government they themselves had created and were now administering was imperiled, they believed, by principles in their very essence subversive of all government and preached by men who, foiled once in their effort to prevent its erection, were now bent upon its overthrow. Where, they asked, is there any trace of true liberty in the proceedings of Frenchmen since 1791? Have they not quickly overthrown their own creation, the Constitution of 1789? Does not liberty imply such a thing as stability? Have they not murdered their King and Queen and multitudes of the higher classes? If this be liberty, its superiority to anarchy is not apparent. Has not the French Republic, after proclaiming that it makes for peace, that it will have nothing to do with conquest, proceeded at once to annex the Netherlands? If this be liberty, at any rate it isn't honesty. Have not the French abolished Christianity; have they not erected Reason into a religion and gone to Nôtre Dame to worship a common prostitute as its goddess? If this be liberty, it surely isn't decency.

From such a conception of liberty as this the Federalists shrank back with horror. Those who were high-minded and those who were narrow-minded were alike alarmed. They had developed order out of anarchy with infinite difficulty. Was it only that anarchy might speedily swallow it up once more? Surely that would be the result if the French principles gained foothold here. As a matter of fact, what had the Revolution done for us? It had, said the Federalists, degraded our politics by placing loyalty to foreign attachments higher than loyalty to our own best judgment and interest; it had foisted clubs upon us whose chief object was to embarrass the government; whose chief result was to render the popular mind discontented, suspicious, irritable and unstable; it had led one section of the country to the brink of treachery,[1] another to open insurrection; it had insulted our Government through its ministers Genet and Adet. The Federalists held that the intrusion of the French Revolution into American life had proved highly prejudicial to the interests of literature; that it had blighted the arts;[2] that it had greatly encouraged infidelity.[3] Believing all this, and much of it was true and much plausible, it was not astonishing that many Americans became inveterate opponents of a movement which they had at first greeted with favor and to which the majority of their fellow-countrymen remained loyal to the end. If the imagination of the Republicans had been aroused by it, none the less had the imagination of the Federalists. If the former peered far into the future, the latter saw deep into the present, understood the wonderfully complicated and delicate nature of human institutions, appreciated the value

---

[1] Genet's schemes in Kentucky and the Mississippi valley. " It is a singular fact that matters as remote as the Revolution in France should have greatly affected the political motives of this young commonwealth." Shaler, Kentucky, p. 129. This significant episode is discussed at length by the historians of Kentucky, Collins, Marshall and others.

[2] "In America the artful intrigues of French diplomatists and the blunders of the British government united to convert the whole American people into violent partisans of one or the other; to such a degree did this insanity prevail that the whole country seemed to be changed into one vast arena on which the two parties, forgetting their national character, were wasting their time, their thoughts, their energy, on this foreign quarrel. . . . In such a state of things what hope remained for the arts? None— my great enterprise was blighted." John Trumbull, Autobiography, 168-169. His great enterprise was the portrayal of the American Revolution, which required for its successful realization official support, which it could not get in such troublous times.

[3] William Ellery Channing entered Harvard in 1794. He has left this description of those days: " College was never in a worse state than when I entered it. Society was passing through a most critical stage. The French Revolution had diseased the imagination and unsettled the understanding of men everywhere. The old foundations of social order, loyalty, tradition, habit, reverence for antiquity, were everywhere shaken, if not subverted. The au-

of what had been historically fashioned out of the experience of the race, divined the necessity of preserving these products of time, saw that pure theory should be held in check and not be let loose every little while to remodel radically the relations of man with man. The Federalists were strong because they stood for law, for order, and in this special case their position was all the stronger because, as Washington said of himself in his Farewell Address, their predominant motive was to endeavor to gain time to the country " to settle and mature its yet recent institutions and to progress without interruption to that degree of strength and consistency which is necessary to give it, humanly speaking, the command of its own fortunes."

The contest between the two principles was terrific, but it was not a contest into which no ignoble elements entered. To each, worthy in itself, was added its alloy of baseness, idealism yoked with narrowness, vulgarity and injustice on either side. There were the scrupulous and the unscrupu-

---

thority of the past was gone. The old forms were outgrown and new ones had not taken their place. The tone of books and conversation was presumptuous and daring. The tendency of all classes was to skepticism. . . . The state of morals among the students was anything but good." Memoir of W. E. Channing, by W. H. Channing, I, 70.

Judge White, a classmate and friend of Channing, expressed the same opinion. " Our colleges could not escape the contagion of these principles " [the " flood of infidel and licentious principles " poured upon the country by the Revolution]; "and I have no doubt that to these and the pernicious books embodying them, much of the disorderly conduct, and most of the infidel and irreligious spirit which prevailed at that period among the students at Cambridge, may be justly attributed. The patrons and governors of the college made efforts to counteract the effect of these fatal principles by exhortation and preaching and prayer, as well as by the publication and distribution of good books and pamphlets. . . . Watson's Apology for the Bible, in answer to Paine's Age of Reason, was published or furnished for the students at college by the corporation in 1796, and every one of them was presented with a copy of it." Ibid. I, 61-62. See also Story, Life and Letters of Joseph Story, I, 66. On the influence of Rousseau on the young men of the time see Story I, 79. On the influence of the Revolution on social forms and usages see William Sullivan, Familiar Letters, 145.

lous, the statesman and the demagogue. But passion
blinded too many; moderation was too rare, vehemence
too much the order of the day. The writings of the time
displayed more temper than truth. Now and then some
penetrating criticism was made, as when John Quincy
Adams said that vanity explained a good deal of the Revolution.[1] But both parties were too prone to lose themselves
in denunciation of each other. "Anglomen" and "monarchists," shouted the Republicans. "Disorganizers," "in-
cendiaries," "anarchists," were among the bitter epithets
freely hurled back by the Federalists upon these men who
shamed not to write coarse drinking songs,[2] to burn the
leading members of the Government in effigy, and even to
circulate printed handbills with coarse woodcuts representing Washington placed upon the guillotine like the King of
France. The hostility of the Federalists to everything that
reminded ever so slightly of the Revolution stiffened gradually into grim, unreasonable and unreasoning hatred, well
typified in Robert Treat Paine. In 1792 he had opened his
Harvard Poem with an apostrophe to France—

"Hail, sacred Liberty, divinely fair!"

Seven years later, in a speech in Boston, his views were
these: "The French Republick has exhibited all the vices
of civilization without one of the virtues of barbarism. . . .
Political empiricism has never attained in any age or
nation so universal an ascendency as at the present day in
the 'Illuminated Republick.' Unfettered by the fear of innovation, and unshackled by the prejudice of ages, the
modern Frenchman is educated in a system of moral and
religious chimeras, which dazzle by their novelty those vola-

---

[1] "The rock upon which La Fayette, Dumouriez, Custine and
innumerable other French generals, as well as statesmen, have
been wrecked, is Vanity. Each of them too hastily concluded himself to be the pivot upon which the affairs of the world were to turn,
and neither had the talent to disguise or conceal the opinion."
Memoirs, I, 69, Feb. 3, 1795.
[2] See Barlow's poem entitled "God Save the Guillotine." Duyckinck, I, 393.

tile intellects, which prescriptive wisdom could never impress with veneration. Every Frenchman who has read a
little is a pedant; and the whole race of these horn-book
philosophers is content with the atheism of Mirabeau, the
historick pages of Rollin and Plutarch, the absurd philanthropy of Condorcet, and the visionary politics of Rousseau.
These are the boundaries of their literary ambition, of their
political science." Turning to the influence of the Revolution in America, he speaks of it as "the melancholy record
of our national degradation." "Who does not remember
the letter to Mazzei or the arrival of Genet? Who has forgotten that dubious era in our history when illuminated
fraternities were scattered, like the pestiferous effluvia of the
poison-tree of Java, from Altamaha to St. Croix? When
anarchy and disorganization were the order of the day and
French consuls and French assignats the order of the night?
When our 'civick feasts' were introduced to celebrate
French victories and our 'watermelon frolicks' to disseminate French principles? When political infidelity was a
paramount title to the suffrages of the people? When Foreign Influence, like the golden calf, seduced multitudes from
the worship of true liberty."

Such, then, were some of the opinions of Americans of
the great French Revolution—opinions to some extent
evanescent, but with their deeply durable influence also,
for they encouraged the Republicans greatly in their way
of thinking and confirmed the Federalists forever in theirs.

The great tempest swept by, but the waves did not
at once subside. Long after the tumult of the hour was
over, men were still talking about it. At the downfall of
Napoleon some arose and shook off the whole horrid night-
mare with an evident sense of relief, as was the case with
Gouverneur Morris, who exclaimed: "'Tis done, the long
agony is over. The Bourbons are restored. France re-
poses in the arms of her legitimate prince." With others,
however, all the superb exaltation of the early Revolution

seemed preserved long years after, as vivid and as ravishing as in those luxurious, hopeful days of '89. This was the case with William Wirt, who broke into this strain upon the occasion of the Neapolitan revolution of 1820: " By-the-bye, did you ever see such a miserable fist as the Neapolitans have made of it? Are these the descendants of Brutus and Cato? O shame and disgrace unspeakable and indelible, in such a cause! I had begun to feel the same sort of throbbing with which my heart beat nearly thirty years ago in the cause of France, and was already panting to go to Naples and take a hand with them. . . . When behold this miserable, mean, pitiful, sneaking capitulation arrives. O how different from the movement of France in the youth of her revolution! Even at this moment my blood runs cold, my breast swells, my temples throb, and I find myself catching my breath when I recall the ecstasy with which I used to join in that glorious apostrophe to Liberty in the Marseilles Hymn—'O Liberty, can man resign thee, once having felt thy gen'rous flame!' And then the glorious, magnificent triumphs of the arms of France, so every way worthy of her cause! O, how we used to hang over them, to devour them, to weep and to sing, and pray over these more than human exertions and victories! And how were the names of those heroes of Liberty 'in our flowing cups freshly remembered' and cele-brated almost to idolatry!"[1]

A passion, the mere reminiscence of which through the haze of thirty years could so thrill and fascinate a man, must have been of surpassing intensity.

When we read that in 1830 the citizens of Charleston got up banquets once more in honor of a new French Revolu-tion, and that William Gilmore Simms composed a poem, "The Tri-Color,"[2] intended to immortalize the same, we seem to feel that we are treading ground already sufficiently reconnoitred.

---

[1] Kennedy. Memoirs of the Life of William Wirt, II, 108-109.
[2] Trent. Life of Simms, p. 58.

BIBLIOGRAPHY.

WORKS.

John Adams. Works, edited by C. F. Adams.—Letters to Mrs. Adams, edited by C. F. Adams.

Fisher Ames. Works, edited by Seth Ames.

Joel Barlow. Political Writings. New York, 1796.

William Cobbett. Porcupine's Works. 8 vols. London, 1801.

Albert Gallatin. Writings, edited by Henry Adams.

Elbridge Gerry. Some Letters of, edited by W. C. Ford.

Alexander Hamilton. Works, edited by John C. Hamilton.—Works, edited by Henry Cabot Lodge.

John Jay. Correspondence and Public Papers, edited by H. P. Johnston.

Thomas Jefferson. Writings, edited by H. A. Washington.—Writings, edited by P. L. Ford.

James Madison. Letters and other Writings.

Thomas Paine. Writings, edited by M. D. Conway.

George Washington. Writings, edited by Jared Sparks. —Writings, edited by W. C. Ford.

AUTOBIOGRAPHIES AND REMINISCENCES.

John Quincy Adams. Memoirs, edited by C. F. Adams.

Charles Biddle. Autobiography, edited by J. S. Biddle.

Henry M. Brackenridge. Recollections of Persons and Places in the West. Philadelphia, 1834.

Samuel Breck. Recollections, with Passages from his Note-Books. Edited by H. E. Scudder.

J. T. Buckingham. Specimens of Newspaper Literature with Personal Memoirs.

G. W. P. Custis. Recollections and Private Memoirs of Washington, by his adopted son.

Alexander Graydon. Memoirs of a Life chiefly passed in Pennsylvania. Harrisburgh, 1811.

Ashbel Green. Life: begun by himself. Prepared for press by Joseph H. Jones. New York, 1849.

William Maclay. Journal, edited by E. S. Maclay.

Gouverneur Morris. Diary and Letters, edited by Anne Cary Morris.

Joseph Priestley. Memoirs, written by himself. 2 vols. 1806-1807.

William Sullivan. The Public Men of the Revolution. 1847.

Ebenezer S. Thomas. Reminiscences of the last Sixty-five Years. 1840. 2 vols.

John Trumbull. Autobiography, Reminiscences and Letters.

Elkanah Watson. Memoirs, including Journals of Travel.

Sidney Willard. Memories of Youth and Manhood.

BIOGRAPHIES.

J. Q. Adams and C. F. Adams. The Life of John Adams.

John T. Morse. John Adams.

John T. Morse. John Quincy Adams.

Josiah Quincy. Memoir of the Life of John Quincy Adams.

William H. Seward. Life and Public Services of John Quincy Adams.

James K. Hosmer. Samuel Adams.

William V. Wells. The Life and Public Services of Samuel Adams.

John T. Kirkland. Biography of Fisher Ames. Prefixed to Ames' Works.

Charles Burr Todd. Life and Letters of Joel Barlow.

Carl E. Oelsner. Notice sur la vie et les écrits de M. Joel Barlow. Paris, 1813.

J. Francis Fisher. Memoir of Samuel Breck.

Matthew L. Davis. Memoirs of Aaron Burr.

James Parton.   Life and Times of Aaron Burr.

H. C. Lodge.   Life and Letters of George Cabot.

William H. Channing.   Memoir of William Ellery Channing.

Edward Smith.   William Cobbett.   A Biography.

G. M. Dallas.   Life and Writings of Alexander James Dallas.

J. T. Morse.   Benjamin Franklin.

James Parton.   Life and Times of Benjamin Franklin.

Henry Adams.   Life of Albert Gallatin.

James T. Austin.   The Life of Elbridge Gerry.

J. C. Hamilton.   The Life of Alexander Hamilton.

H. C. Lodge.   Alexander Hamilton.

W. G. Sumner.   Alexander Hamilton.

William Wirt Henry.   Life, Correspondence, and Speeches of Patrick Henry.

Moses Coit Tyler.   Patrick Henry.

Griffith J. McRee.   Life and Correspondence of James Iredell.

William Jay.   The Life and Writings of John Jay.

George Pellew.   John Jay.

Cornelis De Witt.   Thomas Jefferson.

J. T. Morse.   Thomas Jefferson.

Henry S. Randall.   The Life of Thomas Jefferson.

George Tucker.   The Life of Thomas Jefferson.

James Schouler.   Thomas Jefferson.

Charles R. King.   Life and Correspondence of Rufus King.

F. S. Drake.   Life and Correspondence of Henry Knox.

Bayard Tuckerman.   Life of General Lafayette.

Mme. de Lasteyrie.   Life of Madame de Lafayette.

Robert Henry Lee.   Memoirs of the Life of Richard Henry Lee.

C. H. Hunt.   Life of Edward Livingston.

John Quincy Adams.   Lives of James Madison and James Monroe.

William C. Rives.   History of the Life and Times of James Madison.

D. C. Gilman. James Monroe.
Theodore Roosevelt. Gouverneur Morris.
Jared Sparks. Life of Gouverneur Morris.
Moncure D. Conway. The Life of Thomas Paine.
Octavius Pickering. The Life of Timothy Pickering.
Charles Colesworth Pinckney. Life of General Thomas Pinckney.
J. T. Rutt. Life and Correspondence of Joseph Priestley.
Moncure D. Conway. Omitted Chapters of History.
William P. Trent. William Gilmore Simms.
John H. Morison. Life of Jeremiah Smith.
William Wetmore Story. Life and Letters of Joseph Story.
Henry Cabot Lodge. A Memoir of Caleb Strong.
Thomas C. Amory. Life of James Sullivan, with Selections from his Writings.
George Gibbs. Memoirs of the Administrations of Washington and Adams.
Henry Cabot Lodge. George Washington.
John Marshall. Life of George Washington.
Horace E. Scudder. Life of Noah Webster.
John P. Kennedy. Memoirs of the Life of William Wirt.

BIOGRAPHICAL SKETCHES.

Sir Henry Lytton Bulwer. Historical Characters.
Spencer T. Hall. Biographical Sketches of Remarkable People.
Samuel L. Knapp. Biographical Sketches of Eminent Lawyers, Statesmen, and Men of Letters.
Henry Cabot Lodge. Historical and Political Essays.
Samuel W. Pennypacker. Historical and Biographical Sketches.
J. G. Thorold Rogers. Historical Gleanings.
Henry Simpson. The Lives of Eminent Philadelphians.
H. T. Tuckerman. Essays, Biographical and Critical.
Moses Coit Tyler. Three Men of Letters.

NEWSPAPERS.

Boston Gazette.
Columbian Centinel.
Federal Orrery.
Independent Chronicle.
American Daily Advertiser.
American Minerva.
New York Herald.
Gazette of the United States.
General Advertiser and Aurora.
National Gazette.
Pennsylvania Gazette.
Pennsylvania Packet.
Hampshire County Gazette.
Vermont Gazette.
Vermont Journal.
Connecticut Courant.
Virginia Independent Chronicle.

Joseph T. Buckingham. Specimens of Newspaper Literature.

Frederic Hudson. History of Journalism in the United States.

Isaiah Thomas. The History of Printing in America.

LOCAL HISTORIES.

Josiah Quincy. A Municipal History of Boston.
Justin Winsor. The Memorial History of Boston.
William H. Sumner. History of East Boston.
Charles Fraser. Reminiscences of Charleston.
Montgomery. Reminiscences of Wilmington.
Mrs. Lamb. History of the City of New York.
Scharf and Westcott. History of Philadelphia.

John F. Watson. Annals of Philadelphia and Pennsylvania in the Olden Time.

TRAVELS.

John Davis. Travels of Four Years and a Half in the United States. London, 1803.

W. Priest. Travels in the United States, 1793-1797. London, 1802.

La Rochefoucauld-Liancourt. Travels through the United States of North America in the Years 1795, 1796 and 1797. 4 vols., 2d edition. London, 1800.

Henry Wansey. The Journal of an Excursion to the United States in the Summer of 1794. Salisbury, 1798.

Isaac Weld. Travels through the States of North America, 1795-1797. London, 1800.

CONTEMPORARY LITERATURE.

"Aristocracy, an Epic Poem." Philadelphia, 1795.

Josias Lyndon Arnold. Poems. Providence, 1792.

Ann Eliza Bleecker. Posthumous Works, edited by Margaretta V. Faugeres. New York, 1793.

Richard Bingham Davis. Poems. New York, 1807.

"The Decree of the Sun, or France Regenerated." A poem in three cantos. The first offering of a youthful Muse. Boston.

The "Echo." Printed at the Porcupine Press. By Pasquin Petronius. 1807.

James Elliot. Poetical and Miscellaneous Works. Greenfield, 1798. Copy in Boston Athenaeum.

Fayette in Prison, or Misfortunes of the Great, a modern tragedy by a gentleman of Massachusetts. Worcester, 1802.

Michael Forrest. Travels through America. A Poem. Philadelphia, 1793.

Col. Humphreys. Miscellaneous Works. New York, 1790.

Robert Treat Paine. Works in Verse and Prose. Boston, 1812.

Robert Treat Paine (or J. S. J. Gardiner). Remarks on the Jacobiniad, revised and corrected by the author, and embellished with caricatures. Boston, 1795.

Charles Prentiss. A Collection of Fugitive Essays in Prose and Verse. Leominster, 1797.

George Richards. The Declaration of Independence. A Poem, accompanied by Odes, Songs, etc., adapted to the day. Boston, 1793.

Elihu Smith. American Poems, Selected and Original. Litchfield, 1793.

Isaac Story. Liberty. A Poem. Newburyport. 1795.

John Trumbull. Poetical Works. Hartford, 1820.

LITERARY COLLECTIONS.

Duyckinck. Cyclopaedia of American Literature.

Stedman & Hutchinson. Library of American Literature.

Charles W. Everest. The Poets of Connecticut.

Griswold. Curiosities of American Literature.

Abby M. Hemenway. Poets and Poetry of Vermont.

Samuel Kettel. Specimens of American Poetry. Boston, 1839.

Samuel L. Knapp. Lectures on American Literature. New York, 1829.

MISCELLANEOUS.

Annals of Congress. Gales and Seaton.

John Quincy Adams. The Jubilee of the Constitution.

William Cobbett. History of the American Jacobins in William Playfair's History of Jacobinism. Philadelphia, 1796.

Richard Dinmore. An Exposition of the Principles of the English Jacobins. Norwich, 1797.

William Dunlap. A History of the American Theatre.

George O. Seilhamer. History of the American Theatre.

William B. Wood. Personal Recollections of the Stage.

Timothy Dwight. Sermons. Edinburgh, 1828.

David Osgood. A Discourse. Thanksgiving, 1795. Boston, 1795.—Fast Day Sermon, May 9, 1798. (Some facts evincive of the atheistical, anarchical, and in other respects, immoral Principles of the French Republicans. Boston, 1798.)

James Sullivan (Citoyen de Novion). The Altar of Baal Thrown Down. Boston, 1795.

William B. Sprague. Annals of the American Pulpit. " Eulogies and Orations on the Life and Death of General George Washington." Boston, 1800. Contains several important orations.

James Spear Loring. Hundred Boston Orators.

Gouverneur Morris. An Oration delivered June 29, 1814, at the request of a number of citizens of New York, in Celebration of the Recent Deliverance of Europe from the Yoke of Military Despotism.

George Richards. Oration on Independence, July 4, 1795, pronounced at Portsmouth.

William Smith, M. C. Oration, delivered in Charleston, S. C., July 4, 1796.

James Monroe. A View of the Conduct of the Executive. Philadelphia, 1797.

Alexander Hamilton. Scipio's Reflections on Monroe's View. Boston, 1798.

Alexander Hamilton and James Madison. The " Pacificus " and " Helvidius " letters on the French Revolution and American politics, published entire in Gideon's edition of the Federalist, 1818.

James Sullivan. An Impartial Review of the Causes and Principles of the French Revolution.

Noah Webster. The Revolution in France considered in respect to its Progress and Effects. New York, 1794.

" The Jacobin Looking-Glass," by A Friend to Rational Liberty. Printed at Worcester, Mass., by Leonard Worcester, 1795.

R. W. Griswold. Republican Court.

Rosenthal. America and France.

William Thornton. Cadmus, or a treatise on the elements of written language. Philadelphia, 1793.

Tocqueville. The Old Régime and the Revolution.

Van Buren. Inquiry into the Origin and Course of Political Parties in the United States.

Warfield. The Kentucky Resolutions of 1798.

INDEX.

JOHNS HOPKINS UNIVERSITY STUDIES

IN

Historical and Political Science.

HERBERT B. ADAMS, Editor.

The set of fourteen (regular) series is now offered, uniformly bound in cloth, for library use, for $42, and including subscription to the current (fifteenth) series, for $45.00.

The fifteen series, with fifteen extra volumes, altogether thirty volumes, in cloth as above, for $65.00.

All business communications should be addressed to THE JOHNS HOPKINS PRESS, BALTIMORE, MARYLAND.